# DOVE IN AN IRON CAULDRON

By Hadas Knox

ISBN: 979-8-9922721-1-6 (paperback)

ISBN: 979-8-9922721-0-9 (hard cover)

ISBN: 979-8-9922721-2-3 (ebook)

*For those who feel at home in dreams, in ghost stories, in mist and madness.*

# CHAPTER 1

*T*hey say the banshee cries so loudly when a Traveler dies, you can hear it across the ocean. The night May Connally heard it from inside her wagon, she knew they'd lost another one. She held her hands over her ears, fearing for whom the banshee would sing next, longing for someone to hear her story before it sang for *her*.

But she wondered: who would care? Her story wasn't always a living one, after all. Her life teetered on that delicate edge between reality and myth, what was and what will be.

## Map

SEAWATER SEEPED THROUGH THE FLOORBOARDS. My feet squelched in my worn but sturdy black boots. The air on the ship was thick with the scent of rotten bodies, every breath a reminder that everything, eventually, rots. The scent lingered, though the dead didn't. One by one, they were dropped like cobblestones into the churning silver Atlantic, enough to build a road across our path from Ireland to America.

I crept into my cot, careful not to let the damp seep into the coarse woolen blanket.

Beside me, my husband Francis lay, hands behind his head, staring into nothing. His cold blue eyes didn't blink, didn't look my way. As if I wasn't even there.

Flynn slept at the wall's edge, his breathing soft and steady. He was nineteen, the same as me—a friend from long before this cursed voyage. I remembered him as a lad sweeping chimneys with my brothers, his soot-streaked grin a welcome sight on our jaunts around town.

Now, among the dying paupers crammed into this swaying coffin, his presence was a comfort.

We Travelers stood out, even here, where everyone was traveling. The patchwork colors of our pieced-together clothes marked us, as surely as the lilting Gammon words on our lips. Settled folk shrank from us, their noses turned up at what they couldn't—or wouldn't—understand. They looked at us as though we carried not just hunger, but curses.

A mother huddled in the cot next to ours, her three children pressed close.

"Pray for your sister," she droned. "Pray for her now, so her soul ascends to heaven." Her voice grew shrill as a whistle. She held fast to her bent knees, rocking to the keen of her own voice.

"But, Mammy," the youngest sniffed, "how will we know when God takes her?"

The words scraped at me. My breath caught as I willed Francis to meet my gaze, to give some sign—any sign—that he wouldn't hate me for what I felt stirring within.

But his eyes stayed fixed, empty. As though he couldn't hear the desperate cracking in her voice.

My chest heaved with the pressure of silence. I couldn't speak.

Couldn't reach across the thin, trembling barrier between life and death. Not without him forgiving me first.

And yet, the barrier began to lift—unbidden but as familiar as the murmur of waves against the hull.

If I moved, if I reached through it now, what would Francis say?

We'd stood at my brother John's grave only weeks earlier, Francis's voice heavy with scorn. If I couldn't speak to my own brother, what right did I have to meddle in the fate of strangers? What love could ever blossom between Francis and me if I did?

He wouldn't forgive me.

The ship swayed, rocking the cabin into a fragile daze. I raked my fingers through my tangled mass of brown curls, trying to drown out the mother's cries, the sting of her grief. She spoke of angels and God as if she knew.

*I* knew. That was my curse.

I knew even before the pressure spread to the center of my forehead, before I felt iced over, before the back of my neck tingled as though someone were giving me the softest touch with the tip of their finger.

I knew.

And yet, when it had mattered most, when my brother John lay cold and alone in the earth, I couldn't say a thing.

Perhaps that was when Mammy decided to marry me off to Francis and send us to America. She wasn't a Seer, but I wondered, standing beside John's grave with Francis's shadow towering over me like the *dullahan,* if she glimpsed something in my future.

Another child, gone and buried—perhaps claimed by pneumonia, like my sister Lucy and John, or simply wasted away, swallowed by the earth beneath our feet, the very bones of the land we tread so fervently.

If I'd known what she was thinking, I might have clung to her neck and told her that she was wrong, a match with Francis was all wrong, but—

"Bloody hell, child, am I a priest?" The mother's voice cracked. "I haven't a notion! I dunno why God took her or if we'll see her again.

But will you stop asking me questions about her? I can't take it. Can't you see that?"

She began to sob, her narrow shoulders wracked and bent as she clutched her child's frail frame.

The cabin fell silent, but there was no peace in the stillness. The air thickened, like an open mouth, its scream swallowed in the dark. The soft touch against my skin became dozens of ghostly fingers, clawing at the world I knew, peeling it back like a page of a journal.

I didn't risk another glance at Francis.

The ghost lass appeared before me, her small figure flickering like a candle caught in the wind. She couldn't have been more than three or four, her gray eyes wide and knowing.

I swallowed the fear of my husband's anger and nodded to the lass. *I see you.*

She squeezed her eyes shut and carried me toward her family. Not in the flesh, but in the echo of their suffering. I felt the bones in the mother's fingers as though I were her child, heard them cracking in the cold, like rusted tin.

I glanced at Flynn. His breath was shallow, his shoulders rising and falling in sleep.

Francis would surely make me regret reaching through the veil for strangers when I couldn't reach through to my own brother. He'd accuse me of not caring enough about my own kind, of buttering up to the settled folks because I wanted to be like them and not as I was.

But Flynn? He wasn't keen on settled folk any more than they were on him. He didn't spare a second thought on how they narrowed their eyes on his wide-brimmed hat or heavy cloak, but he wasn't quick to see the worst in me either.

If he heard me telling these folks what I saw, maybe he would understand. Maybe he'd protect me.

They didn't understand our ways, and they could be superstitious. Fearful. No, there was no safety in what I was about to do. No guarantee the family wouldn't turn on me, call me a witch and blame me for every death aboard that ship.

Flynn wouldn't let that happen.

Would Francis?

The wee ghosty closed her eyes, showing me what lay behind them. The images struck like a silver thread of lightning in the dark tapestry of night. She was in her bed, golden dawn outside the window. A wet rag sagged across her forehead. She was almost as pale as she appeared now.

Then, another memory—golden fields of barley, her brother's laughter as he chased her through the stalks.

Finally, a dazzling, endless light. White light, like a winter cloud, with pearly layers of color beneath, as though the sky was painted in stages, first black, then blue, pink, gold, and other colors I couldn't name.

"She's with the angels," I whispered. The mother turned to me sharply, her fingers still pressed into the lad's shoulders.

Flynn stirred and then shot up as though he'd just come back to life in the coffin. His hand was firm on my arm. My stomach lurched.

"May," he warned, his voice low and urgent. "This mightn't be the place."

"For God's sake, Flynn," I gasped. "Weren't you dreaming?"

My heart pounded. Francis hadn't moved, hadn't spoken. Was he even listening? Or was he content to let me ruin myself?

"Well, how could you say a thing like that?" the mother asked, her voice sharp with suspicion as she loosened her grip on the lad's vest.

Flynn's warning glance begged me to stop, but the lass had whispered her name to me.

*Tell my mammy*, she instructed, her eyes wide.

I couldn't keep that name for myself, lest it haunt me. If her mother couldn't be calmed by it, if she called me a *cailleach* or *bean feasa* or even a witch, I'd kneel before her on the groaning boards of our desperate ship and beg for forgiveness. It wasn't much of a plan, but what more could I do?

"Mary," I said, my chest slowing with the release. "Her name was Mary, wasn't it?"

The ghost's whispers were my only comfort, and yet they reminded me of how alone I truly was. To see their faces, to know their names, and yet, no one in this world truly understood me. I could speak to the dead, but I couldn't find the words to comfort the living.

The mother blinked the dust from her eyes. "How'd you know that?" she asked, her voice sharp, her eyes narrowing. "You heard us talking about her, then?"

Flynn opened his mouth, hesitated, then let out a sharp sigh, cocking his head with a resigned air. "If you've got a shilling, this lass here can talk to your Mary for you." Clearing his throat, he added, "God bless you." Flynn was always keenly aware of who he was talking to, and how best to talk to them.

I shook my head, though words wouldn't come. I didn't want her money. I didn't want to be the kind of person who could be bought, who would exploit grief for coin.

And yet, God knew we needed it.

"But how did she know my daughter's name?" the woman repeated, her eyes pressed wildly into Flynn's. "I don't reckon I've uttered it since she passed." A quiet moment followed, the woman's pain swelling in the stale air between us.

"May hears things," Flynn told her, wavering for a moment before resting a hand atop hers and giving it a pat. "She has a gift from God," he added, a faint gleam in his brown eyes.

Like so many before her, this woman stared right through me, searching for her loved one on the other side, like I was more the specter than her lost kin. I was no more than a means to an end, the door you pounded upon with angry fists when you lost the key, fuel for those desperate enough to seek answers.

The woman's trembling hand reached into the drawstring purse at her waist, pulling out a coin. She held it up, her grip firm, her stare unwavering.

My breath hitched as Flynn's hand rested reassuringly on my back, grounding me. The shift was subtle, yet undeniable. A wave of calm washed over me, settling deep. I could smell it, touch it, see it, like the petals of a rose unfurling on a ghostly platter.

"She wants you to know she's doing well. She's doing fine now." I swallowed the lump that was expanding in my throat. "She's with her cousins, and they're getting on well. She wants me to tell you it's not your fault, and there's nothing more you could have done. And…"

I shot Flynn an apologetic glance. I could still come back from what I'd said. I'd given her nothing special, no tale a common fortune teller couldn't spin for a shilling on the side of the road. What I was about to say, however, would wash away that road completely. I sighed, for again I had no say in the matter.

"She forgives her da for shooting the horse. She's glad for it now, for she gets to be with him again, and he makes her feel less alone."

Every word I spoke felt like it tore something inside me. It wasn't just the message. It was the knowledge that the mother's pain would never truly be assuaged, and that I, in my fumbling attempt to bring peace, was only reminding her of her loss. I swallowed hard, trying to hold myself together, but the hollow ache in my chest wouldn't stop. It never did.

We wandering folk saw the worst of the famine as we traveled— unburied corpses ravaged by animals, and the ruins of dwellings even the starving wouldn't go near. I shut my eyes against the memories.

When I opened them, the woman's skin was gray and sallow. Her forehead was lined, greasy. She clutched the coin tightly, her fingers pale. "But how could you know that?" she whispered, her voice brittle with disbelief.

Even after witnessing all the suffering the settled folk went through during the famine, I still wanted to be like them. *Settled*. Fresh thatch above my head and a proper bed to sleep in. A hearthfire to tend. Animals to care for and sleep beside when winter became a villain. A view so lovely it could rip your heart clean out of your chest, but it was yours, every day.

Her question lingered in the stifled air as an ancient-looking man stirred on a cot nearby. He grumbled, his voice rising in a stream of curses, his body a frail shadow of rage as he struggled upright. I barely noticed him until the woman turned rigid, her face tightening in alarm, even the gray draining from her throat.

"Will you pray for them?" she asked frantically. "For my Mary and her cousins? Will you tell them I hold them close in my heart?"

Before I could answer, the old man stumbled toward us, a battered shoe in hand. "Fortune tellers!" he cried. "Swindlers, all of you! There's no one can tell fortunes besides God!"

Flynn stepped forward, calm as ever. "We're owed a shilling," he interjected matter-of-factly.

"Oh, you'll get your shilling from the devil's arse, you sinful people! You dirty Travelers!" He waved his decrepit shoe like a weapon, looking pure fierce for a man in his stocking feet.

"Da!" the mother cried. The old man ignored her, lunging at me with an agility I wouldn't have expected from someone so bent and skeletal.

I looked desperately at Francis, but he had only rolled over, facing the wall.

If Flynn noticed, he didn't say anything.

"Come on," he murmured, his hand steady on my back as he ushered me above deck.

I looked back. The man continued to bicker with his daughter. I thought I heard the mother yell again, "Will you pray for her, then? Will you pray for my Mary?" but I couldn't be sure. There was too much blood rushing in my ears.

I stared out over the railing into the cold starry night. It seemed to swallow me whole, but there was something comforting in it, too. The sea stretched endlessly, just like my thoughts. How many nights had I spent in darkness, wondering where we'd end up? Was there a place for us, for people like me, somewhere on the other side of this long voyage?

Flynn's hand on my back was the only thing grounding me to this world. His calm, his quiet reassurance—it all felt like a tether. I wanted to lean into him, to let my exhaustion be known, but I was afraid. Afraid of what it might mean, of how it might make me feel. But just for a moment, I let my shoulders relax, let the weight lift from them, just enough to breathe.

"Pay them no mind," Flynn said, tousling my hair playfully. His tone was easy, but frown lines creased his face. I didn't answer. My throat ached, and tears threatened to spill. Flynn's voice dropped further, a quiet reassurance. "They'll be no better than us the moment their feet touch American soil. We'll be just as good as them, then."

8

I snorted. "As though such a thing were possible."

He grinned. "Mark my words, Miss May-June-July. We'll be on top of the world soon enough. I can picture it now. You, me, and Francis, showing those settled folks what it means to live large."

I turned my attention back to the sea, as dark and sorrowful as my husband. Francis was twenty-one, but he could have been two hundred, for all the suffering he'd endured. But I'd endured, too. Could I keep carrying this weight for us both, or was I already too broken to continue?

"You know, May," Flynn went on, "I haven't had a chance to tell you yet. I'm truly sorry for the loss of your kin. John and Lucy were lovely folk. I'd never met a pair of twins so alike and a right laugh, too. In a way, it's a mercy God took them both, John so soon after Lucy, so they could stay together. Still, it's a heavy thing, and my heart goes out to you."

Starshine reflected in black waves like swinging lanterns, drawing my mind to the night before I left Ireland, Francis's wide strut as he approached Mammy and me, the tiny sparkle of his lantern illuminating thick black hair. The moon was barely a sliver over the Atlantic —almost as dark as that night that I was bound and unbound, shackled and set free...

"Where'd you go, May?" Flynn asked. It took me a moment to remember where I was. I thought I'd only drifted into the memory for a moment, but from the pinched look between Flynn's eyes, perhaps I'd drifted longer. His gaze narrowed on me another moment before he nodded toward the sea. "Do you see them out there?"

"No," I answered, turning away suddenly. My fingers gripped the railing. "I was only dreaming of America."

He nodded his smile and strung an arm around my shoulders. "You know what they say, Miss May." He grinned devilishly, pulling me close. "Those who live their lives in dreams can't really live."

It was only then I realized how vengefully the cold air rushed through my lungs, and I was grateful for the heat of his body.

"And I say," he went on, "bugger those folks."

My face broke out into what must have been a foolish-looking smile.

"They don't know what dreams can do for a person. Your dreaming will take you far, summer girl."

"Flynn!" I nearly clapped, feeling as right as though I were standing with my own brothers. I let myself lay my cheek against his shoulder. He held me closer.

Maybe he was right. Maybe there was light at the end of the ocean, even for Francis and me.

# CHAPTER 2

# 𝔐𝔞𝔭

*I* might have landed in America with a flicker of hope if the fever hadn't taken Flynn on that cursed ship of gaunt faces. I watched with a tremor as the sailor who sewed up the corpses stuck his needle into Flynn's blackened body. He had to oil the needle, the lad explained without sympathy, so its point would glide easily through the canvas.

A shark waited anxiously below, its fins slicing the waves as my friend's body slipped from a plank over the gunwale. He'd dreamed of being on top of the world, yet I had to watch him sink to the bottom. I envied those sharks. They had Flynn, and I was left with nothing but the ache of his absence.

"Until we meet again," I whispered, but the words fell into emptiness. I didn't feel him there to hear me, just as I hadn't felt John after we'd buried him. The wind was icy, to be sure, but it felt no different than it would to anyone—a slap of cold air, not the ghostly touch I longed for.

"Things will be different when we get to America," Francis said, his voice even.

I stared at him in surprise. Francis had hardly spoken to me since Flynn took ill. Barely even looked at me. And yet I wished he'd said anything else. To look out at that bleak skyline with hope for the future felt like a mockery—a betrayal—of our friend.

But Francis's tone was different from Flynn's when our friend had made a similar assurance. There was nothing playful in his movement, no glint in his eyes. His words seemed hollow somehow, echoing in my chest in a way I couldn't quite explain.

"Things will be different," Francis repeated. "No matter the cost."

He turned and walked away from me then, more of a stranger than when I'd married him. My husband had grown thinner and paler, down to the blue of his piercing eyes, which bulged within dark rims. His black hair seemed duller, too, graying just above his ears.

Back in Ireland, our women teased me for my romantic notions of love. They'd tell me marriage wasn't about love or friendship. It was about partnership.

*Find yourself a man who won't leave you, even after you've given him a few weans. Find a man who will keep to his work and mind you proper.*

But sometimes in our travels, I'd see a man bring a woman flowers or look at her with a hunger that told her she was the only one. I'd watch him stroke her arm with tenderness and note the way she'd melt beneath his touch, like his fingers were fairy wands. I'd try it on myself, curious about the magic of it.

Mammy always said I was foolish for even thinking about what other women had, for expecting something from a man that he wasn't made to give. But I couldn't help wondering: what would it feel like to be touched with love? To feel a man's hands cast spells upon my body?

Now it seemed I'd never know. Francis hadn't touched me at all since the altar in Ireland.

As the ship creaked and groaned beneath us, I caught a glimpse of the first faint outline of land—a jagged line on the horizon, rising from the mist. It was too far to make out anything clear, but I felt something stir inside me. A shift. A ripple beneath my skin, like a breeze before a storm.

Was it the promise of this new place? Or merely the aching hope that, somehow, my fate could change here?

The weeks at sea had blurred into grey skies and rolling waves, but as we neared America, everything sharpened—the air, the wind, the weight of what lay ahead.

When the ship finally docked and the gangplank creaked down, I stepped off and into a world unlike anything I'd imagined. The bustle of smoke and people, pigs and dogs running amok, was a far cry from the quiet hills of home. Stone and brick buildings towered higher than our tallest steeple, and carriages clattered past as vendors called out in sharp, unfamiliar tones. The air smelled of bread and strange spices, making my stomach clench with hunger.

I glanced at Francis. He looked just as grim as he had aboard the ship, not a trace of hope or happiness in his hollow cheeks.

Like most everyone who survived the journey, we sought a place in New York City. A family in Five Points offered to rent us a section of their cellar, but Francis barely stepped inside before shaking his head in disgust and walking out without a word. I trailed behind him like a shadow.

Outside, Francis lingered at the corner of the crowded street. His fingers twitched at his side, as if resisting the urge to reach for something. I watched him, unease creeping up my spine.

"Francis," I began. "Was it so bad? Where are we to settle, then?"

He didn't answer, bending instead to pick up a discarded newspaper. I stared, puzzled. He couldn't even read.

A group of boys pushed past us, their laughter sharp and reckless. One of them bumped into me, sending me off balance. Francis's hand shot out, steadying me with a firm grip. I glanced up, ready to thank him, but froze when I saw his face. His dark, steely gaze locked onto the boys, tracking them as they swaggered away.

One of them glanced over his shoulder and smirked, his eyes darting to the paper in Francis's hand. "Fine likeness!" he called out, his grin broadening as he caught my gaze and winked. My breath caught, and I braced for Francis's reaction.

But he didn't lash out. His jaw tightened, his teeth grinding as he pushed me upright. His knuckles whitened as he clenched the newspaper, his fingers crumpling it into a ball before letting it drop to the mud.

"Not here." His voice was clipped, final.

He strode off.

I hesitated, then bent to retrieve the paper, smoothing it against my skirt. I frowned as I took in the crude drawing of a man with the face of an ape. He was perched on a barrel, waving a bottle in one hand and the flag of Ireland in the other.

Was he meant to be Irish?

Turning the paper over, my stomach knotted further. Another cartoon depicted a fair-skinned man raising his hand as if to strike someone with darker skin. The bile in my throat rose with the sour stench of the gutters.

Francis was already halfway down the street. I let the paper slip back into the mud and hurried after him on sea-weary legs. Each breeze brought a new smell—fish, then rubbish, then excrement—all pure awful and far too reminiscent of the crossing for my stomach's liking.

"Francis, wait! Please." My lungs ached from exertion and the growing cold.

At last, he stopped, turning back as if only just remembering I was there. I spoke before I lost my nerve. "Francis. I know we can find better in time. But for now, please. I need a place to settle for a time. Just a short time."

His gaze swept the street—half-collapsed buildings pressed together so tightly, not even a breeze could pass between them. Horses splashed through gritty puddles, muddying the worn boots of passersby. Nearby, men with dark skin, like in the cartoon, danced on wooden planks to the rhythmic beat of drums. The sound carried a primal energy, quick and stirring, like a hunt.

"Not. *Here.*"

"So where, then?" I wrapped my black shawl tighter around my shoulders, against the quickening drums, the mingling scents, the fear of another night of travel. "What are we to do? Where are we to sleep?"

For a moment, his features softened, like day turning to gloaming. "We're to find work," he said, plain and steady. "We'll have more success if we split up. I'll find out what factories are hiring. May, see who might need help. Weans, cleaning, cooking. Take whatever comes."

I thought he was mad to be so levelheaded when we were down to our last pennies, turning up his nose at the only lodging that would take us in "on time," as folks here called it. But Francis was all I had. I couldn't lose him.

Back home, we Travelers had keen eyes for the lives of settled folk. It was survival. But here in America, I was green as spring, and Francis acted like he already knew their ways. I needed him more than he needed me. We both knew it.

So I nodded, pretending my knees didn't tremble at the thought of being off on my own in a strange city, not knowing my way around or how to talk to folks or what they'd think of me with my tattered clothes and hungry eyes.

I didn't walk two blocks before the smell of baking bread and warm honey nearly knocked me over. I followed the scent to a bakery window. What if it was fate, not hunger, that had brought me here?

I could wash dishes. I'd always helped Mammy keep our things spotless, scrubbing the pots and pans in the stream near camp until they shone like pure gold. Or, if luck was with me, they'd be wanting an apprentice, and I could learn to bake.

Inside, a woman stood stiff-backed behind the counter, her bun so tight it pulled her temples taut.

"Good day to you," I greeted her, forcing confidence into my voice. "Might I have a quick word with the owner?"

Her gaze skimmed my clothes, unimpressed. "For what?" Her tone was rancid and sputtering, like the end of a tallow candle.

"I'm hoping he might be hiring. I'm a hard worker, you see. I can clean and wash and—"

"Can't you read?" she interrupted impatiently.

My stomach dropped. I said nothing, because no, I could not read.

She rolled her eyes and pointed to a sign in the window, then read the words aloud.

NO IRISH NEED APPLY.

Heat rushed to my cheeks. I ran out before she could see me cry.

Once outside, I stopped just long enough to glare at that sign, burning its letters into my memory. I wouldn't make the same mistake again.

In Ireland, I was hated for being a Traveler. In America, I was hated for being Irish. My fate hadn't changed at all. I'd always be living on the fringes, never enough.

Dusk settled by the time I found Francis at our meeting place, a stable in Five Points. Its wooden walls were so weathered, hardly a lick of paint remained. A cracked lantern swung out front, creaking.

The sound, slow and steady, pulled me backward—back to the night we married, when Francis held a lantern just like this one in his shaking hands. My world went as dark as that night, and the memory wrapped its bare-branch arms around me.

Mammy and I had stood shivering outside the church. I was unaware of what was to come. I'd been admiring the stone walls and turrets, fancying that the people who worshiped within had a special stone arm helping them reach toward God and absolution.

Some folk believed the potato blight was divine punishment. That we'd been wasteful, letting crops rot in ditches when times were good.

When I looked up at that church with nothing to light my view except Mammy's lantern, the building's arms appeared to be reaching into nothing but blackness. Even the other side didn't look so black to me as the sky on that night.

That's when I saw Francis. Heard the creak of his rusted lantern. "What's he doing here?" I asked Mammy, my body stiff at the sight of his wide gait. His lantern swung like a sword, attacking the night.

"Get out the way!"

Just like that, I was back in Five Points. A peddler barreled past with a rickety cart, forcing me to stumble back—but my boots stuck fast in the muck, a churn of mud, straw, and manure from the endless press of carts and feet. He missed me, barely. I exhaled, glancing back at the swinging stable lantern. The air reeked of wet filth, smoke from street fires, and the briny bite of the harbor. It wasn't much for comfort, but it was better than facing Francis with my failure.

He arrived soon after, and we stepped into our lodgings for the night.

The inside of the stable was dimly lit, with hardly a streak of light filtering in through the cracks in the walls or the wee grime-coated windows. Though the space was large enough, it felt cramped. The air was thick and tense with the restless shuffling of horses and the stench of their unwashed bodies.

I would have gone to soothe them, but something about Francis stopped me. He was in high spirits. Too high. Smiling wide for a man about to sleep in a pile of wet, rotting hay. He'd even brought me hot gingerbread from a stand by the park, pressing it into my hands with an almost eager cheer.

It should have been a kindness. Instead, it unsettled me.

"Did you find work?" I dared to ask.

"Ah, no," he said absently, tearing a large bite from his pastry. I nearly sighed in relief. At least he wouldn't fault me for the very same failure.

"What's gotten into you, then?"

He grinned, his face all teeth and blue-gray eyes. "Our luck's about to change, May. I know it." Molasses clung to his fingers, and he licked each one in turn. "I found the gambling house."

"Gambling?" My smile vanished mid-bite. Every Traveler woman knew at least one man who was fond of gambling. It never ended well.

"Ease yourself," he said. "I've no taste for it, but the gambling houses are where a man learns what's doing in a new town. I have no money," he admitted, "but I've got something better."

"And what's better than money when you're hungry and homeless?"

"A plan." He raised his brows and grinned, mouth full. Crumbs tumbled to his lap.

A slow dread twisted in my stomach—not just from the butter-rich pastry, but from a Knowing.

It wasn't *reason* I felt, nor was it the hopelessness of our first day in America. This was something else, something foreign and unwanted, shoved into my hands like a sack of stones. And all the while, I was left to carry it.

Exhaustion ached through me, but my mind wouldn't rest. Francis had changed. His silence, his sudden decision to leave the city—none of it sat right. And yet, he was smiling. A real, bright smile, the kind I'd longed for since we wed.

How could I ruin it?

"We'll leave in the morning," he said.

"Leave?" The Knowing pressed deeper into my chest. It wasn't just the idea of traveling deeper into a strange land that seemed to stretch endlessly, though the nearness of the ocean did soothe me. I liked knowing it was there, like I could reach my hand out and scoop up my family just at the other end of the horizon. But it wasn't the loss of my dreaming that plagued me either.

It was something else. A sense of *where* we were going, muddled and sharp and somehow sterile and confining as a cage. The Knowing settled in my ribs, where my heart beat a dove's gentle cry, stifled by wind-soaked skies.

How could something feel so wrong yet fated at the same time?

"Francis, we've only just arrived. Where are we to go?"

He didn't answer right away, instead pulling a blanket from his bag. "Let's get some sleep," he said through a yawn. "By tomorrow night, we'll be in much finer accommodations, away from this vile city and its roach-infested holes these people call homes. Tomorrow it'll be roast chicken and red wine, don't you worry your pretty head about it."

He'd never called me pretty before.

He'd hardly said two sentences to me since John's death.

My whole body screamed at the way he was going on. He must be mad. Chicken and wine? As if he'd found a long-lost rich uncle. As if the world had turned itself inside out overnight.

But what could I do?

I wrapped myself in my shawl and shut my eyes. But the moment I did, I felt something else wrap around me. Not fabric. Not Francis.

Something softer. Darker. Velvety.

I stiffened, eyes flying open.

*Wings.*

Black as a dark angel's. As the space between stars.

No. Black as a *raven's*.

Feathers folded around me, shielding me from sight, from the cold, from everything. A warning? A promise? A piece of home come to find me?

I didn't know, but I felt safe, for the briefest moment. I breathed in, slow and deep. Faintly, impossibly, I caught the scent of jasmine on the cold air. It lingered softly, like the love spells Grandmammy used to weave in secret. She always said jasmine was for those meant to find each other, no matter the distance, no matter the odds.

Then it was gone.

The stable walls pressed back in. The damp gnawed through my shawl. And I was just another impoverished immigrant again, small and shivering, vulnerable to the night.

I didn't sleep much that night, leery as I was of rats or robbers or whatever might come upon us while we slept. But eventually, the cold won out, and I inched closer to Francis, drawn to the faint warmth of his body. He had no fat to warm him, and neither did I. But as I huddled close, careful not to wake him, I could feel my own heartbeat, and I knew my blood was still hot, still moving through me like liquid fire, and again I felt foolish, because I found myself hopeful despite it all.

# CHAPTER 3

## Clement

For just a moment, Clement allowed the heavy ache in his chest to subside. He squinted into the golden fields behind his parents' farmhouse, the biting wind like a tonic, sharp against his skin. There wasn't much left to be done before the final harvest, but Clement preferred to begin his days at dawn, even after a late night.

Only in those newest hours of a frosty morning could he feel connected to the life he was born into—could he look down at his brown hands, dirt permanently compacted beneath the fingernails— and pretend he wasn't the only one in his family with skin that shade.

He spotted his adoptive brother's unmistakable stride in the distance. Clement wasn't convinced that even Rudyard could fully understand why he'd want to remember his former life. His first life.

And it *was* an entire life, in a way. A family had and then not had. A home. A purpose, however despicable.

No, Rudyard could never understand why Clement wouldn't simply grasp his second life as a free man in the city of Hudson, New York with both hands, like the reins of a horse, and run full throttle.

*Don't look back*, Rudyard would suggest shyly. Clement shook his head at the thought. The ignorance. He would *always* look back. Whether he wanted to or not.

"No rest for the wicked?" Rudyard teased, holding out a steaming mug of coffee and a buttered roll.

Clement nodded his thanks, certain that the treat had taken his brother some time to prepare. That morning had been so cold, not a drop of water remained liquid. When Clement had opened the bread box, he'd given the loaf a firm knock before conceding there was no hope for breakfast.

"The potatoes need harvesting," Clement answered plainly, eyes glued to his crop.

He felt his brother's tentative gaze. Frowned. No time for Rudyard's unfounded concern. After the final harvest, their cellar would be filled with all the food they'd have for winter, hopefully enough to stretch until March. But only *after* the harvest.

For the luckiest, the dregs of winter would be little more than a time of rain and thaw. A chance to catch some air without teeth chattering. But for most folks throughout the Hudson Valley and Catskill Mountains, March would mark what their father had always called *The Dying Time*. Even for those with means, it was when meat ran low, and everyone fought for warmth.

He sighed, weary of Rudyard's oppressive gaze. Even though Rudyard had listened to the same warnings from their father, even though more than one winter had passed where they'd been left hungering for an early spring, they'd never *truly* wanted.

Well, Rudyard hadn't. Clement supposed if you'd never known lacking in the way he had, it was a sort of impossible concept to appreciate. The way an empty stomach claws. It's like a beast hunting inside you. A beast with talons.

He ventured a look at his brother. "See how the leaves have died back?" He gestured for Rudyard to look closely. "That means the potatoes are ready."

From where he crouched on the ground, he looked up at his lean-statured brother to see if he was paying attention. With the sunlight directly behind him, Rudyard's light hair looked gray, but his green eyes still sparkled. Rudyard raised an eyebrow, and for a fleeting moment, Clement felt that familiar childlike longing to let go, to shed the weight of everything, to shrug off the memories like a tattered coat—just for a moment—and enjoy his good fortune.

He cracked a smile and rose to take his breakfast with a clap on his brother's back. Rudyard lost his balance only slightly. Clement *did* tower a good half foot above him, and he was broader still.

"Thank you," Clement said earnestly, amused by his own strength. He bit into the roll and held it up approvingly.

"Back to the land of the living, huh?" Rudyard asked, his smile not quite reaching his eyes.

Clement looked at his brother dubiously. He recognized that look. Rudyard had something on his mind. "You know, Rud, if you spent half as much time working this farm with me as you did cracking jokes, we might be living on a real paradise here."

What had Clement been thinking? He could never *let go*. There would be no one left to hold the severity of it all. Someone had to hold it. Bear it.

"Very well then," Rudyard played along. "Pitch in more on the farm, huh? Let me take a stab at it. Give you a break?"

They locked eyes for a second, then broke out in laughter. This was what Clement loved most about his brother. *This* version of Rudyard. The brother who could always—had always—brought him back to the land of the living.

Clement took the final slug of his coffee and pushed the mug against Rudyard's chest. "In all seriousness, I should get back to it. I told Mother I'd have these curing by midday."

No time to wait for a response. He adjusted his pants and returned to his spot on the ground.

Clement *felt* more than *observed* Rudyard's frown. He cocked an eyebrow toward Rudyard, who raised his hat with one hand and combed his sandy hair back with the other.

"In all seriousness, Clem, why don't you take a break? Father said you were with a group last night. He said you didn't get back until nearly dawn. For pity's sake, did you even sleep at all?" Rudyard's eyes glinted, unnervingly bright in the rising sun.

Clement returned the frown. Rubbed the back of his neck. His other hand clutched his trowel. With a sharp thrust, he drove it into the frozen earth.

"Clem, I'm your brother," Rudyard went on. "Talk to me. Tell me what's going on. I know you love to work, and I know winter is right around the corner, but you're running yourself ragged lately. If you're not out in the field, you're building something. If you're not building, you're mending. If you're not mending, you're butchering—"

"I get it," Clement said more sharply than he'd intended. "I'm busy." The frozen soil resisted his trowel's edge. He grit his teeth and dug deeper.

Silence. His brother's eyes bore into the back of his neck.

Clement sighed, setting down his tool. Brushing his hands against his pant legs. Sweat trickled down his brow, despite the icy wind.

"Autumn is no time to sit around idly," he said as patiently as he could. It would be easier to get everything done if Rudyard didn't worry about him. If he'd simply leave him be. "With the river frozen nearly one third of the year, floods in May, snow in June, crops failing, thousands starving... What? Don't give me that look."

He pulled a rag from his jacket pocket as he stood back up and whipped his brother playfully. They were seven again. Just meeting for the first time. Setting off on their second chances with a foolish amount of trust.

Well, their instant bond had proven not so foolish over time, hadn't it?

Rudyard laughed, but after a moment, his mouth curved into something more pensive, as if searching for the right words. Clement waited. Braced himself.

"It's that ridiculous Fugitive Slave Act, isn't it?"

A crow cawed as it landed in the ancient black walnut tree that

23

shaded the farmhouse. Clement shook the feeling away. Though not superstitious, the eerie timing of it, the fog, the withering leaves—all of it made his stomach twist. He sighed, returning his gaze to his brother, who wasn't usually this perceptive.

A wave of guilt washed over him. His mind could be a storm, but he shouldn't let it rain on the one person who cared for him most. If it hadn't been for Rudyard, he wouldn't even be here.

"It's not that I worry about myself," Clement answered carefully. "I've been a free man for seventeen years. I have a life here. I feel safe for the most part. Not a day goes by that I don't think about where I came from and how lucky I was to find our family."

How lucky he was that Rudyard did what he did to bring Clement into the family.

No sense getting sentimental though. He bit his lip closed. His mind could be a storm, and now, its clouds ripened with rain. "But it's all the other enslaved people," he pushed on, "who are miserable day in and day out, who deserve the same right to freedom that I was fortunate enough to find. Now their path is even more dangerous. Now it's not enough for them to escape to the North. They've got to run all the way to Canada. When I left, I barely..." He shook his head. "I thought... Never mind. It's not important now."

He returned to his harvesting, once again digging his trowel into hard earth. Regretting planting the tubers so deep.

When he looked back up, Clement found his brother staring at him, green eyes twinkling with concern and admiration and something else Clement couldn't quite place.

"Maybe I envy you, Clem," Rudyard said softly. "You have purpose. You're a good Quaker. Simplicity and humility are your highest virtues. Equality and freedom for all, your greatest mission. You wear our somber gray and brown uniform with care and comfort, never so much as blinking in the direction of one of Warren Street's latest displays of New York City fashions."

Clement cocked an eyebrow. "They're forbidden," he said plainly.

As forbidden as jewelry. They both knew this, yet Clement looked away guiltily. Just because something was forbidden didn't mean it was forgotten. A man with secrets recognizes a man with secrets.

Clement had a hunch about Rudyard's, just as he knew Rudyard had a hunch about his. Clement was almost certain, in fact, that Rudyard's eye had caught the faint sparkle of a chain around Clement's neck ever so briefly, once or twice, when they stripped to swim in the creek or changed before bed.

But Rudyard had never asked about it.

"You can talk to me, Clement. I know we've never talked about how it was for you... before. Maybe I... maybe I should have asked. I—"

"I know, Rudyard. I know. But I'm fine, truly." Clement plucked a clump of potatoes from the earth with more force than necessary. "And I *will* rest. Just as soon as every caged man, woman, and child knows what it means to fly."

Rudyard's frown deepened. "Well, if you won't sleep, and insist on harvesting all the potatoes *right now*, the morning after the coldest night of the season, mind you, I might as well help you out. You look pitiful out here."

Clement's lips curled ruefully.

His brother delicately rolled up his pants, then shifted his body toward the cold earth. "Hard to keep your clothes clean while you're at it, isn't it?" Rudyard grumbled.

Clement gave him a friendly clap on the back before tossing him a rag. "Pitiful, huh?" he teased.

For a few minutes, they worked in silence. Clement broke up the dirt, gesturing for Rudyard to clean off the potatoes and place them in the basket. Once they'd established a rhythm, he nodded to himself decidedly before asking his brother the question that had been on his own mind.

"What about you, Rud? What is it that you value more than sleep? Surely there must be something beyond illicit fashion and socializing that you're passionate about?"

"I... have my interests. But I fear they're unflattering," he said carefully, as though weighing his words.

Clement avoided his eyes, his throat suddenly dry. He regretted asking.

"Unflattering as these unfortunate square-toed shoes and flat hat,"

Rudyard added, strained levity in his tone. He removed his hat, examining the rim, pulling a stuck feather from the crown. "I know it's called a wideawake but why not call it a fast asleep? Because the design is so boring, it puts one to sleep..."

Clement set down the dirt-blackened crop he was about to pass to Rudyard. The hat and shoes marked them as Quakers—plain, practical, and set apart. A people bound by faith and conscience. Nothing *wrong* with that.

And *unflattering?* Rudyard's choice of words stuck in the spot in his throat where he suppressed a scream. How many times had he heard folks whisper the same about *him* as he walked down Warren Street with a member of his family? As they pointed at his skin? His hair?

"What do you mean?" His voice sharpened when he finally spoke, though he quickly caught himself. "I can't understand that. You have every advantage imaginable. Whatever it is you want can't be that impossible."

Rudyard scoffed, eyes poised on the red spuds. "What if you're wrong? What if God made a mistake with me? If perhaps my soul was meant for another, and—" He quickly checked Clement's face for his reaction.

Clement remained deadpan. He picked up the potato. Wiped it down meticulously.

"Oh, I don't know, Clem. I know how I sound. It's only, you know this whole idea of spiritualism that keeps making headlines? I've been thinking. If there are people, these spiritualists, who can communicate with the other side, perhaps they might know something that could help me figure out why I am the way I am."

Clement wanted to ask his brother which way he *was*, exactly, then quickly decided he didn't want to know. He licked his lips, dry from the morning's exertions.

"Nothing these *spirits* can tell a man that he can't figure out for himself." Clement had said the word *spirits* more mockingly than he'd intended. It was a ridiculous fiddle-faddle, of course. A craze, playing with people's minds and taking a pretty penny from their pockets, at that.

But he regretted speaking harshly with Rudyard. He always did.

"All I'm saying," Rudyard persisted, dropping a shiny potato into the basket, "is that I'd be interested to meet one of these spiritualists. The Fox sisters, for example. They're only in Rochester. I could make that trip in two days. They're part of a Quaker community now. I mean, what are the chances? Spiritualism flourishing within our own community? Well, now that I say so out loud, I suppose it makes sense. We follow the doctrine of *Inner Light*. Any individual can experience divine contact with God. Why not with the other side?"

Clement looked at his square-toed boots. Bit his lip.

"They hold seances for artists, progressives, forward-thinkers, suffragists, abolitionists, you name it!" Rudyard continued. "Clem, you're so focused. *All* the time. You've never courted a woman. You don't even *talk* to women, for pity's sake, though you have no trouble acquiring their interest. You never take a day off from the farm or the railroad."

He exhaled sharply, shaking his head. "We're both twenty-four, but you're the only one of us who is following his own path. I feel like I'm still trying to find where mine begins! This movement is at the forefront of all that's unfolding right now. What if there's a place for me within it? What if it could offer me the kind of purpose you've always had and I've always wanted?"

It was Clement's turn to shake his head. Artists, progressives, suffragists, *and* abolitionists? It seemed like too many different causes for all the spirit world to favor. Rudyard had it right the first time— What *were* the chances?

"The Fox sisters?" he asked, remembering the name from the papers. He'd read the headlines, slick with sensation as the oil that once made Hudson a flourishing community of merchants and whalers. "Those girls who found a corpse in their backyard a couple of years ago? People still follow their story?"

Clement stopped digging. Rudyard looked at the space where the dirty potatoes stopped piling up.

"They didn't just *find* a body," he clarified. "They communicated with its spirit through a sort of tapping system they called rapping. They told the spirit in their bedroom to rap three times if it was injured, *and it did*. They developed an entire way of speaking to him

27

and were able to find out the spirit belonged to a peddler who was murdered five years prior *in their farmhouse.*"

Rudyard's eyes gleamed as he leaned in. "Think about it, Clem. Through the rapping method, people are able to communicate with the greatest minds that ever lived. They can ask questions like, 'Is there equality for the races after death?' and, 'Should women have the vote?'"

He spread his hands, as if presenting some grand revelation. "The spirit realm is answering with a resounding *Yes!*"

"So what happened to this peddler?" Clement asked, skepticism coating his words. If there *was* a spirit realm, his patience was somewhere just as far off. His throat felt dry again in the place where he detected a scream germinating.

He sat down. Crossed his legs. He was in this conversation with his brother whether he liked it or not. There was no way to hide his thoughts on the matter. Only one cause was worth his time and energy—the one that made him into the man he was today—and all others could be left to someone else as far as he was concerned. Not to him, and not to his own brother.

Rudyard remained on his knees. "Local residents came to examine the cellar. They found strands of hair and bone fragments." He gaped at Clement as though he'd just shared the most remarkable evidence. A gust of wind carried the faint anise scent of goldenrod.

Clement gave him a blank stare. "*That's* their proof? Some hair and bone?" He laughed, but bitterness slipped into his voice. "Rud, check our own cellar. I'm sure you'll find more than that from the squirrels alone. Besides, artists, suffragists… I don't know, Rud. Just last month Congress passed The Fugitive Slave Act, and frankly, I don't see how you're able to think of anything else."

"Frederick Douglass attended a seance with the Fox sisters," Rudyard countered, his body stiffening against the wind. His cheeks were red, but Clement couldn't be sure whether it was the wind or his own disregard that caused it.

"There's a link there, Clem. A whole world telling us what side is right and what side is wrong."

"Douglass? Really?" Clement raised his eyebrows, then brushed off the thought. "No. Couldn't be."

Rudyard let out a deep sigh, though really, Clement didn't understand what Rudyard had to be so impatient about. "Clement, there is a world out there waiting to give us guidance. Angels are not just above us but all around. They—"

Clement grabbed his trowel, pushing himself back up to his knees. "I can't listen to this anymore. How can you go on about spirits when your own brother could be sent back to Louisiana?"

Rudyard flinched, and instantly Clement felt a pang of regret. He knew his brother's sensitivity. He knew how blunt he could be; their mother often pointed it out. But life could be taken at any moment—why not speak plainly? And yet…

"Wait," he said, voice softening. "It's just that I don't believe in all those spiritualist sensations. I don't see why Quakers are taking time out of more important causes to entertain the whims of two young girls." He'd meant to apologize, but he could see from the way Rudyard slouched that he'd failed.

"No, you're right. Forget it." Rudyard stood up, brushing the dirt off his knees. "You know, I'm really no good at farmwork. I'll see you back inside, if that suits?" He turned and walked away before Clement could say another word.

# CHAPTER 4

## Olivia

"We *need* a security guard," Olivia pressed, placing a firm, perfectly manicured hand on her madam's milky shoulder.

Maude shrugged it away in a huff, turning toward the kitchen of the Queen Anne house on Diamond Street. The porridge bubbled on the range, filling the small, dim kitchen with the scent of cinnamon and nutmeg. It wasn't Nellie's famous hash and cornbread, but it was the best Olivia could muster up with her very limited culinary skills. No one ever said she was destined for homemaking.

Maude swung back around. "Honestly, Livykins, how can I even *think* of hiring someone new while our dear Nellie is under the weather? Here I am, practically a kitchen maid! And now you want to add even more to my plate." Her dark eyes rounded with sadness, but

Olivia saw right through it. "It's like you don't even think about me," Maude blithered on with dramatic flair.

Olivia crossed her arms and shot her employer a pointed look. "And who's here with you now, waking up early, stirring the porridge herself? Cora? Annie? All I see is me, helping you out when you ask, as always."

Maude blinked, adjusting her posture. "Olivia"—she pouted, the name curling on her lips in that drawn out way that told Olivia she wasn't interested—"I have bigger things to worry about than muscle. You girls handle yourselves just *fine*. Has French Maude ever let anything bad happen to you? Here, help me set the table." Maude pressed a stack of white china into Olivia's hands.

Sighing, Olivia wrapped her long brown fingers around the bowls. As she began to set the table, she noticed that nearly every bowl was chipped or cracked. When did *that* happen? She remembered the day Maude bought that set. They'd been previously owned, yes, but in excellent condition. She pressed her lips together as she laid out the bowls one by one with extreme care.

She could feel Maude's eyes pressing into the back of her ringlets. Olivia *loved* her new hair style. The other girls might tease her about her "unfavorable" complexion, but they couldn't say a word about her hair. Or her nails. *Or* her scent. Olivia took care of herself. More than she could say about the other girls, who didn't seem to care if they bathed each morning or not.

She set, and she waited. It was a battle of wills with Maude, and she wouldn't give in first. The grandfather clock ticked.

"Olivia," Maude repeated.

Olivia's lips twitched. She heard the softening in her madam's husky voice. It was subtle. The other girls would have missed it. But she heard it. She could feel Maude roll her eyes, cross her arms over her ample bosom.

"Olivia," Maude repeated a third time when Olivia went on setting the table, positioning the spoons just so. Olivia held one up and frowned at its dove-gray tint. The silverware seemed in need of an update, too.

"You know I'm the *first* to listen to your ideas," Maude began. "You say I need to read this novel or the other? Well, I've read a few, haven't I?" Maude moved closer, her red hair like a ball of fire in Olivia's peripheral vision.

Olivia snickered. *"Have* you?" she retorted, turning to face the older woman.

"Haven't I?" Maude said somewhat sheepishly. Then she sighed. "I'm tight on cash, honey. Security guards won't work on time. It was a slow summer, and you know how business slacks in autumn. And then winter, well, Hudson is practically a ghost town!"

It was Olivia's turn to sigh. "I wouldn't ask if this wasn't important," she said. "Cora got stiffed twice last week. Annie doesn't know what month we're in, let alone if someone's paid her. And Claire... Claire weighs about as much as a feather. They're not safe here. We need some system of organization. We need a new man. It's been nearly a year since George left."

"You seem to be doing all right," Maude challenged, one thin eyebrow rising curiously high.

Olivia frowned. "I take care of myself," she said plainly.

Maude poured the coffee in one even motion, then handed Olivia a brimming cup. Olivia inhaled the steam, closing her eyes for a moment. Hot coffee on a brisk autumn morning. *Bliss.*

Her bliss ended with a thud as Maude set the percolator on the bare walnut table. Olivia shot her attention back to Maude, who was squinting at her. "What do you care about these girls, anyway, hm? I hate to be the one to break it to you, Livy Baby, but they wouldn't do the same for you."

Olivia set down her cup, then took her time choosing a cup for Maude in the cabinet. The cups, too, seemed to have their fair share of chips and cracks. She grabbed one and filled it, watching the coffee slither like a shiny black snake.

Maude was right, of course. Not one of her co-workers would ever stand up for her.

"That's not the point," Olivia said firmly. She paused, unsure if she should speak her mind. Then she softly set down Maude's cup on its dish and looked up at her friend. Maude was never one to hold her tongue. Why should Olivia?

"This is the right thing to do, Maude. And I know that that matters to you." She held Maude's gaze, even as her throat ran dry. If any of the girls had walked into the kitchen just then, they wouldn't have caught Olivia's meaning. But she'd said enough. She'd said *just* enough.

Maude's frown was broad and deep. "Oh, all right! I'll hire your mutton shunter. But I'm getting someone Irish and cheap this time." Maude took a large gulp of coffee, sputtering slightly from the heat. "I won't even tell the girls it was your idea. How's that?" she added sardonically, lifting her steaming cup in cheers.

Olivia bit back a grin. "Cheers," she mimicked. She took the first sip of her coffee, a sense of pure luxury lubricating her throat. Fortified, she inhaled sharply and placed a hand on Maude's.

Maude sighed a smile, meeting Olivia's eyes. Olivia couldn't be sure what she saw in Maude's expression, but it felt like understanding or compassion or something almost like a mother's love.

Olivia sniffed and cleared her throat, her gaze shifting back to her coffee.

Thankfully Maude seemed to feel the same discomfort. "Well, well"—she broke away, swiping at nothing—"who knows when these Vanderbilt daughters will deign to show their lazy rumps? Get the porridge, will you? No sense waiting all afternoon. Besides, do I have some gossip for you!"

With Maude's usual breakfast prattle, the afternoon carried on as usual. And as Olivia ate her mediocre concoction and watched her madam's vibrant curls sway to the beat of her animated accounts of Hudson's latest goings-on—autumn leaves tousled by the wind—she thought about the china again.

When did they buy it? Was it six years ago? Seven? How could that be?

Business was slow, but surely Maude could spring for a new set. Olivia sipped her coffee in silence, suddenly not so hungry.

If Maude did buy another set, how would Olivia feel sitting at French Maude's, at that same long table, in another seven years? Would she just be staring at the same cracks on different china? Would she look across the table at Maude and notice how the older woman's hair no longer burned the same vibrant flame but appeared withered and dull, more November than October?

And what about her own hair? She changed it every couple of months. What style would her older self choose, and would it be stylish enough to keep her sense of worth?

The question startled her, and she immediately regretted asking it, even silently, even just to herself.

She pressed her cup back to her lips, hiding the thought in peppery plumes.

Yet one thought shone clear against the murky background of questions she knew better than to entertain. With the strangest sense of foreboding, it seemed like buying a new set of china would inevitably lead to the very scenarios she wished to avoid the most.

She coughed, having taken too large of a gulp herself this time. Adjusting her posture, she set down her cup, deciding it best not to draw Maude's attention to the china at all.

# CHAPTER 5

# Map

*I* stepped onto the ferry with trepidation, the same unease twisting my insides as when I first set foot on a boat, months of grueling travel stretching ahead. I swallowed the bitter taste of fear, forcing it down like plain coffee—no cream, no sugar. I stayed above deck, eyes locked on the Hudson River as it carried us onward, a silver ribbon threading through the wind, pulling us toward the namesake city.

I looked at my worn black boots, toes barely covered in their crumbling leather, and smoothed the coarse fabric of my skirt. My cheeks burned with shame at my appearance—shame for how I looked, and then shame for caring so much. Here I was, my boots barely holding together, surrounded by people in silk, laughing as they sipped their drinks—drinks they'd paid extra for—while the fine orchestra played, each note a reminder of how out of place I felt.

"They call the county across the river Greene," Francis told me, his voice steady as we leaned on the deck, "because it's as green as the rolling hills of Ireland. When we look out the window of our new home, we'll see our old one. Our own wee slice of Ireland."

Would I be grateful for the reminder of all I'd left behind? Perhaps. New York City was a metropolis the likes of which I'd never seen. It was overcrowded and reeked of unhappy animals and waste. A part of me was glad to leave it behind.

The ferry bobbed over a rough patch of water. That's when the wind rushed out of me, and the chatter around me dimmed to a low, lazy drone.

So many souls had been lost in that dark river, and to them, it was as if their torment hadn't ended. It gripped me, seeking a way through.

I closed my eyes, and I could almost hear their stories—old, fading voices whispering beneath the surface, as if trying to drag themselves back to living.

I imagined myself anywhere but here. I was on land, walking beside the donkey down another dusty road. In bed, snug between my siblings. On the banks of the Shannon. Cocooned in the wings of a raven...

I longed for anything familiar. Anything that wasn't this cold metal and a crowded deck. Beautifully as the orchestra played, I felt trapped. Francis was the one who believed this was the right path. Not me.

The ferry docked, and Francis extended a hand to help me down. The wind rushed through my frizzy curls, blinding me like the sun—so unfamiliar after months in steerage.

"No farmhouses on Manhattan Island, to be sure," he said, his voice soft but determined, as if he might sway me. "Just hold fast to your dream, May."

The words stole my breath for a moment. They were so much like Flynn's. And yet, something was missing when Francis said them. A softness? A selflessness? I couldn't place it, but my heart ached to believe that the sentiment hadn't died with Flynn.

Francis seemed to know something I wasn't sure I still had the courage to believe in. The dream of a proper home, of warmth, of peace. A dream I wasn't sure I even had the right to hold onto anymore. But Francis remembered it for me. He knew what I wanted most in this world, and I didn't have to explain it. He didn't mock me for it.

For a moment, I let hope rise in my chest, the idea that maybe, just maybe, this would work.

But that Knowing—it came again, cold and uninvited.

*Imagine the worst,* it said. *That's where you'll be safest.*

The city met us with a barrage of carriages waiting to take the important gentlemen and ladies to their homes and hotels. We walked down the paved sidewalks of Warren Street.

Temptations beckoned from every shop window. From the river up to the public square at Seventh Street, shopkeeps boasted home furnishings, ivory goods, bakeries of sugar jumbles, drop cakes, and ginger nuts, bookstores for the latest gossip and romantic novels. I'd never seen such ware and splendor. But none of it touched me more than a pair of wee knit stockings in a quiet shop window. They had a bit of a scalloped lace trim, and I thought they'd look pure lovely on my youngest baby sister.

We walked on. A light snow started to fall. It was the first of November. Perhaps with the fresh month, city, and snow, there could be a fresh start between Francis and me, as well. Perhaps I'd been foolish to feel sorry for myself on the fever ship. Of course Francis hadn't been interested in me after all his suffering, and in the midst of conditions worse than we'd had even on land. Who would be able to focus on love or a marriage in such a state of distress?

I wasn't entirely naive, child though I was. I saw how Francis would look at my brother John. We were all three together by my sister Lucy's graveside when John, not long before he passed himself, gripped his cropped red hair and began pulling.

It was Francis who held him tightly, and they fell to their knees together, until John calmed down enough to accept the reality, the permanence, of his twin sister's death.

It was Francis who wiped the blood from John's nose, the blood that foretold a fate like Lucy's.

There was love within Francis, and maybe he could find it for me, too.

Now I followed close behind as he stopped to ask passersby for directions. The night came on quickly. We spent the last of our savings on a wee room in a cheap inn at the edge of town.

I slowly stripped down to my shift as I faced the clouded window. Francis was already in bed, beneath the cover. It was the first night he would have the chance to make me his wife not only by priest but in body as well. Our first night alone, in a room of our own, where strangers weren't packed in like sardines.

A part of me longed for those strangers. Another part of me wondered… What would it feel like to be touched by a man?

Gazing in the mirror, I parted my hair down the middle with my fingers, smoothing each half down the front of my body just as Mammy had done for me the last night I saw her.

I didn't want to think again of that eerie night, the swinging of Francis's lantern, the urgent, strange tenderness in Mammy's eyes when I'd asked her what we were doing at a church while the rest of the family slept huddled in our wagon.

Yet that's exactly where my mind drifted.

"What's he doing here?" I'd asked Mammy desperately, teeth chattering.

The words echoed in my mind, the same ones I remembered outside the stable where we'd spent last night. As I gazed at the fractured mirror, I wondered if I was destined to keep hearing those echoes—seeing the swing of Francis's lantern, feeling my teeth chatter —each time I looked into cracked glass. Was that who I'd always be? Fragile, broken, haunted by shards of the past.

I'd clung to Mammy's sleeve as I'd asked the question. She began to finger the rosary beads she always wore about her neck.

A bantam crowed somewhere off in the distance. It was a curious, fearsome sound at that hour. It meant something was about to go wrong.

Mammy stiffened at the sound, but she made no mention of it. Instead, she turned to me and looked me straight in the eyes. I couldn't remember the last time I'd seen her look at me like that, truly look at me like she was searching, *needing* an answer.

"What are *we* doing here?" I asked next. "What are we doing at the church in the middle of the night? Why did you pack me extra stockings? Why didn't we tell anyone we were leaving?"

I had more questions but by then my throat was closed and I felt the tears coming. Mammy reached over my shoulders to draw my hair into a bundle, then split it in half like two loaves of bread and smoothed each half across my collarbones.

"Listen here, May Connally. I know what'll become of you if you stay. If you survive, in a year or two you'll marry. Your husband will have you going door to door with your sixth sense.

"If he's kind, he'll use you until your cup runs dry as a broomstick. If he's anything like some of ours, he'll give out to you until you turn to the drink like I did, and like your grandmammy before me. You'll have yourself twelve bonny children to look after by the time you're younger than I.

"And your talents? They'll feel more like a curse, so bone tired will you be that your eyes flutter closed to the good spirits and open wide to the evil ones. Naw, I won't have that for you."

She stared off for a moment, then looked back at me with a haunted expression. Her eyes were pale and sharp. "You stand a chance in the world. Our people know a sadness the likes of which the settled people will never know. A beauty, too, aye, but there's a biting sadness that comes with it. Do you understand me, May?"

"No," I admitted freely. I'd never heard her speak this way before. She was always practical, her mind as rooted on the next task as the forest paths we traveled. "I haven't a notion of what you're talking about. What do you mean, 'if I stay'?"

Silence.

"Mammy, where am I to go?" My voice sounded small and faraway.

"Give me your hand," Mammy ordered, ignoring my questions. She placed a small purse of coins in my palm and closed my fingers around it. "May, you're to go to America. It's only a short walk to the port. You're to buy yourself a ticket. Leave and make a life for yourself. I've seen too many of my children dead in this God-forsaken land, God forgive me for saying so. I won't lose you, too. Not when you've a gift like yours that shouldn't go wasted."

She turned her gaze toward Francis, now just a few paces away. "Francis will marry you, so you won't be alone. I've already discussed it with his mam. It's a good match, and the two of you will fare well together. Mind you don't mix with the others there. Don't go mixing with anyone different from you."

"But, Mammy—" I tried to interrupt. I wanted to tell her that I didn't love Francis, and never would, nor would he love me. Our bond might deepen, but he'd never look at me like he'd looked at John. But before I could speak the words, I knew how foolish of me it was to think of love. Love was a privilege for those who had not been abandoned by God.

I swallowed my words. Instead, my only plea was that she keep the money. "You need this," I told her.

"Naw, May. *You* need this. You take this now, and when the time comes, you'll help us in kind." She gave a single, sharp nod. She wasn't often one for words, but when she had something to say, that changed. She spoke as though she were possessed, like the words couldn't tumble quickly enough from her parched lips.

"Now listen. When you get to America, you don't forget your little brothers and sisters, you hear me? I need you to work hard and send for them. And God forgive me for doing it this way," she said, her voice trembling but firm. "Hauling you out of bed in the dead of night and marrying you off without your family here. But what choice have I? You know your da would never allow it. Thinks we need you here, scraping by on readings for a shilling." She paused, the lines on her face etched deep. "But it's a woman that sees the road ahead. We need you *there*. You understand?"

My head was shaking rapidly then, more rapidly than I thought I had strength for. "I can't, Mammy. I can't do all that. Send Eileen or—"

Mammy's grip tightened on my shoulders. "You listen to me, May Connally. It's you that's going. Not your sisters or brothers. You're my eldest, and you're here for a reason none of us know yet. You're the one that's to go. I made mistakes with you, being my first, but this—I'll get right."

Her voice rose, a shriek into the quiet night. "I don't have what you have. I read palms and tea leaves like your grandmammy showed me, but your gift, May—it's like no Connally woman has ever possessed before. You were born with it, and you're not to waste it. Has this famine taught you nothing?"

I wished I could paint color into her sallow cheeks, that I had fingers gentle and magical enough to do it.

How could I feel so loved and so alone at the same time?

A single sob broke free before I nodded, swallowing the rest of my fears like a bitter draught. The truth of the matter was, I'd never been so afraid in all my life, nor so filled with a wild, trembling excitement. Finally, I could see a road out of hell, where the spirits were surely more numerous and starved than anyplace else.

Friar Hoare came next, solemn as the grave. He conducted the ceremony, and he did so briefly. When the moment came for Francis and me to kiss, Francis just looked down at his feet, stock still. Finally, I looked him square in his white, windburned face and laid a small kiss on his mouth. His lips never moved at all. They remained still and cold as a fish's. Only his eyelids fluttered up, revealing eyes like shards of ice, piercing and still.

That was my first kiss.


I FIXED my shoulders down my back and gazed once more into the inn's cracked mirror. My hair was parted neatly down the middle, but there was no hiding the tension in my face or the heaviness in my eyes. The weight of my promise pressed down on me like a stone. I had to make a life in America, one that was worth the sacrifice my family had made. I turned around to face Francis.

He lay still with his back toward me. I crept to the bed, sitting silently beside him. After a moment, I cleared my throat in case he hadn't felt the slight sinking of the mattress. His head shifted just slightly, and he raised an eyebrow in my direction.

"Goodnight," he said simply.

I thought I might have heard the tiniest drop of tenderness in his voice. I stared at him as he turned back around. Perhaps I was only imagining the tenderness.

"Goodnight," I said softly.

Sleep came slowly. I don't remember it coming on at all. Just that tough, stuffy feeling in the eyes as I lay on my back listening to Francis's strangled snores.

We left without ceremony the next morning, as though the night hadn't passed and we were still continuing on from the day before.

The city was something else entirely. I tried to take it all in as I trotted behind Francis, the heels of my boots clicking against the uneven stones. A lovely patina of brick and stone townhouses stood shoulder to shoulder, lining the streets. Men and women in fine clothing and polished boots crossed the wide dirt streets, chasing away a few stray swine and hurrying into the pretty shops that glittered with chandeliers glowing in the windows.

A flash of color caught my eye—a tiny rainbow darting across the cobblestones, cast from the light of one of those chandeliers. Without thinking, I reached out as though I might catch it, my fingers hovering just above the ground. But it vanished before I could touch it, melting into the gray morning.

I pulled my hand back quickly, feeling foolish. What was I thinking? To be sure, there'd be no leprechauns on the other end here in this city.

Still, a smirk tugged at my lips when I spotted a few men lingering outside the grog shops in the early light, their steps slow and tipsy, indeed giving me a taste of home.

As we turned off Warren Street, I gaped at the row of elegant houses shaded by chestnut trees. There were homes with wide pillars, cottages devoured by red ivy, and mansions with round-arched windows and low-pitched roofs. Marble stoops boasted iron scrapers for the quality folk to rid their boots of muck. I imagined myself employed by one of these families, in charge of keeping their floors swept, sanded, and shined. I'd do the dusting, the polishing, even the cooking. Maybe one day, I'd be doing it all for myself, in my own home, my family there with me.

At the corner of State and North Seventh, one building caught my eye. A monstrous brick structure with six chimneys, a fanlight above the front door, and three gables, all surrounded by a black wrought-iron gate. Only when I stopped walking did Francis notice. He followed my gaze, and though he might have seen the color seep from my cheeks, he hurried me along, his focus fixed on our final destination.

"Diamond Street?" he asked a man passing by in a dark frock coat, top hat, and polished leather boots.

I held my breath, wondering why Francis had to ask for directions from such a wealthy man of all people.

The gentleman made a strange sound, almost a *humph* in the back of his throat. He looked from Francis to me with the pinched expression I'd have expected. He was judging us, of course. Our clothes were ratty, and we were overdue for washing, but still I felt an indignant fire in my belly. He swiftly pointed across a deep gully in the road ahead before shaking his head and marching off.

"Diamond Street," Francis noted upon arrival, looking around proudly like he was Henry Hudson himself.

Two rows of shabby houses lined the dirt road, which was cloaked in a thin, chilly mist rising from the river and casting a gray haze over the bordering cobblestone. The air, dense and damp, smelled of smoke leftover from the previous night's fires and lanterns. A pig grunted at us before scurrying off. Otherwise, the block was quiet but on edge, as though waiting for the day's clamor to pick up.

We approached a large house with a taupe doorway, where a couple of lasses lounged, wrapped in house coats over fancy gowns.

Francis, seeming to have found exactly what he was looking for, turned to me.

"I'll be right back. Wait here," he said.

I watched as he pushed his way inside, shoulders squared with purpose. When I turned back, I found myself under the scrutiny of the lasses. Their eyes were puffy, half-lidded, the kind that came from too little sleep and too much drink.

"I thought he was your man," one of them said, a cigarette dangling lazily between her teeth.

"Beg your pardon?" I asked. I pulled my shawl tighter around my shoulders. Next to them, I must have been a sorry sight, shivering in rags, unwashed and wild-haired.

"That was my guess," the lass continued, voice casual, though there was an edge to it that pricked my skin. "We saw you coming and made our guesses about who you were to each other." She studied my face, noting my blank expression. Her mouth curled. "Cora here thought he was your pimp. Guess I owe her a drink."

The one called Cora exhaled smoke through her nose, smiling slyly.

I had never seen a woman smoke before. The sight of it threw me; the smell even more so. Mammy used to try to steal puffs from Da's clay pipe, but he'd slap her hand away, snapping for her to keep her ugly mouth off his tobacco. That scent—woody and bitter—wrapped around me so completely that, for a moment, I forgot where I was.

The lasses were staring at me.

"No, you're mistaken," I stammered, words tumbling over themselves. "He *is* my man. My husband. Why—"

Before I could finish, they locked eyes and burst into laughter.

"Oh, honey," the first one said, shaking her head. "And here I thought *we* had it rough. You poor thing." She flicked her cigarette, embers tumbling into the street. "He takes his turn too, I hope? Fine, tall man like that. Bit skinny, though."

My heart pounded so hard I thought it might crack my ribs. *I'm alive, I'm alive, I'm alive,* I told myself, as if the words could still the trembling in my chest. Whatever was happening, I was *alive*, and so I was fairing better than John and Lucy.

44

*Perhaps.*

I wasn't so sure anymore.

I turned, looking through the house's bay window. The eaves were lined with sweet, gingerbread brackets. I couldn't make out anything inside except the black, oily glisten of the parlor stove. My gaze shifted back to the lasses. Their paint was thick and stale, the kind worn too long, through too many hours.

"What is this place?" I asked, my voice barely a whisper.

The house had an elegance to it, with intricate engravings that hinted at former wealth, but time had not been kind. The paint peeled. The lantern hanging from the portico was missing a pane of glass. The banisters were wobbly, the wood rotting. Now that the mist had thinned, I could see that the rest of the buildings on the street fared no better. Sagging roofs. Faded red curtains. Shadows lingering in doorways.

I watched as Cora, her straight black hair falling like a sleek curtain over her shoulders, frowned and her expression turned distant. "You don't know?" She had an accent—not thick, but foreign enough. Yet it didn't stop her from sounding utterly American. "There's only one thing people come to Hudson for."

"Well, two," the red-haired girl corrected. She looked younger than me, freckles scattered across her cheeks like Lucy's. "These bawdy houses or the gambling parlors. But most who come chasing one vice end up indulging in both."

"Three if you count the saloons, Annie," Cora added.

"Most lawless city on the river," the redhead—Annie—chimed in, gesturing dramatically as if quoting a headline.

Then the door swung open.

A woman filled the entire frame, spilling over an unlaced corset. Her red bustle shimmered, silk catching the dim light. She held my gaze, and for a moment, I felt like I was staring into the heart of a decaying rose garden—beautiful in a way, but tainted and rotting. Her hair was red as blood, crimped and curled, matching her heavily painted lips and cheeks. I couldn't tear my eyes away, but the sight churned something in my stomach.

"That's your honey?" she asked Francis, looking me up and down.

"Pretty little thing. Strange blue eyes. And we'll have to do something about that hair. Well, come in, darling. Don't let the cold blow in."

I met Francis's eyes, and in that moment, something shifted inside me. I knew Mammy had sent me out of one hell just for Francis to pull me down into another one. That all the glitter and glamor that had caught my eye when we docked was an illusion—skillful brush strokes on rotting canvas. Dust in the sunlight. This city was cursed.

Back home, we called them "strolling women." They were the ones who walked the roads, begging or selling what they could to survive. Many of them were unwed mothers, cast out of society and left without means of supporting themselves and their weans. Some of them would end up joining us on the road. We'd take them in, for who were we to judge? Life could be cruel.

When I was a child and too guileless to know better, I'd ask them awful questions like what was it they missed most about settled life.

It was the settled life I was after. Not the strolling one.

And now?

Now, I ran.

I didn't know where I'd go, but I turned on my heels and bounded down the slick cobblestone with the meager strength I had left. Tears blurred my vision, and the world spun, leaving me stumbling into passersby who barely noticed as I dashed by.

Through the chaos raging in my head, I could hear Francis calling my name. I'd never hated the sound of my own name more. Mammy had named me May, for that is the month when the fairies are most likely to be seen. It's a liminal time, when nature comes back to life.

I was five years old when she told me that what I'd described as a ripple in the world's still waters—like when you've tossed in a pebble —was called the Sight.

"Every few generations, a Traveler is born with it," she'd said, her voice soft yet filled with mystery. "But only Travelers have the Sight."

"Why only us, Mammy?" I'd asked her, pulling idly on a particularly bouncy curl with one hand, haphazardly feeding a mealy apple to our donkey with the other.

She thought for a moment, her eyes the shade of midnight, alight with flecks of peach pie filling. "Settled folk are too new," she answered at last. "Their feet don't tread the earth like ours do. Their roots are stunted. Ours stretch as far and wide as the roads we travel. Theirs are not connected to the Old Ones."

"Old ones like Grandmammy?" I'd asked. Mammy's eyes flitted to mine, and then something unusual happened.

She laughed.

It was a rare sound, but a pretty one, like seagulls in November. "No, lass, much older than she. The Old Ones are the *sidh*, or the fairies, and because traveling people were the first mortals to walk the land of Ireland, some say they mated with the fairies, and we carry some fay blood in us still. For some of us that means nothing. But others, like you, are born with the Sight because of it."

I wrinkled my nose. "And that's a good thing, then?" I asked cautiously.

Mammy shrugged, and her eyes turned slate gray. She used her apron to wipe her hands clean of the soot from our fire. "Mind you don't give away all our good apples to that ass."

All these years later, running down the road of an American city, I couldn't help wondering what might have been if she'd chosen a different name for me. Would I still carry the weight of fairy blood, or would I be normal? If she'd named me Marie or Gillian or Brigit, what would I be doing at this very moment?

Grandmammy used to say, "Change a name, change a fate." It was hard to imagine I'd still be running from a street called Diamond, married to a bitter, grieving man named Francis, and living a nightmare. It was no use outrunning him, but that didn't matter. I'd run if my whole heart burst in the process.

I'd made my way back to Warren Street when I ran straight into someone, nearly knocking him over. Luckily, he was tall and broad-shouldered, and it was only me who fell back onto the sidewalk. Still, I was mortified by my clumsiness.

"Are you all right, Miss?" the stranger asked in a low, gravelly voice, extending an arm to help me up. The concern in his tone was enough to still my racing heart for a moment. I looked from his brown hand up to his amber eyes. I smelled jasmine, then realized we were outside the florist's. I took his hand, warm as a bear's, despite the cold fog. As he helped me up, I had the strangest sensation of home.

"Sorry," I stammered. "I wasn't looking where I was going. I was lost in thought—"

"You sound like my brother," he began. But he stopped talking once I'd returned to standing and our eyes met, and for a long moment, neither of us seemed to know what to say. I felt something so familiar, like I was being pulled into a memory that didn't quite belong to me.

"Your brother?" I prompted.

"Well, yes," he replied. "His mind is always busy, for better or for worse," he added wryly.

"Then he's lucky he has you to look after him." I meant to sound quite unbothered, but my throat caught at the end. How had it been for my own siblings, waking up the morning after I left to find another one of us gone?

The man gave me a curious look. I blushed and looked down, then met his eyes again. They were captivating—a true amber, so pure you could preserve a dragonfly in it. He seemed about to say something, but that was when Francis caught up to me. He paid no attention to the man behind me as he grabbed my arms and spun me around.

"Look at me," he demanded, his voice tight.

My breath shook as I looked once more at the stranger. He had a focused look in his eyes, a wide mouth, and strong cheekbones.

"Are you all right, Miss?" he asked again. "Do you need any assistance?"

Now Francis noticed him, too, and eyed him like a tear in the calico cover of a wagon. "She's fine," he said gruffly.

He snaked his arm around my shoulder and began to lead me away. My feet moved only out of a strange numbness, for my mind was still telling me to run the other way.

I glanced back at the stranger, taking in the neat simplicity of his attire, the dirt beneath his fingernails, and again I had that odd, gnawing sensation of home. His eyes locked with mine, and for a moment, I could've sworn I saw something more than just concern there.

What was his name? I found myself wanting that answer more than anything, but Francis's grip remained firm around my arm as he pulled me along, the weight of it a reminder that there was no escape —not now, not ever.

I exhaled shakily as I turned my head to face forward, my breath misting in the chill air, mocking my lack of courage.

We didn't speak at first. Perhaps Francis figured he'd won me over already, but I was still thinking of a way out. When the tightly packed buildings of Diamond Street came into view, I took a step back, releasing myself from his hold.

"Francis, give me a chance to find another job," I pleaded. "You said yourself I can cook and clean. And besides, can't I go back to doing readings?" Fresh tears stung my cheeks as they froze immediately in place. I was mortified, and I hated him for making me feel that way.

He frowned, and his eyes narrowed on me.

Slowly, lazily, the street began to wake. A lad carried a broom outside a saloon. Yawning, he began scuffing its muddy front step. A couple of others passed by, wrapping their cloaks tightly around themselves, their heads down, paces brisk, as though they could walk off the shadows of the night before.

"People here must know loss, too," I said, trying again. "Maybe not like in Ireland, but they must be interested at least in *some*one on the other side."

"Now listen to me," Francis said sternly. He gripped my shoulder blades, so tightly I felt they might snap in two. "That Seeing of yours? It's not going to work here. I'm your husband, and I've taken the liberty of asking around what kind of work a lass like you can get. This is your best chance, May. Do you know what a lass in a brothel on that street makes? More than a constable. More than a doctor. Think about it."

He leaned closer, his breath hot against my cheek. "You'd be making more than those cabbages who chased us out of campgrounds back home. More than the doctors who couldn't save your brother, your sister. My da. Any of the poor, starving souls we left behind. Wouldn't you like that?"

I didn't say a word, though my knees threatened to buckle under me.

"That farmhouse you're always on about, that dream of yours—have I forgotten it? No. You could buy that yourself, May. With your own earnings. Bring your family over. Start your life the way you've always said." He paused, the weight of his next words heavy in the air. "All you have to do is lie down on a bed and rest your weary bones for a while. You can do that, can't you? For the life you've dreamed of?"

His tone became tender then, and it frightened me more than his stern one. I never knew him quite as well as John did, but he seemed so changed since my brother's death. At least there was honesty in his demands. I didn't know what to say. Everything in me screamed that no, I could not do what he was suggesting. I still had my principles. My pride. Visiting the poorhouse back in Ireland was one thing. We were starving, and it was survival.

The poorhouse was one thing. A whorehouse was another.

Still, I kept my mouth shut as Francis held my gaze, his towering presence and owl-like stare silencing me before I could even find the words. Why bother? I'd lose an argument with him before I even spoke.

"May," he continued. "I didn't want to scare you last night, but I'll be honest about what I've learned here. New York isn't like back home. The people here aren't simple, God-fearing folk who might chase you off with a few curses and a broom if your readings spooked them. These are people of *science*. Do you remember that brick building you were staring at earlier? The one with all the chimneys? That's an asylum. The doctors here—" He paused, as if reluctant to say it. "They'll come to your door and lock you away if they decide you're not right in the head. Do you understand what I'm saying? If you tell anyone you can speak to the dead, they'll brand you a lunatic. You'd be trapped in there, May, no better than a wild dog."

His tone shifted again, pity slipping into it like oil on water. "They don't take well to *different* here. They'll call you a hysterical, weak-minded woman," he pressed on, his words like stones piling on my chest.

50

My exhaustion grew heavier, deeper, until it felt like relief to let his voice guide me. There was relief in trusting him. There was rest.

"They're not like the doctors back home who gave Lucy a pitcher of boiled lemons when she was dying. Here, they don't respect women's cures. Your mammy's herbs and medicines? They'd laugh her out of the room. You think it was hard back home, trying to keep your tongue in check every time a spirit wanted to talk through you? I understand, May. I do. Better than you think."

I thought of the woman on our ship, the one who'd lost her daughter Mary. I wanted to ask him why he hadn't even looked at me when I'd needed him if he understood so well. It had been Flynn who'd come to my side, Flynn who'd held me steady. Not Francis.

"But here..." He tilted his head, feigning a sympathy that didn't reach his eyes. "Here, it would be worse than you can imagine. I've been cold to you, and I'm sorry for that. I'm man enough to admit when I've done wrong. Those days are over. This is a fresh start for both of us. I won't be your enemy, May. It's those doctors you have to fear. But don't worry. I'll protect you."

"How will you do that?" I asked him bluntly, though my voice still shook. I felt childish as I folded my arms.

"Because I got work here, too. Madame Maude was in need of a man to watch over things. Didn't I tell you I was sorting things out for us at the gambling parlor? That's where I found out her last man flew the coop, and she's after hiring an Irishman. See? Didn't I tell you our luck would change? I'll be right there with you if anyone gets out of line."

I could only stare at him, wondering what line he meant and what it would take for someone to cross it. Was not having strangers take his wife to bed, let alone before he had himself, line enough?

America wasn't supposed to be like this, but maybe the road to my own heaven wouldn't be paved in gold. Maybe it would just be wood slabs over dirt roads, scuffed cobblestone, and eventually, my family beside me, all under one roof, preparing for Christmas together by this time next year.

Maybe that was all I could hope for.

When we arrived back at the house, the madam greeted me with open arms, as though it was perfectly ordinary for a new girl to sprint down the block just before getting hired. Francis mumbled some excuse about needing to gather things for our room and left without another word, abandoning me to her care.

"Come along now," Madame Maude said, ushering me inside as though I were an old friend. She guided me into the parlor, a dim but cozy room scented with wood smoke and faint traces of perfume. Her maid—a moon-faced woman some years older, introduced as Nellie—brought me a steaming cup of tea and a plate of fried eggs and sausages. The smell alone was enough to set my stomach rumbling.

I sank into a pale pink sofa with frayed seams, my hands trembling despite the warmth of the teacup between them. I set it down and smoothed my skirt.

"The other girls are having breakfast in the kitchen," Madame Maude said, her voice low and honeyed, with a crinkled edge. "I'll introduce you in a bit. Anyway, you can call me French Maude. That's what everyone calls me."

"Are you French?" I asked, surprised by her unusual but assuredly non-French accent.

She brushed the question away like a pesky fly. "I know enough," she said, settling deeper into her chair with a practiced ease, her ample frame shifting like a willow dipping its branches into a pond. Then she leaned forward, her eyes gleaming with mischief. "I used to whisper some sweet nothings to my clients back when I was a working girl like you. I even whispered some Gaelic," she added with a wink. "Make the men think they'd found something rare and mysterious."

She raised her eyebrows at me, and for the briefest moment, my mood shifted, and I felt the pull of a smile, despite the nerves still smoldering in the pit of my stomach. The room felt like a dream—soft around the edges, neither good nor bad exactly, just not quite real. None of it made sense. How could I be sitting here in a bawdy house? Surely, it wasn't my own husband who'd brought me to such a place.

And yet, the house was tidy enough and warm, the breakfast was divinely greasy and salty, and nobody had yet chased me away or hassled me for a reading. No one even knew I could *give* a reading. It was as though I was bearing witness to a wee miracle. Not one person —besides Francis, of course—knew me. For now, at least, I was just a lass sipping tea in a quiet parlor.

I glanced around the room, taking in the details: the cream-colored wallpaper with its tiny red floral print, the ornate carpet with worn edges, and the wooden floors beneath, swept but unpolished.

"You like what you see?" French Maude asked, her tone somewhere between pride and challenge. "Everything here, I bought myself. Other madams get into business with a man who fronts the coin and takes most of the profits. I worked for what I have, and I bought it all myself, some of it on time, some of it in exchange for favors. Don't look so surprised. I was the belle of the ball when I came down to New York at your age, maybe younger. How old are you, anyway?"

"I'm nineteen," I replied, my voice steady despite the unease curling in my stomach.

She shrugged as if to say it didn't matter much. "You'll do just fine. I tell all my girls: you work hard, you'll do just fine. We have weekly visits to the physician, and one day a week off. I don't allow extra work. My girls need their rest." Her words hung in the air, and I realized she meant to sound motherly, but there was a calculated edge beneath the surface.

"And if a man gets out of line?" she continued. "We have our system. You come straight to me if you need to, and I'll take care of it."

I nodded, unsure if I should be grateful or terrified.

"Prices are set on a menu," she said briskly, as though discussing the cost of a loaf of bread. "BJs are a dollar. Amorous congress"—she raised her eyebrows pointedly—"is double. Anything unusual has its own price, and I work that out with the client beforehand. You'll get your wages each morning before breakfast. And speaking of breakfast, we eat together here, like a family." Her tone softened, but the word *family* rang hollow. I didn't know what to make of any of it.

"Does all that sit well with you, May?" Her gaze fixed on me like a hawk waiting to see if its prey would dart or freeze.

I nodded, lucid dreaming, afraid to ask what made an act "unusual," what all the other words meant—amorous congress and beejays? Perhaps something to do with birds?

Her gaze narrowed for another moment before she gave the faintest nod, as though sealing her decision. "It's settled then, we'll give you a shot. Come meet the girls."

She led me through a narrow hallway into the kitchen, where Cora, Annie, and another lass were gathered around a table, laughing and chatting as they ate buttered toast and eggs. The scent of fresh coffee reached me, rich and inviting, and for a moment, I hesitated. I knew, in the back of my mind, that this couldn't possibly work out for me, that I would have to escape somehow, start over on my own if need be. Move silently through the night and camp out by day. I was no stranger to hard travel, after all.

But the lasses—*girls*, I reminded myself—were sipping that hot coffee. *Real* coffee, with fresh cream and sugar. I hadn't had anything like that in years. I made up my mind to sit for a bit, warm myself through, and then figure out a plan.

Annie nodded in my direction as she carried on with her story. I fidgeted awkwardly while the maid placed a steaming mug in front of me, as if it was the most ordinary thing in the world for me to be here. I edged my face above the cup before sipping, feeling the steam like kisses against my skin.

"So then," Annie said, smirking, "he had me tie the rope around his John Thomas, leave him standing there, naked, in the backyard—you girls remember how cold that night was?—and hold the other end all the way from inside my room, *second floor*, tugging until he finished! Aside from some rope burn, easiest dollar I've ever made!"

"You didn't even touch him?" asked a thin girl with enormous black eyes, almost too large for her gaunt face.

"Not one finger." Annie's smirk widened. "I kind of liked him, actually, a bit touched though he was."

"The client is always right," French Maude chimed in, raising her voice like a toast. "The madam and then the client. In that order!"

The girls burst into laughter, nudging one another with knowing looks. The sound felt strangely disarming, almost comforting, though I wasn't sure why.

"This is May, everyone," Maude said, cutting through the mirth as she returned to business. "She'll be joining us."

"You're pretty," said the waifish girl. "I'm Claire." She extended a limp hand to me, and I shook it awkwardly.

"You all live here together?" I asked. "Cora, was it?"

"Dông," Cora replied, "but no one here can pronounce it right, so I go by Cora. And yeah, all of us, plus—" She looked up as another girl hurried in with a thick book tucked inside her elbow.

"Did I miss breakfast?" she asked, breathless from running down the stairs. She adjusted her eyeglasses, waiting for a response that didn't come.

My own breath caught for a moment. She was striking, with brown skin, full lips painted a soft red, and dark, expressive eyes that reminded me of a fawn's. Her glossy black hair fell loose down her back, and though I guessed she was only a few years older than me, there was a quiet elegance about her that made her seem years—lifetimes—ahead.

Cora pulled a chair out for her with a begrudging scrape against the floorboards, and the girl sat down.

"Hi, I'm Olivia Johnson," she said, her voice calm and measured as her gaze met mine. "Are you a new girl?"

The chatter paused for a brief moment as the other girls exchanged glances of amusement and curiosity.

"Don't mind Olivia," Annie said, breaking the quiet as she turned to me. "She's desperate to talk someone's ear off about whatever *romantic* novel she's reading. Ignore her, or she'll bore you to tears."

"You can read?" I asked Olivia, in awe of the ability. Travelers had little use for quill and parchment, and books were an impractical luxury to carry with us on the road. I didn't know what kind of education the women in America might have had, but if Olivia was educated, then why was she working at French Maude's?

The other girls snickered.

"I'm sorry," I said quickly. "Of course you can read. It's me that can't. I was stupid to assume." I blushed violently.

"Not stupid," she assured me. "What's your name?" Her smile was kind and gracious.

"This here's May," Annie responded for me. "Irish May."

"Hey, May?" Cora said next. "Can you teach us some sweet Irish nothings to whisper into our men's ears tonight?" The group burst into laughter, clinking their mugs together before resuming their lively conversations.

Across the table, Olivia caught my gaze. "I can help you get settled after breakfast if you like," she offered.

I hesitated, the weight of my plan—my escape—pressing faintly against my chest. I didn't intend to stay, but at that moment, the pull of companionship was stronger than the call of the road. I nodded, letting her kindness tether me there just a little longer, even if only for now.

# CHAPTER 6

# Olivia

Olivia gathered her purse and cloak from her bedroom. As she turned to leave, her gaze caught the newcomer still lingering by the doorway, hesitant, almost shrinking in the frame. May smoothed the hem of her skirt with trembling fingers, eyes darting like a frightened bird. Olivia felt inclined to offer her a smile. She'd been new once, too. She knew what that was like.

"I'm afraid I can't yet afford a new dress," the Irish girl confessed, her voice barely more than a whisper.

She was all skin and bones. Probably a victim of the potato famine Olivia had been reading about. *Just awful.* Olivia had never gone hungry before, but she knew what it was like to not be able to afford a new dress. She'd help the girl get sorted. It was easy enough—after all, she had more dresses than she could ever need. The right thing to do would be to help her find her footing.

But deep down, she knew what would happen. Once May got comfortable, she'd turn her back on Olivia just like everyone else. Everyone always did.

Still, today wasn't about that. Today was about giving her a moment of grace. May looked so lost and out of place in her filthy black shawl and boots that were tearing at the seams. Her hair looked like a bird's nest and not in a fashionable way. But her eyes were a startling shade of blue, somehow deep as stormy waters and cloudy gray at the same time. Her lashes were naturally thick and long, and if Olivia squinted past the dirt on her face, she could almost imagine a fairylike sort of beauty in the delicate arch of her brows, the curve of her lips, and the innocence that still clung to her.

Olivia sighed, the weight of the gesture settling heavily on her shoulders. "I assumed as much," she said in a tone she might have used with a younger sister. "You'll have one of mine. I'll only have to pay for the alteration, so it's no trouble."

She rummaged through her armoire, eyes flicking over the collection of dresses she no longer wore, until her fingers paused on a simple white tarlatan gown, its soft pink stripes adding a touch of sweetness. She held it up against May's tiny form, the fabric practically drowning her, then shrugged. "We shouldn't have to lose too much. Just a bit around the middle, maybe the bust."

May's eyes rounded like a puppy's. "I'll pay you back," she promised, her voice thick with sincerity.

A wave of sadness washed over Olivia, and she had to look away, unsure whether to laugh, cry, or scream. "Of course you will," she said, forcing a tight smile.

It didn't really matter to her, anyway. She had plenty of money and no shortage of clients. Money didn't seem to matter all that much when she thought about it. As the thought sank in, the urge to scream overpowered any desire to laugh or cry.

If money didn't matter, then what the hell was she doing with her life?

She threaded her arm through the new girl's. "We better get going if we want this dress before your first shift."

They stepped out into the chilly air, Olivia's arm steady at May's side. The Irish girl's head turned at every window display. She said "no thank you" to each salesman and paper boy who called out their wares. She couldn't seem to make it a few feet without stumbling on some stray animal or child's makeshift ball or person who crossed her path. Olivia narrowed her eyes. For someone so small, she left a wake of confusion behind her.

Had the girl ever been in a city before?

Had Olivia looked this lost on her first day in Hudson?

When they arrived at their destination, Olivia swept the door open, holding it for a flustered, red-faced May, who hesitated as though she didn't quite trust the threshold. The girl was a patchwork of contradictions: light eyes full of wonder but fists clenched with unease.

Olivia placed her gown into the seamstress's calloused hands, her tone clipped and firm. "We need this finished by tomorrow night, tonight if you can." Her words brooked no argument, and the seamstress gave a short nod.

May, however, seemed to have been struck dumb. The girl was gaping at the shop's tables and shelves stocked with rolls of cotton, wool, and silk fabric, spools of thread, chalk, paper patterns, and a couple of foot-treadle sewing machines. Her mouth hung open in awe as if she'd stumbled into a treasure trove.

Olivia stayed close as May stepped into the gown with obvious discomfort, shifting like the fabric itself was too fine for her skin. Then came the tear—an audible rip that made the seamstress gasp.

May's face went pale. "I—I'm so sorry—"

"We'll get the hem taken in, too," Olivia cut in, her voice casual. No use making a scene. Her attempt at nonchalance earned a raised brow from the seamstress, though the woman wisely stayed silent.

After twenty minutes of measurements, pins, and quiet promises of a quick turnaround, they left the shop with the doorbell's chime marking their exit.

"That was much too kind of you, Miss Olivia," May insisted. "I hope I didn't embarrass you."

Olivia shook her head. She looked in the direction of Maude's, where rain clouds seemed to be blowing in, then out toward the river. "We have time," she said, almost to herself. "Do you want to see the Parade?"

May blinked, her head tilting like a curious bird. "A parade?"

Olivia couldn't help the chuckle that escaped her. "Not *a* parade. *The* Parade—our promenade," she clarified. "It's... just a place where people walk."

The simplicity of the explanation made May's confusion all the more apparent. Her nervous energy was palpable, the girl's slight frame practically vibrating beside her. Olivia's amusement faded.

"It's a staple," she added, leading May toward the park overlooking the Hudson.

"And... where are they going?" May asked hesitantly.

Olivia blinked. "Nowhere," she said finally, the word landing flat and hollow, even to her own ears. "They just walk."

Was this how she had been, once? Wide-eyed and clumsy, trying to make sense of a world that felt just out of reach? The thought was unsettling.

Still, it wouldn't be long before May grew accustomed to all of it—before she distanced herself, just like the others. That was simply how things worked. Olivia's shoulders squared as she quickened her pace, leaving no room for argument.

"They just walk?" May asked, her fine features twisted in confusion.

"And people watch. It's where folks go to show off their fripperies."

Olivia followed May's gaze down to her tattered plaid skirt, then back up, her cheeks burning. "But how can I go in these?"

Olivia chewed on a frown.

May was right. Her clothes looked ragged, her stockings had gaping holes, and the leather of her boots was even more woefully frayed than Olivia had first noticed. One fleeting encounter with a puddle would do her feet no favors.

But Olivia shrugged away that thought, too. Enough feeling sorry for the girl. Let her see what people say. Better she knows now than later. That's what Olivia would have wanted for herself. If she'd ever been that shy and naive and painfully innocent, she would have wanted someone to warn her about the world. About *people.* About... him.

Maybe then she wouldn't have been so foolish.

"Oh, who cares about that anyway? Let's just take a stroll." She threaded her arm through May's.

The stares pounded like a flash flood. Not only from small children, who had yet to learn manners, but from men and women in expensive frocks and matching suits. Olivia kept her gaze steely, her chin high, as she trotted forward, even as she felt May stiffen.

"Ah, Miss Olivia," May murmured, her voice almost lost in the hum of chatter and the crunch of gravel underfoot. "Perhaps we should head back to the dress shop? Might it be ready by now?"

Olivia considered it. Maybe May was right. Why subject themselves to prying eyes? Why give these folks the satisfaction? She stared back at a heavily mustached man who lifted his gaze so high up, his nose stuck up straight to the air. The disdain radiating from him was almost comical in its transparency.

No. Why let them win?

She tightened her grip on May's arm, offering a calm, unbothered smile. "Don't mind the stares," she said lightly. "We have just as much a right to walk as anyone else."

"We do?" May asked. Her voice squeaked with uncertainty.

Olivia kept her gaze ahead. "Of course we do," she said firmly.

An irksome tenderness toward the new girl stirred in her chest. A part of her wished that May would never learn who Olivia was in this city, that they might even be friends. But that would be impossible. Ridiculous. She shoved the thought away.

"Have you read many novels?" May asked suddenly, her voice cutting through the tension like sunlight through clouds.

Olivia blinked. Of all the questions... "You really want to know?" she asked, arching a brow.

May's storm cloud eyes widened. "I want to know everything," she said. "I have an endless list of questions about America, Hudson, bawdy houses, men, beauty." She sighed. "But most of all, I want to know your stories. I haven't heard a really good one since my grandmammy."

"That's sweet," Olivia said, a hint of sadness curling her words.

"She passed during the first year of the famine," May added hesitantly.

The girl really did seem sincere. But it didn't change the *fact,* and it *was* a fact, that soon enough, she'd act just like the others, competing with her for clients and snickering about her bookish nature every chance she'd get.

"In Ireland, we'd all tell tales to each other during our long rides in the wagon, me and my siblings huddled together, and in the evenings after we made camp. I'd help Mammy with the cooking while we told stories. We cooked outside, naturally, and I promise you, even when the fare left us wanting, I could savor each tale like an oily broth."

Olivia felt another tug at her heart. A desire to hear more, to write down May's stories in ornate strands of poetry—no, simple would be best. Simple, clean, perfect words that would highlight the beauty of the moments themselves. Words that wouldn't describe an open fire, but make you feel like you were sweating beneath its dancing limbs, have you breathing in the peppered breeze, its coolness tracing paths along your scalp.

Suddenly, her chest felt hollow. A pinprick of poison. She tugged back. Nothing good could come from following her heart. From writing anything at all ever again. She'd learned that lesson the hard way.

"Well, I hate to tell you, Miss May, but I'm no storyteller."

May's face fell.

Despite herself, Olivia added, "But I do think words contain the only real magic left in this world. I'm just not the person to wield that wand."

May stopped walking and turned to face her. Olivia held her breath, waiting for May's face to crumple with disappointment—or worse, to mock her for her "poetic nonsense."

"Miss Olivia," she exclaimed instead, "you're a dreamer, too, aren't you?"

Olivia exhaled sharply, hesitant to meet May's eye as they reached the edge of the promenade. The view of the Hudson River was unparalleled. The water was still, a silver mirror reflecting a cloudy sky.

"Nothing good can come of two dreamers banding together," Olivia advised. Her tone was light, though her heart thrummed as she let herself speak the fear out loud. Words were powerful, after all. She knew that better than anyone else at Maude's.

"Those who live their lives in dreams can't really live." May sounded lost in a dream of her own.

Could it be possible they had more in common than she'd presumed?

"I've always wondered what it's like to read," May mused. "You must feel like the whole world is open to you."

Olivia's gaze flicked toward her, sharp as the wind off the river. "You really can't read at all? Not a word?"

"You must think very little of me," May said softly.

For a moment, Olivia didn't know what to say or where to look. May had it all backwards. The girl's confession landed somewhere between heartbreak and farce. This whole conversation felt as untethered as a paper boat on the Hudson.

"I'm sorry," Olivia offered. "I don't think any less of you. It's just—" she hesitated, glancing at the churning gray water. "I just feel sorry for those who can't. Without my books and poetry, I don't know how I'd face the world, cold and gray as it can be." She shrugged, glancing back at May's pale, open face. "You weren't taught, that's all. We're women—God forbid we carry an intelligent conversation. God forbid we're inspired."

Her own sincerity made her snap her mouth shut and clear her throat.

May tilted her head, her pale eyes full of something Olivia couldn't quite place—innocence, maybe, or a gentleness too tender for this place. "So America is not so different from Ireland in some ways," she mused.

Olivia started walking again. Her pace quickened, as though she could outpace the tightness spreading through her muscles. She felt May's flurry of skirts brush the dirt behind her as she tried to keep up.

*To hell with it.* She would just tell May how it was, plain and simple. They were grown women. They worked at French Maude's, after all! What was she doing entertaining idle prattle about dreams and novels, and as if they were in the same position, no less!

"Let me tell you something about this country, Miss May," she said, her voice turning brisk. "'All men are created equal,' they say. What they mean is 'white men.' And if the Know-Nothings had their way, both of us wouldn't be here at all."

When she heard no response, she stopped walking and turned back to May, waiting for her to catch up. Olivia searched her pretty, symmetrical features for signs of understanding.

May nodded slowly. "Know-Nothings?" she asked tentatively.

"Mhm." Olivia nodded firmly.

She turned on her heels, threaded her arm through May's, and continued walking. The air was congested, black with smoke, and the Parade smelled faintly of dead fish. The landscape had a fierceness to it, as though the river was home to mysterious monsters with whetted teeth, just waiting to bite.

And yet, she could see what the local painters saw in her city when they set up their easels in that very spot. She couldn't look out at that silver ribbon without feeling a sense of something holy and unspoiled. She just couldn't.

She turned her gaze to May, wondering what May saw when she stared out over the railing. Did she see the same towering mountains dotted with trees and shrubs, the same modern marvels crossing the river, sails that whispered of possibilities in foreign lands with every billow? Just cross the dock, pay your fare, and soon you'll arrive...

By the look on May's face, Olivia assumed she only saw the monsters.

Olivia pressed her lips together before continuing. "Know-Nothings called themselves a secret society at first, saying they 'knew nothing' whenever someone asked them a question. But their views are clear enough. Drain all the color from America; no foreigners allowed." She laughed bitterly. "We're lucky French Maude doesn't give a damn for politics. She knows her business, and the very things

Know-Nothings hate most—people like us—that's who they love the most when no one is looking."

"I'm not—"

"Oh, I know," Olivia interjected. "You've got that husband of yours. Strong, silent type. You wouldn't be the first working girl to have a man waiting in the wings, and you certainly won't be the last."

She felt for May, she really did. But the fact was May didn't have it any worse than the other girls at Maude's. Not really. Of course, it was terrible that her husband had arranged her position at Maude's. A sweet girl like May might have even believed in love at some point. But men were who they were. Brutes, plain and simple. Always looking for the next best—the next step up on the ladder.

Olivia softened her voice. "Remember what I said about all men being equal? That doesn't mean us. We're at the bottom of the ladder, May. But if you can't read, you'll never climb it at all. You'll never be sovereign."

May looked at her with that same, uncertain glance, a sky unsure if it would rain or snow. "Sovereign?" she repeated slowly, as though testing the word's shape.

"Autonomous," Olivia replied carefully. If May took anything from their conversation, it should be this. "Able to take care of yourself. That's what I don't mind about our line of work. You know that seamstress altering my dress for you? In one hour, we make what she makes in a day, and she knows it. It's not always pretty in our line of work, but we care for ourselves."

She followed May's gaze back toward Warren Street. It had cleared out. Perhaps folks feared the cloudy skies. A flock of ravens flew through the air. A few shop windows darkened. Those that remained open boasted small, flickering glows through tall, rectangular windows.

Strangely, May didn't look so out of place anymore.

Olivia sensed another question on her lips, parting slightly, like a child trying to catch snowflakes on her tongue.

"What is it?" Olivia asked.

"I just wonder," May began, eyes darting nervously, "do you not feel lonely?"

Olivia stiffened. May had broken one of the cardinal rules of Diamond Street. *Don't talk about your past. Don't talk about your future. Don't talk about your feelings.* No one had ever asked her that question before, even though she was always alone.

"Come on," she said briskly. "We'd better hurry before the shop closes."

# CHAPTER 7

## Map

The streetlamps in Hudson remained unlit under the waxing gibbous moon, leaving the city cloaked in shadows and silver light, a hazy darkness that felt almost like home, like where I belonged.

I walked down French Maude's staircase in silk and rouge, smelling like rose and honeysuckle, fingers trembling against the banister. I looked nothing like the lass that had stepped off the steamboat only a day earlier.

Francis stood by the front door, ready to let in customers and collect their money. His glassy eyes barely lifted to meet mine. When they did, disgust twisted his features. He quickly looked away, his lips pursing as though to keep from speaking.

My cheeks flamed. I felt like a prized pony on display. My hands fumbled for fabric to cover myself, but there was none to find. The thought of running gripped me—the sound of my heels clacking against the sidewalk, the rush of cold wind through my pinned-up curls.

But I still had no plan, no place to go, no money to my name.

The other girls hooted and clapped, their approval of my transformation almost mocking.

I stood there, heat prickling my skin, and realized with a sharp clarity that nearly stole my breath: I wasn't leaving. Not just yet, anyway. My fate hadn't changed at all, though I'd traveled across the world. I was still me, a lass on the fringes, barely able to balance as I walked across a delicate edge in Olivia's fine clogs, two sizes too big.

The other girls seemed to know how to move, how to smile, how to flirt. I watched silently, able to hear my own uneven breathing.

And then, a sharp smack on my rear startled me, and I turned to see French Maude grinning. "This one's yours," she called, waving at a middle-aged man. His sour scent of juniper and rotting citrus reached me before he did.

I hadn't even caught my breath when I found myself alone with him in a dim, slate-colored room. The sparse furnishings included a washstand with a clay vase of dried white roses. Everything felt muted —white roses, white vase, even the light seemed drained of its hue. I swallowed. What had happened to all the colors in the world? Where were the yellow garden roses and mulberry vases and wallpaper patterns shining like halos around the sconces? My chest tightened, my thoughts spiraling as I hovered on the brink of panic.

The man approached without hesitation, his mustache and goatee extending well past the limits of his narrow face. I flinched as he moved to kiss me. It would only be my second kiss, yet I knew that kissing wasn't supposed to feel like this—as void of feeling as two clouds passing by each other but without the softness. It couldn't possibly.

I stumbled back onto the bed, every nerve in my body on high alert. He hesitated only briefly before climbing onto the mattress beside me. His puckered lips came toward me again, and I squirmed away.

"What is this game? I didn't pay for this," he declared. Mistaking my silence for the end of the game, he leaned it for a third attempt.

That's when it happened.

Mammy used to tell me that threes are lucky. Now I understood that rule for myself, for the moment his lips neared for the third time, my vision exploded with blinding flashes of light. Images rushed into my mind—a woman dabbing crumbs from his mustache, the scent of a burned Christmas ham, her anger and his yelling. She never apologized, though she wished she had.

I wasn't in the room anymore, not fully. My mind floated above it, caught in the spirit's memories. Her grief weighed heavy on my chest, pressing until I thought I'd suffocate. But I knew this feeling—knew it from the countless other times spirits had found their way to me.

Once I spoke for her, she'd release me. Until then, I was trapped, my breath shallow, my heart beating like a frantic bird in a cage. I longed for the moment—just that one moment—when she'd finally let me go.

"It won't bring her back!" I blurted.

"What?" His lazy indignation shifted to utter befuddlement. "Bring *who* back?"

She hadn't given me her name yet, but I could see her clearly—her pale hair and pleasant, tired eyes. Her long face and small mouth. It was all coming together before me, between us.

"She knows you think of her daily," I continued quickly. "Even now you're thinking of her, in this room with me. But I can't be her for you. She's still with you, you see." I finished without any bravado. It was a shot in the dark, and he'd either grow angrier with me or run in fear and turn me into the lunatic hunters Francis had warned me about.

That fear twisted in my stomach, but what choice did I have? I hadn't planned to see the ghost of his wife. When a spirit stands between me and the person she loved, I can't hold back. Everything in me aches to be her lips, like I'll utter no words of my own until hers bubble up like a spring. No, like a burning pot of tar.

The name began to form. "Catherine? Clara?" I ventured, my voice low, almost a whisper, reaching out to whoever would answer first.

"Caroline?" he said, his eyes ablaze, his voice trembling with the force of realization. Even his mustache seemed to stand on edge.

"Aye! Caroline!" I confirmed, a chill rushing through me. "She needs you to know that she's with you still. That it's time to love again. But... not like this." My cheeks burned as the words spilled out. "She knows she acted jealously in the past. She found something in your desk drawer—a kerchief? No... Oh." My breath hitched. It wasn't a kerchief. I could feel the heat rise in my face. "But she's not jealous anymore. When you begged her forgiveness, it took time, but she did forgive you, even though you always wondered. She wants you to find real love, like the kind the two of you once shared."

The expression of someone who knows they've spoken to a spirit can be described in no better way than looking as though they'd just seen a ghost. Truly, that's how it is.

This man, whose name I didn't know, who was about to be my first experience of lovemaking, began to cry. Without hesitation, he leaned into me, his head on my shoulder, his tears soaking through the thin silk of my gown. I sat there in stunned silence as he wept and wept, his mustache like seaweed against my bare skin.

By the time we descended the staircase into the parlor, his tears had subsided, and my trembling fingers had steadied enough to glide smoothly along the banister. The other girls glanced up with knowing smirks, their eyes flicking between us, assuming I'd kept him busy in an entirely different way. French Maude glanced in our direction, frowning, undoubtedly ready to demand he pay double for the extended time.

Before she could speak, he rushed to her, throwing his arms around her shoulders. "I'm a new man! I'm alive again!" he cried out, his face flushed and streaked with tears.

Everyone stopped their chatting and flirting and stared at him. Then they stared at *me*, their faces a mix of approval and something more suffocating and primal.

Yet again, I blushed. A twist of panic coiled in my stomach at the thought of my secret slipping free. The fierce brick walls and iron-barred windows of the lunatic asylum blazed in my mind, a fate far worse than shame.

"She's a miracle!" he continued. "I didn't think it was possible, but she spoke to my late wife Caroline! Why, you didn't mention she's a spiritualist!"

"A what?" I asked, willing him to be quiet. Let them think me a woman of the night. At least that sin belonged to the living. At least that left me free of locks and keys that were not my own. Free of suspicion and false judgements.

An eerie grating sound scraped at the edges of my mind, pressing against my temples, trying to force its way in.

Francis's towering figure came thundering through the room. "Time to leave, sir. We'll have none of that slandering in this establishment." He was skinny, but at that moment I saw him as someone pure fearsome. This poor man would be wise to move away from my husband.

But he didn't see what I saw in Francis. Instead, he craned his neck, peering around him like a mouse sniffing for an opening in a wedge of cheese, all too eager to tell the room what I was.

"Hold on," said Maude, pushing her way to the center of the crowd that had grown tighter around me. "Is this true, May? Are you a spiritualist?"

"I… I don't know," I stammered.

She squinted at me. "You don't know, or you won't tell?" she asked, so close to me now, I could see the fine hairs above her upper lip.

"I don't know," I repeated. "I don't know what that means."

I'd known exhaustion before, but now I felt tired in a different way —tired of feeling like a fool, never knowing what any of these Americans were talking about. I'd traveled my whole life but never to a place as new as this one, and I wanted nothing more than to curl up in a tight space and sleep for years—sleep until my family was safe and with me, and we could all travel on together and settle down in a home whose simple beauty would not leave us sore for the hills of Ireland.

"A spiritualist who works at a brothel," chortled another man. "Now that's a fine bit of humor!"

I felt like an even greater fool for dreaming of my farmhouse then.

"Tell me, May, and don't lie to me," Maude pressed. She narrowed her eyes to slits, giving me that same huntress look she'd given me during my interview. "Do you see anyone around me that nobody else can?"

I looked to Francis, desperate for guidance, but Maude took my face in her hands and tilted it back toward her. "Don't look at anybody else, lovey. Just tell *me.*"

I closed my eyes and drew in a slow breath, willing the room to disappear. The cold I stepped into was not crisp or cleansing but sharp as iron, biting at my skin like forbidden ground. Shadows formed behind my eyes. Details came into focus, scattered and disjointed, colder than the air itself. Pieces of something metallic, edged in crimson.

Piece by piece, they locked together, and then I couldn't look any longer. I couldn't bear it.

A spirit. A baby. So small, so blue.

Like a winter's night.

*Death.*

Dead before it was ever born.

I looked up at my employer, unsure if I could speak the truth aloud. A lie might protect me, but exhaustion tugged at my resolve. Lying felt like scaling a mountain.

"Whatever it is, May, just go on and say it," Maude said, her voice tight despite her attempt at courage. "We've all lost someone here, am I right?" She cast her question to the room, but the tremor in her words betrayed her.

I licked my chapped lips, searching the room for a pitcher of water. My throat was too dry for what I had to say. "He's fine," I murmured, almost too softly to hear. "He doesn't fault you for your choice. He knows the first breath of life wasn't meant for him."

Her eyes widened, and in that moment, she looked older, and somehow softer and lovelier and slighter.

"Anything else?" she asked, her voice steady now, though her gaze pinned me in place.

I shook my head, unsettled beneath her stare. "He's at peace," I admitted reluctantly. "He says what you both went through was part of God's plan, and it was necessary to prepare him for his next life."

The tingling behind my neck began to fade. "That's it. I lost him. He won't say anymore right now." I paused, unsure whether to apologize. "Sorry."

It's hard to describe what it's like when a spirit leaves. I have no control over it. It's like they open or close a fence gate to me just as they please. I can't remain on the inside any better than I can break a wild horse. I would have explained that to Maude, but after doing the two readings side by side, I was drowning in a sickening fear and a bottomless hunger. I can't say which was deeper.

The room was so silent, I could hear Francis's heavy breathing. I saw the puzzled glares of the other girls, and the curious looks of the men who hadn't noticed me when the night began. They wanted intrigue and mystery in a world that was always the same, save for the weather, which was dreadfully unpredictable. Well, here I stood, so mysterious I couldn't even make sense of myself.

"I knew it was a boy," Maude said at last, her voice low.

I looked at her blankly.

"And what of it?" she asked, daring me to judge her.

"What's going on?" the men murmured, their voices overlapping. "Can she really speak to the dead?"

Then they pressed in tighter, their eagerness turning feverish, their voices clamoring, their hands reaching, offering larger and larger sums of money.

Francis's face hardened into stone, and Maude's lips curled with a predatory hunger.

I realized then that what Americans called *Spiritualism*, I had always called my plight. It was just a new name for what people had always believed. *My* people, anyway. Yet here in America, speaking to the dead was treated like another modern marvel, no different from steamboats and railroads.

An entire religion was beginning to take root, and I could see only its fragile beginning, like a spider stretching her legs before weaving her gossamer bedsheets, unaware of who she would one day ensnare.

Francis met my gaze, and something shifted in his stony expression. Bewilderment? Hesitation? He was supposed to have all the answers. Some foolish part of me believed he would protect me, that he would send the men away and let me be. But he knew the rules. The madam was always right. Then the client. In that order.

And me? I was just another pawn in a larger game. Worse still, I was cursed with the Sight, and no mortal can stand up to a curse. At least, not without the help of a wise woman witch or a knight in shining armor.

All I had was Francis.

And truly, I was beginning to realize that all I had was myself.

# CHAPTER 8

# Rudyard

*R*udyard's heart raced as he stared up at the imposing limestone building on Warren Street. He took his time approaching the tall double doors, polished to a gleam and adorned with brass fixtures. Above the doorway hung a carved wooden sign, gilded lettering spelling out Central House Hotel.

He lowered his gaze before entering, hoping to avoid eye contact with anyone who might know him. Not that he really expected to see another Quaker at the upscale hotel bar. But better safe than sorry. Only at the last moment did he remove his hat before opening the door.

He let his eyes adjust to the dim, open room, decorated with the rich warmth of dark mahogany. Somber portraits of stern-faced men in gilded frames loomed from the deep red walls. He walked past the small round tables, each occupied by men of varying stations—some nursing glasses of gin, others hunched over their pipes, tapping ash into cut-glass trays.

Rudyard perched on a stool at the bar, the polished surface reflecting the glint of decanters lined up behind it. The wideawake hat in his hands felt damning, its very presence exposing him. The barkeep's gaze flicked to the hat, then back to Rudyard, amusement barely concealed in the quirk of his mouth. Too late, Rudyard realized he should have left it on the rack by the door. Jaw tightening, he hooked it under the bar, then smoothed the fabric of his coat, as if that might erase the moment.

"What can I get you?" the barkeep asked with a raised brow. He wore a crisp white shirt and black waistcoat, wiping the counter clean with practiced efficiency as he waited.

Rudyard gazed at the shelves, stocked with fine crystal glasses and silver decanters, alongside bottles with ruby and amber-hued spirits.

"Cider," he managed.

He waited quietly, strumming his fingers against the bar. He tried not to look around too much. He probably stuck out enough as it was.

At last, the barkeep sent his cider sliding down toward him. But before Rudyard could curl his fingers around the glass, a large and calloused hand beat him to it. Reflected on the bar counter, he saw a pair of impervious blue eyes and strong, defined features. Rudyard lifted his gaze. The actual eyes were even bluer. How had he missed *those?*

"For me?" the man said playfully, his words tinged with an Irish lilt.

Rudyard felt his face flush hot. Mortified, he stumbled over his response. "Fine, if you like," he managed, fumbling to cross his square-toed shoes beneath the bar stool.

The Irishman nodded his thanks, his grin growing wider as Rudyard sat frozen. *Say something, you fool.* But his tongue refused to cooperate. There was something devilish, almost wolfish in the fellow's smile. The eyes were icy, strikingly vivid, almost impossibly so. And yet, as this man returned to his table, Rudyard felt a pang of regret. Why hadn't he thought of anything clever to say? Something witty or smart? He must be the least worldly person in all the city.

The Irishman took his seat with a group of equally boisterous companions by the slow-burning fireplace that dominated one wall. Rudyard's gaze lingered. They were a raucous lot, their laughter and shouts rising above the orchestra. One pair leaned over a game of backgammon, while others gestured animatedly, calling for more food and drink. They seemed entirely at ease, taking up space as though it belonged to them.

Rudyard found himself envious of their ease. Clearly, they all knew how to enjoy themselves. How to have a good time.

He thought of the rabbit stew his mother had made for dinner. They always ate rabbit on Mondays.

"Another cider," he motioned to the barkeep.

His cheeks still burned, but he buried his embarrassment in the amber liquid, nursing the glass, occasionally catching a few words from the tall man's table. The room was lively for any Monday he was familiar with, slowly filling with traveling merchants, local gentry, and well-dressed businessmen.

And yet, his ears seemed to prick in the direction of that one round, white-linened table by the fireplace.

"Your steak and baked potatoes on my tab, Francis, honey," a waitress cooed.

Rudyard's ears perked at the name. *Francis.* The name suited him, Rudyard decided—regal, but not without mischief.

Francis's voice rose above the others, boasting of a seamstress who had made him a frock coat "on time," and then, *what the heck*, on the house. His companions roared their approval, toasting to "Mr. McMurry" with cries of "*Sláinte!*" and pounding the table in triumph.

By night's end, the barkeep, suspicious of Rudyard's presence at first, had been utterly won over by Francis. Rudyard watched as Francis tipped his chair back, made a few well-placed compliments about the bar's decor, and lent a sympathetic ear to the barkeep's complaints about his lady. Drinks flowed freely in return.

Rudyard slumped lower in his seat, the cider turning sour in his stomach. His gaze kept returning to Francis, despite himself. The man's charm was maddening—a skillful performance, effortless and magnetic. He seemed to know precisely what people needed from him: a word of praise, a hint of hope. He could roll them out like dice, and even more so, for they cost him nothing.

How could a person rouse so much admiration, and so seamlessly at that? And someone so loud and vulgar, no less! For Rudyard had to admit, after hours of observing him, the man *was* wolfish.

And yet, there was more to him than manipulation, wasn't there? Something in the glint of Francis's eyes, like a crack in ice, or perhaps in the roughness of his laughter, hinted at genuine warmth beneath the bravado.

Rudyard grimaced, knowing he could never replicate such charm. He wasn't born for it! He had always tried to be dignified, to present himself as someone worthy of respect, but where had it left him?

Alone at a bar, brooding over a man who had barely even noticed him.

The paned-glass windows revealed that it was closer to morning than night when the barkeep cut him off. He slapped his money on the counter, then looked back at Francis's table. Most of the men remained, but Francis was gone.

His stomach sank.

Remarkably, he felt even more miserable than when he'd first sat down. He lifted his hat off its hook, deciding to hold on to it a bit longer before placing it back on his head. Then he stumbled into the brisk November night, oblivious to his open coat that flapped in the wind with the threat of frost bite.

Typically, he would turn left to make his way back home, but tonight, struck by a peculiar sound in the alleyway, he turned right.

What was that sound? A wounded animal? A stray dog? No, it was decidedly human.

*A moan.*

*Francis.*

He recognized Francis instantly, even with his back turned. The dark smudge of his hair against the crisp night air was unmistakable. For a fleeting moment, hope surged in Rudyard's chest. This was his chance—a rare opportunity to say something clever, something charming. To prove he *could* be the kind of man who turned heads. What luck to catch him alone. A second chance, thank you, God!

Rudyard stepped forward, words already forming on his tongue. But then—

Curious strips of yellow glowed around Francis's head. Rudyard blinked, his vision snapping into clarity.

Francis wasn't alone.

Rudyard froze.

Francis leaned over another man, his broad frame angled protectively, almost possessively, around him. The other man, smaller and blond, tilted his head as Francis's lips brushed the curve of his neck. The blond man's eyes fluttered shut, but when they opened again, they landed squarely on Rudyard.

Rudyard's breath hitched. The blond man pushed Francis back just enough to break the moment. A pair of blue eyes swung toward him. Francis's gaze met his, direct and sharp, and Rudyard felt like a rabbit caught in the jaws of a wolf.

He stumbled back, heart pounding, and fled down the block. His square-toed shoes scraped against the cobblestones as he turned the corner, finding refuge against the nearest wall. He pressed his hat to his chest, struggling to catch his breath. What had just happened?

His heart pumped faster than it ever had before, and he couldn't make sense of it. He had seen Francis—*really* seen him. Not the polished charm, not the easy grins or rakish confidence. He'd glimpsed something raw, something unguarded. And he couldn't decide which unsettled him more: the act itself—a dangerous defiance of everything society demanded—or the gnawing fear that it might be contagious.

Whether he hoped that it was.

Whether he'd never hoped for something so fervently in all his life.

*For pity's sake!* Rudyard squeezed his eyes shut and tilted his head up toward the wind. The man was brusque and rude and clearly an opportunist. And yet, Rudyard thought as he willed himself not to cry, he was like Rudyard in a way no one else had ever been. And, God help him, that must mean that his heart was like Rudyard's.

He swallowed. It didn't hurt that Francis was easy on the eyes. Terrifying, yet easy. His breath quieted, and for a moment, he thought he heard the moaning again, as though the wind had carried it to him as a sordid joke.

He swallowed his heart, put on his hat, and made his way home.

# CHAPTER 9

# Clement

lement passed the brick jailhouse at 364 Warren Street. It was a tall, handsome building that always gave him an odd sort of chill. The kind of building that swallows up a man like a whale.

He continued toward his destination, wondering if he might see the small, blue-eyed woman again.

Instead, he saw face after unfamiliar face. Was there some sort of fair in town? Hudson crowds typically thinned out before the quiet of Christmas. Now the town seemed fuller than ever with new faces.

Just not the one he wanted.

It had been weeks since she'd run into him, and though he'd been busy, he couldn't quite escape the quiet moments—walking the well-trodden path to town, tending to the animals, checking his appearance in the mirror—when he'd catch himself wondering how she was doing, and if he should have done more to ensure her safety.

Bells chimed as Clement stepped into the general store on Warren, shaking off the cold.

"Good afternoon, Clement. What can I do you for?"

He nodded at the shopkeep, adjusting his hat as warmth seeped into his bones.

Though times were hard, Hudson was still a town of quiet seasons —seeds in winter, harvest in fall, swimming in the creek come summer. A place for simple pleasures, for fishing, for toys in shop windows, for quiet talks around the stove.

And sometimes, when a man wasn't looking for it, a place to fall in love.

"Spring seeds," Clement said, clearing his throat as Mr. Theobold disappeared behind the counter to fetch the catalog. He removed his hat and set it on the counter, watching the shopkeep shuffle through his stack of books.

He frowned, shifting his weight.

Love—of all things.

It wasn't the first time he'd thought of it in recent weeks. Worse still, every time the notion crossed his mind, it came with dusk-colored eyes, framed by chestnut curls. Even now, standing here for the sole purpose of preparing for planting, that face lingered, vivid and unwelcome.

He stiffened. Shoved his hands into his coat pockets.

A breath slipped from his lips just as Theobold returned, catalog in hand. "Got some new varieties of apples I think you'll like," the shop-keep droned.

Clement lifted a brow. "We've got plenty of trees in the orchard already."

Theobold shrugged. "Nothing finer than an orchard. Why, you could always invite folks in for picking if you end up with an excess."

Clement considered. "Well, all right then. Let me see what you have."

*This* was what Clement loved about his town. Simple, everyday pleasures like new varieties of apples and picking them in the fall. Life was simple. Wholesome.

Clement flipped through the catalog. A prickle at the back of his neck alerted him to the shopkeeper's sidelong glance.

He looked around, wondering if there was something in the shop he was supposed to notice. Dry goods, spice shelves, tools, candy baskets, dried corn husks, and pumpkin decorations. Nothing out of the ordinary. When he looked back at Mr. Theobold, the older man leaned in.

Beginning to understand that he had something of a more private nature to discuss, Clement leaned in, too.

"You heard all this business about French Maude's rising star?" the shopkeep asked, hardly glancing up from behind thick spectacles.

"No," Clement said. His brow furrowed deeper. "Mr. Theobold, what are you talking about?"

There was no need to mention anything relating to the town's lascivious underbelly. The brothels were the one minor tear in the Quaker fabric of the city. Sure, citizens turned a blind eye to them—just as they forgot the Parade was once a banquet ground for Henry Hudson and his men before mutiny left them stranded to starve.

*If the river could speak*, he mused sardonically.

But sometimes a blind eye is exactly what's necessary. An effective way to see the world the way one wants it to be. The way it *should* be.

"She's a medium," Mr. Theobold said, his tone casual as he marked the ledger with neat strokes. "Making waves in this community, I'll give her that, and for such a tiny little thing."

*Christ.* Clement tensed. First the mention of a brothel, now this. He couldn't listen to any more talk about mediums. Was no one interested in honest conversation anymore? All he wanted to discuss with his old friend was whether the edge of the family property had the right soil for cherry blossoms.

He sighed quietly, forcing himself to keep a polite veneer. "You've seen her, then?" he asked.

"Oh yes," said Theobold evenly, setting his pen aside. "Nice-looking girl, too. It's easy to see why she's become popular."

Clement frowned, his patience wearing thin. "As a... medium, as you call it? Or"—he cleared his throat and then lowered his voice—"a scarlet lady?" He couldn't get the story straight. First Rudyard, and now Theobold—trusty old Theobold—prattling on about mediums. And *this* one worked at a brothel of all places. Had the world gone mad?

The doorbell chimed. He turned to see another customer hobble in on a cane.

"Can I help you?" Theobold called out, his tone sliding easily into practiced hospitality.

Clement remained silent, his jaw tightening. The interruption was a welcome excuse to let the absurd topic drop. Still, the mention of the medium lingered in his thoughts like an unwelcome draft, stirring something he didn't care to examine too closely.

"Yes, you can. Pound of sugar." The customer limped to the counter beside Clement, tipping his hat as he introduced himself. "C.L. Blood," he said. Tufts of frizzy black curls fell out of place despite his strong smell of pomade.

"Anyway," continued Theobold lazily as he measured the sugar, "to answer your question, Clement, she's a medium, nothing more."

"Talking about that little Irish lassie at French Maude's?" C.L. raised his eyebrows to the men, as though the two of them were also clandestine customers of Maude's.

Clement felt a tug at the word "Irish," but he pushed the thought from his mind. Irish immigrants were arriving by the day. There was no way they were discussing the same woman who had bumped into him on Warren. Whom he hadn't gotten out of his mind.

"We are," Theobold replied with a curt nod, pouring the last of the sugar with precision.

The customer cocked his head to the side. "That lassie's a medium, absolutely. She spoke to my great auntie Sue, may she rest in peace." He looked up at the other men.

Clement grimaced, knowing C.L. was waiting for them to validate his grief with a nod or a "Sorry for your loss." He would receive neither.

"Anyway," C.L. continued, clutching his hat by his long, scrawny middle, "she's as real as they come, and I know real. I'm in the business of making things look real, should you need anything looking real, you know what I mean?" He winked, leaving Clement with the distinct feeling of needing a wash.

Ignoring Clement's grimace, C.L. smoothed his black mustache, the only hair on his otherwise clean-shaven jowls. "Yes, siree, that's right! I know a fraud when I see one. And she's no tart, no, siree. Believe me, I'd sample that sugar if it were for sale, if you know what I mean, hehe." He let out a whistle that made Clement cringe. Theobold looked at the sack of sugar disconcertingly as C.L. lowered his high-pitched voice even more, so that Clement and Theobold had to inch down toward his face. He smelled of cheap gin.

"That madam won't sell Miss May for anything. You can't even sit alone with her. Always got someone watching. That half-rat security guard, or Miss Olivia—also a rare treasure—or the fiery madam herself. But she's worth the beans. Have either of you fine gentlemen had a reading yet?"

Theobold looked sideways at Clement, eyebrows raised with curiosity.

"No. I don't believe in mediums," Clement said shortly. "When you're dead, you're dead," he added for good measure.

C.L. laughed, a nasal sound that rang through the shop like a discordant bell. The other customers stared. Even the children stopped rummaging through the candy basket to see what the commotion was all about. Clement scratched the back of his head, which suddenly felt warm and prickly. The city really had gotten crowded.

"Oh, you haven't had a reading yet!" C.L. yelped with irritating confidence. "That's for sure as a slamkin! One minute with her, and you know she's a miracle. The real deal, no doubt, hehe." He nodded to himself wistfully, then looked up at the ceiling. "Aunty Sue, glad you're doing dandy in that great big garden in the sky." He slapped the money for his sugar on the counter and shuffled out the door.

Clement watched him leave, thinking of the conversation he'd had with his brother back in October before the final harvest. He'd already thought Rudyard should be above all this spiritualist nonsense. But now, seeing Rudyard *and* Theobold—reliable old Theobold—joining the likes of the common forgers, men who visited brothels and possessed manners worse than his family's goats... It was inconceivable.

Clement's gaze shifted back to the seed catalog in front of him, though his mind was elsewhere. He could stay, pay for his order, and go home. Forget the fraudster. Go on with his life, steady and respectable.

He sighed.

But none of that would help Rudyard.

His brother wasn't just interested in spiritualism; he was looking, desperately, for guidance. For salvation. He was chasing answers that didn't exist and wouldn't stop until he thought he'd found them. Rudyard would always wonder. Always believe in this fake religion until he found definitive proof otherwise.

Perhaps Clement had been thinking about this the wrong way. Keeping Rudyard away from spiritualism hadn't worked, but maybe confronting it head-on could. It was a fraud good enough for a man like C.L. Blood. A waste of time. A distraction. If Rudyard could see for himself what had been clear to Clement from the start, their life could continue on as usual. The creek in the summer; harvest in the fall.

Decision made, Clement turned to Theobold. "Hold my seeds for me, will you?" He dashed out the door before the shopkeep could ask when he'd return for them.

"Wait!" Clement called after the tawdry customer.

C.L. hadn't made it far.

"This house." Clement lowered his voice once he'd caught up. "The house of ill repute. Where the girl works. Miss May. Where is it?"

The man flashed a crooked-toothed smile.

The fellow who answered Clement's knock on the taupe door was tall. Even taller than Clement, with haunting, clear-blue eyes and a large, full mouth. He looked familiar.

"We're not open," he said, attempting to close the door in Clement's face.

Clement instinctively reached a hand on the inside of the door. "I'm not a customer," he corrected. "I—"

Clement hesitated under the Irishman's impatient glare. He cleared his throat. "I'm not here for...You see..."

He didn't have a clue what to say he wasn't there for. Relations? Comfort? Women? He couldn't care less for any of the three, all vices as far as he was concerned. His mission was clear. Once he could prove this Irish girl was as fraudulent as they come, he could set Rudyard straight and put an end to his brother's foolish dreaming. Before it got even more out of hand.

He had come for his brother, but how could he explain that to the unnerving bawdy house security?

With the twitch of a frown, Clement thought about Rudyard moping around the farmhouse like a ghost, disinterested in the family's commitment to abolitionism or in finding any sort of fulfillment at all, it seemed. Last week, Clement had gone to bed before his brother had returned home from town. The next morning, he caught the stale scent of cider on Rudyard's breath, though he'd never known his brother to drink.

He'd solidified the plan on his walk to Diamond Street. As soon as he could meet this so-called medium and prove her to be a charlatan, he would bring Rudyard to meet her. Then Rudyard would see for himself that what mattered most in the world was change. Freedom. Liberty. The American Dream. And then, the two could go on being brothers again without the thick fog that had settled between them. What his brother lacked was purpose. He had simply lost sight of it.

The surly man began to close the door again. "I'm here for the spiritualist," Clement said at last, resenting the term.

"And I said, we're not open. Come back after dark like everyone else."

Visit a bawdy house after dark? Out of the question. Clement was a Quaker, an abolitionist, a conductor on the Underground Railroad. To be seen at *that* house, no less during the half of the month when not a drop of gas glistened within the streetlamps, *could not* happen.

"I'll pay double," he offered.

The burly man stared for a moment, then extended his palm. "Triple. $3. You have twenty minutes."

Clement balked, then reached into his pocket, producing the money. The Irishman snatched it up with practiced ease, tucking it into the pocket of his ostentatious coat before ushering him inside.

As Clement stepped into the dim foyer, he glanced through a doorway that revealed a parlor crowded with women. They lounged on sagging furniture, their housecoats loosely belted, makeup smeared as though it had been worn for longer than the recommended amount of time. The room appeared neat enough, though shabbily furnished. A faint stale scent emanated from the large, frayed settee when one of the women plopped down.

He felt their eyes on him, speculative and unabashed, as he followed the Irishman toward the staircase.

"Madam's acquiring some new furnishings for the house today," the Irishman said lazily. "Miss Olivia will sit with you instead. Don't be trying anything funny, then. We'll all hear about it if you do."

Clement didn't respond, but his shoulders stiffened.

As they passed by the parlor, he caught snippets of a hushed conversation behind him, the words just loud enough to reach his ears. He couldn't be sure, but he thought he heard one of the girls mention something about accepting all types of men now.

"More handsome than the usuals. I wouldn't mind if he took *me* upstairs when he's finished with baby May." He heard that loud and clear, just as the red-haired girl who'd said it clearly intended. She smiled at him with what might have been intended as charm.

"What usuals?" a black-haired woman snapped, her tone sharp with irritation. "I wouldn't mind if *any*one took me upstairs. This place has been cobwebs and dust bunnies."

"Except for May," the redhead retorted, clicking her tongue.

"You sure you want to bother with the little witch, honey? We can take you right now if you want some real fun."

Clement turned, offering them a curt nod. His frown deepened as he cleared his throat. "No. Thank you."

It wasn't the first time Clement had been the object of unsolicited attention. He'd long since come to understand that some women found him attractive, though it was rarely a sentiment he returned. Dismissing their advances, however, often seemed to have the opposite effect, fueling their determination.

Someday, perhaps, he would take a wife, but she would have to understand that marriage would always be secondary to his work. A wife who accepted such terms wouldn't be easy to find.

At the top of the stairs, a spirited giggle spilled from the nearest room, followed by a woman's voice reciting what sounded like poetry. Clement paused, caught off guard by the sound. For a moment he forgot his mission and simply wanted to stand outside the door and listen. It was a sweet, silky voice that made him think of honeysuckles, and the cadence of her words carried an unexpected intimacy that sent a faint chill up his spine.

"For God's sake." The Irishman scowled, dragging Clement back to the moment. He was clearly not as enchanted. Without bothering to knock, he shoved the door open.

# CHAPTER 10

## Map

Joy was something I hadn't felt in a long, long time. As a child, it had come so easily, slipping over me like a dream —an intoxicating state where I was neither fully awake nor asleep. In those moments, I'd lose track of what was real and what wasn't. I'd be free. A moon-chasing, barefoot-dancing, gently flying dove. I'd be in the right place at the right time, and the world would feel no heavier than a midsummer haze, threaded with the shy chatter of white-throated sparrows.

That's the best way I can describe joy, unburdened and unbroken.

And for a fraction of a moment, I was back there, listening to the song of a white-throated sparrow drifting in from the maple tree outside my window.

"Did my heart love till now?" Olivia's voice was low and honeyed as she read from her favorite play. "Forswear it, sight. For I ne'er saw true beauty till this night."

I frowned, cutting in before she could continue. "This Romeo lad sees a perfect stranger and forswears everything else of beauty in the world? It sounds pretty, but I must be the daftest lass alive, because I can't understand it."

Olivia's eyes widened in disbelief, then softened, her lips curving like bleeding-heart flowers. "You're not *daft*, May. No one's taught you before now. But you have me here. I'll teach you."

She thought I was only talking about poetry, but I wasn't. I would have listened to Olivia read for hours if she dared. I had only learned some letters by this point, but it was thrilling. She was a good, firm teacher—one who'd giggle with me when I didn't understand something, rather than make me feel ashamed.

When she read to me, I felt myself carried back home on a woodsmoke wind, my little siblings cuddled in the warmth of my arms as Grandmammy told her stories; as Mammy watched the fire, quick to read omens in the shift of the smoke, in the way the sparks flew.

*Read to me, Olivia, until my eyelids give up and sink heavily, like a body sprawled out upon the moss, warm and green.*

Green. The color of things that grow. The color of things that die. Most people think of green as new life, forgetting it's just as much the color of death. Green is springtime and the last bright burst before autumn; it's regeneration and decay; it's a bridge between this world and the next.

And wasn't that what Olivia was offering me now? A bridge—however small—between who I had been and who I might become?

*Read me across this bridge and I will follow.*

No, I wasn't talking about poetry when I told her I didn't understand the play. In my own way, I could understand Shakespeare's language just fine. It was love I couldn't understand. A love that changed the way you saw the world in one brilliant, shining moment.

But I was too shy to tell her all that, so instead I followed her line of thought.

"Is there really a point to reading, Olivia?"

I knew the answer in my own bleeding heart—the beating one inside me, not the flower—but I asked, needing her to confirm it. "What can we do with all these pretty words, anyway? We'll never be seen as anything but women. No one cares if we can read or write or recite poetry."

Olivia's eyes gleamed with mischief. "You know," she said, "some say Shakespeare stole his plays from a woman named Amelia Bassano, also known as his Dark Lady. They say she had dark skin and might have even been a working girl. Makes you read these lines completely differently, doesn't it?"

"How do you know all of this?" I marveled.

"Just because I'm a fancy lady doesn't mean I'm uneducated, May McMurry."

We laughed. Again, I wondered about her past, though by then I'd picked up on the unwritten rule in the house. *Don't talk about the past.*

"Besides," she continued, "you don't need an education to be a poet. You just need eyes, and a heart, and a longing deep within for *something*. Anything, really. Just that longing. And you've got all three, Miss May, so don't sell yourself short."

"I have?" I asked, unsure. "But what am I longing for?"

I knew, of course. But how could I admit it? That a poor Irish girl like me still dared to hope for something beyond this house? That I dreamed of love and family and freedom?

"You tell me," she said earnestly. Her gaze was a warm, steady invitation. For a moment, I thought to break the rule and tell her everything. That my marriage was a sham, that I'd been kissed but the one time—and even then, it was more I that had done the kissing—and that I was saving every penny for my family, half-dead in Ireland.

Heat crawled up my neck. "I couldn't hope for much," I said instead. "But what about you? Do you dream of something beyond this house?"

Her expression turned sour. "I'm not a poet," she said, a sharp edge in her tone. Then, as if brushing away the blade, she smiled faintly, looking at me with those same wildflower-honey eyes. "I'm just a reader. But there's something special about you, May. *You're* a poet. And one day, I'll be reading your words."

I chuckled nervously. "Oh, give any Irish person a bottle and you'll find the lot of us are just as poetic as the next."

I wrung my fingers together, downplaying the little leaps and somersaults I felt in my chest.

It was bizarre to hear her put herself below me, for all I saw was a role model, her profession aside. She worked in a brothel, and wasn't ashamed of it, either. But I didn't see her that way. She was different. *More.*

"Well, I'm calling *you* a poet now," she said resolutely.

I smiled, though it was a fragile thing. As much as I wished to believe there was something special about me, I couldn't. After what I'd gone through since the famine began, I was no longer able to cradle the sparrow's melody in my heart. All I could do was hope I'd feel some sense of worth once I brought my family over.

That I wouldn't be too late.

A floorboard creaked in the hallway. A second later, the door to my bedroom flung open, and my breath caught.

Francis stood there, shoulders hunched, but he was not alone. A shadowy figure lingered just behind him. The moment I saw him, the room seemed to tilt. Faces blurred, distant and dreamlike, and for a breathless instant, I felt unmoored from myself.

Yet a strange, undeniable joy bloomed in my chest, the kind a bird must feel when a song rises through its throat.

I panicked.

A joy like that didn't belong to someone like me. It wasn't safe.

"Hello," said the figure in my doorway.

His voice was deep and steady, pulling me back to the ground like a weight tied to my ankle. Shadows draped over him like a heavy cloak, but they felt familiar. They felt like *home.*

Around him, ancestors hovered—dewy, translucent figures trailing his every muscle twitch.

My heart pounded as he looked at me. But it wasn't the vacant, hungry stare of those who came seeking answers. His amber eyes held something else entirely.

Something that felt as if it bridged two lives.

Our eyes locked. My breath tangled in my throat. Did he feel it too?

Then another sensation crept over me. *Recognition.*

We'd met before.

On the sidewalk, outside the florist's. He wore the same plain Quaker attire, the rim of a flat-top hat held neatly between his fingers —a man set in his ways, deliberate in his movements. His coat, though simple, fit snugly across his frame, hinting at a life of labor, the kind that shaped a man's shoulders through years of work—perhaps farming.

But now, as he looked down, his expression unreadable, I saw no flicker of recognition.

Perhaps he didn't remember me at all.

Let alone as deeply as I remembered him.

And the memory *was* deep. I hadn't been able to shake his eyes since the first time I saw them. I thought of them as I dressed for work, staring hard at my own reflection, wondering what he might see when he looked at me. I'd asked Olivia to help pin back my hair, rubbed the rouge from my cheeks and lips, thinking maybe a Quaker would prefer a more natural-looking lass. Then, just as quickly, I painted the color back on, because Maude wanted her girls painted.

"May, this fellow would like a reading," Francis announced abruptly, shattering my thoughts.

"A reading?" My voice barely rose above a whisper. A prickle spread from my face down my arms. Had I been mistaken? Had the door not just opened to a change of fate, to a silent prayer answered? "Right now?"

"Yes," the man said hoarsely, clearing his throat. His gaze met mine again, calm and deliberate.

The small round table Maude had set up in my room stood between us now, with two chairs waiting. He crossed the room and sat down, his movements unhurried.

"My name is Clement. Clement Stoker," he said, his voice as careful as his gaze.

The way he spoke, the patience in his tone—it both infuriated and thrilled me. Did he know me? Was he searching for something, or was it merely my own longing filling the space between us? At least now I had his name.

Olivia cleared her throat and nudged me, a subtle reminder that it was my turn to speak. I collected myself immediately.

"May. May Conally. I mean, McMurry." I blushed, remembering my married name. My eyes flitted to Francis, who looked like he was about to growl. "May McMurry."

Olivia continued to stare at me with a devilish smirk. Francis's scowl hardened before he sighed impatiently. He'd looked disgruntled since that first night at French Maude's, the frown lines around his mouth and across his forehead deepening.

"Pleased to meet you," Clement said evenly, his words simple yet laced with a quiet intensity that left me fumbling for a response.

I felt my lips part again, but I couldn't muster the words. I understood how Clement might not have recognized Francis. My husband had been on American soil just a few short weeks, and already he had filled out significantly. He was no longer the scrawny, gawky lad who'd narrowly escaped hunger. He was large and brooding now, putting on an impressive amount of weight by the day.

What I couldn't understand was how Clement didn't recognize *me*. Had I, too, changed so greatly? Or had I simply made so little an impact?

"If you lassies don't mind, I'll be leaving now," Francis offered flippantly, breaking the silence. He turned to Olivia with a raised brow. "Olivia, you'll be staying, will you?"

It was Maude who made the rule that someone stay in the room with me when I did my readings. She'd seen enough of them to know they could leave me so weak with hunger I'd occasionally faint, and she wasn't one to take risks. Whether it was my well-being or the success of the reading she was more concerned with, she never said— but Maude didn't believe in wasted efforts.

"You're the new favorite," Olivia had teased in a sing-song voice. "Enjoy it while it lasts."

I didn't think she was envious. If Maude did favor me, it was only because I brought in new clientele, though it hadn't earned me any kindness from the other girls. They seemed to see a target on my back, snickering at my unruly hair or my small stature when I was close enough to hear, but far enough not to defend myself.

"Mhm, I'll stay," Olivia answered smoothly as Francis flipped his hat off the mantle and left, the door clicking shut behind him.

We'd been sharing a room at the brothel, maintaining the facade of husband and wife, a bizarre arrangement that somehow made sense to Maude and the others.

At night, though, we didn't touch. We didn't even lie close enough to share warmth.

In Ireland, on cold nights, we'd curl up with our families—even the cattle, if a farmer was kind enough to let us sleep in his barn. Here, in my own marriage, I was worth less than a cow.

That thought kept me awake, knees hugged to my chest beneath wool blankets, shivering in the dark. And when the loneliness bit too sharp to bear, I'd tiptoe down to the kitchen, snatch a bannock to nibble on, and sit by the stove, listening to the embers sigh as the night faded to ash. Anything to chase the cold that lingered beside Francis.

Now, in the glow of lamplight, Clement's gaze lingered on Olivia for a moment before shifting to me. A sudden shame prickled beneath my skin. What a foolish thing, to imagine I could belong with someone like him. Someone good. I knew he was good; I could feel it in the way his spirit moved stiffly through our house of ill repute, in the quiet longing he held for the ancestors who still loved him fiercely.

But when he looked at me, did he see my heart as good, like his? Or did he simply see a lass who earned her wages in a brothel?

I swallowed hard, forcing my voice into something steady. "You came for a reading, then?" It came out dry, thinner than I meant it to. I pressed on, ignoring Olivia's knowing glances. "Is there someone in particular you wish to connect with?"

"I was wondering..." His voice faltered, trailing off as he rubbed the back of his neck.

Remembering myself, I rose from the bed and pulled out my own chair across from him. The moment I sat down, I felt the warmth of him, solid and close, and my pulse stumbled into a war beat.

"What is it?" I asked him, settling into the rhythm of a reading. The first moments always required effort, like feeling for the current beneath still water; but once I found it, the work carried on as naturally as breathing, as waves rising and falling in hypnotic, salty hushes.

He cleared his throat, eyes locking onto mine. That same sensation flickered between us again—sharp, electric, like the snap of a daguerreotype capturing something neither of us could name. Something real. Something lasting.

"Could you...? Might you...?" His fingers tightened where they rested on his knees. "Would you maybe just tell me what you see?" A breathless laugh escaped him, self-conscious. "I don't really know how this works, Miss May," he admitted. Then, quickly, as if catching himself, he added, "Excuse me—Mrs. McMurry, is it?"

"You were right the first time, sir. Miss May is just fine." I smiled, careful to remain polite but firm. I couldn't stand hearing my name tied to Francis's anymore, especially now that he was gone from the room.

Olivia leaned back on the bed with a blithe expression that was almost impossible to ignore.

Well, we all had our secrets at French Maude's. I could see it in the driftless eyes of the other girls as they moved through their routines—swishing hips, batting lashes, shining eyes—all mechanical and hollow. They were here, and not here. And in that, I understood them.

We all came from somewhere, even if we didn't speak of it. Memories have a way of returning, of resurfacing like ghosts, driven by a will of their own. They arrive when we least want them, or when we need them most.

Olivia's voice broke through my thoughts, laced with wicked mischief. "Are you sure about this, *Miss May?*" She tipped her head toward Clement. "You know how Maude feels about working extra. Perhaps we should see if this fellow can come back *at night.*"

I didn't answer right away. There were things between Olivia and me we never spoke aloud. Some stories, once told, lose their distance and become too real to bear. But right now, I knew what I had to do: earn money, and earn it fast. Maybe Olivia had found a way to close the book on her past, but I was still mid-chapter, caught between what was and what could be. If I couldn't let go of my past, then at least I could rewrite my present. My name, included.

My gaze drifted back to Clement, the space between us suddenly too heavy. I could see nothing but the darkness in him then, a cloak of shadows billowing at his throat. But seeing the dark was not the same as seeing *in it*. Not entirely.

"I do see something," I began, a Knowing blooming in my chest like an ink stain on cloth. "Your kin. You're more protected than just about anyone I've ever seen."

I hadn't quite noticed it the first time. My own spirit must have been too bothered, taken up too much space. But now there was no *unseeing* it. His eyes widened, but there was a blankness behind them, like he didn't believe a word I was saying.

"Grass? Fields? Such a distance of fields..." The images were coming to me in faded bursts of green and red. "Blood?"

He shifted uncomfortably.

"Cold metal."

He flinched.

"Chains." I gasped, looking back at him. My voice faltered as the visions sharpened. "I see an older woman. A grandmother? And another woman her mirror image but younger. A mother? She's here," I said softly, her presence tugging at me like a gale. "She's telling me she's always with you."

His face fell, and I wasn't sure if I should continue. He looked as though he might crumble where he sat, and I nearly stopped to fetch him a glass of water. But his mother's presence was insistent. She had a message, and she wouldn't let me go until I delivered it.

"She wants me to tell you something quickly, because she knows this is something you wouldn't normally do."

He looked ready to bolt, his body taut as a bowstring. I didn't need his mother to tell me he was far outside his comfort; it was written in the pallor of his skin, the tightness in his jaw.

Sometimes I forgot how strange and wondrous the other world seemed to others. To me, it was as real as the ground beneath my feet, as constant as the rise and fall of my breath. But for someone like

Clement, the notion of life after death—a presence that could reach across the veil—was enough to make the earth beneath him shift.

His gaze followed my fingers to my throat, to the small figure charm tied on a black ribbon. I held it between my fingers, tracing the worn grooves. It had been Grandmammy's once. A protection charm, she'd called it. I wasn't sure I believed in such things anymore, but I wore it still. Now, with Clement watching, it felt heavier than usual, a tether between what I saw and what I knew.

My grip tightened as I nodded, recognizing the presence before me.

"Your mother is asking me to touch this necklace," I said, my fingers lifting the charm, "and to tell you she's as close to you as this ribbon is to my neck."

But there was something more, something just out of reach. I forced myself to focus, grasping at the impressions she sent me. They came in faint flashes, like candlelight in a draft.

"She's thanking me for holding the necklace. And..." I hesitated, the next piece slipping through my fingers before I could catch it. "I can't quite make this part out. Does a necklace mean something to you? Was it significant between you?"

Only then did I look back at him.

He was sweating. His eyes shone with something too raw to name. Slowly, his hand lifted, fingers trembling as they reached for my necklace. His knuckles grazed my skin as he took the charm between his fingertips.

I didn't want to move away from him. But I had to; he wasn't touching me for me. He was trying to touch his mother.

I knew the spell he was under. I had unknowingly cast it, yet I wanted no part in it.

I flinched, the movement barely more than a quiver, but it was enough. He dropped the charm as though it had burned him, his hand recoiling in shame.

"I'm sorry, Miss May," he said hurriedly, his voice frayed. "I should not have asked. I should not have come."

Before I could respond, he stood and was gone, a rustle in the leaves outside my window.

Olivia gave me a knowing look. "Strange one," she said lightly.

I reached for the charm, half hoping he'd left behind some warmth, some trace of his presence.

"Don't, May," was all she said next. Her words were bitter from a voice of lavender honey.

"You sound like my mammy," I responded distastefully.

She turned to me, her dark eyes steady, daring me to deny it, to claim I hadn't fallen for a man I had no business loving.

For a moment, we stood there, suspended in an unspoken understanding. Then, as though some invisible thread had been snipped, we broke into laughter.

I couldn't say why she was fond of me or why she trusted me, but from then on, something shifted between us. Perhaps it was a recognition that we were both human, prey to the same unbearable longings as anyone else, keepers of the secrets and stories that had brought us here, united by something stronger than place and time.

Whatever it was, it felt inevitable. It felt like fate.

We were kindred. She'd read poems to me in the afternoons—beautiful poems about delights I couldn't imagine and a sadness that pulled like the strings of a golden harp. Poems about the immortality of the heart, odes to a nightingale, the terror of a raven.

We'd surprise each other with penny sweets from the general store, small gifts wrapped in wax paper and tied with ribbon.

On our days off, we'd walk arm in arm along Parade Hill, laughing as though the world were kinder than it was. The respectable ladies would stare at us as we passed, their looks heavy with disdain, but we'd ignore them.

I almost wished my farmhouse seemed like a greater impossibility, for having a true friend was the only gift I knew that wasn't just as much a curse.

One afternoon, as we strolled along Warren Street, arm in arm, I was overtaken by the sharp, resinous scent of rosemary.

"What's the matter?" Olivia asked.

It could have drifted from the apothecary, but I immediately thought of Grandmammy. Rosemary had been her favorite herb. "Dew of the sea" it meant. I could still see her wrinkled, sun-spotted hands plucking the fragrant leaves as she spoke to me through cool, clipped words.

"She needs very little water to survive," she'd said. "She lives on the wetness in the air. And she's a healer, mind you. A bath with rosemary can cure near anything." Those words were from a time before the famine, but still, with the scent now lingering around me, I felt Grandmammy's presence as clearly as if she'd taken my hand.

It was a message, I thought—though what it meant, I couldn't say. I'd never been able to summon the spirits of my departed family, though I often wished I could. Rosemary could mean anything—or nothing. But somehow, I believed it had something to do with memory. Memory, like rosemary, needs little to blossom.

Mammy's memory followed swiftly behind Grandmammy's, though as far as I knew, she still walked with the living. At that moment, I had been thinking—*wishing*—to remain by Olivia's side. Mammy used to say, "Be careful what you wish for, May Connolly." The words, once familiar and almost comforting, now felt like a warning I hadn't heeded. The echo of her voice, once so grounding, now vibrated with a chilling weight, as though the past was trying to catch up with me.

I couldn't place my finger on why, but the knot that formed in my chest wouldn't let go.

Something was shifting. A price to pay for wanting things to stay the same. Something dark and inevitable was pressing in, and I was already too close to see it coming.

# CHAPTER 11

# Clement

*C*lement pulled his coat tighter across his chest as an icy wind made a joke of his layers. It had been weeks since he'd last ventured into town, and he'd nearly forgotten how the wind rolled off the river, snaking artfully between the shops this time of year. Caused a chill that stayed in your bones long after a door closed against it, and you rubbed your hands together by the fire.

"Afternoon, Mr. Theobold," Clement greeted, stepping into the warm interior of the shop.

Theobold, peering over his spectacles, looked up with wide eyes, not bothering to hide his surprise. Clement had avoided town, it was true. Who needed holiday crowds and city noise anyway?

But today he had business he couldn't very well put off. The bell on the door chimed as a woman with two small children followed behind him.

"This is Mrs. Davidson, the woman my father was telling you about," Clement said.

Theobold straightened and adjusted his spectacles, his expression softening into something warmer as he approached. "Ah, yes," he said, his tone kind. He extended his hand, which Mrs. Davidson hesitantly took. "Pleased to meet you, ma'am. Have you ever worked in a shop before?"

Mrs. Davidson glanced nervously at Clement. Her dress was plain wool tartan, her black hair parted neatly down the middle and twisted into a tight knot at the back of her head. Her eyes, red-rimmed and shadowed, betrayed exhaustion, though she held herself upright with quiet resolve.

"That's all right, Mrs. Davidson," Clement said gently. "You can speak freely here. Mr. Theobold's an old family friend."

"Well, no," she admitted slowly. Her children clung to her legs, the boy on one side and the girl on the other, their small faces peeking out cautiously. Clement swallowed hard. His stomach twisted. The boy looked nearly the same age as he was when he'd escaped. But this boy still had his mother.

"I've never worked in a shop exactly," Mrs. Davidson continued. "But I can clean, stock, sell—whatever you need me for. I'm good with numbers, too. I used to help my former mistress with the book-keeping."

Clement gave her an encouraging nod.

"Former," she added, a faint smile tugging at her lips. "Sounds strange to say it."

Theobold studied her for a moment, his large nose tilted slightly downward, then broke into a broad grin. "That's grand! God knows I could use some help keeping these books in order. Come on around the counter, and I'll show you the ropes."

Mrs. Davidson hesitated, her hand brushing against her son's head as if she couldn't quite bring herself to let go. She looked to Clement, her eyes brimming with uncertainty.

"It's all right," Clement said quietly, his voice low but firm.

He inhaled deeply, the words catching in his throat. What he wanted to tell her was that everything would be fine now. That the hardest part was behind her. That she and her children—still together, still bound by the fragile yet unbreakable ties of family—would have the life they deserved. But he couldn't say it.

Instead, he met her gaze and gave another brief, reassuring nod, hoping it would be enough.

The bell on the door chimed again. Clement turned absently, only to feel his chest tighten and his throat go suddenly dry. Parched.

It was *her*. The charlatan from French Maude's, dressed in a periwinkle silk that matched the curious shade of her eyes.

"Afternoon, Miss May!" Theobold waved.

Clement balked.

"Good afternoon, Mr. Theobold," May called cheerily. But when her gaze settled on Clement, her smile faltered, dimming into something unreadable.

Clement cleared his throat, willing himself to speak evenly. "You two know each other?" he asked, his tone betraying more judgment than he intended. He regretted it immediately. He had no right to pass judgment. After all, he and Miss May knew each other as well.

Thankfully, Theobold didn't seem to notice. "Of course! Miss May has become one of my best customers," he said warmly. Then, turning to her, he added, "Oh, Miss May, you're in luck today. I've just received Miss Olivia's favorite tarts, delivered fresh this morning."

"Lovely," May replied. Her tone was cool, but her dimples could thaw the morning's bread. Clement needed some water, indeed. "You're very kind to think of us," she added. Gone was the wild fear he'd seen in her when they'd first met. Now, she seemed entirely at ease, her confidence disarming.

Her gaze brushed past him again, and he found himself struck by the contradictions she seemed to embody. Eyes cold as ice in a face as creamy and delicate as a magnolia. She made no sense. None at all. What he was feeling was fiddle-faddle to the highest degree. And what right did she have to look at him as though he were a stranger? No one here could guess they'd already met—not once, but twice. He should have felt his shoulders relax at the thought, but somehow it felt... regrettable. He swallowed harder.

"Oh, hello!" May beamed suddenly, her voice brightening as her gaze landed on Mrs. Davidson's children. The two little ones were staring at her, wide-eyed and curious. Before Clement could interject, May had knelt down to their level, giggling with them, asking their names and ages as though nothing else in the world mattered.

Clement cleared his throat. "These children have had a long night," he began firmly. "Now is not the time for games—"

Once again, she was a step ahead, her eyes sparkling with playful mischief. "A long night?" she cooed to them. "Then I'm certain you must be too tired for a ride upon the ferry, aren't you?" Their faces lit up with delight. May turned to their mother with an eager smile. "May I lift them? Just for a moment? My siblings used to love this game."

Mrs. Davidson hesitated, then nodded.

And before Clement could protest, May had one child perched on her shoulders and the other balanced in her arms, whistling a tune as she paraded through the aisles like a ship cutting through waves.

Clement realized, in horror, that he was smiling. An unfounded, frivolous grin stretching across his face. He cleared his throat, something insufferably caught in it. He'd prepare a tea of slippery elm first thing he got home. For now, time to put an end to the madness.

"Miss May," he said sharply, though he softened when the children burst into giggles. "Mrs. Davidson was just about to begin her training for her new job—"

"Oh!" May exclaimed. She stopped abruptly, making the children, still on her person, giggle even harder. She turned to Mrs. Davidson with a sudden seriousness. "Then you'll be needing someone to watch your darling children?"

"Well..." Mrs. Davidson began, glancing uncertainly between Clement and May.

"I'll watch them," Clement interrupted quickly.

"You won't be needing any help?" May asked, setting each of them down beside their mother. She released them slowly, ruefully, as though with a great deal of compunction. Then she brightened again, her gaze turning to Mrs. Davidson with such untethered hope, Clement almost felt a tug of longing himself. "I'd love to treat them to a hot cocoa. My little siblings are so far away, and—"

"That won't be necessary," he interrupted, tethering the hope for the two of them.

"Please, Mama," the children begged, jumping up and down and pulling at her dress. "Well," Mrs. Davidson said hesitantly, "it's fine with me if you're sure you don't mind?"

Clement looked at the clock, then sighed. Hot cocoa. With May. "About an hour, Mr. Theobold?"

Theobold gave him a cheerful salute. "Take your time."

"We'll take good care of them," Clement said to Mrs. Davidson, his voice steady and reassuring. Then, with a stiff resolve, he followed May out the door, the children clutching each of her hands as though they'd known her their whole lives.

"Save two tarts for me?" May called back to Theobold as an afterthought.

"Sure enough, Miss May!" He waved.

The wind hit them the moment the door swung open. It sent May reeling, her small frame bending as though she might be blown back into the shop. Clement stepped forward, his long arm bracing the door.

"Thank you," she said, her voice soft as her gaze lingered on him. Clement wondered what, or whom, she saw when she looked at him.

They walked in silence down the bustling street, the children skipping ahead now and then before rushing back to May's sides. The air was alive with the chatter of shopkeepers, their voices rising above the howling wind. They called out boasts of fine jewelry, the newest fashions just in from New York, a hair-straightening liquid that worked like magic. If a bit of baldness ensued, you could purchase "The Magic Fluid" to prevent more hair loss, lest you prefer a wig from William Green.

As a boy outside the shop called out the advertisement, Clement noticed May reach absently for a stray curl, tucking it behind her ear. He felt the oddest desire to assure her that her hair was just fine as it was.

As they stepped inside the bakery, the warmth of the ovens greeted them. The room smelled of fresh bread, pastries, and cinnamon. He'd never been here before. Didn't care for sweets. But the children's wide-eyed delight was unmistakable. They scrambled to a small wooden table with mismatched chairs near the window. Though the panes of glass were fogged from the warmth inside, they offered a glimpse of the street beyond, where passersby braved the cold Hudson wind.

May ordered four hot cocoas. She even splurged for croissants.

Clement stiffened as their waitress appraised the odd assortment at their table. Himself: a man of simple, practical dress, a Quaker farmer by every visible account. The children: too thin, tired, their clothes patched but clean. Perhaps she would think these children his? And then May: wearing an umbrella of a gown. Skin as pale as a white dove, save for her windswept cheeks.

He felt unmoored by the scene, as though he were watching it from some place outside himself.

His gaze returned to May, her hands moving like a flutter of wings as she turned to the children. "What's your favorite dessert?" she asked them brightly.

They exchanged blank stares. "We've never had dessert," the boy said at last.

"Never had dessert?" May asked incredulously. She looked at Clement, clearly seeking confirmation that the notion was ridiculous.

Clement looked down at the table. What could he say? This hardly seemed the time to explain that these children had arrived on the Underground Railroad only the night before. The weight of the truth seemed to settle in the air nonetheless, and when he looked up, he found May's eyes fixed on his. There was something raw in her expression, something he couldn't name.

And yet, to his surprise, he didn't feel defensive under her gaze. Odder still, he felt... well, it was an unfamiliar sensation. Like an afternoon when there's no work to be done. Or the first snowfall. Opening the window when the June bugs dot the blackness.

*Open.* He felt open.

May exhaled softly, her face unreadable. Then, as if by sheer force of will, she brightened again, turning back to the children. "Well," she said, her voice light and musical, "you're in for quite a treat. Hot cocoa is my favorite."

They walked back toward the general store at an easy pace. The earthy aroma of cocoa still clung to May, emanating from each swoosh of her gown. The boy had returned to his post on May's shoulders, and his younger sister slept in her arms. Somehow the children made her look even smaller, not larger.

"Why not let me carry her," Clement offered.

"Oh, no," May replied lightly. "I'm happy to, really. I miss this. I used to go door to door with my mammy in Ireland, selling trinkets to the farmers' wives. In one arm she'd be carrying the basket of swag. In the other, my little sister. Tied to her back would be a bag of clothes she'd gathered for the weans, and right between her teeth, she'd hold the milk can with the lid on tight. We'd walk for miles like that, and I'd be beside her, lugging oats for the pony and household wares, heavy dishes and the like, stuffed into another large basket. I'm the oldest of nine so—" She stopped abruptly, her breath catching.

Clement felt an immediate pang across his chest. He wanted her to keep talking. She'd been smiling as she'd described the scene, right up until that last moment. He wanted her to keep smiling.

"Oldest of seven, I mean," she corrected quietly, her smile fading.

The silence fell like a curtain between them. Clement nodded once, his jaw tightening. She was still a charlatan, a fraud of the worst, of the most heartless variety. Yet he found himself asking her what happened. Wondering if she was all right.

Reminding himself not to stare at her hair.

"Oh, it was fever that took my twin siblings, not long before I left Ireland."

Clement swallowed. Loss was loss, whether you were a charlatan or not. "I'm sorry," he said simply.

"We all have our burdens to bear," she told him. "I still catch myself forgetting from time to time. I think of what I'd like to show John and Lucy once I bring them over, and then I remember..." She trailed off, her words vanishing like breath on glass.

That's when he noticed how tremendous her curls really were. Though she wore her hair pinned back, stray ringlets escaped, shimmering like honeysuckle branches in the wind. He immediately looked away.

"It's never easy losing someone you love," he ventured. *Don't.*

She nodded, her gaze softening. "I think it's really kind, how you're helping Mrs. Davidson," she offered. He noted the quiet attempt to shift the subject. And again, he caught himself staring at her. The bridge of her nose had a smattering of Venetian red freckles, the sort of detail one might miss in passing but couldn't forget once noticed.

"When I first came to America, all I wanted was for someone to be kind to me," May continued. "To help me get settled. You're doing that for Mrs. Davidson. She must be very grateful to you."

Clement's stomach turned at her words. He remembered—more vividly than he would like—how he'd felt when he'd first arrived in New York. Though it wasn't a new country, it might as well have been. He'd been luckier than most when he'd met Phillip and Molly Stoker, and Rudyard, of course, who called him "brother" and gave him a second chance at life. Yet that heavy, chilling, cold sweat sort of fear that rode him all the way to New York—well, he couldn't simply shake it off.

"I imagine you must have felt... alone," he said, at last settling on the word. Maybe it was the pain so clearly in her heart that mirrored his own. He didn't know what exactly was happening, but when he looked at her, he saw something that scared him.

When he looked at her, he couldn't heed his own warning.

The general store came into view across the street. As soon as they were inside, he would hand the children back to their mother, ensure she had what she needed, and return his focus to what mattered.

"Don't be lonely, Miss May," the boy on her shoulders said suddenly. "We'll be your friends." His voice was sweet and innocent. Why Clement did what he did. Preserving that innocence. Heck, giving it a chance.

She tilted her head up to grin at him, her dimples deepening in a way that transformed her face into something vibrant and full of life. A picture that someone—*not him*—could treasure.

"That won't be necessary," Clement responded before May could say another word. His voice came out firmer than intended. "Miss May is all settled now. She's doing just fine."

The silence couldn't have lasted for more than a second, but it stretched.

"That's right, laddie." May smiled politely, her tone light but measured. "I'm all settled now." She gave the boy's thighs a gentle squeeze, making him break into a giggle. "But we can still be friends," she added with a smile.

Clement held the door open for the trio. Watched May carefully pass the sleeping girl back to her mother, then kneel to hug the boy goodbye.

He couldn't see spirits. Didn't believe in them, for that matter. And yet he could almost swear he felt hers. Pure and contagious in the very best way.

It was only a twitch. The slightest inconsistency in his worldview. The faintest whisper. But something was telling him that he might have been wrong about her.

# CHAPTER 12

# 𝔐𝔞𝔭

"That's it, May," French Maude said with a decisive sweep of her hands, as though wiping them clean of me. "I can't have you doing your readings anymore. You understand, don't you? It's nothing personal. I enjoy them. You're very good at what you do. But I can't have it. Business is business."

Her gaze drifted upward, landing on the chandelier—a gaudy, glittering thing she'd recently installed. Her newest prize, paid for with money I'd drawn in for her.

The change at French Maude's had been subtle at first. I'd noticed the glances from the girls, sharp as glass shards, but had brushed them off as nothing more than jealousy. Olivia, ever candid, was quick to fill me in on the whispers behind my back. They were unoriginal, the same tired slurs I'd heard a hundred times—mostly that I was Irish (as if that was a surprise), and that I was changing the place, ruining the men who came and turning them into "soft sacks."

"Don't take it personally, May," Olivia said one evening. "I'm sure they still talk about me in much harsher terms. I've taken business from them before, don't get me wrong. But you?" She laughed, low and warm. "You could put all the working girls in Hudson out of business. End the industry entirely. And with nothing more than your *mind*. Even *I'm* impressed."

There was something about the way she said it, the way her dewy brown eyes shimmered with admiration and whimsy, that caught me off guard. Olivia wasn't like the others. Not only more beautiful, educated, and refined, but when I felt her spirit, it was velvety with a honed edge, the kind that made you want to lean in, not away.

God intended for people like her to be artists, people wooed by even the simplest of pleasures like sun showers and misty dawns, yet able to create as furiously as though under a spell. Mammy might have called her an "evil genius." I didn't think she was evil, though. She was complicated, like a story with no clear ending, something you're meant to listen to, not pick apart.

As curious as I was about her, I never asked, just as she never asked about my marriage or my past in Ireland. We were united by something deep, something you can't easily pinpoint or place a label on, something that coursed through breath and blood, that most others will never notice, even when that blood runs red as everyone else's.

But now, it seemed my time in her story was coming to an end. The other girls had made sure of it. They'd complained that their clients, even their most loyal ones, had started drying up after visiting me.

That's the funny thing about closure. It doesn't need much—a kind word, a touch, a reading that gives someone something to hold onto. The holes these men carried with them for years weren't patched by what I said, but by what they believed. And belief, I'd learned, was the most powerful thing of all.

I'd seen the sadness in their faces, the quiet ache etched into every line. Famine, disease, violence. They could have come to me in a brothel, a tavern, or the general store. It didn't matter the place. Their pain was written into the air we shared, lingering like smoke in a dingy room.

Very few escaped an untimely death.

Still, Maude wasn't about to lose her business over it.

She'd gone so far as to import her niece from Montreal. The girl, Madeline, was truly a girl, all of thirteen years old but three years above what the law considered suitable for the mature responsibilities of a girl at French Maude's. If she couldn't sway customers away from me, then no one could.

So said French Maude.

For a night or two, it seemed the place might go back to normal. Men trickled in, enticed by word of a new girl, fresh as a snowdrop. But soon enough, word of my readings reached the spiritualist press. Visitors began arriving from as far away as Boston and Philadelphia, hoping for a glimpse of the otherworldly. A glimpse of me.

The complaints from the other girls returned in full force.

"You have to choose, Maude," Annie declared one evening, her tone a thorn's tip. "Is this a house of spiritualists or good old-fashioned tarts?"

Maude's decision was swift, though the faint tightening at the corners of her mouth betrayed her annoyance.

"I'm not kicking you to the curb," she said to me later, her words breezy but firm. "You can have your old job back—just make up your mind by tonight. Stay and work—and no more of those readings—or leave by the end of the week. Nothing personal, doll face. It's just business."

I kept my eyes on her, though the shadow of Francis loomed behind her, a dark smudge at the edge of my vision. I didn't need to turn to see him; his satisfaction was a pulse in the room, a cloying smugness that made my stomach twist.

I didn't answer Maude right away. The air in the room was thick with expectation, almost suffocating. I could feel every detail, like a second skin—the dust settling on the velvet drapes, the stale scent of spilled gin rising from the frayed carpet.

Beneath it all, there lingered something older, something far more ancient than this house or the people in it.

I thought of the Mohicans, the first people to walk this land before the Dutch carved it into parcels and sold it off. They believed everything had a spirit: the trees, the rocks, the creeks. I didn't need to believe; I knew—*Knew*. The spirits were still here, their rage woven into the house's foundation, their cries carried on the draft that snaked through the room.

I could feel Olivia, too. She was trying to hold her composure, but her spirit betrayed her—a persistent ache, the kind of loneliness that sinks into your bones and lingers. She'd never admit it, not to me and certainly not to herself, but she didn't want me to go.

The other girls, though? They were restless, their amusement like a prickle against my neck. I didn't need to hear their laughter to know they wanted me gone. I'd seen their glares, heard their whispered taunts. I understood their resentment, even when it stung. Their lives were raw, jagged with pain, and I could feel it all—the crimson of their wounds, their silent hopes for something better, their bitterness at a world that never gave it to them.

Often, my Sight felt so raw that it hurt. These girls were hurt, too. I could feel that most of all.

# CHAPTER 13

# Olivia

*O*livia ripped another piece of paper from her leather-bound journal, tore it in half, crumpled both sides together, and stifled a scream before chucking the ball of garbage onto the floor.

She'd been *good* at this once, hadn't she? And even if her talent had been nothing more than a delusion, at least her passion hadn't. She was still happiest alone, save for the company of her poetry books.

Wasn't she?

She remembered the first book of poetry she'd ever read—a collection by Heinrich Heine. It was a gift from her public school teacher, Mr. Martin Wilbur, and it had blown the hinges right off the door of her mind. There were others, she realized then, that thought and felt as deeply as she did. If it hadn't been for her teacher, maybe she'd still be living under her parents' roof, or married with a few children by now, or...

*Don't go there, Olivia,* she told herself. *Don't you dare.*

And yet, as she stared at the crumpled, pathetic attempt at poetry on her bedroom floor, her mind began to drift to days at her parents' modest farmhouse, the seven acres that was their pride and joy, long walks to the one-room schoolhouse, two braids down her back.

After school, her teacher would lend her book after book, from Robert Browning to Alfred Tennyson. He trusted her with rare translations from the Golden Age of Russian poetry. Her favorite was Pushkin. Pushkin understood the monotony of life and opened his heart to a holy muse. He seemed to understand *her.* After devouring his poems, Mr. Wilbur gave her a thick, annotated volume of Shakespeare. She kept it on her bedside table, occasionally opening it just to see his own neat handwriting pressed into the margins.

"Some believe his plays were written by a woman named Amelia Bassano, better remembered as 'The Dark Lady,'" he told her one afternoon. All the other students had gone home, but he'd lingered behind the schoolhouse with her. He ran his hand down the length of one of her braids. It was November—she remembered the quiet shades of brown—but it might as well have been May, because in her mind's eye, she'd seen fields of bluebells and basked in sunlight. She had never imagined that a woman with skin like hers could actually publish poetry. True, a white man had stolen the credit for it, but the representation gave her hope.

Mr. Wilbur must have known he made her feel the world could open up to her like a rosebud.

"I want to be a poet," she whispered, breathless.

He asked to read something she'd written. Even all these years later, she still felt the same pounding of her heart as she rushed home that afternoon, rifling through her journals to find the perfect example of her talent, a promise sealed in unstinting ink.

"Knock knock," Maude crooned. Olivia was so lost in the memory, the thump on her door made her jump. "Bad time, honey?" Maude's husky voice on the other side was tender.

"Just a minute," Olivia called, gathering together her quill pens, brass inkwell, and journals. She tried to open her desk drawer, but it was jammed closed. *Of course.* Thinking quickly, she slid her writing supplies unceremoniously beneath her bed. *Shit.* The inkwell spilled, staining the wooden floor black beneath the four-poster bed. Deciding she'd clean it later, she hurried back to her seat by the desk, crossing her legs as she said, "Come on in."

Maude swayed through the narrow doorway like a fish slipping through water, her skirts trailing behind her like fins.

"Olivia!" Maude exclaimed, her face lit with that unmistakable glimmer of fresh gossip. "You won't believe the story I have for you! Did you hear? Old Duffy's on the hunt again!"

Olivia frowned and sighed internally. *Old Duffy.* Again. It was always the same: some new tale about the constable and his exploits, some scandal that thrilled Maude and made her eyes shine. For Olivia, it was exhausting. Another distraction, another reminder of the narrow world she inhabited on Diamond Street, hemmed in by whispers and the steady grind of customers.

She wanted to close her door and get back to work, to dreaming, to anything that would take her far away from this place. But Maude was beaming, her energy buzzing through the room like a spark looking for tinder. And maybe Olivia's so-called work, her scribbles and daydreams, were pointless anyway.

So she played along.

"The constable should really come here for pleasure, not work, one of these nights. Might make this town a happier place for us all." Her tone was easy, her delivery flawless. Maybe if she played along long enough, she wouldn't be playing anymore. Maybe one day, she'd feel the way she used to feel: *fine.*

Maude plopped onto Olivia's bed, the springs groaning softly beneath her weight. She immediately began to toy with the satin pillows, smoothing them with her fingers.

"This story really is tremendous, Livy," Maude began, her voice thick with excitement. "You'd have heard it already if you'd joined us for breakfast instead of doing whatever it is you do up here alone all afternoon. Anyway, I heard this tasty morsel from Mr. Van Buren last night." She winked. "You know how last week a group of drunks beat up Old Fluffy Duffy and left him to bleed in the mud outside Central House?"

Olivia nodded, already weary of where this was going. "You really get too much satisfaction from his pain. He takes your bribes," she reminded Maude. "What is he to you, anyway?" She knew the comment would irk her madam, but she was annoyed about the interruption, the insufferable tugging on some unidentifiable part of her body.

The question hit its mark. Maude stopped petting the pillows and fixed Olivia with a sharp look, the kind that could cut through iron. Olivia instantly regretted her comment, but before she could soften it, Maude inhaled deeply, brushing off the barb like stray lint on her dress.

"Well," Maude continued, her voice bright again, "he returned to the Central House on Sunday with a gun. A whole group of churchgoers watched the entire thing, running outside for a small taste of drama in their tiny pathetic lives!" She slapped her knee and cackled. A tear escaped the corner of one eye, and she wiped it away with a swirl of her pointer finger.

"The group of bawdy Irishmen were still drunk and enjoying themselves, picking fights with whoever they could. Duffy had apparently enlisted his nephew to help him, and the two of them set off firing their weapons into the air right outside Central House!"

Olivia leaned forward despite herself. "A gunfight outside Central House?" she asked. "Was anyone hurt?"

Maude smacked her scarlet lips. "The drunkards were prepared, darling. Apparently, they'd seen two magpies and a crow hopping about the night before, or some such nonsense that made them believe coppers were coming. When Duffy began to fire, they fired back, until both sides were out of bullets."

"Was anyone hurt?" Olivia repeated, her interest now fully piqued.

"Not one person! Well, one of the drunkards got shot in the face, but just a graze. Duffy's nephew fired the shot, naturally. As if Duffy were capable of such a thing..."

As Maude continued to prattle, Olivia's focus drifted back to the place it always went when the world around her felt too small and stifling: back to her first mistake. *The poem.*

Why had she shown Martin Wilbur that damn poem?

She'd searched for the perfect one. A poem that would reveal her brilliance, her heart, and her dreams all at once. The one that he'd read and fall in love with. The one that would tell him she was *meant to be a poet*.

She'd chosen a soft, lovely piece she'd written only a few nights prior. It was inspired by Queen Mab, the fairies' midwife who assists sleepers in giving birth to their dreams, mentioned in her favorite play of all, *Romeo and Juliet*.

Queen Mab was undervalued, just a wispy reference in a secondary character's banter. Olivia had wanted to change that.

She'd spent one lonely evening lying in her bed, imagining how else the tiny queen might have played a part in the greatest tragedy ever written. What was it like for Juliet to fall in love so deeply and thoroughly that she would take a dagger to her own heart?

That was her second mistake. *Curiosity*. She'd wanted to be a poet but let the question of love begin to cloud her mind.

"What do you still do at this desk, anyway, Livy? You haven't written a poem in years."

Maude's husky voice cut through her reverie. Olivia blinked, realizing Maude had stopped talking and was now squinting at her with suspicion.

Olivia bit her lip. "Sorry. I was distracted."

Maude's sharp gaze softened. "Best not to start that writing business now, Livy dear. You're doing so well here. The girls hardly tease you at all anymore." Maude gently touched beneath Olivia's chin with her bejeweled knuckles.

"Hm," Olivia murmured, noncommittal. Maude meant well. She always had. But Olivia didn't care about teasing. She'd been teased since childhood, not for being the only student with her skin tone, but for being a bookworm. "You know, my parents once thought I'd become a teacher."

Amusement played at Maude's round features.

"Of course, I had no interest in teaching," Olivia added quickly. "I didn't like children."

They laughed. "Well, who does, honey? Certainly no one who works here." Maude guffawed and Olivia chuckled.

What if she had never written that stupid poem? The question pounded at the back of her mind, demanding attention.

She'd sat in her childhood bedroom like a fool, thinking of Romeo and Juliet, picturing her own breasts, bare and broom-colored, with the silver dimple of a blade pressing in between them. She'd been so lost in her imagination, even now she could remember the feel of cold metal, a pressure so minute, yet oppressive enough to rattle her breath, like an icy waterfall beating down her back.

She felt her ribs knit around the silver dimple, her heart pound irregularly. The poem she ended up writing and showing to Martin Wilbur came from *that* depth of imagination.

No wonder it was cursed.

A story about Queen Mab visiting Juliet in her darkest moment, convincing her to take one last doze before ending her life. Juliet agrees, and Queen Mab gifts her a dream of a second husband, a second chance at love. When Juliet wakes, she bids Romeo farewell and starts her life anew.

The poem had been charming, written in delicate iambic pentameter, with just enough humor to balance its sorrow.

When she handed it to Martin, she'd been terrified, but his reaction had been everything she'd ever wanted.

"You are no teacher, Olivia Johnson," he had said, his dark eyes smoldering. "You are the poet that others teach."

Those words had sunk deep, had eaten her alive like a great whale. She hadn't realized how badly she'd needed to hear them until they left his lips. She swooned in their vibrant, illusive, soaking-wet belly.

When he kissed her, she was surprised, though she'd imagined it before.

But those thoughts had been the innocent musings of a child, akin to Romeo's puppy love for Rosaline. Now Olivia was feeling the stirrings of womanhood—the thickening of blood and racing pulse and desire to be seen completely, bare broom breasts and all.

Womanhood, with all the power and fragility that came with it.

Maude's husky voice tore her back to the present. "I still remember the day I decided to approach your little poetry stand on Warren Street," she mused. "I kept passing it day after day, and I recognized something of myself in you. This big city of ours can often feel like a small town, and I thought: that pretty baby is on her own. I'd never seen anyone drop you off or stop by at the end of the day to walk you home. You'd have this lonely look in your eyes when you'd stare after passersby for just a moment too long."

Olivia had thought she was in love. Had thought she could have her husband and her poetry and a life that was poetry itself. She could be queen of the fairies, inspiring girls like her, both in color and of mind, to dream.

He'd married another girl from her class that same year.

Instead of letting the rejection extinguish her dream, it seduced her deeper into it. She saw herself in Icarus, reveling in the ecstasy of his flight before the inevitable fall. Her misfortune became a lullaby, and she rocked in it and cried herself to sleep for weeks.

But finally, she decided she didn't need Martin. She didn't need public school or classmates who called her odd and pretended she didn't exist at lunchtime and never invited her to their parties. She was clever and imaginative, and she could birth her dream into reality on her own.

She stole money from her father's wallet, packed a bag, and left her small farming town of Claverack for Hudson. There, she found work as a kitchen maid, scribbling poetry in the brief moments she could steal between her duties. She wrote with the fierceness of someone determined to prove everyone else wrong. She wrote of treachery and deceit and revenge, of poisonous violets and charcoal skies.

She set up a makeshift poetry stand on the sidewalk, offering to compose quick verses for a penny apiece. A few passersby stopped, more amused by the novelty of a young girl writing poetry than by her talent. Older women would pat her head or tug her braids, tell her they really ought to bring their granddaughters over to see her.

Olivia felt her cheeks flame at the memory and Maude's mention of it. She looked down, then back at her madam. "Maude," she began reprovingly. What was Maude *doing* bringing up a memory like that anyway? She knew the rules. Hell, she *made* this one! *Never talk about the past.*

"Now, now, just wait," Maude went on as though reading her

thoughts. "It wasn't your loneliness that made me approach you. We've all been lonely, from time to time. There's no shame in it. I came over because I knew you were a fighter, industrious, smart, and strong, unfazed, for the most part. You and I wore a similar cloak of mystery, *mystique*, even—so hard to find in working girls these days. And just between us, I know a woman spurned when I see one. A happy woman—a complacent woman—has no place in a house like mine. But a woman who has loved and lost, who wants more? *That* sort of woman fits in at French Maude's like wood in a stove. That's why I offered you this job."

*Wood in a stove.* The turn of phrase didn't sit just right.

Maude had promised her time to write and clients who might be interested in sponsoring her. The price of exchange was a pittance, Maude had said. Olivia would only have to give up her nights.

"I didn't have to think about my answer," Olivia admitted. Her nights were the worst part of her life, when she was utterly alone, not even a shadow to comfort her. The darkness was where Martin Wilbur haunted her most. She'd lie in blackness and see his wife's white wedding dress, a dizzying swirl of silk and lace. She'd see him kissing her neck and praising her homemaking, a skill Olivia had never excelled at, for she hated chores and preferred organized chaos.

She didn't have to think twice. She was only too glad to give up her nights.

"I'm not sure anyone ever said yes as quickly as you did, Livy dear."

Even then, Olivia was no longer the naive child she'd been before Martin. She'd known who Maude was and what the nights at her house would entail, but she hadn't cared. She'd already given herself away once. She'd never be a rosebud again. Novembers would just be Novembers, and good riddance to that girl, anyway. With Maude as her guide, she'd become an entire thornbush of black roses, and she'd earn more money than Martin ever would, and she'd write and publish all the poems he never would. He was a coward, hiding behind the words of others and never declaring his own.

The ones he did declare, he didn't mean. *Worthless words.*

"Can you believe that was seven years ago, Livykins? Seven years since you and I first saw how we could help each other. Now you have more regulars than any of the other girls. You're always requested first, and I still think you could really make something of yourself."

Olivia's eyes widened as she looked up at Maude.

"Not as a poet, of course," Maude quickly added with a swipe of her hand, "but as a madam." She looked at Olivia with a mother's pride.

Olivia nodded. "Seven years," she repeated thoughtfully. "That's a long time."

*The ticking of a grandfather clock. Cracked china.*

She had stopped writing almost immediately once she'd started working for Maude. The darkness that had once inspired her quill had become her life. She got what she wished for, in a way. Her life had become her poetry, only now it was dark as a dreamless sleep.

Until May arrived.

May had stirred her from a slumber so deep it felt, in retrospect, like a witch's curse cast into the ink of that damn poem. May made her remember Martin and fairy midwives and dreams and pain and love. She made those memories rise to a boil, and suddenly, Olivia felt like she was standing on the edge of a cliff, on the brink of an important decision.

She could choose life.

Maybe some gifts were worth holding on to. Maybe it wasn't too late to sharpen her pen. Maybe curses were meant to be broken.

May was changing her, and she didn't want it to stop.

But May was also a problem. A glaring, unavoidable one. The reason Maude had come to her room today. Maude would do what she had to do to fix the problem. And then, May would be gone.

"You and May have a special bond," Maude said, breaking into her thoughts, "and here I am, mean old Maude, forcing her into a corner. Work like the others or be on her way." She wagged her finger playfully, mimicking her own tone.

Olivia shook her head. "I don't think you're mean, Maude. You're a businesswoman." She sighed, her eyes flitting toward the space beneath her bed, where the spilled ink had spread just enough to be visible. "It is what it is. And Maude? I *am* grateful you approached me that day."

"Of course you are, dear."

Suddenly, a question occurred to her about Maude's earlier piece of gossip. Perhaps she'd missed it, but now she found herself needing to know.

"And was he arrested?"

"Who?" Maude asked absently, pursing her lips. "Whoever it was, I certainly hope not."

"The man Duffy's nephew shot. Did they catch him?"

"Nope!" answered Maude with another lip smack. "Still at large."

"Hm," Olivia mused. "Kind of poetic, in a way. Like a badge of courage across his face."

"Hm," Maude said in a very different tone. "That's my cue, baby doll. Come down soon. I had Nellie keep your breakfast warm."

Olivia watched Maude's wide, fan-shaped hair disappear out the doorway, listening to the fading clatter of her footsteps. Once they were gone, she glanced at the pool of ink beneath her bed. For a moment she thought about pulling out her work, cleaning the ink, and refilling the inkwell.

Then she sighed, stood, and followed Maude's footsteps, quietly closing the door behind her.

# CHAPTER 14

# Map

"What are you going to do?" Olivia asked me.

I stood by my window, gazing out. It was almost sunset, and the view was pure lovely. I could see the sapphire silhouette of the Catskill Mountains, their jagged peaks dotted with young pines. Above them, the sky was painted in the softest shade of pink, so delicate you'd wrap it around a baby's head for warmth.

Soon the lantern above French Maude's taupe door would flicker to life, signaling the start of business.

"I don't know," I admitted.

Olivia came to stand beside me, her reflection faint in the glass. "Well," she sighed, "help me with this necklace, will you? Not all of us can get by on our wits."

I turned to her and tied the lace at the back of her neck. As I did, she flinched. That's when I saw it—a deep, dark bruise blooming behind her shoulder blade.

"Liv!" I gasped, my hands freezing mid-knot. "What happened?"

"Oh, that?" she replied, brushing me off with an uneasy laugh and turning away. "Just one fella from last night. A brute, that's all."

Neither of us spoke for a moment. Silence felt heavier with Olivia. By now, she'd learned there wasn't much about someone's present that could stay hidden from me. I didn't know her past, but I knew she was suffering now.

"The tall one with the dark eyes? That dandy?" I asked, thinking back to the man from the night before. Something had felt wrong when he'd walked in, but there wasn't a thing I could do once he'd taken her to her room.

"Handsome ones are the most trouble, aren't they?" She attempted a joke, but when our eyes met, her smile faltered, for we both knew my husband was handsome, just as we knew we didn't talk about him.

"What did he do?" I asked quickly, shifting the focus back to her.

"Oh, May. You're sweet, but don't trouble yourself. This is the business I'm in."

I wasn't going to let her shut me out that easily. "Well maybe it'll be the business *I'm* in, too, by the end of the night. What did he do?"

She pressed her lips together and sighed before sitting down on the edge of the bed. "May, I don't want to talk about it, understand? He was rough, that's all. Made me feel... made me feel my place. That's it. He's a fucking coward, and he'll go to hell where he belongs. One day, right?"

I stared at her, my thoughts swirling as I tried to figure out what to say. In the end, all I could think to do was sit beside her and drape my arms around her neck.

Contact like that still felt foreign to me. I was more comfortable with the contact between person and spirit than person and person. No feeling of a pulse or a heartbeat; no heat from a body; no softness at all. My connection with the other side existed within a cold world of tools. It was the phrases the spirits would speak, or the images they'd give me, like bubbles about to pop, or a Knowing that would hit me in the gut, carving it hollow like a gourd. Those were my tools for connection. Not touch.

Olivia stiffened against mine, but I didn't let go.

"You wouldn't tell a copper?" I asked, already regretting the question. In Ireland, we had the Constabulary, and all they ever seemed to do was harass us, chasing us off streets or accusing us of crimes we didn't commit. Law wasn't for people like us—it was against us.

Olivia sniffed and scoffed bitterly. "Hardly. They'll turn a blind eye to what we do if we pay them enough. But stick up for us? No chance."

Her voice cracked on those last words, and I felt her begin to soften as she leaned into me. A moment later, her head rested on my shoulder. I could feel her light, choked sobs, her pain vibrating through me, and the wet warmth of her tears against my collar.

It was a kind of connection I had never known before. I savored it, but I couldn't help fearing for myself, at the same time. If I stayed at Maude's, I'd be just as vulnerable. Even *Olivia*, brave and strong as I knew her to be, couldn't always protect herself. And me? Wispy, mercurial creature that I was? I wouldn't stand a chance.

I felt trapped, suffocating in the small room, caught between my cold, hollow marriage to Francis and the looming threat of being shoved into a room with a stranger, forced into something I couldn't bear. For a fleeting moment, I thought of opening the window, leaning out, and gulping down the chill, sharp air. But Olivia needed me, and so I stayed.

After a few minutes, her sobs subsided, and she pulled back to dry her eyes. They still glistened as she described, in vivid, merciless detail, all the things she'd do to that dandy if she ever saw him again.

And slowly, as my bedside taper burned to a stub, she came back to herself, the Olivia that had saved me, in turn, from many a sad night when my readings were done, and I was left drowning in fear for my family, sorrow for my siblings on the other side of the veil, the emptiness of my heartless marriage, impossible dreams of a few acres to call my own, and the white December sky above a blue mountain silhouette so vast it could eat your heart with loneliness.

"Listen, May," she said firmly, wiping away one last tear. "I'm not telling you what to do, but don't do this job." Her voice was low, urgent. "Go out on your own." She shook her head, still sniffling, and fixed me with a steady, burning gaze. "Rent a shop up in Capital City, or even Manhattan. You've saved enough money, haven't you? Rent a legitimate shop. For your readings. Start fresh."

Her gaze locked with mine, and I couldn't help but wonder: did she know about Francis? Was she hinting I should leave him too? The weight of her words hung in the room, as if the walls themselves were leaning in. My mind spun with questions. Could I really leave Francis just like that? What would Mammy say if she found out? Was I giving up too easily, and did he deserve another chance?

But the more I thought, the more the possibility of freedom gnawed at me, bright and alluring, like the edge of a knife.

"But..." Was I even strong enough to work for myself? The only woman I knew who ran her own business was French Maude, and we were nothing alike.

"Don't think too much, May," Olivia urged. "Just do it. Open your safe, take your money, and go."

I blinked. *Don't think too much.* I'd never been good at that. My head was a storm of possibilities, of endless paths, each one more terrifying than the last.

But Olivia was offering me a window. A chance. I glanced at her, then turned to the small safe, the cold metal glinting under the flickering gaslight.

Could I really leave Hudson, leave *everything* behind?

I'd walked the city streets by Clement's side, close enough to feel his warmth, to see our breath dissolve into one new cloud for heaven. There had been a child in my arms and another on my shoulders. I knew how outlandish it was to think of this as Olivia told me to think *less*, but that visit to the general store had turned into a glimpse of a life I wanted. I'd never felt so settled as when I'd told Clement about what I'd lost and seen a hint of understanding cross his face.

But I'd also seen his shoulders tighten when I'd asked Mrs. Davidson permission to watch her children. I could hardly blame him. He saw who I really was: a woman who conjured spirits and worked in a house of sin. He didn't want the children acquainted with the likes of me. Rightly so, perhaps. I had to lie and tell them I was all settled, when in fact I wasn't settled at all. I didn't belong in Hudson, nor anywhere for that matter.

Perhaps I *was* better off leaving.

"Are you sure I can?" I asked Olivia, the words almost choking me.

"It's your life, May. Go. Now. Do it."

Her words snapped something inside me. I didn't hesitate. My feet moved of their own accord, crossing the room to the safe, my hands shaking as I turned the dial. My heart pounded. This was it. This was the chance I'd been waiting for. By now I'd put away a good deal of money. More would be better, but what I had was enough. I could leave tonight and keep my virtue. My hope. My spirit.

*Seven, Fourteen, Twenty-one*—the numbers we'd picked for luck. *The luck of the Irish*, Francis had said. I whispered the phrase under my breath now, but it tasted like dust on my tongue.

The safe creaked open, and I froze. My breath caught in my chest. My heart slammed against my ribs, and a cold sweat broke out across my back. I could feel my blood redden my ears, my face, my neck in hot patches of poisonous, itchy color.

Olivia stepped forward, her own breath catching as she peered inside. She turned to me, her eyes widening, her expression unreadable. "Where's your money, May?" she asked, her voice a rusty whisper of disbelief.

Now I was the one who didn't want to cry.

The money I'd saved—every hard-earned cent—*gone.*

# CHAPTER 15

## Clement

"*I* can't believe you've met her *twice* already, and I haven't met her even once!" Rudyard exclaimed, practically skipping beside Clement as they approached Diamond Street. Clement grimaced. "And now I'm finally going to meet her! And I have my brother right here with me, knowing her personally. What could be better?"

Clement sighed. "I don't know her, Rud. Like I said, I've only *met* her. We've spent less than a few hours together." *And I've actually met her three times. But maybe the first time when I helped her up doesn't count. She probably doesn't remember it, anyway.*

"A few hours is nothing to sniff at, Clement old chum," Rudyard said with a playful nudge.

"Even so," Clement said slowly, "it's not enough to trust her."

Rudyard shrugged. "Well, that's not saying very much. You don't trust anybody."

Clement shot him a mock-serious glare. "That's not true. I trust *you*."

Rudyard nodded sagely. "Ah, well, you're a poor judge of character then." He grinned. "I hate to break it to you, Clem, but I know you pretty well. There's a part of you that believes in her."

"You mean, *in her abilities*," Clement said a little too defensively.

Rudyard chuckled. "Of course. What else would I mean?"

Clement cleared his throat, looking straight ahead. "Well, I hate to break it to *you*, but I don't. What you think she can do is impossible."

They walked on in silence, the town coming into view through a haze of chimney smoke and freshly painted brick. The lull didn't last long. Rudyard's face took on a familiar expression of determination. Clement braced himself for another of his brother's spiritualist sermons.

"It wasn't long ago, my dear brother," Rudyard began dramatically, "that the first message was sent across a telegraph. The words 'What hath God wrought?' made it from Washington D.C. to Baltimore. Now I ask you, if taps across wires allow people to communicate with each other, then why can't a sort of spiritualist telegraph allow people to communicate with the other side? Why can't a person, a *medium*, act as a form of wire herself, conducting the energies from another world? The world is changing, right before our eyes! What was once impossible is now becoming possible."

Clement shook his head, baffled by Rudyard's misplaced intellect and enthusiasm. "I suppose next you'll tell me about the railroad and steamboats—"

"Like floating palaces," they said at the same time, in very different tones. Clement had heard the phrase too many times before. He sighed, shooting his brother an accusing look. Rudyard shrugged, unrepentant.

"I'll admit," Clement began cautiously, "that she is very convincing." *And kind, and sweet, and breathtaking.* "But you need to be careful around her. There's something I still can't trust about her."

"Didn't we just have this discussion?" Rudyard teased, raising an eyebrow.

Clement hesitated, a thought surfacing that he couldn't shake. "She introduced herself with different names. She was May Connally. Then May McMurry. Then just Miss May." He furrowed his brow. "I mean really, Rud, what kind of person besides a con artist has three different names?"

When Rudyard didn't respond, Clement glanced at him. His brother's face had gone pale, his cheerful expression frozen.

"McMurry, did you say?" he asked quietly, avoiding Clement's eyes.

"I think so. Why?"

"Oh. No one. Nothing. No reason." Rudyard snapped his mouth shut and looked out toward the horizon, the afternoon sun glowing a bold amber. After a moment, he shrugged. "Spiritualists have stage names. I wouldn't think anything of it."

"Hm." The explanation actually made sense. "But she works in a brothel, Rud."

Rudyard's gaze skewed toward him, wary and assessing. "And? For pity's sake, Clem, you don't have to *like* her. You just have to introduce me to her."

Clement chuckled as though it were entirely obvious, but Rudyard's words struck a nerve. Was "liking" her what he'd been resisting all this time?

Was "liking" even the right word for what he felt?

They sloshed through the gully that separated Diamond Street from the more respectable parts of town. The shift was abrupt. Stately homes gave way to narrow, grimy streets, thick with the smell of alcohol, manure, and cheap coal smoke. The air itself felt heavier here. Tinged with a sense of urgency and lawlessness. Polluted with raucous laughter that spilled from the taverns.

And yet, there was nowhere else he'd rather be.

The last time he'd seen May, he'd felt like... like maybe he really *had* seen her. Mrs. Davidson's children had trusted her instantly, and wasn't it said that children could sense a trustworthy soul? It must have been instinct that drew them to her. That, and her kind smile. And her heart-shaped face. And her compassion...

They stopped in front of the taupe door. Clement swallowed, his pulse quickening.

He was in trouble.

# CHAPTER 16

## Map

Time had never felt so foreign as it did in Hudson. Back when we were on the road, time had a pulse, alive like the earth itself—growing, shifting, stretching in every moment. The way the seedlings pushed up through the soil, the way sap warmed in the veins of ancient trees, how salt turned to glass and the rawest ingredients transformed into medicine. Time was the changing curves of the moon, the owl's midnight hoot, a fawn's first nibble of dandelion greens. Time was an endless circle, a wild, unhurried flow.

But here, it was different. Time had become something painfully human—linear and scarce. It made every moment feel like a debt owed.

I lay on my bed, a cold sweat slick across my forehead. I was waiting for Francis. But it wasn't just his return that gnawed at me. It was the feeling that I was not using my time right. I was not living right, like a selkie forced into a fish tank for someone else's amusement.

Selkies live in the seas surrounding Ireland—half human, half seal, fairies of the ocean. Lustful fishermen steal their skins, trapping them on land after glimpsing them in their lady forms, naked and radiant beneath the moonlight. When my Sight failed me, when the future blurred and the right path slipped from view, I understood their longing. I, too, felt caged, as if some unseen hand had stolen my own skin, leaving me in a life that was no longer mine to shape.

Time was Francis's tool, and he used it to get what he wanted. For me, it was always running out. Time was a punishment, dry and rotting, lightness as it puts on weight and turns to burden. Now I had the burden of knowing there was little time left before I would be forced into work I barely understood, let alone wanted. The thought seemed to stop time around me, though I knew it would keep ticking by.

With the money gone, there was no other way.

How much time did I have to earn money for my family before they all wasted away? How much time until I would be forced to spend cold nights with even colder strangers?

I thought of the traveling men I'd seen touch their wives with tenderness. I swallowed, placing a hand to my cheek as though I were one of those wives, and my hands were my husband's. I closed my eyes, savoring the feeling for just a moment. Searching for the magic of it.

The creaky turn of a brass doorknob startled me back to my reality, the one in which I'd never know a man's touch in that way.

"Francis!" I bolted out of bed as he walked in. "Where have you been?"

"Out," he said flatly. "Did you—" He spotted the open safe. "Oh." He shrugged, removing his coat. "Guess I beat you to it, didn't I?"

"Francis," I said, narrowing my eyes, "what did you do with our money?"

How foolish I'd been for trusting him when he'd promised to protect me. He began to put his coat back on. It was a new black frock coat, perfectly tailored. It must have cost him a fortune. *My* fortune.

"On second thought, I'm going out again. I'll be back in time for customers." I watched him open his dresser drawer, pull a pistol from his coat's inner pocket, shove it beneath his clothes, and push the drawer closed. I didn't even know he owned a pistol.

"I take it you've decided to stay? Don't have much of a choice now, do you?" he asked casually.

"Is that why you took it?" I couldn't believe what was happening, how blind I had been to who he was. How blind I was still. Mammy had once told me you never really know a person. My longing for her competed with my hatred for Francis, swirled together in my throat like oil and water, and I didn't know whether I wanted to scream or cry.

Then, in the dim light, I noticed it—a fresh wound slicing across his left cheek, red and raw, as if from a knife or a bullet's graze. For a fleeting moment, instinct took over, and I almost reached for a kerchief to wipe it clean. But then my fingers curled into my skirts, and I gritted my teeth instead.

"You took it so that... I'd have to stay and work here? As a *scarlet lady*? What difference does it make to you anyway? You never wanted me to do my readings. Why? Was it because I couldn't talk to John for you?"

"Couldn't or wouldn't?" he said quietly.

I blinked. No words found their way to my lips.

"I didn't take it for that," he added, still focused on the doorknob. It was then that his voice changed. He sounded meaner than I'd ever heard him before. "Never speak of John again."

I stood dumbfounded, my next words blocked by competing flickers of guilt and compassion. I bit my lip. *No.* I would not let him shake my resolve. I sunk my toes into my slippers.

"Then why'd you take the money? Where is it?" I demanded. My words were thin, strangled. The temperature of the entire room was rising because of me, as though I were not a lass but one of the new parlor stoves advertised as the most elegant piece of furniture. *Let him that hath no stove rather sell his chimney and buy one.*

This was money *I* had earned, on my own, for myself and my

family. I'd never seen him put a penny of his own wages in the safe. His earnings wouldn't have lasted him any longer than the night.

"Where is it, Francis?" My words came out thin and wispy, burning my throat.

"It's gone!" he blurted. "I lost it all at the gambling parlor. It's gone, and I can't get it back. Are you satisfied now? All you can do now is get to working and we'll earn it back in time."

*Gone.*

The word hit like a candle blown out in a storm—sudden, final, leaving only smoke. My mind reeled, scrambling to find a way around it, as if I could undo what had already been done. I gripped the edge of the dresser to steady myself, but the room still swayed.

"We'll?" I screamed. "*We'll* earn it back? I'm the one that's to do all the work. I'm the one that's to sell all I have in the world that's mine, while you stand by the blasted door and pocket money! But it's not really mine, is it? It's yours, *husband*, though you won't even look at it!"

"Shut your mouth, May!" he shouted back. "You want the whole house to hear you?"

"I don't care! I don't care anymore! I hate you, Francis! You're a stupid drunk and a lousy gambler! You lost everything. You come home like a half-rat with blood dripping down your face."

I paused, waiting for him to fight back, to say something—*anything* —to make this less of a nightmare. But he only stood there, silent.

Quietly, for my own indulgence, I asked him, "How am I to send for my family now? They'll all be dead before I earn back the money."

The tears fell, fire down my face. My breath came too fast and too sharp. A part of me still searched his face—some pitiful, desperate part of me that thought he might see that I deserved better.

For half a second, he hesitated. Looked at me.

Then, with the same hollow, careless voice, he said, "You're to work."

He took off, slamming the door behind him.

Where would he go? There was no money left to gamble or drink away, but by then he knew just about everything in Hudson could be bought "on time."

I stared at the door, so far from my instincts, I could scarcely remember how to live in the sun and sleep beneath the stars.

Hudson was corsets and crinolines, and I wished to be free and held at the same time. I knew it made no sense, but I wished for both at the very same time.

Even then, when I should have been thinking about my family and nothing else, I thought of love. The kind that is worth everything, that is immortal, that runs deeper than human time. It wasn't in that room with Francis, I knew that much at least.

Would I ever find it?

# CHAPTER 17

# Rudyard

"$S$he won't be doing any readings tonight," the Irishman barked at Clement as he shoved past them, his broad shoulders nearly grazing the doorframe of French Maude's.

Rudyard immediately ducked behind his brother, his heart pounding as though it might break free of his ribs. There was no mistaking Francis McMurry. The thick black hair, just beginning to gray above the ears. The way his presence seemed to drain the air from the street. Rudyard's mouth went dry, a wave of heat rising from his chest to his cheeks.

He tried to steady his breath. What would he tell Clement?

He certainly couldn't tell his brother what he'd seen Francis doing in the alley outside Central House. Or that Rudyard had been there at all.

But now, seeing the Irishman again, Rudyard realized he'd been right about the name McMurry. There was some relation between this man he'd seen at the hotel tavern and the spiritualist he was about to meet. Siblings, maybe?

Peering cautiously past Clement, Rudyard watched Francis disappear down the block. The sky above Hudson was shifting to a pale, feathered gray, the light dimming just enough to blur the edges of Francis's silhouette until it dissolved completely.

"Everything all right?" Clement checked. His voice was clipped, laced with agitation. "You still with me?"

Rudyard hesitated, ensuring the Irishman was well out of sight before stepping out from behind his brother.

Since that night at the hotel bar, he'd hoped he'd never see Francis again just as much as he'd hoped he would. And now, he didn't know what to feel. He swallowed down the memory of what he'd seen. It was neither here nor there, and best left forgotten.

He turned to his brother. "Let me try knocking," he offered in a forced breezy tone, brushing past Clement toward the door. Clement gave him a skeptical look but said nothing. Rudyard's fingers trembled slightly as he rapped on the door.

This time, a beautiful woman with brown skin, dazzling peach cheeks and long, straight black hair answered the door.

"It's you," she said. She sounded as surprised as she appeared.

For an instant, Rudyard wondered if they'd met before and how he could have possibly forgotten a face like hers. But then he realized she wasn't looking at him at all. Her eyes, sharp at the edges but warm at their core, were fixed entirely on Clement.

Clement cleared his throat and adjusted his collar. "You remember," he said uncomfortably.

Rudyard arched a brow, his curiosity piqued. What *exactly* did she remember?

The woman—she smelled delightfully of rosewater—flicked her gaze briefly to Rudyard, but her focus remained on Clement. "Well, you heard the big man," she said coolly. "She's not reading tonight."

"Why not?" Clement asked.

Rudyard was touched by his brother's tone: concern under the guise of indignancy. Clement cared more deeply for him than he let on. Placing a hand on Clement's shoulder, he stepped forward.

"Excuse me, Miss," he said, fighting to keep his voice smooth and polite. "Might we continue this conversation inside?"

The woman cocked a brow but stepped aside with an exaggerated sweep of her arm. "Why not." As they passed, she shut the door behind them and leaned against it, arms folded. "I do have to get ready. For work," she added dryly, giving them both a pointed look—just in case they'd somehow forgotten where they were.

Inside, the hallway was dimly lit, the air heavy with the mingling scents of tobacco and fried meat. Girls in loose housecoats drifted past, casting fleeting glances at the brothers.

Rudyard's pulse quickened as he realized he'd made it through the door without drawing the attention of any large, ruggedly attractive Irishmen. And now, incredibly, he was on the verge of speaking to a renowned spiritualist. A flicker of excitement lit in his chest.

The women's glances didn't bother him in the slightest. He met them with an easy smile, dipping his head in small bows of acknowledgment that only made them giggle. For a moment, Rudyard allowed himself to believe he belonged here—poised, charming, and perfectly at home amid the faint glamour of it all.

Unlike Clement, whose movements stiffened to the point where Rudyard wondered if he'd rust stuck that way. He tugged once more at his collar, the front door apparently of great interest to him. Bending toward the woman who'd let them in, he lowered his voice. "Listen, my brother must speak with her. He's been... obsessed, frankly, since I told him about my visit. I know as well as you that it's a trick. But he feels he must see it for himself. Is there any way...?"

She let out an amused chuckle. "Your brother? Really?"

Rudyard, sensing the heat spreading across Clement's face, interrupted. "Adoptive brother," he clarified, his tone light. "Rudyard Stoker. Pleased to meet you. I'm sorry, we didn't get your name. I'm afraid in the haste to see Miss May, we've abandoned our manners completely."

Clement cast him a curious look, one that seemed to see, for the first time, the true depth of his fascination with the Spiritualist Movement, perhaps even the lengths he'd all too willingly travel to find his way in. He felt the weight of that gaze but chose to meet it with an air of calm determination; perhaps it might conceal the turmoil beneath.

The woman raised a brow, her lips curving into a faint smile. "Olivia," she said simply. No "Miss," no formality—just the word, grounded and matter-of-fact. Rudyard's eyes widened in admiration. There was something striking about her directness, a quality he couldn't help but envy. He'd always been so cautious, so restrained, afraid to claim anything too boldly for himself.

But this? It felt different. Invigorating. He was chasing after what he wanted, already feeling more alive than he had in years. Perhaps adopting some of Olivia's forthrightness might suit this new version of himself.

"Miss Olivia?" he replied with a slight bow, intent on proving that he could be every ounce as charming as any man who didn't spend his nights alone at Central House. "Well, that's a grand name! Is there any way at all we can speak with Miss May? Just a few minutes, perhaps? We're prepared to pay for the privilege."

Olivia looked around, a small wrinkle between her dark, long-lashed eyes. "May could use the money right about now," she said at last with a soft sigh, her tone devoid of pretense.

Rudyard felt a jolt of excitement surge through him. He thought of the world's modern marvels, and wondered if it wasn't steam and electricity that powered them, really, but this very feeling. Life force. Energy. Possibility.

Olivia turned slightly, glancing at two girls lounging in the parlor. He couldn't see her face, but he could imagine it, for a moment later, they shrugged and wandered off. Olivia tipped her head toward the grand staircase.

Rudyard looked up the steps with a faint recognition and a blazing hope that every footfall might draw him nearer to his fate. He had already skirted dangerously close to uncovering a hidden part of himself. Would this spiritualist be able to see his deepest longings, raw as they were?

He ascended, his heart thudding in time with the creak of the worn wooden steps beneath him. Glancing back, he saw his brother following, his movements growing increasingly stiff and mechanical.

Rudyard only hoped Ms. May wouldn't see *too* much—for he carried one secret he wasn't ready to face. Not with his brother, and perhaps not even with himself.

# CHAPTER 18

## 𝕸𝖆𝖕

You'd be daft to underestimate the wind. Anyone who'd spent even a day in Hudson would understand its danger. They'd have at least a dim, hazy knowing, like the light from a candle in the afternoon or a memory of childhood melancholia. A waft of rosemary as it dries from the kitchen beams.

I sensed something of the city's past each time I encountered the wind, when it tousled my hair as I stepped off the gilded steamboat that brought me from Manhattan Island to Hudson, or when Grandmammy came to visit through the scent of rosemary. Or now, when a gust blew through my window the moment Clement Stoker walked back into my room.

My heart was so broken, it barely leapt when I opened the door to find him standing there, meeting my gaze with wide, hesitant eyes.

Behind him, Olivia whispered with a man I didn't recognize—

sandy-blond hair, an eager smile that didn't suit the heaviness in the air. She laughed at something he murmured in her ear, as though they were old friends.

Then she noticed me, and her expression shifted instantly. Maybe it was the swollen eyes or the sticky streaks on my cheeks that gave me away. She gasped.

"May! What happened? I saw Francis—"

I was quick to wipe away the dampness from my painted cheeks and shook my head. "Forget it," I told her, my voice thin. "I've made my choice."

I turned on my heel before I had to hold Clement's gaze for another moment. I couldn't bear it. If he hadn't respected me before, if he hadn't *cared* for me before, he certainly wouldn't now.

I crossed the room and sank onto the bed, the weight of my skirts swallowing me.

Olivia hesitated before gesturing quietly for the men to follow her in, shutting the door with deliberate care as though sealing off the world outside.

"Um," began the blond man, "forgive me, but I must ask—you truly speak with spirits? I need to know. I need to see. If—"

"Shh!" Olivia cut him off and sat beside me on the bed. The men were left standing awkwardly, waiting. The blond one rocked on his toes, *too eager*. Clement, on the other hand, was stiff, his hands uncertain, his lips pressed together.

"May, what happened?" Olivia's voice was gentle but insistent. "He spent it all, didn't he?"

"Of course, he did," I said bitterly. "Every penny. And now I have to get ready for *work*." My voice cracked on the word *work*, and I didn't miss Olivia's flinch. I hoped I didn't offend her.

"So you *are* working? Splendid!" said the stranger. I didn't have the heart to look at him, presuming which kind of work he thought I meant. He wanted a reading, and I couldn't offer him one anymore.

Olivia tossed him a blazing look, God bless her, and mercifully, he clamped his mouth shut. Across from him, Clement swallowed, the slight tremor in his throat betraying him.

"We've come at a bad time," he said uneasily. "We should go."

"What do you mean?" his companion asked, incredulous. "She said she's working!" He was slenderer than Clement but wore the same plain, somber clothing. A Quaker, no doubt. A friend of Clement's?

"No," Clement said firmly, though his eyes flicked toward me. Was my distress so loathsome that he couldn't wait to escape? Was I always somehow too much and never enough?

"Just… wait," I said, pressing the heel of my hand against my brow. I didn't want him to leave. "I need a second to breathe."

Olivia placed a hand on the bare skin of my shoulder where the silk of my dress didn't reach. I knew my shoulder was hot as fire. My whole body was, and Olivia pulled back her hand just as quickly as she'd extended it. "Tell me what's happening, May. We'll figure it out."

Their eyes were on me now, watching, waiting.

All I could do was look down at my lap. My skirts shimmered in the candlelight, a sea of periwinkle silk above layers of petticoats. "To match my peepers," Maude had said when she commissioned the dress. That had been back when I was still worth something—when my readings brought in steady coin.

Now, the sight of it made me feel hollow. I wore my wealth while my family starved.

"Who are you, anyway?" I asked the stranger. I must have sounded overly blunt, for he flinched.

"Rudyard Stoker." He stepped forward with a determination that bordered on desperation. "Clement's brother. He told me about your skills, and I've been waiting since word broke out about the Fox sisters to speak with a spiritualist, and now here you are!"

I frowned, first at him, then at Olivia. "Why does everyone think I'm a spiritualist? I'm Catholic."

"Oh." Rudyard faltered, blinking rapidly as though trying to reconcile the contradiction. Collecting himself, he gave a small bow, begging my pardon, before pressing on. "Would you read for me?"

"They're prepared to pay," Olivia interjected, her tone steady and expectant.

I sighed heavily, feeling the weight of the moment settle on my shoulders. I didn't know if I had the strength to focus. And Clement…

Clement was watching me. Any hope I'd ever had of earning his respect would be gone with the bath water.

And yet, the thought of him leaving was the worst pain of all.

I was trapped. In this house, this city, this marriage. Trapped in my own body. If I had to get ready for work, then work could wait.

"Please sit," I said to Clement, my voice quieter than I wanted it to be.

"I'm just here for my brother this time, actually," he said, not moving an inch.

I looked up at him with clear eyes.

"It's not up to you," I said, my voice honed to a quiet, steady blade. The words felt foreign, as if borrowed from someone braver, someone who had nothing left to fear. I was drawing on a courage I didn't know I possessed, the kind you scrape from the bottom of a dry well when there's nothing left to lose.

"It's not up to me, either," I went on, the weight of certainty settling into my words. "It's up to whoever is on the other side. If you want me to read for your brother, you have to listen to your *mother* first. She's the one showing up here. If it's meant to be, she'll guide me to whoever's coming for your brother."

Clement and Rudyard exchanged a look, the air between them heavy and unspoken. I caught the flicker of fear in Clement's eyes just before he tried to mask it with a scoff.

"All right then," he said stiffly, easing himself into the chair across from me. "But I'll be honest, I've had some time to think this through, and I don't believe in any of it. I'm here strictly for my brother to see for himself. He's easily influenced, and I want to make sure he doesn't get taken advantage of."

"You're worried about her being a fraud?" Olivia scoffed. "Is that what this is? Or are you scared she's telling the truth?"

My jaw tightened. I was seconds away from boiling over like a tea kettle. He had come here to disprove me, to strip me down to nothing more than a liar.

And once, not so long ago, I had imagined he might see me for who I really was, as someone worth knowing, worth caring for.

"I've never heard of a Catholic working as a spiritualist before," Clement countered, eyes focused on Olivia.

I'd already cried over one man today. I wouldn't cry over another. No. There comes a point in every woman's life when she decides she's done—done giving her power away, done begging the world to be kind. It's a dangerous brink to teeter. Choices feel insufficient. Irrelevant. All she can do is react from the smoldering ashes in her belly.

I let the ashes burn at the back of my throat, a fire I refused to feed. With a slow exhale, I crossed my legs and licked my painted lips, still salty.

"When did your mother die?" I asked Clement, my voice calm but deliberate.

"You tell me," he shot back.

For a moment, the air seemed to still. My breath caught as a cold shame swept through me. I saw it now—why he'd looked afraid before. His mother was here, clear as day, shaking her head, eyes full of a deep, dark sadness.

He hadn't known she died. Hadn't known... until I'd told him in his reading. I swallowed.

"Your brother. I'll read him first." I kept my voice steady, though my throat was tight.

Clement glanced at me, a question in his eyes, but he didn't protest. Rising, he surrendered his chair to Rudyard, who sat swiftly, his face flushed with anticipation. His hands trembled slightly as I took them, brushing my thumbs over his palms. They were soft—too soft to be a laborer's—with neatly trimmed nails and the faint scent of floral soap clinging to his skin.

I didn't need to communicate with the other side to sense what was different about him. And yet, the other side was there with me in the room, drawn to me like moths to a flame. Or perhaps I was the moth, drawn helplessly to their light.

"You've always felt different," I began carefully, doing my best to study the entire canvas before tracing the shape of each brushstroke. "You and your brother shared an instant bond."

"That's right!" Rudyard exclaimed, his excitement spilling out before he glanced nervously at Clement, whose expression remained stoic. Lowering his voice, Rudyard continued. "I knew right away he was the brother I'd always wanted. We were only children when we met. My parents were supposed to take Clem here to a new home, but I begged them to let him stay with us instead."

I nodded softly, feeling the truth of his words ripple through the air. "Your parents..." I hesitated, trying to feel my way forward. "Did they lose someone? A son?"

Rudyard's face lit up with astonishment. "Yes! We lost my younger brother. When Clem came, it felt like our family was whole again."

I snuck a glance at Clement. He'd been watching me with that same careful expression I couldn't help savoring. He quickly looked away.

I looked back at Rudyard, who was staring at me with his mouth open. For a moment, I wasn't sure how much to say with Clement and Olivia still in the room. A part of me wanted to blurt out exactly what I knew and send the brothers back to their lives and out of mine, where hungry shadows chomped down on me at the first slice of sunlight.

And yet, I was who I was: a gentle dove—the silly, daydreaming lass my da would scold for coming home from a reading with nothing to show for it but the wildflowers I'd picked along the road and a withering hunger in my belly.

Recognition shone in Rudyard's face. He must have known I could see his deepest secret, and he turned to ice.

"You should be yourself," I said gently, trying to soothe him. "Despite your differences, you and your brother are alike." I allowed myself the faintest hint of a smile. "There's a grandmother here for you. But you never knew her, did you?"

"That must be my father's mother," he said thoughtfully. "She died before I was born."

I nodded. "You would have gotten on well with each other. She was like you, too. In a different way than your brother is like you."

Rudyard looked like he wanted to press for more details, perhaps ask me in what way I meant, but he didn't. "Does she have a message for me?" he asked instead.

I chose my words with care. "She says she knows it's hard, but you should find a way to be yourself. She went through life pretending she wasn't different. She wasn't truthful. She doesn't blame herself. She says it's not right how the world makes you hide, and one day, it will all be different."

A silence settled over the room. Rudyard's lip trembled.

Clement shifted beside him, his voice cutting through the moment, harsh and skeptical. "The things she's saying could be said to anybody, Rud. Who doesn't feel different from time to time? Who doesn't have a secret of their own?" He turned to me, eyes relentless. "Tell us. Different *how?*" he demanded.

I met Clement's scrutinizing glare with one of my own. The silence stretched for a moment before he wisely looked away. Whatever judgment he carried didn't matter; this moment wasn't for him. I turned back to Rudyard.

"Mr. Stoker?" I began, aiming for calm authority.

"Please," Rudyard interrupted with a faint smile. "You're speaking to my late grandmother. I think we're beyond formalities. Call me Rudyard."

I nodded. "Very well. Rudyard, nobody else in this room needs to understand what I'm saying except you. I admire your bravery for coming here, and through your grandmother, I'm giving you permission to be who you are, because... you won't give it to yourself."

A single tear broke free from his eye, tracing a path down his cheek. He squeezed my hand, and I could feel his gratitude in that small, rooted motion. Despite the ache in my chest, I squeezed back, if only for a moment, before pulling my hand away and standing. "Well, if you'll both excuse us," I said, my voice tight with exhaustion, "we have to get ready for work."

"Wait. What do we owe you?" Rudyard asked quickly.

"Nothing," I told him. Olivia tried to intercede, but I was firm. I'd take no payment.

Clement's expression shifted, surprise flickering across his face. The disbelief there stung more than it should have. He'd clearly thought that a charlatan like me wasn't capable of rejecting his money.

"What work do you have to get ready for?" he asked, an edge in his tone. "I thought you said you weren't reading."

"I'm *not*," I replied, a breath of defiance rising in my chest. It dissolved just as quickly. What had I expected?

"You're right. I'm not special. I work here like everyone else. The other girls complained I took their business, so now, their business is mine. Your brother was the last man I'll be reading for. No more deception for you to worry about."

"But you can't stop!" Rudyard's outburst startled me. His hands reached for mine again, gripping them with a pleading urgency as he had during the reading. "You have a gift. A remarkable gift. You can't waste it."

Mammy's parting words echoed in my ears. *I won't lose you, too. Not when you've a gift like yours that shouldn't go wasted.* But Mammy wasn't here. And the reading was over.

Whatever connection I'd shared with this man moments before had already faded. I slipped my hands free from his and turned my back on him. On both of the brothers.

Olivia, sensing the shift, stepped in as my shield. "It's time for you to leave," she said firmly.

"Please," insisted Rudyard, quite determined. He took a step toward me, speaking to me through my back and the protective barrier that was Olivia. "I know we've only just met, but I believe I was brought to you for a reason."

"Rud." Clement's voice was low, a warning. He stepped toward his brother. "You don't need her to tell you to be yourself. I could have told you that."

"But you didn't," Rudyard snapped, his voice thick with emotion, as though he'd been holding on to that frustration for some time. Clement closed his mouth and swallowed. That brought me a bit of satisfaction. "Don't you see? No one has ever told me it's acceptable to be who I am. You always shy away from the topic, any time I've tried to tell you. Even now, you don't want to know. I can tell. You don't."

"I—" Clement faltered, his jaw tightening as he searched for words that didn't come. He looked almost grateful when Olivia stepped in.

"Look, fellas," she said, drawing herself up to her full height. Next to me, she was the shortest girl at French Maude's, but she could have fooled us at that moment. "I'm glad you had a nice reading," she said to Rudyard. "*You* should learn some manners," she told Clement. "And now, it's time for both of you to leave."

"Miss May," Rudyard pressed, "I'll gladly leave if you want me to. But you've given me a gift, and I would like to return the favor. Just answer one question for me. Do you *want* to work at French Maude's?"

I laughed—a short, bitter sound that escaped before I could stop it. What did it matter what I wanted? Regardless of what I did with men upstairs, my body was and had been my business. How had I failed to see that?

"What is the point of your question? I have nothing in this country. A woman has to find a way to survive."

Rudyard exhaled, a soft sigh of relief, as though he'd been waiting for me to admit it. His emerald eyes shimmered with something I couldn't quite name—hope, perhaps, or determination. "What if spirits weren't just voices?" His voice lowered as if he were speaking a secret. "What if they could be seen?"

"What are you getting at?" Olivia and Clement asked him simultaneously. They looked at each other, then away, determined to find no common ground.

"Materialization seances," Rudyard grinned. The room seemed to lean in, waiting.

"You want to run a ghost show?" Olivia's voice broke through the stillness. "Rich men paying to be spooked out of their wits?"

"Not just a show," Rudyard said, his eyes a storm-lit sky. "If Miss May can start leading seances, everyone in this house can get what they want." He turned to me. "You can continue to use your talent, *and* you'll bring in more business for the other girls than they can manage."

I crossed my arms in a gesture that probably made me look more innocent than I'd become. "I don't know what that means," I admitted.

Rudyard grinned.

"The seance, my friends, is the heart of the spiritualist religion. And I know all the rules," he began, his voice trembling with life. "Two hours beforehand, sitters must bathe and change into fresh clothes—black suits for men, white dresses for women. They gather around a circular table, balanced by temperament and gender. A light meal is served—no meat, no alcohol."

Olivia snorted softly, shooting me a look that said, *as if that's possible in a place like this*. Rudyard didn't seem to notice. His face was flushed with inspiration as he spoke, and despite my doubts, I felt myself being drawn in. His words conjured something that felt fresh and new, like slipping under clean tartan blankets after a long day's journey.

"Light vibrations must be filtered through orange glass or linen, just like in a photograph," he went on. "Hands rest palm-up on the wooden table, which, once charged, becomes a conductor. The medium—in our case, Miss May—is the receiver through which the forces are focused."

He carried on, oblivious to Olivia's skepticism and Clement's thinly veiled disapproval. Still, they let him speak.

I hardly wished to admit my curiosity had peaked. Spirits flocked to me unannounced and uninvited. Like a secret dream, they beckoned just on the other side of the veil. Friends or villains, they were familiar. I had spent most of my life teetering on that ghostly line. But the idea of *summoning* them—controlling them, rather than being at their mercy—was something else entirely.

If there were others like me in the world, using their gifts as tools rather than *being* the tools themselves, what could that mean for me?

And yet, I couldn't ignore my practical concerns. My safe was empty, and if I wanted to keep my relationship with God intact, I'd have to be prudent, even wise, with my next step.

"There's still something I don't understand," I said finally, breaking the spell of his words. "The other girls complained I was taking their business with my readings. Why would this seance notion be any different?"

"Your readings give people peace." Rudyard's response came in one cool breath. "I feel like a weight has been lifted off my chest, and my brother won't admit it, but he felt the same thing when you read for him. He came home a different person." Clement opened his mouth, then closed it. "You did!" Rudyard pressed, turning to his brother. "Less hurried. Less… sprinting to the next task."

"What's your point?" Olivia asked, crossing her arms.

"My point is," Rudyard continued, undeterred, "of course May's clients don't want the other services your establishment offers. After sitting with her, why, nothing will ever be the same. They don't need the comfort of the flesh anymore, because May soothes the spirit. A seance is something else entirely. It's not closure—it's hunger. It's danger. It's flesh."

The brothers sighed simultaneously. But where Rudyard's sigh conjured wistfulness, Clement's harbored distaste.

"But *how?*" I asked. "I don't know how to conjure spirits. I can only communicate with them, not... materialize them."

"You can learn," Rudyard said quickly. "The Fox sisters didn't start with materializations either—just knocks in the dark. They figured out the rest over time."

I swallowed, unsure how to respond. The push and pull of hope and despair was exhausting, like an eternal dance with the fairies, tripping over steps I couldn't master.

"Fine, but what's in it for you?" Olivia interjected, crossing her arms. "Maybe Maude would agree to this, and maybe May could do it. But what do you care? And don't tell us you just want to return a favor. Everyone in this town has a motive. Women like us are the ones who see it most clearly. What's yours?"

Rudyard hesitated. Clement studied him, his gaze as laden with suspicion as Olivia's.

Rudyard was no different from any other person desperate to believe. He saw me as something more—Hudson's own answer to the Fox sisters, someone who could inspire wonder and reverence. But as I searched his eager face, I found myself wondering: what did I see in myself?

"I understand why he cares," I said before either man could respond. My voice carried a new authority, one that silenced the room. Even Olivia didn't dare press me.

Rudyard turned to me, his breath catching, as if he hadn't expected me to voice what he had barely admitted to himself. His lips parted, then closed again. When he finally spoke, his voice was quieter, more careful. "My brother and I know someone who might be able to help you." He looked at Clement, who sucked in his cheeks dubiously, the skepticism returning.

"Very well," I said firmly. "How can I meet this person?"

Clement finally spoke, his voice measured. "Listen, Miss May. My brother's intentions are good. But this person he's referring to isn't exactly the kind of man—"

"Come on, Clem," Rudyard interrupted. "Put your own feelings aside. I know this isn't your cause, but let's help her."

Clement's jaw tightened. I could see the war in him—the fight between his principles and whatever history he had with this mysterious man. At last, he exhaled. "I don't like him. I don't trust him. I don't agree with half of what he stands for." He looked at me then, his gaze heavier than before. "But if Rudyard needs to see this through… maybe it could help you, too."

His shift made me pause. Was it simply Rudyard's persuasion? My tentative benefit? Or was there something more—something Clement needed to settle for himself?

He was still watching me, his expression schooled into neutrality. I held his gaze for a breath longer than I should have, something wordless stirring in the space between us. Uncertainty? Understanding? A dare? I couldn't tell, but it sent a pulse through me all the same.

"We're meeting him tomorrow, as a matter of fact," Clement added. "I'll write down the address for you."

"Well then, write it and get on your way," Olivia said, effectively dissolving the heat I felt rising between us. "I have some parchment in my desk."

She moved to fetch it, but I offered to do so myself. Without a word to Olivia or Rudyard, Clement followed me through the winding hallway. His footsteps were quiet, purposeful, as if he hadn't intended to follow, but found himself drawn along anyway.

My chest tightened with confusion—why was he trailing me? What was about to unfold in Olivia's room? Only one sconce lit the hallway. Its dim light spiraled around my mind like gray smoke.

# CHAPTER 19

## Map

"How is Mrs. Davidson settling in?" I asked, my fingers brushing through Olivia's desk, though my mind remained entirely elsewhere.

"Fine," he replied flatly, before adding, "The children still ask about you."

This made me smile, but I didn't look up from the task. His presence was an undeniable weight in the room, his nearness pressing on my skin like a heated whisper. I could almost sense the contours of his body without looking—the texture of his wool coat, the subtle shift in his stance. Even so, I didn't dare turn toward him.

"Why didn't you read for me?" he asked next, his voice low.

My hesitation lasted just a moment. "I'm a fraud, remember?" It was a challenge more than a question.

He didn't flinch. "I'm not so sure," he murmured. His scent—earth and pine, damp leather—settled around me, rich and lingering.

Instinct propelled me to look at him then, half expecting what I'd felt between us to be gone, a spark that never caught. But instead of fading, the feeling between us intensified. I saw the way his amber eyes had turned dark in the gloaming and how they stared at me now —not through me—and it scared me.

I took a slow breath, trying to steady my racing heart. I could no longer avoid his question. Why *didn't* I read for him?

"I thought you knew," I began, searching his eyes for hints. "I thought you knew your mother was gone. I was certain she was telling me you knew. But you didn't, did you?"

The sun hovered just above the horizon, casting the room in a burnt orange glow. I reached for the candle on Olivia's desk, my fingers shaking ever so slightly as I lit the half-burned taper. The flame flickered. Long, wavering shadows surrounded us.

Suddenly, I felt the creeping unease of darkness closing in. Maude's doors would be opening soon. Francis could return at any moment. If he found me here, alone with Clement, he would report to Maude that I was still giving readings, and I would be forced to leave. Perhaps I'd choose to leave, anyway, but I wanted that decision to remain mine.

"I knew," he decided gingerly. "I could feel she was gone, not long after I last saw her." He met my gaze, his own filled with something unreadable. "That must sound insane."

"Did you forget who you're talking to?" I replied with a wry smile.

The upward tug at his lips made my heart leap. I looked away, trying to regain my composure. But then, his tone shifted, becoming more serious, more reflective.

"I was born into slavery, Miss May. Though I think you know that?" He glanced at me for a moment, the memory of the reading I'd given him thick between us like a sky about to pour rain.

"I was to be transported to a new enslaver," he continued, his voice distant, as if the past still clung to him. "From New Orleans some-where up the Mississippi. My mother cried the night before, tears flowing like the river itself. Then in the morning, she took me to the house of a woman who worked for the Underground Railroad. She told us how to make our way to freedom."

He paused for a long moment, uncertainty wavering in his eyes. His words landed between us, filling the space and leaving no room for anything but his story.

"The night we set out, one of the guard dogs bit my mother in the leg." His voice was raw and vulnerable. "She told me to run on. Promised she'd catch up with me later and not to turn back for anything."

A shiver ran down my spine, for I already knew how the terrible story would end, could feel it lingering between us, unspoken, trembling at the edges.

Clement continued, his voice softening as he spoke, a strange peace in his words. "Just before I took off, my mother gave me a necklace, fine and gold, to get me started when I made it to New York. I didn't want to take it. If I did, it'd be like admitting I knew she wasn't coming. But my mother ordered me to take it... so I did."

I waited, hardly breathing, unsure if he was going to continue. I thought of the coins Mammy had pressed into my palm just before she sent me away, and I wondered how my own story would end. How *hers* would.

For a fleeting moment, I thought Clement might run off again, but instead, he moved his hand to his coat pocket.

"I don't know where she got the necklace from," he said, a sigh slipping from him like a broken promise. "But I have an idea. I think it was a gift from our enslaver, from years earlier. I think he arranged my sale when it started to become obvious who my father was."

His hand emerged. My heart ached as the soft glint of a gold chain with a silver key pendant caught the candlelight. "I never had to sell it though. When I got to New York, I met the Stokers, and they took me in and raised me as their own. Now it's all I have left of my mother."

I shook my head. That wasn't all he had. But the way his mother's spirit looked at me with her neck held high, I knew he was right about his father.

Clement caught my gaze, his eyes searching mine. Then his shoulders relaxed, and he actually laughed. All I could do was stare, not knowing at all what was passing through this man's mind and heart. I must have looked completely awkward, standing there gaping at him, for next he said, "I'm sorry, Miss May. It's just I've never told this story to anyone before. Not even my own parents, the folks who took me in and raised me from then on. Not even Rudyard knows the whole of it."

I wanted to throw my arms around him like butterfly wings—to tell him his secrets were my secrets, cocooned within my deepest core. But I stopped myself, because it wasn't the time. Instead, I chose to hover my butterfly self above him, for I felt myself in a garden of wildflowers, and it was enough.

"How did you know she was gone?" I asked, my voice barely more than a whisper. "What did it feel like?" I wanted to know everything there was to know about him.

"Just a feeling." He shrugged. His shoulders fell, broad and heavy. "That feeling when you're truly alone. But I've felt the same feeling before, and it didn't mean anyone was dead. It just meant I was alone. So I couldn't be sure."

His eyes met mine, locking me in place, stopping my breath as they swept over me. I wanted to tell him to keep speaking, to ask what he meant, to touch his cheek and tell him our hearts were the same. But I was paralyzed. A comfortable warmth seemed to gather from the words unsaid.

"I'm always alone," he murmured. "Always on the fringes. Folks that look like me assume I think I'm better because I live with a white family. They don't like that I walk around with Rudyard like he's my brother. White folks look at me like I'm less-than, like I should be thanking God each day I was taken in by white folks. Even Rudyard doesn't understand what it's like. To him, I'm just a brother, even though I was the only Black student in our school, and I can't go with him to the polls, and..." His voice faltered slightly, then grew steady again. "And I certainly can't ask a pretty Irish girl out to tea."

I flushed something fierce, turning my face away from the candle-light so he wouldn't see. "We have something in common, you know," I said, trying my best to steady my breath. My heart was a lost cause. That couldn't be steadied, but at least he couldn't hear it.

"What's that?" he asked. I could hear the half-smile in his voice.

"We were both sent to Hudson, and we found our own way. Alone as we are."

A pang of guilt plucked at my ribs like a mandolin string, for I had lied—or told a half-truth. I wasn't entirely alone. I felt alone, sure enough, but I did have a husband with me, and I couldn't bring myself to admit it. If I did, I'd lose Clement before I even had him.

He pulled a piece of parchment tied with ribbon from the stack I found in Olivia's desk. Then, with careful precision, he dipped the quill and, as promised, wrote an address, his script neat. He blew softly on the ink to dry it before handing it to me, his fingers grazing mine in a fleeting touch that threatened to undo me completely. Then, without a word, he reached into his coat pocket, producing a small change purse and emptying its contents onto the desk.

"What's all this?" I asked, my brow furrowing in confusion.

"Don't work tonight," he said simply.

I shook my head, though the temptation tugged at me. "I can't accept this."

"You read for my brother," he replied. "You earned it."

My throat tightened as I stared at the coins, still unsure. "But what will I tell French Maude? She expects an answer from me tonight."

He shrugged lightly, his expression unreadable. "Give her a cut. Tell her to give you a week, and you'll transform the place with a new model for readings. Tell her to trust you."

"But how can you be sure these seances will work? How can you know Maude will be open to the idea at all?" I asked him these questions, but the only ones I really wanted answers to were *"How can you trust me?"* and *"You mentioned tea...?"*

The silence between us deepened, and his eyes softened, searching mine with a quiet intensity. "I see you, May," he said, his voice low and steady. Then, with a movement so swift it took me by surprise, he stepped closer. "At least, I think I'm starting to."

I didn't have the heart to tell him I couldn't read the address he'd written down. I just curled my fingers around the paper and nodded. He slipped out with his brother before the last crumbs of sunlight were swept away by the mountains and the streetlamps were lit. I placed a hand on my cheek, and I didn't give up on my dreams entirely, after all.

I realized the next morning, as I looked out my bedroom window, that I hadn't gone out that early since unpacking my small sack of belongings at Maude's. The sky was still layered with sunrise, gold then white then sapphire, so that we might have been beneath it or under water, swimming like mermaids through glittering beauty. The bare trees reaching up might have been sea anemones, and the houses caves, where mysterious creatures wrapped themselves in a homey darkness.

A raven landed on my windowsill, startling me from my reverie. Its brown eyes met mine, and it released a hoarse croak.

I looked back at Francis snoring loudly in our bed. The last time we'd seen a raven, we'd stood together at my brother's grave. What would he say if he could see another raven return to me now? My chest constricted as the memory surfaced, dread forming like a lump of clay in my stomach. Was that the moment he'd changed? One minute he was my friend, and the next, a stranger.

I could still see us there, the grave soil damp beneath our feet. Francis had begged me to speak with John. "Is he at peace?" he'd asked me, his voice raw as the wind nipped at his straight black hair. We were the last two standing by John's grave. Mammy had hurried off to tend to the rest of the children. As the oldest of the seven still living, she needed me, too. But I hadn't been ready to leave. I had wanted a moment alone with my brother, my closest friend.

Francis, pale as a snowdrop, save for his windburned cheeks, had waited beside me. His eyes were the iciest blue as they searched mine. A screeching gust of wind swept my curls across my face, forcing me

161

to pin them back with one arm. "I don't know," I answered, a familiar grip on my throat, stealing the air I'd need to exhale smoothly.

Five years had passed since the blight had swept across the land like a plague. I was bone weary and weak and couldn't hear the dead in the same way I could when I was younger and better fed. Wouldn't it be my luck that a raven swooped down and landed right at our feet. Its tawny eyes, so like this American raven's eyes, darted between us.

Francis stared at the bird, and his expression hardened. "You don't know?" he hissed, his scowl cutting across his face. "Even the raven knows you're a Seer!"

His words stung. I pressed my fingernails into my palms. The ragged edges sent relief as they sank into soft skin. Ravens are drawn to Seers. Though I hadn't a notion why it had come to me then, when I was in no state to See anything.

Calmer, I sighed, glancing up at Francis, pity softening my glare. In another life he might have looked like a child, so innocent and even were his features. His lips looked a lovely shade of red and his smile was handsome. But our way of life and the times in which we were living had weathered him. His face looked sallow, tired, and lonesome.

I flinched. I'd accidentally dug too deep and scratched through the skin, an angry red line blossoming on my palm. I attempted another deep breath, but the unexpected heat of pain unfurled the temper I'd been holding back.

So a raven had come. What of it?

I shifted my gaze toward the horizon, squinting to hide the breaking of tears. My throat burned like I'd swallowed sea water, the words clawing their way out. "I can't see anything. It's too soon!"

"So that's it, then?" His voice was low and steady, void of its usual fondness for volume. When we'd sit around a fire singing at night, back before death began coming for us swift as a hare, you could always make out Francis's voice above the rest, or perhaps below it, for it vibrated like a stirring in the earth. "He's just gone, and we don't know how he is or if he's still with us or anything? That's it, then?"

I'd never seen Francis, nor hardly any of our men, cry before. It was like ice melting down a river. My heart thawed for him, so I took his hand, remembering how I'd seen him hold John's the day we buried my sister Lucy. John was *my* brother, but Francis had loved him, too.

I closed my eyes and took a slow, deep breath, waiting for any familiar sensation. An image, a symbol, a whisper, the slightest tingle at the back of my neck. *Anything* that would tell me John had found peace, or give me some reassurance to offer Francis. Even as my eyes squeezed shut, I could feel Francis staring at me. His long fingers tightened against mine in expectation. I swallowed, the sound of silence thick in my ears.

I heard nothing. I felt nothing.

My eyes opened to blue frost. His lips were slightly parted. I cleared my throat. "He's still with us," I lied.

Francis wore the oddest expression. He squinted ever so slightly, and his frown lines deepened, though his mouth didn't close. Could he tell I was lying?

"May." It was Mammy's voice. Startled, I turned around to see her wasted, shadowy figure behind me. "It's time to go now, lass."


I PUSHED my bedroom window open, hoping the wind would carry away the memory's bite, the guilt I still felt for failing to give Francis more when he'd needed it. For lying to him. The draft prompted him to pull the blanket over his head, but he didn't wake up.

Tentatively, I reached my hand out to stroke the bird, still perched on my windowsill. It let me glide my fingers softly over its silky feathers. "What do you want with me?" I asked quietly. "Am I being punished for my wrongdoing?"

It croaked before flying away, another piece of home to leave me. I swallowed down the loss, gazing back at the slumbering city street.

Back in Ireland, people would talk about the streets of America being paved with gold. Only now, in that odd winter light, which lasted just long enough for me to notice and cling to it, did I understand where that saying came from. The streets were nothing more than swaths of dirt, littered with human and animal waste. When you sniffed, you found they still held the faint memory of the fish carcasses that were once Hudson's glowing industry. But in those early morning hours, all I smelled was air, crisp and new, and all I saw were mountain silhouettes, a gray so aglow they looked magenta.

"You'll come with me, won't you?" I begged Olivia. The morning light filtered through the curtains, catching the sheen in her coiled hair as she buried her face in the pillow.

"Please, Liv," I went on. "What if I get lost on my own?"

She rolled over to face me. I'm sure I was a pitiful sight, kneeling by her bedside with my clasped hands, half-laced bodice, and hopeful grin. I could have made my own way—asked for directions from passersby or memorized the shape of the numbers and letters I didn't know yet. But the truth was, I hated being alone. Hudson felt too strange, too foreign, too ready to swallow me whole.

"Maude let me be last night, but if I don't find a way to materialize a spirit in a week, I'll have no choice but to work. Not that there's anything wrong with that," I added quickly, not wanting to offend her.

Olivia groaned and rolled her eyes. "Oh, May. You're not cut out for this business. We both know that."

I grinned.

"Let me see that address," she sighed, reaching out with a reluctant hand. Her eyes scanned the parchment. "It's not far, just a few blocks."

"I'll make the coffee!" I offered brightly, already rising to dash to the kitchen.

"May." She sounded hesitant as she stopped me before I could dash out the door. I turned, finding her sitting up now, fingers knotting together in her lap. "Are you sure there's no one else you need to ask before you go?"

I paused for a moment, feeling my back stiffen. I licked my lips, suddenly dry at the thought of my husband. Just yesterday she'd urged me to leave the city. She'd almost certainly meant Francis when she said it. Now I had to second guess myself. Had she changed her mind after the Stoker brothers' visit? Or had I misunderstood her all along?

The pause hung between us, stretching long enough to make her brows knit. But I forced a tight smile, certain of my answer.

"Quite sure."

We turned the corner of North Third onto Union. Olivia glanced down at the address I showed her, then tilted her head toward a modest white chapel ahead. Through the narrow windows, a group of Quakers sat in silent worship, their plain frock coats and straight-legged trousers muted against the warm glow of morning light. Heads were bowed, and not a sound escaped the building.

"Oh no," Olivia said, taking a step back. "I cannot go in there. That's a Quaker meetinghouse!"

"Please, Olivia," I begged. I wasn't entirely sure what being a Quaker was all about, but I could guess how one might feel toward women dressed the way we were. "Please, please, please. I need you."

She peered through the window again, shielding her eyes with a hand.

"That's George Van Buren," she said, stepping farther away and shaking her head of perfect, glossy curls. "He's a client. He'll recognize me."

"And you'll recognize *him*," I countered. "Come on, Liv. Even I know the golden rule of bawdy houses. You'll both pretend you've never seen each other before."

She sighed, perhaps mildly impressed. "If I'm about to go into that room with you, after everything I did last night, then you have to at least answer me something, *Miss May*." She said the name in a way that evoked the half-truth I'd told Clement. She wasn't going to say anything about it, *yet*, but she'd made it clear that she could.

"Why does that Quaker dandy with the pretty cat eyes care a penny for what happens to you?" she asked. "I know you work your miracles, but he got what he came for. Why is he trying so hard to change your fate?"

I exhaled slowly, choosing my words with care. "I think he sees in me a struggle he faces himself. He's… trapped, in a body that feels like a mistake. His spirit wanted something different."

I let out another deep breath. In Ireland, I had never spoken so much as I did here. Survival didn't leave much room for conversation. But in Hudson, I had my basic needs met. Food, shelter, even friendship. Time to think was a new luxury. Someone to listen to my thoughts was madness altogether.

"We're different from each other, of course," I added. "I've only just arrived here, and I'm poor and Irish and Catholic."

"And a woman," Olivia reminded me.

"Right," I agreed. "But he doesn't fit in either. Not the way he's supposed to. He can fake it easier than I can, but it won't do his soul any favors."

Olivia arched a brow, skepticism etched into every elegant line of her face. "So it's really just your kindred nature that makes him want to help?"

"No," I admitted. "Not just that. I think it has to do with these seances and the kind of people they attract. I get the sense that spiritualists, the ones everyone keeps mistaking me for, are his kind of people. Artists, writers, outsiders. I think he sees me as a bridge to community or belonging. And, in a darkened room…" I hesitated, letting the thought unravel. "I imagine you can be anyone you want to be."

I glanced at Olivia, not expecting her to understand. Who would she want to be if the choice was hers? If she had every door open to her, and no one watching which one she chose?

Her reply surprised me. "That makes sense," she said with a shrug, her tone lighter than I expected. She sighed and, with a flick of her wrist, gestured toward the door. "Go on, then. After you."

We tiptoed in.

The air was cool, the modest stove struggling to chase away the chill. Wooden benches faced one another in stark symmetry, the arrangement as unadorned as the brick walls that surrounded us, bare of even a lick of whitewash. Thankfully, we spotted empty seats not far from the door. Our silk skirts swooshed as we filed towards them.

The Quakers greeted us with a ripple of blank stares and fleeting, downcast glances. The children, though, couldn't hide their curiosity, their giggles barely muffled. The wee lasses sat bonneted and kerchiefed, their dresses simple but pure lovely in their own dove-colored way.

At the front of the room, a man stood on a raised platform. He had light-brown skin, and his black hair was combed back smoothly over a high forehead. I drew in a breath at the sight of his eyes, dark and intense like holes in the heavens. His voice, rich and resonant, filled the otherwise subdued space, the only lively thing within those stark walls.

Olivia sighed deeply in my direction, but we remained, the fine clothing of successful fancy ladies flashing in a room of simply clad Quakers. Parrots among pigeons.

The lecturer spoke of a Fugitive Slave Act and the need to help enslaved people escape to freedom. About the plight of the Black folk in America, not only in the southern states but in the north as well. He described how they were treated as less-than, dehumanized in the newspaper cartoons, the cruel stereotypes perpetuated in everyday life, and the prejudice that refused to loosen its grip.

"Indeed," he said, his voice rising with conviction, "the millions of Irish immigrants have done little to advance this cause. They fled oppression, abandoned by British imperialism, left to starve and die in unspeakable poverty. Yet here, in America, they seek access to whiteness. They shun the enslaved, resent the Black man for working the jobs they covet. They say, 'Do not come North to take our jobs. Stay in slavery in the South.' They turn their backs on abolitionists, striving to separate themselves from the oppressed."

Olivia was very still now, her earlier impatience gone. She didn't look at me, but I felt the shift in her. A thought taking root, a quiet, measured consideration.

"But we must strive to educate them," the lecturer continued, "to help them see that we are all God's children, brought here on different boats but, ultimately, in the same boat."

I sat as frozen as Olivia. I'd never heard Irish people called intolerant before. Ireland didn't have the same mix of folks as America, but I'd never known us to care if someone looked a bit different.

When I was just a lass, on the eve of the great famine, my family traveled through Dublin. The houses where I did my readings and Da did his sweepings buzzed with talk of a man named Frederick Douglass. He wasn't a Traveler like us, but more of a visitor, all the way from America. His story of escaping slavery captured everyone's attention. People spoke of his courage, his cause. Some even purchased his book. The Irish embraced him, condemned the injustice of slavery. Even our leaders supported his fight, refusing money from American donors who tried to buy our country's freedom with the blood price of the enslaved.

Now I could hear no more of this man's speech in that plain, echoing meetinghouse, so tired was I of being discriminated against myself. Right there, where I sought refuge and hoped for a key to my freedom, again I was no more than Irish, and words—hateful words— were being put into my mouth.

I got up and headed straight for the door. Olivia followed suit. We must have been an obvious sight, the two of us racing out with our enormous silk skirts bustling and trailing after us like pastel storm clouds. If Clement hadn't noticed us before, he did now, for he followed immediately after.

I folded my arms tightly across my chest as I stepped into the blinding white light. The chill wind cut through the silk of my dress, but I barely noticed over the dull roar of my anger and hurt.

"Wait, Miss May!" Clement's voice called out as he caught up to us outside.

I turned to face him, though I couldn't meet his eyes. The wind was blustering, and I would have regretted coming, except that to feel him beside me felt—just for a moment, against all logic—like home.

"I'm sorry," he said, his voice low. He moved closer, searching for my eyes until I couldn't avoid his anymore. "I didn't know he was going to talk about that today."

My throat tightened. I searched for something, anything, to focus on, my eyes landing on a horse-drawn carriage as if I'd never seen one before.

"Well, you didn't say anything to stand up for me, either," I mumbled, mortified by the tremor in my voice.

"He isn't wrong," Clement answered. I could feel his eyes searching for mine again. "Next to the Know-Nothings, the Irish show no support for our cause."

The carriage turned the corner, disappearing into rows of gray trees reaching their bare arms into vibrant white. How was this man, who seemed to trust me only the night before, now defending a lecturer who had put me down just for being Irish? I didn't know anything about politics outside of what I'd just heard, but I knew what I'd been through. What the Irish *were* going through still. And we had a right to feel nervous for our livelihood.

"Excuse us for fearing for our jobs," I said, voice sharp, "when we could barely afford sugar for our tea back in Ireland."

"Then you do look down on me, just like the rest of Irish Americans," he countered, shoving his hands deep into his coat pockets.

"No!" I yelled, heat rising in my chest. I steadied myself with a deep breath. "Look down on you? How could I look down on someone whose heart is like mine?"

I watched the lines of his face soften at my words. We stayed like that for a moment, each just looking at the other, and in my case, trying to remember to breathe.

Olivia cleared her throat, and I realized how close he and I had moved toward one another. I quickly took a step back.

"Look here," I said. "I'm not defending the Irish who would see anyone in chains. How could I? I'm one wrong answer away from chains myself."

He inched back, scoffing and crossing his arms in defiance.

I gave myself a moment to listen to the bustle on the street as it droned in varying degrees of noise, for I could sense my temper rising. If I didn't bite my tongue, my rage would get the best of me.

"When I landed here," I continued, my voice steadier, "there were nineteen questions I had to answer before my papers were stamped. A friend of mine on board had warned me about them beforehand." I ignored the pang of an awful memory. Flynn in a large brown sack. A needle diving in.

"The officer asked if I had any mental disability. I told him no, for a 'yes' would be a 'yes' to a return ticket home and a certain death. But who could have gone through what we did and land on the other side in the right state of mind? Not one person answered that question truthfully."

His mouth twitched, like he was chewing on my words, but he shook his head. "That's not chains," he said quietly. "We're not in the same situation. You can change your clothes and become someone else. Maybe you feel like you can't, but for me, it's more than a feeling. It's impossible. Slavery in this country is something you will never understand. No matter how poor you are or how much prejudice you face, you'll never know what it means to have dark skin in America."

His voice was gentle but serious, and I could feel the truth in it. I looked at Olivia, who seemed to agree with him despite herself. The weight of my ignorance sank in my stomach like a stone. Mammy had warned me not to mix with others. I'd seen open minds back home in Ireland, but that didn't mean all minds were open. Folks on both sides of the ocean could think they had me figured just by looking at my clothes or hearing my voice. But Clement, Olivia... It was different for them, and I'd been blind to it. I'm certain I flushed something fierce.

"You're right," I said at last. "I'll never understand. What is happening in this country is different. I only meant that it's *you* who must look down on *me*, Irish and poor as I am. Living in a brothel..." My eyes started to sting, and I couldn't go on.

His arms unfolded. "I don't look down on you, May."

I looked back up at him, unspoken words tickling the tip of my tongue. His eyes searched mine for an answer, and all I wanted to do was give him the right one and make him believe it. I didn't notice

Olivia staring at the two of us with her own mouth open until she broke the silence.

"Well, great," she said with a showy smile. "No one looks down on anyone else here. Now that's settled, can we meet this friend of yours who will teach May to conjure spirits? Some of us have jobs to get to at some point today."

I'd never felt this way before. Never been in love, not even close. My da had set the standard for me, and it was a low one, so low I wondered at times if I'd do best on my own. He'd try to clip my butterfly wings and tell me to wake up from a dream. I still wonder: how could he do that to me? Dreams were all we had back in Ireland during the blight. Reality was a curse. Dreams were all we had.

But I realized now that my disinterest in men only went as far as the men I'd known. In reality, I had only been waiting for Clement. Dreaming of him. There was no one else for me but this one particular man. The way he cared for others—for families like Mrs. Davidson's and for his brother—was unlike any amount of caring I thought possible.

Clement faltered. "About that," he answered sheepishly, one hand rubbing the back of his neck. "This man who can help? His name's Paschal Randolph. And... he's the one who's speaking in there now."

# CHAPTER 20

# Clement

Clement watched carefully from across the room as Paschal spoke with May. Olivia was talking beside him, offering her thoughts on how the conversation seemed to be going, but Clement barely registered her words. This was supposed to be a meeting of the minds—a gathering of abolitionists who understood that slavery was more than the cruelty of individuals; it was a system that had to be dismantled.

And yet, his mind was lost in the wild fields of May's buckwheat honey hair, wondering how far down her back it fell when loose, in the slight starriness of her blue eyes, her sweet pink mouth that curled ever so slightly as she spoke, so that she always seemed amused, even when she wasn't. She was a mystery. Before he knew it, a chuckle escaped him.

"What are you smiling about?" Olivia asked, cutting into his thoughts.

She was more tiresome to ignore than Rudyard when he wanted attention. That was when Clement realized he had been staring. He cleared his throat and turned to face Olivia.

"I'm just making sure he's being respectful." His lie was obvious. "I don't like the fellow," he said next. That, at least, was true.

Though Paschal was known to lecture with the Friends, Clement had never considered him a friend. Their shared abolitionist cause was where the similarities ended. Paschal had once accused Clement of being too bogged down by what meets the eye. Clement, in turn, had labeled Paschal a charlatan—obsessed with debauchery under the guise of healing. Paschal called himself a "sex magician," of all titles, yet still paraded into meetinghouses as if he belonged there.

But Clement now had to admit, the man could help May out of a situation that made him burn with jealousy under the guise of rage. It was with a strained cordial smile that he'd introduced May and Paschal to each other at the end of the meeting.

"You don't like him because he has a bad personality or because of the way he's all over May?" Olivia asked, her pointed tone breaking through his thoughts again.

Clement scoffed, absently. Before he could say more, Mr. Van Buren approached him, nodding a greeting. The respected gentleman's perfectly round face was framed by tufted white mutton chops. He was otherwise bald. As he neared, Van Buren's eyes flicked to Olivia. His double-take was unmistakable. Olivia met his startled look with a cool, raised eyebrow. The man hesitated, then turned sharply on his heel, walking away with his nose in the air.

Olivia nodded to herself with a disconcerting sense of satisfaction. What did he just witness between Olivia and Mr. Van Buren?

"Mr. Stoker, I'm going to ask you a question," Olivia said, blocking his view.

"Call me Clement," he replied absently, his attention drifting back to May.

Olivia sighed. "Clement, what exactly are your intentions with May?"

Her bluntness left no room for avoidance, and his laugh felt as forced as his lie. He wished he could redo it. Olivia's stare didn't waver. The room suddenly felt much warmer.

"I don't know," he admitted finally, deciding honesty would serve him better with May's straightforward companion. He acquiesced his full attention. The problem was, Clement didn't know his intentions. He didn't know what was possible. And yet, he was undeniably interested in continuing the conversation.

"You can't have her," Olivia said flatly.

Her words made him want to say *watch me*. But a light-hearted approach, he decided, might be more prudent. "Is there a law against it?"

Neither one of them was light-hearted.

"Neither one of us gives a damn about the law," she replied.

To an outsider, they might have seemed like two friends sharing a casual conversation about the snowstorm that was sure to follow soon after the past few temperate days, or perhaps their Christmas plans—the Stoker Christmas would be a quiet, contemplative affair, though most Quakers wouldn't celebrate at all.

To any outside, but May, that is. Could she feel the tension slice through the air from across the room? Was that part of her talent?

"I'm talking about her *life*," Olivia went on. "Your own speaker said as much. She has a chance at whiteness. She can be somebody in this country. Wouldn't you give up some fairytale dream of love for that chance? If you care about her, you'll let her do the same."

Clement found himself speechless—first by the way the word "love" sent a wave of panic through his chest, and then by the thought of whether Olivia might be right.

He closed his mouth and stole one last glance in May's direction. Nodded his head in consideration. From across the room, the red of her freckles stood out even more against the white of her skin, like holly berries in the snow. His lip twitched in a smile.

Olivia's persistent gaze pulled him back. His brow furrowed. His throat felt dry. And he found himself regretting he'd never counted those freckles.

# CHAPTER 21

# 𝕸𝖆𝖕

𝒯he room began to thin as the clock struck noon, enticing folks toward their midday meal. I watched Olivia and Clement speak. Their bodies were stiff as though on guard, and they weren't quite facing one another, as though reluctant to admit they were actually having a conversation. Clement's brow was furrowed, and Olivia was flushed.

What were they talking about? My mind reeled with the possibilities. I wanted so badly to trust both of them, for the people I cared for to care for each other. I hoped Clement would see Olivia's soft heart beneath her hard shell, and that Olivia would see how Clement was different from the other men we both knew. Most of all, I wanted them to see the way I might fit into his world.

Mr. Randolph leaned in toward me. It wasn't a natural movement, like the bend of a tree, but more like a sharp extension from the waist.

"So, you're the Irish spiritualist Rudyard has told me so much about."
He stood a hair too close, like he was desperate to command my
attention.

"Er, aye," I said distractedly. Clement's shoulders, usually proud,
were sloping downward, and Olivia was leaning in, her doe eyes more
like those of a huntress. "Wait, no. I'm not."

"You're not?" He cocked an eyebrow, a smirk spreading across his
wide, full mouth. His lips were pale and smooth, and when he pressed
them together, they formed a cupid's bow, giving him an almost feminine air.

"No, Mr. Randolph," I corrected myself. "I'm Catholic. But I
suppose I'm what folks here would call a medium."

Mr. Randolph's tone was playful, though his body continued to
move as rigidly as a tin soldier.

"Speak to spirits?" he asked me next, as casually as if he were
asking my favorite color. "A lot of folks claiming the same these days,
Miss May. With a face like yours, you could be the match to spark the
flames to change the fate of a nation. Only question is: what fate
would you push?"

His gaze felt like a beetle crawling up and down my body.

"There's power in beauty," he continued, though I wished he
wouldn't. "And where there's power, there's danger. And let's not
forget, you're Irish!" He laughed. The sound ended abruptly, without a
gulp of air to follow. "You're the enemy." He winked, as though he'd
just told me a grand joke.

I tried to smile politely, yet I felt like screaming. Why must I cower
to his mockery? Why did I let him speak to me so? I bit my lip, for I
didn't have a great deal of choice in the matter. I needed his help,
after all.

"Oh, you know I'm only teasing, dear May," he went on, as
though we were old friends. His lips twitched, or perhaps he
smirked. "And please, call me Paschal. Now, let's see what you can
do. Put you on the spot, shall we? Who would like to communicate
with me here?" He spread his long arms in a wide, theatrical
gesture.

It took me a moment to grasp what he meant. My mind stuttered, catching up with the challenge in his probing eyes. His lips twitched again, tickling the wispy hairs of his goatee.

"Right now?" I asked. His nod was gracious, almost courtly, but his gaze poured down on me like a spatter of hail, testing me with an unrelenting focus. "Very well, then. Let me see," I began.

I took a deep breath, falling easily into familiar sensations. A cool yet satisfying tingle spread across the back of my neck. The world softened, dimmed, and shifted as I surrendered to the pull.

"It's funny," I began, my voice distant even to my own ears. "I'm seeing the sea." *I'm smelling salt in the air, feeling buoyant, seeing a woman whose hair is wet and knotted, black except for the white, salt-stained ends that tumble across her shoulders.*

"And why is that funny?" he asked crisply, almost impatiently.

"Because..." I hesitated, searching for the words as the image grew clearer. "There's something feminine about the sea. It feels... maternal. I see it cradled in a mother's hands. You lost your mother, didn't you?"

His cutting expression softened just slightly. "When I was a boy," he admitted.

"And you had nothing," I murmured, the words coming unbidden.

"Grew up in Five Points. Spent my childhood in the streets. Just about every house hosted a grocery below and a brothel above." His chuckle was wry and hollow, a brittle shell for the pain beneath.

A chill swept through me as I remembered my one and only night in The Five Points. The cramped cellar we might have called home. The roughhousing lad who winked at me. The bakery and its awful sign. The mildewed hay we'd laid on.

Paschal had spent his entire childhood there. He had a faraway look in his eyes that helped me piece together the rest of the story.

"Your mother was your whole world," I said softly, "and when she died, you went to sea."

"I ran away," he corrected, a long finger wagging. "I had to. Had no means to support myself. Didn't come back until—let's see—five years ago, maybe."

My head felt heavy, stuffed like a pork pasty, but I pressed on, the message straining to be delivered. "Your mother is still with you, you must know. She's sorry for how her choices hurt you." I faltered, unable to meet his gaze. "She knows you struggle with your parentage. She… she thought her husband was dead when she met your father."

She showed me a man with the gait and stature of thirty or so years, dressed in a fine coat with tails. His collar was buttoned tightly, all the way to his cleft chin. He was shadowed at first, a silhouette drawing my attention to a prominent nose. As he turned to face me, or perhaps Paschal's mother, his dark eyes examined us before crinkling slightly. His straight chestnut hair was combed and parted neatly down the middle. He was so clearly Paschal's father; the eyes gave it away; they were gentler, kinder, but set the same way and burning with the same focused attention.

A flash, and the vision shifted. Another man stood before me now. This one bore a heavier presence. He was her husband, I was sure of it. His features were rougher, his stance more rigid, but there was something in his eyes—loss, perhaps, or anger—that spoke of a deeper story still hidden in the folds of time.

"When your mother's husband returned, very much alive, she was shocked," I continued. "You were just a baby. She'd hoped he'd stay, but he wouldn't."

I could see her in my mind's eye, tugging at his arm, pleading, crying. "He needs a father!" she begged. He slammed the door in her face.

When I looked back at Paschal, my vision dissipated in frothy white waves. I stumbled, feeling disoriented. Paschal helped me to a seat, dutifully courteous but clearly fazed. I hoped I'd proved him wrong about me. I didn't wish to be anyone's enemy, least of all the one person who could help me now.

"I must apologize," he said, a slew of theatrical gestures returning. "I should have invited you to sit."

"I'm fine," I replied, my voice a little shaky. "Only hungry."

Paschal's laugh was jarring, like thunder breaking through a quiet, misty haze. His moods seemed to shift in the blink of an eye, without any warning or transition. I, on the other hand, could linger in a mood for days, even weeks.

"Come on, then. I'll take you to lunch."

"Oh, I couldn't," I stammered, looking back to where I'd last seen Olivia and Clement. Now Olivia and Rudyard seemed deep in conversation, and I couldn't spot Clement at all.

Paschal followed my gaze. "They'll be fine," he insisted, drawing out the word 'fine' longer than I thought possible. He leaned in again, his opaque gaze as impossible to read as the twitch of his lips. He offered me his arm. "Come on. I know how readings can work up an appetite."

Something in me was screaming to leave the room and catch some air, like Paschal was a storm about to blow in and keep me stuck indoors. I wasn't nervous, exactly. If anything, his odd mannerisms had a strange way of settling me, like an anchor in a sea of uncertainty. If he was a storm, I was the white winter sky, bright and steady, a thing that knows what it is. A storm, however, is indefinable. It's wind and rain and lightning and thunder, chaos with the power to uproot trees and sink ferries. But I wasn't afraid of it. I knew if I was ever going to make my dreams real, I couldn't hide away from the storm. I'd have to face it head on.

We sat at a wee round table covered in clean white linen at the Central House Hotel. Paschal ordered for us—two of the famous steak and baked potatoes and a mince pie to share. The large hearth crackled, yet I felt little warmth, and though the closed velvet drapes blocked the wind from seeping in through the tall windows, they also created a sense of seclusion, of being quite stuck indoors.

We waited for our meal, conversation as stilted as his movements.

When the food arrived, our conversation ceased entirely.

The rich aroma curled around us like a decadent fog—melted

butter glistening on golden pastry, the kind of meal I would have scarcely dared to imagine in Ireland. I felt guilty even drawing it into my lungs.

I crossed my hands in my lap. One wrong move and I might turn him even further against me. He didn't care for the Irish; that much was plain. And as for what he thought of my reading, I couldn't say. His expression had been a cipher, impossible to unravel. All I knew was that I desperately needed his approval.

"Eat," Paschal invited, opening his arms in a gesture of invitation.

Ravenous as I was, I didn't need to be told twice. I took a bite, and the flaky crust dissolved on my tongue, warm and buttery, buzzing with flavor. With every swallow, my guilt faded, replaced by the steady rhythm of hunger finally being sated. I ate without restraint, my fork diving into the pie again and again, and washed it down with thick gulps of tea.

The silence between us stretched once more, broken only by the gentle clink of silver against porcelain. My stomach felt like a bottomless pit, yet I'd put on only a bit of weight in America. I looked healthier, and there was more color to my cheeks. Regrettably, I still had few curves, and what shape I did have owed itself entirely to the curious inventions of crinoline and corset.

It was then I realized Paschal had been watching me eat more than he'd been eating himself. His eyes gleamed with quiet amusement, his posture unnervingly upright. The way he sat, thin and angular, made him look even taller than he already was, like a figure sketched in ink and stretched to life. Heat rose to my face as I hurriedly dabbed my mouth with my napkin, suddenly self-conscious.

Paschal broke the silence. "So," he said, setting down his tea with a lifted pinky. "You were right about everything. I was married just this past year, and hopefully my mother will see her grandchildren grow up, in the way that she can, of course."

There was a twinkle in his eye when he spoke of the other side. It was as if he longed for it, or for anything that wasn't the present. It seemed to me that he ached for escape, for release from the man he was. At the drop of a hat, his voice would change from a raucous booming to a soft purr, his posture would straighten and then slouch, and his gestures, once small and clipped, would open wide, as if he sought to occupy more space than his body allowed.

He was an enigma, perhaps even to himself. But I couldn't say I was keen to solve the puzzle of Paschal Randolph. No, the only mystery I wanted to untangle at this luncheon was materialization. How was it done? Could I do it? And most pressing of all: would he help me do it?

"Congratulations," I said, swallowing the large bite I hadn't quite finished. I cleared my throat with a sip of tea, extending my pinky just as he had.

Perhaps he would decide I wasn't strong enough to hold a seance of my own. After all, I nearly swooned from a simple reading. Whatever his thoughts on the matter, they were either complicated or private. Why else would he want to take me to luncheon to deliver them?

Paschal sighed. "Are you ever going to ask for my help?"

I choked on my tea before looking into his eyes—two inkwells. I couldn't help but wonder if he saw right through me, if he knew the depth of my longing, of my quiet desperation.

I did not wish to solve the mystery of Paschal, but did he wish to solve the mystery of me? What would he uncover if he tried?

Would he see Irish May, barefoot and half wild, hair tumbling to my waist as I searched for fairies among the wildflowers?

Or would he see the May I'd become since the blight, the girl whose hair knotted and tangled in the screeching wind, who'd seen my most beloved family plucked away like decayed roses from a bouquet?

I looked down at the crumbs on my plate. Both versions of my former self felt lost to me now, and I couldn't for the life of me figure out if I missed either one of them.

I shifted uneasily. Perhaps, in his eyes, I was simply a woman. An American. Desperate.

Suddenly, the calm I'd felt before was gone, replaced by a quiet storm gathering in my chest.

"Er, aye," I replied, setting down my warm porcelain cup with a slight clatter. *A woman. An American. Desperate.* "I don't know how much you're aware of my situation..."

He smiled without joy, waiting for me to continue. The table across was staring and whispering. I did my best to ignore it. We had just as much right to be there, I told myself. That's what Olivia would have said. We even looked the part, he in his well-tailored burgundy frock coat and green silk vest, and I in a shiny garment of my own, blue silk with ruffled sleeves.

"Right," I went on. *Thunder rumbling.* "I need to learn materialization. My employer, you see, is intrigued by the idea of holding seances at her, well, establishment. But I haven't a notion how to materialize a spirit. I didn't even know that was possible until Rudyard told me so. Can you do it? I mean, do you know how?"

My heart pounded in my chest as I waited for his reply. It would change everything for me. Either way, a storm would break.

Paschal clasped his fingers together on the table. "Why, Miss May, you're as innocent as a butterfly wandering into a flower garden!"

I blinked, stunned. "I am?" It was a silly question, but how else could I have responded to such a remark?

One of the ladies at the next table pointed at me as she whispered something to her companion, who giggled in response. Paschal's gaze followed mine, and he leaned back in his chair, his posture languid and easy. "It's hard to ignore, isn't it?" he said.

I glanced briefly at the gossipers, then back at Paschal. The tension had broken with the surprise of his butterfly remark, yet it hadn't disappeared. Instead, it reconfigured, like a broken arrow, except this time it was aimed at these ladies.

"What are they talking about, anyway?" The question slipped out before I could stop it. I knew I should steer the conversation back to materialization, but my thoughts had fractured, splintered. I was tired —so tired—of always being the dove, soft and small, while the world belonged to the lions. And in this case, to these fine ladies, who circled and devoured with nothing but a glance.

"Us," he said, his voice bold and just a touch too loud. "A white woman and a Black man, sitting together, having lunch."

"I'm not white," I corrected, just a hint too defensively. "I'm Irish."

Paschal smiled coolly. "And I'm English, French, German, Native American, and Malagasy. But *they* don't see that." Surreptitiously, he pointed a bent finger toward the other tables, his eyebrows raised in silent question.

"This country doesn't make any sense," I murmured at last, picking up my cup only to set it down again with a clatter. "In Ireland, we all shared the same skin color, yet we welcomed those who looked different. Here, everyone's divided."

Paschal was silent for a moment, his gaze piercing, yet somehow, unnervingly, patient. I felt his silence beckon my thoughts, urging me to speak.

"You and I are mediums," I went on, perhaps against my better instincts. "We possess a rare ability. And yet I see how the papers portray both Irish and Black folk as too simple-minded for a single cultivated thought. What's wrong with everyone here?"

There was no answer at first. The room thickened with the low hum of chatter and the rattle of dessert spoons. The air smelled sickly-sweet of warm custard and brandied pears. Then Paschal's boom of a laugh echoed through the hall, drawing eyes toward us. My cheeks burned as I lowered my face toward my plate as much as my neck would allow.

"Go on, eat," he said almost kindly. "Look, Miss—"

"Please. Just May."

He nodded, raising his eyebrows. It was another one of his gestures that was impossible to interpret. "May. There's a great deal I can teach you. I'll be in town often going forward. My wife and I are starting a farm in Stockbridge. It's a distance, but not so far that I won't be back for lectures and meetings." He dabbed his mouth with his napkin. "The abolitionist movement is growing here, and whether you call yourself a spiritualist or a Catholic, people like us know right from wrong, and we're at the forefront of it."

*People like us.*

Relief filled me, and I couldn't help but think that maybe, just maybe, we could trust each other.

But then—the floor seemed to drop out beneath me.

"May," he said, his voice flat, almost apologetic. "I can't teach you materialization."

The words landed like a dull thud. All that hope, that fragile thread of belief, snapped in an instant.

"I'm not saying it can't be done," he continued, dabbing at the other corner of his mouth as if he hadn't just torn something open in me. "But I can't do it. I use my gift for healing. There's some showmanship involved, of course, to make a living. But materialization... It's outside my expertise."

I had faced the storm, and it had devoured me. My head was spinning. *A woman. An American. Desperate.* The words blurred my vision like twilight shadows. *Not enough. Never enough.*

"And you don't think it could be in *mine?*" I asked, grasping, grappling, not caring if he saw into the depths of my desperation.

"It would certainly be a feat, truly the most spectacular and remarkable evidence of life after death." The twinkle returned to his eyes. He believed it was possible. Maybe he even believed I might have the winning combination of courage and power to do it.

"Then help me," I said, breathless, the plea escaping before I could stop it.

He leaned in closer. I gazed into his dark, murky, unblinking stare. His lips twitched, and for a moment I saw him as he might have looked as a boy, visiting his mother in the hospital. He looked sweet, even innocent, and I couldn't figure out which version of him was the real Paschal, and which was the false one.

His eyebrows rose, erasing the glimpse of another person I might have seen. "Why not come to Stockbridge?" he asked smoothly. "Work the land with us, learn how to use your talent for healing. Mediumship is a gift. Don't waste it putting on performances for lustful flapdoodles." He snickered. "There's so much more you can do."

He poured me another cup of tea, the fragrant steam curling between us like a fragile bridge, before sitting back in his chair and opening his arms wide. "What do you say, May? Will you accept my offer of sanctuary?"

I sat still, my hands resting lightly on the edge of the table, as if the porcelain cup before me were an anchor. The question of truth and falsehood unrolled in my mind like a creased map, impossible to smooth completely.

Sanctuary. Was it safety he was offering, or a kindness that concealed a cage?

The offer was tempting—I'd have been a fool to deny it. A place to work an honest job, free of judgment and whispers. A place to bring my family. Yet I couldn't shake the feeling that the storm hadn't passed at all. The air was too still, the sky too quiet. The worst of it was still out there, waiting.

# CHAPTER 22

# Map

*There's so much more you can do.*

Paschal's words echoed through my mind, settling into an ache I'd carried for as long as I could remember. It was Mammy's voice I heard beneath his, laced with the same quiet reproach she'd wielded before marrying me off and shipping me across the world.

Why was I never enough? Not for my da, whose disappointment fell as steady as rain. And then, the bitter revelation: Mammy didn't think I was enough either.

Mammy had always kept busy—taking care of the wee ones, cooking, cleaning, scrubbing our little home spotless even with all the grief she carried on her narrow, sloping shoulders. She had the oaten meal ready each morning before my da awoke, the evening meal boiled before he returned from his laboring.

Now it was my turn to carry the burden, to save the family and somehow survive in the process. But no matter what I did, it was never enough.

And Paschal—with his knowing eyes and gilded words—couldn't even teach me the one thing I truly wanted to learn. My one hope for salvation.

He was offering me a way out, true enough. A home on his farm in western New York.

I told him I would think on it. Part of me wanted to run away from the entire loathsome life Francis had chosen for us. The thought of settling down on a farm, of starting over somewhere far away, held a quiet appeal. Yet my gut gnawed at me, sowing doubts about the man and his intentions.

Even if my heart had sung with certainty about him, I don't think I would have gone. Even as a Traveler, this land felt foreign and wide.

How could I move forward when I couldn't even find my footing standing still?

The thought of starting over again filled me with dread. I didn't know who to trust, and worse, my senses—usually piercing and clear—had felt tangled since giving Paschal his reading. But one thing came into sharp focus, undeniable and absolute, when I returned to French Maude's.

Just outside, hands buried deep in his pockets, stood Clement.

I couldn't leave.

I stood rooted to the cobblestones, staring at the back of Clement's head. The lamplighter was making his rounds, his torch casting a brief, dancing glow as he lit the gas lamp outside Maude's. The faint hiss of ignition gave way to a steady flame, and the lamp's light spilled over the street, chasing back the creeping shadows of dusk.

"Pardon me, Miss," the lamplighter said, his torch pole swaying as he strode past to light the next lamp.

Clement turned at the sound, his face catching the soft glow. I smiled instinctively at the sight of him, his calm presence grounding me beneath the flickering light. But then the memory of my frustration surged forward, pulling my smile into a scowl.

"Where did you go?" I demanded, crossing my arms tightly. "You left me at the meeting *you* invited me to." My tone was sharper than I'd intended, but I had my pride, after all.

Clement's expression softened with regret. He pulled his hands from his pockets and made a gentle gesture, something between an apology and an appeal for understanding. "I'm sorry," he said, his voice low and earnest.

I opened my mouth, ready to argue, but the moment our eyes met, the words caught in my throat. His gaze held mine, steady and unguarded, even as his throat bobbed with a swallow. He stood neither straight nor hunched, but open, waiting, leaning just slightly towards me. He made me wonder what it would feel like to stand just as open. No, to *be* just as open.

"What happened?" I asked at last, my voice more tentative than I intended. I planted my hands on my hips, trying to appear more confident than I felt.

"Your friend said something to me. I had to think for a minute. I *have* to think." His words were clipped, his tone careful. He shook his head as though to clear it, then pivoted. "But never mind that. How did your talk go with Paschal? Is he able to help you?"

The question settled over me like a weight, and I shook my head, swallowing hard to hold back tears. A horse-drawn cart clattered past, leaving a cloud of steam in its wake, thick in the cold air. "No," I said finally.

Before I could say more, Olivia stepped out of French Maude's, closing the door with a soft clack. She pulled her housecoat tightly around her as her eyes moved between us. Her gaze lingered on Clement for just a second longer than seemed casual. Then she turned in my direction. "I saw you leave with Mr. Randolph. How'd it go?"

I couldn't bring myself to answer.

"What's going on?" she asked next, her tone clipped, though she attempted a strained levity. "What's everyone whispering about?"

Clement glanced toward the street, his lips pressed into a line. "Can we go inside to talk?"

My eyes followed his. The uneven cobblestones beneath us were slick with slush, littered with scraps of food, broken glass, and the telltale evidence of horse traffic. People bustled past, cloaked in layers of wool, their heads bowed against the chill. Laughter and faint music drifted from the open tavern doors, mingling with the scent of pipe and coal smoke, sweat, and cheap liquor. A pair of men stumbled into view, each with an arm around a woman whose painted cheeks and brightly colored dresses stood out garishly against the gray backdrop of the dimming day.

"Inside?" Olivia crossed her arms. "Is May working for you for free now?"

"Liv—" I started, startled by her tone. But before I could question her, she threw up her hands and turned on her heel. "You can talk in my room," was all she said over her shoulder, disappearing into the darkened hall.

Something was bothering her, but I couldn't put my finger on it. Was she upset with me? Or was it Clement? A strange thought flickered in my mind: was she trying to prevent something between us? But why? I was beginning to see what others might say, but I couldn't see what Olivia might hold against us.

We entered the safety of her understated room. While the other residents of French Maude's decorated their rooms in bold shades of wild cherry and port, Olivia preferred muted tones. Her bedroom was a summer garden of peach and creamy white, polished mahogany, and sheer curtains. The furniture was sparse and carefully chosen, soft yet strong.

Clement seemed to take it all in for the first time, eyes scanning the silk chaise and yellowed pages of poetry pinned above her worn desk. On a small shelf, a few well-worn books leaned against one another, their spines cracked from age and frequent reading.

Olivia sat at her vanity, idly brushing at her hair with a deliberate nonchalance, though her eyes flicked toward Clement. He hesitated, unsure where to sit, his hands drifting toward his pockets again before stopping. I stayed near the door, taking in the tension between them like a clock wound too tightly, ticking closer to an inevitable break.

"So what happened?" they both asked at the same time, turning to me in unison. The moment stretched awkwardly before they looked away from each other, Olivia busying herself with her brush and Clement shifting his weight to the other foot.

I let out a long breath and sat down on Olivia's bed, running my hands over the tufted blanket as if smoothing it could also untangle the knot in my chest. "He can't do materializations," I admitted finally. "In fact, he warned me against them."

"Warned you? How?" Olivia asked, setting down the brush.

"That good for nothing..." Clement muttered under his breath, his jaw tight.

I didn't feel like rehashing the afternoon. I was tired and feeling sorry for myself, like nothing had worked out for me since I'd arrived in Hudson. Maybe since I was born. It was an awful state. I could feel it taking over my body, yet I lacked the tools to stop it.

The Sight was a curse—I knew that now. All I wanted was to vanish, to become a ghost myself and drift beyond reach, so neither of them would have to look at me and see the wretched, cursed thing that I was.

I smoothed the blanket again, the motion as fervent as it was pointless.

Mammy used to scold me for being too dramatic whenever I'd swoon after a reading, especially once the blight hit and there was rarely even a crust of bread to steady me. She said I needed to toughen up, to ground myself, as if a bird could simply decide not to fly.

But at that moment, I almost felt lucky to be among people who hadn't yet tried to clip my fragile, airy wings. Clement and Olivia had built their lives despite the obstacles, their beliefs unshaken. I respected them for it. But they were wrong to believe in *me*.

What did they see that I couldn't? How could they trust me when I could barely trust myself? The absence of faith in myself was suffocating. It was like being locked inside a glass case—able to see the beauty of the world, close enough to touch it, but forever separated by an unyielding barrier.

"He said that I should be doing more with my ability than performing for flapdoodles. That I should learn to heal. To help people."

Olivia gasped, set down her hairbrush, and shook her head. "He's *daft*, May."

I laughed softly, appreciating her attempt to cheer me up, though it didn't quite take.

"Men don't understand what it's like," she continued, her voice gaining fire. "You're doing everything you can just to survive—and help your family, no less. What does he expect? That you'll study medicine and become a female physician? Half the population doesn't even believe in the Summerlands, and the other half, if they'd even *trust* a woman, might call you a witch instead of a healer. The world isn't built for you to 'do more.' It's barely built for you to stay afloat."

I raised my eyebrows. I'd been among the grieving in Hudson long enough to know about the Summerlands, the place where spiritualists believed souls travel following their death, an in-between sort of lavish garden that hosts them before they travel on toward their next life. But Olivia?

"What?" she asked, catching my look. She shrugged, a touch sheepish. "I picked up a copy of the *Spiritual Telegraph* on my way home. A girl has to know what she's up against."

My chest ached at her small but thoughtful gesture. She'd gone out of her way to understand something she didn't have to. My friend was remarkable.

I ran my thumb over the worn edges of my figure charm, tracing its familiar shape. The weight of Paschal's offer settled over me again, thick and cloying. Could I really leave? Did I even have a choice?

I swallowed a pang of nerves and finally said it aloud. "Paschal offered me a place on his farm."

Clement had been quiet since his initial reaction. I braved a glance at him. A shadow passed over his expression. "Maybe that *is* the best thing," he said at last. His voice was low, measured.

He looked at Olivia, and a pulse of understanding passed between them that only deepened my unease. He sat back on the chaise with a quiet sigh, his shoulders softening, as if he'd made peace with something. "Maybe starting over is what you need. If Paschal can teach you something valuable, that might be the best path forward."

My heart sank for the second time today. The only thing that kept me from drowning completely was the quiet sorrow in his voice.

Now Olivia fell silent, studying her stockinged feet with sudden intensity.

"Right, then. Look," I said, feeling myself grow hot. "I don't know what's going on between the two of you, but it's not for either of you to tell me what I should do."

They both looked up, startled by the sharpness of my tone. For weeks, I'd been waiting for the right moment to tell Clement about my marriage, but it was too late to find the perfect words.

Of course, a part of me wished I'd never have to, but the other part of me knew: there's no escaping the past and no escaping who you are. It was Mammy who had me marry, and I couldn't dishonor her by running off now and becoming an adulterer or farmer or healer or whatever anyone thought I should be.

*Could I?*

No. The truth was already out there between us, waiting to explode. I let out a cold, clear sigh. "It's my husband's choice. I can't do whatever I want or what either of you think is best because I'm bound to the will of my husband, for better or for worse."

I braced myself. If he'd thought I'd never understand him before, perhaps now he'd realized how little he'd understood *me*. Perhaps we were simply meant to be mysteries to each other, and the odds of our friendship were stacked too high against us.

Clement froze. His mouth opened slightly, as if he couldn't quite believe what he'd heard.

"Your husband?" he repeated. His voice was gravel, tinged with disbelief and something deeper, something that twisted painfully in my chest. For a moment, I thought I saw anger flash in his eyes, and it startled me. No one had ever cared enough to be angry on my behalf before.

I'd made a mistake—perhaps many mistakes—that I couldn't take back. I'd been foolish to think there was such a thing as a right moment to deliver news like that.

I'd asked myself if I missed the person I'd been in Ireland. Whether I did or not, the confession I'd just blurted made it all too apparent that she was not quite so lost to me after all. The desperate American woman I was becoming was still bound to my roots, for as Mammy once told me, my roots stretched as far and wide as the roads I'd traveled.

Clement looked like he was trying to remember something as he rubbed the back of his neck. "To your security guard?" he asked next, gaze hard against mine.

"Technically," I admitted weakly, a feeble attempt at undoing what cannot be undone. I wanted to move closer to him, to explain properly, but my body wouldn't obey. "It wasn't love. It was desperation. Our mothers arranged it so we wouldn't be alone in this country."

His expression grew distant, his thoughts churning in a place I couldn't reach.

Was this the storm I'd feared? I hoped so, for my heart felt like stone, too heavy for my body. If this was not the storm, then surely I would find myself crushed completely when it broke.

"But I don't have Francis at all," I continued.

Grandmammy once told me about sirens, sea creatures with golden hair and shell-adorned combs who lure sailors to their doom. The sound of the combs is so mesmerizing, the sailors can't resist getting closer, drawn in by the siren's magic. If I'd been a siren, with all my power in my hair, I still would've torn it out if it could've turned back time, allowing me to tell him the truth differently.

I felt powerless. All I had were words, and so words, any words, tumbled out.

"Francis has *me*. And all the money I've earned so far. He took it all and lost it in the gambling parlors. And now I don't have anything or anyone to rely on." I could scarcely breathe, and my gravestone heart was cracking. My red-rimmed eyes challenged him to run away. Without him, I'd have one less complication in my life. I was barely maintaining composure as I waited for his response, hoping he'd stay and run in equal parts.

Olivia continued to look down, but she'd picked up her hairbrush again. Her gaze practically burned a hole through her stockings as she fervently picked at the hair in her brush.

"Your husband," Clement said to himself. "The security guard... who pulled you away the day we met."

Olivia looked at me with a mixture of surprise and hurt, undoubtedly realizing I hadn't been completely open with her, either. I could have cried at that moment if it wouldn't have made everything even worse. He remembered. He remembered meeting me on the sidewalk the day I'd arrived at Maude's, and felt entirely hopeless, felt I'd been given the wrong name, and was cursed because of it. He remembered.

"So you'll stay," Clement said, his focus unwavering. "And you'll find another way to do these materializations."

I looked at him questioningly.

His eyes shone with the same intensity, but the warm honey flecks had dissolved. Now his eyes were murkier, harder to read. He didn't flinch or turn away from my gaze. He remained steady, but he was no longer there with me in the way he'd been minutes earlier. I'd lost him. Gone like the raven by my window just that morning, though it felt like a lifetime ago. Gone, and I had no one to blame but myself.

"Paschal isn't the only medium in New York," he said flatly. "Rudyard will find you another spiritualist. He's dead set on joining the movement one way or another. Pardon the pun." His tone was sardonic, humorless. "You'll earn back your money, and you'll start over—with your husband."

"Clement—" I tried to get in a word of comfort or apology, but he wouldn't allow it.

Olivia set down the new objects she'd begun to fiddle with. The perfume bottle and rouge hit her vanity with a clank so hard I hoped the glass bottle hadn't cracked. "Sure, maybe he can find someone else to train May, but we're nearly out of time already. This Paschal told you not to perform, right? Well, what if we do the opposite? Forget the training and go straight to the performance."

"Fake the whole thing?" Clement asked, narrowing his eyes.

She nodded, hints of mischief brightening her eyes.

"Liv, I can't fake it. I'm not an actress."

I could tell she was lost in thought because she began to chew her perfectly manicured nails. Olivia took exceptional pride in her nails, soaping her hands in warm water with ritualistic regularity before pushing back the hard skin at the base with an ivory tool, then filing the edges of her nails into a gentle curve that matched the outline of each fingertip just so, all before buffing with powder.

"You don't have to be an actress," she said, her voice gaining confidence. "*I'll* be your actress. I told you: I read up on these seances while you were at luncheon. Rudyard can fill us in on the details. But from what I've learned, sometimes the medium sits behind a curtain while spirits come out before the sitters—that's our audience.

"*I* can be that spirit. We'll set up a trap door behind the curtain leading down to the cellar. I'll hide below until it's pitch black, and then I'll give the men a performance they'll never forget. You know I can, May." A smile touched one corner of her matte, mauve lips.

"But why would you do all that?" I asked, my voice catching. "You'd go through all that trouble just to help me?"

One of her shoulders rose and fell like an evening tide as she shrugged. But when our eyes met, there was nothing casual about the moment, for there is nothing casual about two people seeing each other completely. It's like an entire ocean with all its glistening seashells and creatures that shine light in the darkest depths, when most people go about keeping their shoes clean of the sand. She took my hand.

"May, do you realize you're the first person to show me a drop of kindness since I came to French Maude's? To treat me as an equal. Besides," she added, her voice dropping lower, "imagine the possibilities. A dark room where a spirit can't be held accountable for its actions. We can take back our power, May. We can put on performances they'll never forget. Trust me."

I glanced at Clement, wondering what he was thinking—a Quaker and an abolitionist, sitting on a silk-upholstered chaise in a brothel worker's bedroom, discussing fraud. His expression was unreadable, but the tightness in his jaw made my stomach twist.

"I'll tell Rudyard the plan," he said after a pause, his voice flat and distant. Standing, he buttoned his coat with quick, deliberate movements. "He'll be able to help you from here on."

He couldn't have made a faster escape. He'd thought me a charlatan from the beginning, and now, I was proving him right.

I wished to be alone and cry the rest of the day away. But there was no time for that. Olivia and I had an act to prepare.

"May," she said with hesitation, "is your marriage really that cold? Does Francis never... even touch you?"

I turned toward the window, hiding the tears that began to spill freely. The view of the ever-constant mountains blurred through my grief. "He's never laid a finger on me," I admitted through a sob.

"Oh, May," she soothed, coming up behind me to place a hand on my shoulder. "*He's* the flapdoodle."

I choked on a laugh.

"Just do me one favor," she said, her voice gentler now.

"What's that?" I sniffed, wiping away my tears with the backs of my hands.

"Find a better spot to hide all the money you're about to make."

"Welcome, gentlemen, to the first official seance at French Maude's." Olivia's voice was clear and professional as she stood in the parlor. The rest of the women of what was quickly becoming the most notorious brothel in Hudson stared at her with wide, coal-rimmed eyes.

Maude shook her head, tutting with distaste. "You're too stiff, Livy dear. You need a little verve in your voice. A little more... *charme*. Watch." She pushed herself up from the settee to stand beside Olivia, wiggled her hips and spread her arms to reveal her squished and ample bosom, then bellowed the introduction, forming two firm fists at the end like an autumn tree shedding its leaves in one final, ecstatic crimson burst.

Her niece giggled, sounding her age for one brief moment. Then the moment ended as Madeline said, "Aunty, this isn't the theater. It's a house of tarts. Have Liv bend over a little and we'll be the talk of the town."

Maude frowned.

"Relax," offered Cora. She stood up and placed a hand on Maude's arm. "This will be fun." *Her* smile, on the other hand, looked incongruous upon her melancholic face.

I couldn't help smiling myself, though a dark feeling lingered in my gut. The other girls were excited to play their parts, their eyes sparkling despite the dull smudges beneath them, ghosts of the night before. For a moment, I let myself believe; maybe we could actually pull off this charade. Maybe, soon, I'd be sending for my brothers and sisters.

At first, the girls had had their doubts, but in the end, it was Annie who swayed their opinions. With a shrug that turned their heads like a feather in the breeze, she'd said, "Well, maybe it'll beat tugging a man's roger by a string from my bedroom window."

With Annie's endorsement, the others were pleased enough to jump in with their own examples of clients with specific needs—a man who ate from a plate of pork chops during the deed, another who insisted his caged bird remain in the room. That last one made me bite back a grin, solving the mystery of the strange squawking I'd heard the other night. In the end, we were all cackling together like a coven of witches at midnight.

Several rehearsals later, and with the performance just a few hours away, the house buzzed with the confidence of a new moon, knowing her light would only grow.

*Imagine the worst,* a Knowing whispered. *That's where you'll be safest.*

My summer-sky glimmer of hope grayed into dusk as soon as Francis opened the taupe pocket door. He wore a jolly grin on his ever-widening face. He'd grown at least two stone since we'd arrived in New York, and his cheeks stood out round and ruddy as a sun against the clouds he brought with him.

"May! You're home. How splendid to see you, darling."

"Darling?" I asked, more than a wee bit dumbfounded. He'd never called me that before, let alone been glad to see me. Something was most certainly, dreadfully, wrong.

By the heavy door just behind him stood a man in a long white coat. It took me a minute to realize he was wearing the uniform of a physician, and suddenly the grave whisper—the Knowing—began to make sense. I turned to Olivia, who offered a look of quiet confirmation, her worry written plainly across her face. Then, I turned to Francis.

"Francis, you didn't. You called that man here?"

"I did no such thing," he said with feigned hurt. "He came of his own accord. Must have caught wind of the marvelous performances you lasses are planning to put on. He's asking for just a couple minutes of your time. I only said you'd be glad to oblige."

"I told you we shouldn't advertise in the press yet," Cora said stiffly, ribbing Claire in her bony side.

Claire pouted, her thin pink lips like wilting rose petals. "So sue me. I thought we'd get the word out," she said, lifting her slender shoulders into a sheepish shrug.

"And what's next?" Olivia mumbled loud enough for everyone to hear. Her eyes were locked on Francis. "You'll have Nellie make Sawbones here something to eat while he interrogates your wife?" Her arms were folded tightly across her chest. Francis glared at her. She glared back harder. They looked like two dogs who didn't care for the other's scent.

I was too nervous to even sigh, but not too nervous to glue a scowl to my face.

The physician cleared his throat before introducing himself as Dr. George Worth Edmonds. "Nothing to lose oneself over," he said plainly to all of us, now crowded into the hallway. "I've just come for a little talk on the subject of Spiritualism."

At the doctor's request, Maude ushered her girls away, albeit reluctantly, inviting me and the slim, bespectacled professional to sit in the parlor. He took the settee, upholstered in a once-lush velvet, now worn thin and patched. I sat carefully into one of the high-backed chairs across from him and looked around, taking in the space as though seeing it through the doctor's eyes.

Tufts of stuffing peeked through where my chair's fabric had split. A fire crackled in the soot-stained marble fireplace of the otherwise silent room. Not much had changed since I'd arrived. At first glance, the room still had the air of opulence, though dulled by time and constant traffic. I'd grown accustomed to the scent, but I knew it lingered—stale perfume, burning oil, cheap tobacco, and the faint musk of bodies. The wallpaper peeled near the ceiling and corners, revealing patches of plaster underneath. The heavy velvet curtains might have once kept out the winter chill, but they'd lost their plush, and a draft from the window cracks made the dim light of the gas lamps flicker.

"Mrs. McMurry," he began, assuming a formal tone with me, but I stopped him quickly.

"Miss May will do, if you please," I insisted.

He cleared his throat, slightly flustered, but nodded his acknowledgment. The low lighting made the room seem almost dreamlike, yet it also brought out the shadows. Perhaps in these shadows, I hoped, the doctor might miss some of the unsavory details of the room's wear.

"Very well," he said stiffly, as though I'd just told him to call me Queen Victoria. "Miss May," he continued, launching into a barrage of questions.

*What is your religious affiliation?*

*Have you ever acted violently toward yourself or another?*

*Do you ever have spiritual visions?*

*Do you claim to exteriorize the substance known as ectoplasm?*

On and on he went.

I felt weak and wobbly, as though I was newly landed in America again, and any wrong answer would send me away. It was clear as the side table's gin decanter and mismatched set of glasses that my sanity was in question. I thought of the large brick asylum I'd passed that first bright day in Hudson. Compared to the feeling I had as I stood outside its wrought-iron gate, mesmerized and terrified in equal proportions, Maude's Queen Anne was a cozy cottage.

Once the questions were complete, I rubbed my face, exhausted.

"Now it's not surprising you would have these sorts of delusions," the doctor went on, acting as though he was the kindest of men. "Given where you work, of course."

"What's that supposed to mean?" I snapped, suddenly sitting quite upright, ready to defend the house and its faded grandeur as though I were Maude herself.

He jotted something down in his wee leather notebook.

"What are you writing?" I'd thought my nerves were on edge already, but the tiny scratches of his quill felt like hail down my back.

He looked at me with a half-smile, then closed his book. "I can write my notes later, if you prefer. Now, it's clear to us in the medical establishment that spiritualist aspirations are no more than heavily disguised venereal passions."

Seeing my confusion, he continued as though speaking to a wayward child. "It is my professional opinion that it is either hysteria or insanity that is causing you to believe yourself a psychic medium. But you, a weak-minded woman, are not necessarily to blame. Rather, the culprit is this whole business of femininity gone awry."

With wide swirls of his ink-stained hands, he gestured toward the room we were sitting in. His face crumpled a bit, like he'd drawn up the foul odor from the rug. It, too, frayed at the edges. Its once intricate pattern was blurred by dirt and use, though the center remained bold, the curling vine and rose design still visible.

I looked from the oval rug to the oval face of the doctor, gaping. He stared back, like I should be grateful he was open-minded enough not to blame me for my fiendish ways. But I wondered: who did he think he was?

I made sure to keep my mouth shut, lest he use my own words against me in claims of hysteria. It was an awful feeling—one I didn't expect to soon forget—to feel caged like that. Like nothing I could say would make a thimble of difference. Like my fate had already been sealed in wax.

"Terrible places to work, these bawdy houses," he went on, intentionally sniffing the air like he'd never smelled tobacco and yesterday's flat ale before. Nellie did a fine job cleaning up, but those smells were hard to be rid of.

Dr. Edmonds looked at me again with that fatherly expression. "I want to be overly fair with you, Miss May, because I know you Irish don't have as many choices when you get here. I am, you should be grateful to know, progressive of mind. I understand the plight of the lower classes."

He leaned in closer to me, smelling strangely floral and sweet, mistaking my silence for the gratitude to which he felt entitled.

*How lucky I am to be interrogated by a doctor who understands the Irish plight. How lucky to even be considered human, in light of my Irishness, my poverty, my stupidity.*

Was that how I was supposed to feel? Well, his tone only made me all the more feral, ready to fly off in any direction there was air and space.

"I did take a few minutes to speak with your husband before I arrived," he continued, lifting his reading glasses to the top of his nose. He reopened his notebook and scanned his notes. "Ah, yes. He's told me you've referred to him as a tyrant." He shut the book with a clap and looked straight at me. "Well, my dear, such symptoms of anti-socialness, such disregard for the sanctity of marriage, I must tell you does not bode well for the case of your sanity."

I was utterly speechless. And what did selling his wife into prostitution bode for the sanctity of marriage? I no longer trusted Francis about most anything, but I did believe what he told me about the asylums. They were a worse prison than any, where I could be locked away on but one doctor's referral, which was really just one man's referral, for doctors are just men and not the gods folks make them out to be.

On one man's whim, I could be erased, never seen or heard from again. The worst of it was, I'd have no hope. No one to save me. My own husband wouldn't lift a finger to see me set free. For all I knew, he was the one that called on the doctor in the first place.

My worry overshadowed my Sight, but it didn't darken the ability completely. There was someone knocking on the door of my mind, trying to reach the doctor. I bit my lip.

*Not now. Go away. Please.*

Opening the door for her would surely be my quickest path to ruin.

"Now, Miss May, what are we going to do about these so-called seances you're set to put on? We can't have people believing in such anti-social, anti-religious ideas now, can we?"

At that moment, French Maude, who'd quite clearly had an ear pressed against the door, burst in.

"Now, now, Dr. Handsome," she said, forgoing any pretense of having given us privacy. "Surely you're not going to tell us to stop our performances before they even get off the ground, are you? Our dear May is a professional. A *darling* in the community. Our little circles won't hurt anybody. They're harmless!" Her voice rose to a near squeak. "Just a little fun, a little *amusant* as they say, in *Pari*. Why, you'll put us out of business if we stop now, with a week's worth of shows lined up and nearly sold out already!"

The doctor stared for a moment with mild disgust. He rubbed the bottom of his nose, a perfect triangle in the center of a potato-shaped face. "Are you admitting, then, that your seances will be fraudulent?" he asked clinically.

"Real, fraudulent, they're whatever you like, honey. The customer is always right," Maude said with a swish of her hips, flashing a gap-toothed smile.

The doctor's lips twitched, but otherwise he did not move, continuing to stare at Maude as though she were a sideshow attraction. Maude didn't notice or didn't bother herself over it. She continued to beam in his direction, waiting expectantly for him to get up and leave.

"Right," he said, as though finally coming to a conclusion. "I will review my notes and pay another visit soon."

He was gone with the loud smack of the front door behind him, most likely too confused by the scenario to know exactly what to do next. Maude, polite smile still plastered on her face, brushed her hands together with a "good riddance to you, you gillygaupus scum bucket." She gave me a self-satisfied nod before shimmying into the kitchen, unceremoniously inquiring after Nellie's sticky buns. "That's it for rehearsal, girls. We'll run it once more before the house opens."

The girls, now deprived of their entertainment, and with some extra time on their hands, stopped their eavesdropping. Madeline and Claire trailed after Maude, lured by the scent of warm sugar, while

Annie and Cora stepped outside to smoke. Olivia said she had to get ready in her bedroom and left me with a hand on my arm and reassurance that we'd talk later. Francis, smug as I'd ever seen him, was on his way, too.

That left me alone, a ghost that might fizzle off into the wind. Alone in the once-grand parlor of the Queen Anne, where illusions were kept alive for those who wished to believe, but the truth was never far from the surface.

I no longer wished to put on the show. Wouldn't we all be playing with fire? No one else seemed to give the doctor a second thought. No one else had their lives at stake, nor the burden of their family's lives.

I rubbed the skin above my brows and slumped onto the settee. Even its jewel-toned arms were threadbare.

A wise person might have told me to keep looking forward, but I was a person who talked to the dead about their past lives, which often made me feel lost and directionless, if anything more accustomed to looking back. I only hoped I wouldn't look back on that moment with regret for allowing the show to go on.

"Welcome, gentlemen, to the first official seance at French Maude's."

Olivia was dressed for work and looked exquisite with bright red lips and rouge that glittered like broken seashells beneath the sun. Her corset was an impressive display of whale bone and steel, accentuating her natural curves that would make any woman jealous.

The parlor had been transformed from an ordinary space to hang your stockings and gab on the settee into a vision of the eeriest magic. Candelabras decorated the mantle, the heavy curtains were dusted and drawn closed, and sconces reflected plum and alabaster rainbows on every wall.

Rudyard and Francis stood next to each other by the door that separated the parlor from the entrance hallway. Clement, I wasn't shocked to see, had chosen not to attend.

Maude had permitted us a trial run. The other girls had spread the word in low, teasing whispers by their clients' necks and ears, and the line of men interested in attending the first seance was more than Maude could fit in the room. She was entirely delighted by the turnout.

"Don't embarrass me," she'd whispered to me and Olivia, a smile glued to her face.

I'd been too nervous to eat all day. Already I felt dizzy, but our act was solid, and I trusted Olivia's confidence. I trusted *her*.

I didn't know what to expect when the curtain closed and the lamps extinguished. I didn't know what men and women did in the dark, at least not from experience. But I took a deep breath, reminding myself that none of that mattered. Olivia knew enough for the entire seance.

She stood before a tight circle, with last-minute additional seats squeezed in for extra payment, and readied the audience.

"What you are about to experience will be unlike anything you've ever experienced before," she warned playfully. "You all know of our radiant resident spiritualist, Miss May. But today, in just a few moments, you won't see her at all.

"No, today, as you can see"—she motioned to the other girls to begin tying me to my seat—"our girl will be restrained completely."

A bawdy laughter erupted from the audience.

"We will seal her ties in wax. There is no way for her to get out without disturbing the wax, which we will check at the end of the seance. From behind her curtain, she will summon the spirit realm right here to this circle. She has no control over who will arrive. That's up to the spirits."

She looked around the room for dramatic effect. "Anything will be possible," she continued. "How will the spirit feel? Will it be of flesh and blood, like you and I?

"I invite you to touch, to taste, to experience for yourself. It will be the very material of your fantasies, your dreams, for the spirit that chooses this seance knows precisely where it is and has come with a fervent desire.

"Now, without further ado, I will blow out the lamps, and sing our lovely May into a trance state."

She opened her mouth, interrupted by a loud throat clearing from wee Madeline. With the slightest of frowns, Olivia bent over, lifting her skirts with one fell swoop. The audience hooted and cheered. With a look that said "Fine, you were right" to Madeline, Olivia began to sing.

On cue, Madeline scurried down to the larder by way of the scullery steps. She'd be first to emerge from the second staircase beneath the parlor trap door.

Being so close to Christmas, Olivia chose *Silent Night*, gesturing for the room to join her. The parlor echoed with the rich vibrato of song. It was a strange, eerie feeling to witness a display of piety in the heart of a brothel.

In the pitch-black silence, wee Madeline made her reentrance, slipping out from behind the curtain like a snowdrop emerging through frost. She had dubbed herself Minnie for the night, a name as delicate as her porcelain form. Giggling softly, she started the circle off by sitting in the laps of the men, tickling them with feathers and giggling. Though I couldn't see their faces, I could hear the echoes of longing acutely. I could feel them bounce back to me like an arrow coated in my own poisonous longing.

And I did ache from longing. I ached for the one face I *did* see behind the curtain.

As the men that had waited in line to enter French Maude's brothel began to moan and gasp and lick their lips, I, too, began to feel something stirring within me. I, too, could feel my fantasy coming to life before my eyes.

I thought I had understood my feelings for him, had kept them neatly contained. But now, in the velvet shadowless parlor, they unraveled, raw and sprawling.

I didn't just want him close. I desired him, in a way I'd never desired my husband or any other man before, and that desire burned low and steady.

Madeline departed with a flourish of blown kisses and the soft pitter-patter of her stocking feet scampering off.

One by one, the other girls entered, each slipping into her role like a whisper through a keyhole. There was Pocahontas, a native child who went by Poca, and Cissie, another spirit child, similarly playful and mischievous. Their voices, high and teasing, rang out like flutes above the droning hum of the men's growing enthusiasm.

Finally, Annie swept in, her presence commanding even in the darkness. Tonight, she was Ahmos, or Mosey, an Egyptian queen reborn from the night itself, regal and untouchable until she wasn't. A delighted gasp from one of the men broke through the tension when she leaned down and planted a loud, exaggerated kiss on his cheek. His voice, thrilled and high-pitched, announced his victory to the others: "I've been kissed by a queen!" The laughter that followed was brash, thick with ale and awe.

Behind the curtain, tied and unseen, I listened to the performance unfolding, its rhythm pulling the men—pulling me—into its web. The air was saturated with the scent of pipe smoke and clove oil, mingling with the heat of bodies too close, too eager. Though it was only a show, a crafted illusion, the energy it conjured was real, primal, and undeniable.

I didn't know what men and women did in the dark from my own experience, but I was beginning to imagine it, to sweat at the very hint of it.

Clement's face appeared in flashes before my eyes. It was so dark behind the curtain, I couldn't tell if my eyes were open or closed. Yet I saw him there, sitting across from me at the bakery, standing thoughtfully with his hands in his pockets, buttoning his coat before leaving, and me, wishing I could reach out to him and make him stay. Imagining his lips crashing down upon mine like ocean breakers, breathing in his scent of sun-baked earth and pine and fire.

Then his image was gone.

In its place, I saw unfamiliar faces. So many of them. I felt fingers clawing, grasping, pulling. My breath shook heavily, raggedly, thickly, each gulp of air harder and harder to draw in. There were too many ghosts—all attracted to me at the very same time.

I squeezed my eyes shut, tried to shake my head free of them. I didn't dare cover my eyes with my hands, lest I break the wax seal binding and ruin the illusion we'd worked so hard to create.

*Leave. Leave me be!* Teeth clenched, I spat the words silently. *Go away! I don't want to know you!*

And then, as suddenly as they had appeared, they were gone. A flash of emptiness replaced the chaos. Breath came slow but unsteady, my body drained beyond anything I had expected.

Cora was the last to perform. I knew her bit well from rehearsals. The thin material of her dress had fallen off one shoulder, revealing a faint outline of a golden curve, like the first glimmer of a waxing moon. She'd planned to take a sitter's hand and place it on the bare skin of that shoulder.

"I can feel it!" the lucky sitter exclaimed, his voice tinged with both wonder and disbelief. "I'm touching her."

"What do I feel like?" she asked, her voice ethereal, delicate, and utterly feigned.

"Like a real person," he stammered. "I can feel your pulse!"

"Oh," she replied in a coy, sing-song voice, drawing the moment out. "I've never been touched before. I'm still pure, you see, and I've come back for longing."

This man sat closest to me, and I could sense her movements as she guided his hands across her body, over her breasts, and then lower. He was shaking, his breath trembling audibly.

"Tell them what you feel," she coaxed sweetly.

He could scarcely make out the words. "She feels just like a woman. She feels so real," he stammered. "It's like a real lady's conch!"

A chorus of jealous gasps rippled through the sitters, their hunger unmistakable.

Cora's voice was suddenly light and childlike, a perfect mimicry of innocence. "I'm afraid I must go now. Thank you for helping me."

"Wait!" he cried again. "Will you be back?"

With a giggle, she was gone, leaving the audience spellbound and aching for more, no doubt ready to pay any price for it. As I sat there, tied and invisible, sweat cold and slick across my brow, I realized with a heavy, sinking clarity: Rudyard had been right.

Olivia stepped forward to draw the seance to a close. With a practiced elegance, she lit a single candle, its small flame flickering against the suffocating shadows. She invited the men to continue upstairs with the girl of their choice, to pick up where the evening had left them.

But before they rose, she pulled back the curtain, revealing me, the medium, still tied and sealed to the chair. I could feel my face drained of color and my long hair must have looked wilder than usual, as though rubbed with static electricity.

The men clapped, their applause hollow in my ears.

As soon as Olivia untied me, I staggered to my feet and retreated feebly toward my room—across the scuffed floorboards of the narrow hallway, past its wooden wainscoting and flickering oil lamps, past the men who smelled of parlor gin and unwashed bodies, who no longer noticed me now that my only use to them was complete.

But just because they were engaged in the oiled curls and rouge-stained cheeks of the other girls, that didn't mean their departed loved ones would be. I braced myself against the inevitable pull—the begging, the clawing—for one more chance, one fleeting moment of connection. The seance had cracked open a window for them, and now that it was over, surely they would rush back in, desperate and relentless.

I climbed the creaking staircase as swiftly as I could, my steps hurried, almost frantic, as though I were racing the dead themselves. Each groan of the wooden boards beneath my feet felt like a reminder that they were close behind, their unseen hands reaching.

Yet when I reached the top, I paused, breath caught in my chest, and realized something entirely unusual.

I didn't feel a thing.

No whispers. No tugs. No ethereal eyes boring into me from beyond.

I'd simply passed, unhindered, as though I were just... ordinary.

Was this what it felt like to be normal? To walk through the world untouched by fairy blood or curses? I swallowed, the strange void more oppressive than the tobacco smoke that began to fill the house in gray and black patches.

Would it last? Did I even want it to?

The quiet should have been a relief, but instead, it left me unsteady, unsure of who I was without their pull.

The next morning, the house buzzed with the afterglow of success. Rudyard stopped by for breakfast at Maude's own invitation to discuss strategies for the future. The other girls included me and Olivia in their chats and jests and began to plan the next circle.

With a seance six nights a week, there would be no shortage of business for them. Men would travel from up and down the river, they fantasized, for a chance to gain a seat at French Maude's, the most opulent bawdy house on the street.

Rudyard swore he'd make our seances the most captivating theater performance in the state, and perhaps beyond. "One day," he predicted with a wide grin, "we'll take this act to London. Mark my words, London will be the bedrock of Spiritualism and materialization. You'll be famous there, all of you."

The household was merry for the first time, joy and hope peeking in through the cracks in frosted windows. I should've felt it too—the warmth, the possibility. After all, I could see my means to an end beginning to materialize—the money I needed for my family and our homestead, even friendships.

And yet, I felt no lighter.

Worst of all, I couldn't rid my mind of thoughts of Clement. I saw him clear as ice, warm as amber, sweet as honey. I wanted that man so much I almost forgot the obstacles that lay between us. I almost forgot how lost he was to me now.

Once, he might have seen me. The real me. But now, I remained very much alone, the lass everyone looked through like glass. I felt delicate as such, too. I longed for a way to fade into obscurity, to be seen only for my heart, to be enough, and yet God seemed to be pushing me in the opposite direction, directly into the limelight, where I might sizzle and fall like Olivia's beloved Icarus.

# CHAPTER 23

## 𝔐𝔞𝔭

𝒯he profits from our seances were so good that even Francis couldn't find a word to complain. In just two weeks, despite Maude and Francis's cuts, I'd already saved enough for one ticket to America. But Francis, ever practical, said I ought to wait until I had enough for at least two. "You can't let any of them make the journey alone," he told me, his voice carrying a rare note of earnestness.

I barely shrugged in response, though deep down, I suspected he was right. A single ticket wouldn't do much good—not for what I was trying to accomplish.

"And where," he added, leaning back in his chair as though he'd already won the argument, "do you plan to house them when they arrive? You think you'll cram them into this Queen Anne on Diamond

Street? Or maybe you'd prefer a hovel in Five Points?" His smirk was sharp, but his words cut deeper.

He was right about that, too. I'd need more than tickets. I'd need a home, a real home.

A place where my siblings wouldn't have to scrape and hustle the way I had. A place where they could get settled and rest and recover without the pressure of either making money right away or else continuing to starve.

So I swallowed my impatience, reminding myself that this wasn't just about getting them across the ocean. It was about giving them a chance. A real chance.

A part of me couldn't help but wonder if any place, even Maude's, was better in the winter than the wagon in which they were getting by now. Winters could come hard and fast, and I could imagine the canvas walls of that wagon doing little to keep out the bitter winds or the creeping frost. They wouldn't have the coin to rent a small dwelling, and the snow would make travel impossible.

Maybe it was foolish to think so, but I sometimes caught myself wondering if it would have been better to send whatever I'd saved straightaway, bit by bit, to ease their burdens even slightly.

But the thought was a fleeting one. Even if I'd wanted to send the money, Francis wouldn't allow it. I couldn't so much as lift a finger without his approval. And the moment I tried to outsmart him, he caught me.

Francis was as clever as he was cold. Each morning, he counted our savings, and when he noticed a few coins missing, he came storming after me. His anger flared like a match struck too close to straw.

"You thought I wouldn't notice?" he hissed, his face pale but his eyes burning.

"I was going to send it to them," I said, trying to hold my ground, but my voice shook despite myself.

"To them?" His voice rose. "How could you hide money from me, May? After all I've done for you!"

Before I could respond, his hand came down hard across my cheek. My breath hitched, and for a moment, the only sound between us was the crackling of the fire in the hearth. He stood over me, trembling with anger—or maybe guilt—but he didn't speak again.

Neither did I, at first.

Normally I would have had a Knowing about something like that. A faint vision of a rosebud torn apart or a treasure chest sinking beneath the sea. Some vague image that wouldn't make sense until it did, when the thing it foreshadowed came to pass.

When Francis had found my money, or when he'd slapped me, I should have felt a loose Knowing tied up like a ribbon. Yet I didn't.

"It was just enough for a boat fare," I said at last, keeping my voice steady. "In case anything should happen to it." I stared hard at him, my hands clenched at my sides. Only the smallest tremor in my throat might have betrayed the fear I felt. He'd be angry for what I was about to say, but I said it anyway.

"You can't blame me, Francis, after what happened last time."

His face darkened, and for a moment, I thought he'd strike me again. My hands flew up to protect my face, but he stopped himself, lowering his arm with a sharp exhale.

"That was one night's bad luck," he said through gritted teeth. "It could've happened to anyone. Don't worry about what I'm doing, May. The only one you should be worried about now is yourself."

"Myself? What have *I* done?" I asked him.

"It's not what you've done, but who you're doing it with."

We stared at each other coolly. In moments like this, I saw glimpses of the lad I'd grown up with. No pretenses, no airs. We understood each other, despite everything. And yet, I knew he enjoyed this—putting me in my place, making me doubt myself.

"If you've got something to say to me, Francis, just say it."

He sighed, dragging it out like a martyr forced to carry some unbearable burden. "May, those people you're spending all your time with? They're not your friends. They're not your people." He crossed his arms, his posture triumphant, as though he was the clever man and I the green, guileless woman; as though his words were not of his own small mind but of a priest's.

Rage rose in me. What did Francis know about friends? About

loyalty? But I swallowed the words, keeping my expression neutral. If I pushed him, he might lash out again.

Taking my silence as an invitation to keep talking, he did so gladly. "May, you're a wee lass. You don't see the world the way it is. I'm the one out in town, talking with our own folk at Governor's Tavern, hearing what it's really like here in America.

"And what are you doing? Huddled in this house, nose buried in some rubbish book. You're not going to get the truth from a wagtail lass like Olivia Johnson.

"Don't you see, May? She doesn't care about you. None of them do. They see you as nothing more than a brute. They look at our struggles, our poverty, and think they're better because they've been here longer."

I wanted to tell him it wasn't true, but what was the point? He'd never hear me anyway. His hate ran too deep—not just for people who were different from him but for the whole bloody world. He had a fire in his belly. I could hear it in the mornings. A kind of fire that sent everything up in fits of acid coughing, and he'd have an appetite fiercer than mine trying to fill it back up at breakfast with angry forkfuls of eggs and sausage.

If I disagreed with him now, I'd only start crying hot tears of frustration—only proving him right about me. I wouldn't give him that satisfaction.

"Well," I said as steadily as I could, "you don't have to worry about me. Olivia might see me as you say, but she's been a friend to me, and Clement doesn't come by anymore, so."

Francis's expression shifted, an odd glint in his eye.

My stomach clenched as I realized my mistake. He hadn't mentioned Clement.

I bit my tongue, wishing I could take the words back. I didn't want him thinking Clement meant anything to me at all. It's not that I feared my husband being jealous, though traveling men could be a jealous breed, prone to watching their wives carefully. I was afraid because I knew he was territorial, which I suppose isn't so different from jealousy, only one comes from the heart and the other from the gut. And the man standing before me was ruled by his gut.

Worse, I feared the implications of my own blindness. I hadn't seen any of this coming. No Sight, no Knowing since the first seance. What else might I be missing?

*Things will be different. No matter the cost.*

His words from aboard the coffin ship thudded into my mind. Before me was a man who would protect what was his, callous to any price. I'd never seen him act viciously before, yet his expression reminded me eerily of the shark's in the great Atlantic Ocean, the one who devoured our Flynn.

I prayed Francis didn't see my feelings for what they were, but in my heart, I knew he did. I could see it in the way he looked at me, putting together the pieces of my secret longing. Panic tightened my chest. I had to distract him, steer his thoughts away from Clement.

"You know," I said, my voice laced with forced confidence, "you and his brother, Rudyard, have more in common than you think. I know you're after seeing yourself as Irish and everyone else as against you. I know you're after forgetting where you come from at the same time. But you and Rudyard are alike. Sure, the two of you could understand each other in a way that most men can't. Not with other men, anyway."

The moment the words left my mouth, I regretted them. I felt sick. I'd managed to shift his attention away from Clement, but had I planted a far more dangerous seed?

"Hm." That was all he said, but the sound lingered in the air, unsettling as a nail dragged against glass. His lips curled into the faintest, most satisfied smile, and my stomach dropped.

When he turned and left the room, I stood frozen by the hearth, staring into the embers. My chest felt hollow, but it wasn't a Knowing that told me everything was about to go wrong. It was something worse: a bone-deep certainty that no matter what I did, I wouldn't be able to stop it.

# CHAPTER 24

# Olivia

Olivia unlaced her corset and let it drop to the floor. With a long sigh, she sank onto her bed. The first light of dawn peeked over the mountains, slipping through the crack in her drapes and brushing the room in soft gold. The house was quiet now, save for the faint rustle and murmur of the other girls settling in after another bustling night.

She closed her eyes, taking in a deep, corset-free gulp of air, ready to fall asleep in her chemise. But the crickets outside sang too loudly, their chorus threading through the walls and pulling her from the edges of sleep.

With a groan, she pushed herself up and crossed the room. Drawing the drapes wide in surrender, she let the dim light pour in. Dust glittered in the narrow space between her and the fogged windowpane.

Her mind wandered to May, who looked so tired after each performance.

What had life been like for her as she'd traveled through Ireland? May had shared pieces of her past, more than anyone else ever dared to in this house, but the fragments weren't enough to form a clear picture.

Olivia tried to imagine the beginning of May's story, how she might weave it aloud in her lilting, musical voice.

*Where I was born in Ireland, there wasn't a glen, loch, or cliff that wouldn't make your heart sore and tender. But I knew where to find the sea queen's throne at the edge of the Atlantic, and where the trade winds carried the scent of honey.*

Olivia could almost hear May whispering behind her, the words so vivid they might as well have been her own memories.

May would tell her the Hudson sky was a lonely one, but as Olivia looked out her window, she felt a strange tugging, like half her body was dissolving into that endless purple-gray unknown, and the half that remained in the dim room was all the company she needed.

May's stories about the *sidh* and *sluagh* were terrible and beautiful, one of Olivia's favorite combinations. Perhaps Olivia had stories within her, too. She had been a poet once, her public school teacher calling her a prodigy.

Even now, as a performer, she showed no less promise, captivating an entire room's attention with a vitality these men could never have expected from the dead. Olivia knew she could write. She could write *well*. That ability had never left her.

It had grown dormant, perhaps, like an ember buried under ash, but it could still ignite—could still awaken, like a spirit after its last breath.

She opened her desk drawer and pulled out her journal, brushing aside scattered perfume bottles, hair combs, and loose candles to clear a space.

Words began to press against her chest, demanding release. The pen felt heavy in her hand as she dipped it into the ink. In the low, flickering light of her oil lamp, she began to write.

*The men who visited Maude's never spoke of it in the daylight. That was the rule that kept them Christians, Quakers, respectable citizens, and loyal husbands. It was a code, and if broken, humiliation would spill from its cracks like blood.*

She paused, rereading the lines with a frown. Something felt off, the words too stiff and hollow. She dipped her pen again.

*Hudson was a cold and wicked city, its residents thirsty for thrills at any cost, even a life.*

She set down her pen. Again, she paused, reread, and frowned, but this time, she dipped her pen only to cross out the words in a fervor, ripping through the rough, yellowed paper with the point, adding more scratches to the desk underneath.

She sat back and exhaled sharply. She was a *poet*, not a storyteller.

May could craft grand, sweeping tales that had inspired Olivia to want to tell her own. But Olivia's gift was different. She wasn't meant for arcs and endings. She thrived in fragments, in glimpses, in images that flickered like candlelight—half-formed but alive.

Sometimes there are no heroes, no journeys, no transformations. Sometimes there is just a wild, cherry-red stirring that turns to black ink. A perfectly manicured hand reaching within, pawing at a secret world even if no one else will ever understand it.

She looked at the wreckage of her story. For good measure, she crumpled the page into a ball and threw it into the wastebasket.

Writing used to be her solace, her joy, but now it felt like an anchor dragging her into darker waters. The words tasted bitter on her tongue, and every thought seemed to carry the ghost of Martin Wilbur.

She closed her eyes, imagining her mind as a blank canvas.

Just as quickly, she opened them.

In the darkness there was Martin, kissing her shoulder, calling her a poet, making her feel like queen of the fairies. There was Martin, dancing with the tall blonde girl that sat in front of her in class. And there was Olivia, penniless and broken, selling bespoke poems from a makeshift stand on Warren.

She had loved writing then—hadn't she? Or had it always been for Martin, to prove him wrong, to show him what he'd missed out on, what he'd thrown away?

Her pen hovered over a blank page. She wanted to write about the light and the dark that animated a night in her city. She wanted to be free and keep herself company through her own words, not for profit or accolades, nor for Martin Wilbur or anyone else. She wanted to write because there was a rich and wild world inside her, ever-evolving—it would be gone before she could ever tame it into words —but she had to try.

Again, she closed her eyes, willing herself to conjure a blank canvas.

Instead, all she could see were May's stories, her voice weaving images so vivid they seemed to shimmer in the air. She saw Brigid, May's goddess of fire and inspiration, standing in her mind's eye, arms crossed, gaze unrelenting.

A few words began to bubble up. *Ghostly dalliance. Midnight tryst. Witching hour.* They felt more like Olivia than the story she'd just tried to write, but they still weren't right, as though scraped with a rusty scythe from the corner of her mind.

Why couldn't she find the words? Once, they had come so easily. How long had it been since writing felt possible without the ghost of her only love looming over her?

A realization made her inhale sharply. She didn't enjoy writing anymore. In fact, she hated it. Perhaps there was a time when she loved it, but now the words soured in her mouth, turning to vinegar before she could even shape them. The only words that brought her any spark of joy these days were May's—May's accent, May's stories, May's characters.

May saw something in Olivia that Martin hadn't. May saw the real Olivia, while Martin had seen the false one. He'd seen naivety, a play-thing, something to treat carelessly. What did May see? Olivia chewed on her nails. She had to figure that out for herself.

Silently, she thanked Brigid before shooing her away. Then she closed her eyes, inhaled the faint traces of dawn, and listened for the echoes stirring within her.

There was life inside of her. It was dripping over like paint on a blank canvas. She could be queen of the fairies without Martin's permission. She could be anything at all. The seance had shown her that.

Still there were no words resounding through her mind. It was saturated, instead, with images.

She'd seen some of them before, and others she imagined in so much detail that they could have been real. She felt like she was half-asleep, and whatever she dreamed would be so vivid, she'd believe the dreams were memories the next morning.

She saw girls with feathers on their breasts and apples caressing their darkened lips, angel wings and naked backs, looks of longing, innocence, and seriousness offset by thick thighs and heavy pendants. Women laying out on the rocks of Spook Rock Creek, airy as breath themselves, phantasms melting into the landscape.

She dipped her pen into ink, and she began to draw.

# CHAPTER 25

# Map

"You've been naughty," Olivia's silky sweet spirit voice cooed, brushing the dandy's ear like a cold wind. He stiffened, his facade cracking for the briefest moment. We'd both recognized him the moment he walked in, paying his entrance fee to Francis. My stomach churned at the sight of him. He'd looked around with a peevish air, as though he knew he wouldn't be welcome after what he'd done to Olivia.

Normally, when a man overstepped like that, the victim would tell French Maude, who'd pass the word to Francis, who would be pleased to give out to those types of men—pigeon-livered muttonheads, as he'd call them—if only for the pleasure of a quick brawl.

But Olivia hadn't told a soul. Not Maude, not Francis, not the girls. Only me. Her strength was her shield, and she clung to it fiercely. I think the idea of someone fighting her battles would feel like another assault. Another way for a man to take something from her.

But her silence didn't mean she'd forgotten. The memories lingered, surfacing when she'd drop a plate out of nowhere or her fingers would shake when she laced my corset.

Had Francis known, I have no doubt he'd have relished the chance to give the sly dandy a good walloping. But Francis didn't know, so he took the man's money like everyone else's, letting him join the line of men eager to experience the "new religion" at Maude's.

"Liv, you don't have to go out there tonight," I whispered, my voice tight. "I'm sure someone else can play your part or do their own a little longer."

But Olivia was adamant about continuing with the show as planned. "He's not going to stop me." Her voice was resolute, her posture tall as she smoothed her skirts and stepped into her role.

When she addressed the room, there was something different in her tone, something I couldn't place my finger on.

"You've all come tonight because you know that death is not to be feared," she began, her honey-sweet smile spreading as the audience leaned forward, spellbound. "It is to be welcomed. All the same, we hope it doesn't come prematurely." The men nodded and chuckled softly on cue. "Now, without further ado," she said, extinguishing the candle, "I leave the master, our very own spiritualist, Miss May, to her miraculous work."

The room dimmed to pitch black. The trap door beneath us creaked softly as, one by one, each girl slipped through to perform. I could barely focus on anything but the faint trace of unease, like the last breath of an unfinished dream at dawn. Olivia was set to end the performance, after Annie, and the hour dragged on unbearably as I waited for her moment.

When Annie finally finished, the room stilled, humming with an eerie, expectant silence. It was Olivia's time. Behind the curtain, she changed without a sound, slipping into her ghostly costume. Tonight, she'd crafted a new persona for herself: Queen Mab.

It was not the playful, fairy-like being we'd expected. We could feel it, even before she stepped into the circle. Something eerier had come forth, as though crafted of darkness itself.

"I am a spirit of poor tidings," Olivia whispered, only the faintest glimpses of a sheer white robe floating through the black air. "Is there someone here with a rotten soul?"

The audience tittered nervously, unsure whether to laugh or shiver. Who among them didn't wonder, even for a fleeting second, if their soul was rotten?

She moved slowly, the rustle of her gown barely audible as she extended a delicate hand. Her fingers brushed the knee of the man nearest me, lingering for only a moment before gliding to the next. One by one, she trailed her touch down the row of men, each breath in the room held taut with anticipation, until she found her target.

Her hand paused, her voice lilting like a dark lullaby. "It's you," she sang. "You've been naughty."

The dandy shifted, his discomfort palpable. He tried to laugh, but the high-pitched strain gave him away.

"You've been a naughty, naughty boy," Liv purred, her voice as sweet as sin.

The dandy gasped and then moaned with pain.

"Oops. I'm afraid my spirit hands don't know their own strength. Why, I've grabbed him by the berries!" Her innocence dripped with mockery, and the room roared with laughter. "Grabbed him awfully hard, I'm ashamed to admit," she continued, her tone still that of a maiden's, wide-eyed and blameless. And then, with a quick and deliberate motion, she kneed him soundly in the same spot.

The sharp intake of his breath was unmistakable, followed by a faint, choked wheeze as he doubled over, reaching for something. The surrounding gasps were so loud I almost missed it, yet over the din, I thought I caught Olivia's whispered, venomous warning. "Return, and I'll pick them off the bush."

My breath snagged in my throat, and for a moment, I was sure Maude would storm in with a candle, blowing the whole act to pieces before the coppers arrived to investigate another murder on Diamond Street. But Olivia didn't give her the chance. She vanished in a breath, as swift and silent as the *morrigan*.

Most knew the Celtic phantom queen as a harbinger of war and doom, but the women in my family spoke of her differently. To us, she was a queen of fate. Mammy's tales painted her as a shapeshifter, one moment a crow, the next a beautiful woman, washing the blood-stained garments of her enemies, guarding her people and her land. In other tales, she appears as a banshee, red-haired and red-eyed, heralding the death of a Traveler.

Perhaps Olivia might have seen her as a goddess of sovereignty, a guardian of power stolen and reclaimed. Tonight, it seemed the *morrígan* herself walked with her.

We were all at a loss for what to do next. The tension in the room hung heavy as a new set of velvet drapes. Finally, Maude threw Madeline back into the ring to buy some time and shift the mood. Within minutes, Olivia reappeared, serene as a saint, dressed in her fine clothes as if nothing had happened.

She closed the circle with flawless composure and a faint but knowing smile. The men clapped and cheered, still basking in the relief of not being singled out as "rotten." Some even rose to their feet, puffed up with pride for having witnessed what they deemed a miracle.

Olivia came to untie me, tossing me a quick, triumphant smirk. I attempted a smile back, for my friend was victorious in her efforts. She had taken back her power, and I should have been entirely glad for her.

Perhaps I was just tired. Perhaps it was knowing that Olivia still had another shift to work that night, and I would be left alone. Whatever it was, I was in no shape to meet her excitement just then.

The men were still applauding as the rest of the girls filtered back in, dressed for their second shift. That's when I noticed Francis. His arm was slung over Rudyard's shoulder, and he was whispering something in his ear.

I blinked in surprise. As far as I knew, they'd barely exchanged a word before tonight. Francis had warned me against Rudyard as company. Yet now they seemed almost familiar, slipping out the door together into the dead of night. It was a waxing half-moon, which meant the streetlamps were unlit. Like the cry of the banshee, such things never boded well.

I must have slept the moment my head hit the pillow, for I didn't struggle to fall asleep as I usually would. I was so weary, I didn't even finish my tea or grab a bannock from the kitchen. Nellie was always kind. She took to preparing bannocks in my honor, thinking I might be missing the Irish cooking. With a bitter irony, the ghost of a smile had touched my lips the first time she'd prepared them. If only I could send them off across the sea. If only a rock dove would swoop through my window, clever and steadfast enough to carry them to my family like secret notes to a distant lover, scrawled feverishly in red ink.

I could have slept the whole night through, prurient noises from the other bedrooms notwithstanding. But before the rest of the house quieted for the short remainder of the night, Olivia crept into my room and shook me awake.

Dazed at first, I stared up at the ceiling. All I'd wanted, since I was old enough to remember, was four walls and a roof. To wake up in the same place I fell asleep, sure in the knowledge that it wasn't going anywhere. To know that one day I'd be gone, but the house would still stand, a beautiful relic, a poem of stone and wood and thatch.

Now the walls of my small room were closing in around me. The air felt damp and slick, and a line of snow gathered along the floor by my drafty window. For a moment, I had been happy. The whole house had been happy. Now that joy in the big house on Diamond Street felt stale as disease, and I was certain I'd stayed too long in one place.

"May! Are you awake?" Olivia asked, flushed. "No Francis?"

It was then that I came back fully into my body, looking beside me for a familiar imprint on the bed.

"He hasn't come back yet," I said, sitting upright. That wasn't unusual; Francis often spent the night elsewhere. But dread curled in my stomach as I remembered what I'd seen earlier, at the close of the circle. "He went out with Rudyard."

"Hm," Olivia murmured, thoughtful. "I didn't realize they were friends."

"Me neither," I said bitterly.

She hesitated, a frown playing at her lips, as though she was weighing whether or not to say more.

"What is it?" I asked her.

Fidgeting with her skirt, she glanced at the open door. "Come downstairs for a minute. If Francis comes back, I don't want him to hear us talking."

"Downstairs? Can't we just go to your room?"

"It's a mess right now." She took my hand and led me to the settee in the parlor, then looked around to see if anyone was listening. We could hear the low chatter of the girls in the kitchen, enjoying a midnight snack of gin and buttered bannocks, which they had to admit were delicious—*for Irish fare*, of course.

"I know you've said Francis is a gambler," Olivia began, her tone measured. "And how did you put it? 'Fond of the drink?'"

I chuckled, for whenever she used an Irish expression, it felt like a brief moment of home. But it was brief, indeed.

"Well," Olivia went on, "I was curious if Rudyard had ever seen him out on the town and what he'd been up to, ever since Francis robbed your safe. So I asked Rudyard if he'd follow him after last night's seance."

"You *what?*" My voice rose in alarm.

Olivia shifted in her seat, unperturbed by my tone. "He was dodgy about it at first, but eventually, he admitted something. He said he'd seen Francis out before. Once. It might've even been before we met Rudyard."

My heart clenched. "Seen him?"

Olivia looked at me solemnly, eyes warm and tragic as a fawn's. That's when I knew.

"Rudyard saw Francis with a man, didn't he?"

Olivia's look of pity confirmed my suspicion. I swallowed.

"Anything else?" I asked. There was always more to a story. Better to know the whole of it before deciding what comes next.

"Only that Francis saw him, too. At least, Rudyard thinks he saw him. But they never spoke of it. And maybe now they're both pretending they never saw each other at all."

I rubbed my temples, not knowing what to make of this new information. What Francis did at night was his own business, unless my money was involved. There was no love between us, after all. But if Rudyard knew about Francis's preference, and now Olivia did as well, then...

My heart thudded with possibility. Then it was only a matter of time before Clement did, too.

Of course, there were other factors to consider, other ways any sort of kinship between Francis and Rudyard might pose complications. But none of them mattered to me. All I could think of was how to prove to Clement that my marriage was no barrier between us.

"You knew, didn't you?" Olivia asked softly. "You don't seem surprised in the least."

I grimaced. "My only shock is that he wasn't more careful about it."

She fell silent, likely piecing together fragments of past conversations, making sense of it all.

"Never mind about all that," I said hastily, interrupting her thoughts. "If Clement finds out the truth, then he'll know for certain that my marriage is a sham. Then maybe he'll forgive me for withholding it from him."

She shook her head, her curls swaying slightly. "Oh, May, you're still hung up on Clement Stoker?"

The look in my eyes must have been answer enough.

"Look, May, I had to tell you because I just found out before the show tonight, and I'd never keep a secret like that from you." She hesitated, her gaze dropping to her lap. Her hands fidgeted, twisting the hem of her dress. "Let sleeping dogs lie, hm?"

I couldn't tell if she meant Francis and Rudyard, or Clement and me. Either way, I nodded. I had enough to unravel without chasing after fresh troubles. My mind wandered to Rudyard and Francis and what a friendship between them might mean. Something fearsome, perhaps, for Francis was not to be trusted. Or something unexpected —gilded and beautiful. If Rudyard found happiness and Francis let me go, then perhaps I, too, could hope for a happy ending.

"Well," Olivia said, no longer interested in speculating about what these men did in the dark, "my shift is done, and all that's left for me to do is celebrate our success with my very best friend. I held my enemy's eggs in my hand and squeezed. *Hard*. And that, Miss May, means we're drinking."

I decided to put my concerns aside and followed her into the kitchen to grab a bottle of Maude's best diluted whiskey. But I paused at the threshold, glancing down at my nightgown. "I'm dressed for bed, not the drafty parlor. Can we go to your room instead?"

She hesitated, her brow furrowing, but before she could refuse, I took her hand and led her up the stairs. "I don't mind a mess," I assured her.

A smile tugged at my lips despite myself. Perhaps my fate might still change for the better. And besides, my friend was happy, and happiness has a way of spreading quicker than a fever.

Inside her room, she lit a candle and uncorked the bottle. My eyes roamed the space, and I froze. We hadn't been inside her room together since we'd started the seances.

Now that a friendship was blooming between us and the other girls, we'd taken to spending our time in the parlor and kitchen with the others. We'd exchange stories all together in the late morning when winter's brightest sun would filter through the windows and Nellie would be clattering pots and pans or chopping by the range. We'd sit around the wooden table with cups of tea or gin and laugh about new ideas for spirit characters or poke fun at unsuspecting clients.

I hadn't even had a poetry or reading lesson with Olivia, so busy had we been with the planning and executing of our grand charade.

Now I looked around her room, unable to understand what I was seeing: papers and papers filled with sketches, scattered pell-mell.

I picked one up to examine it and nearly choked on my breath. It was a self-portrait of Olivia, draped in her white spirit robe, arms over her head like the porcelain ballerina atop a fine box of jewelry, fingernails long and pointy. She appeared in the drawing as a silhouette in front of a stained-glass door, yet I knew it was her. The energy of it thrummed like a heartbeat. A strange combination of femininity, flowers, and royalty.

I looked up at her, my voice barely above a whisper. "A mess?"

She shrugged shyly.

"Olivia," I breathed, "this is marvelous. I've never seen a drawing so pure lovely in all my life. You never told me you're an artist."

She looked as luminous as the drawings, cheeks glowing a burnt rose in the candlelight. Incredible how just one small candle can illuminate an entire spirit; change a person completely.

"You think so?"

I nodded, lifting another sheet.

It was Annie, plain as day, except she wore angel wings and feathers in her hair. She knelt on mossy ground, her hands clenched together by her breasts as though praying or pleading.

"I think so," I managed at last, still nodding.

Olivia pressed her lips together in a small, thoughtful smile. "I always thought I wanted to write poetry," she admitted, her voice hushed as though sharing a secret. "But these circles... I don't know what it is about them that inspires me so. My senses feel heightened. I'm alive again, like when you walk through the woods in the middle of winter, and you've been dreading the cold, only to realize how fresh it makes your cheeks and how warm your heart beats against the wind. These images have been coming into my mind at all hours, and I can't wait to get back to my room after everything and make them... materialize."

She looked up at me from her seat on the bed, her smile stretching all the way to her eyes, which glittered like twin secrets. "It's like magic, May. You've brought magic here."

I grabbed the whiskey bottle and took a slug, pretending to clear my throat as I sputtered from the fire of it. I couldn't tell her that magic always comes with a price, and the price of her new gift was mine.

At first, it had felt like a dull headache, the kind that fades with food or rest. But deep down, I'd known since the night of the first seance.

After the headache, there was only emptiness, like a blue sunset you watch from your bedroom window, while all the world passes by on the streets below.

And then, it was just black. Silence, like a telegraph line gone dead. Someone might be sending a message from the other side, but until it reached me, I'd never know what it said, or if it was coming, or if it had ever existed at all.

People called the telegraph an invention of science. That's fine and all, but was it not also one of faith?

Now when I looked at people, all I saw was the one pulsing figure before me—a miraculous concoction of water, breath, earth, and spirit —but just the one, nonetheless. There wasn't a single soul surrounding them, needing my voice, tugging at my hemline like an impatient child. I thought I didn't want to be used by the spirit realm any longer, but to feel of no use was an even more miserable feeling.

The spirits of the seven spheres had abandoned me—that much was clear now. With that realization came another: I was no longer the Irish Catholic girl who had boarded the ship to America. I'd left her somewhere in the middle of the Atlantic, perhaps with Flynn; or perhaps on the dock when I first stepped onto foreign soil. Spiritualism had become more than a trade, more than a mask to wear for the seance-goers. It had grown into a way of seeing the world, a way to mend the endless fractures of pain and injustice.

But somehow, in my pursuit of survival, I'd strayed from that purpose.

Maybe the spirits were angry with me for ignoring their calls to heal and comfort, for using my gift for deceit rather than solace, and for banishing them, in the midst. Whatever the reason, I was no longer a medium but a regular Irish American woman, and a fraud at that.

"Have you shown anyone else your drawings?" I asked Olivia, desperate to shift the weight of my thoughts. "Surely you could sell these? Have some fine, rich person frame them in gold and silver above their mantle?"

"Not yet," she said thoughtfully, the corner of her mouth quirking up. "But I've been thinking about showing them to Rudyard."

A crease formed between my brows. "Rudyard?"

"I like him, May," she admitted, answering the question I hadn't asked aloud. "He cares about all the same things that I do. Art, beauty, poetry, travel. I do think someday we could go somewhere together. London, even."

I bit my lip.

"Oh, don't look at me like that," she teased, swiping the whiskey bottle. "I don't mean it like that." She tilted the bottle to her lips, swallowing a mouthful of fire. "Rudyard's the queerest man I've ever met, and I didn't need to take him up to my room to be sure of that."

"Oh," I said, hearing how daft I sounded.

Olivia's gaze softened, though her brows knit slightly. "I don't mean any harm in saying so. I love him just the same, no matter who he loves. Don't you?"

I managed a weak attempt at a smile, though it felt more like a grimace.

"What's wrong?" she asked me, handing me back the bottle. "Something's up. Why are you not happier?"

"I *am* happy," I lied.

I couldn't tell her the truth about the loss of my ability. If she knew, she'd tell me to stop the charade and get it back. I couldn't take away her inspiration, just as things were finally going her way.

Or worse, she might *not* tell me to stop the charade, and the vision of the friend I held so dear would slip through my fingers like silt. I wasn't prepared for that either.

So instead, I told her another truth, one equally unsettling. I told her that I missed Clement—as mad as that made me, because I hardly knew him. "But he'll never come by again, because I'm married. He must think I'm some sort of..." I trailed off, but Olivia could read my thoughts.

"Scarlet lady?" she smiled kindly as my head slumped down. "Look, May, there's something else I should tell you," she said with hesitancy. There was no trace of her bright smile any longer.

I braced myself, feeling wobbly at the thought of any more secrets. "What is it?"

"There might be another reason Clement hasn't come by," she confessed. "When we were at the meetinghouse, I—I told him he should leave you alone."

For a moment I couldn't make sense of anything. The room washed over me in sickening, crashing waves, like when you wade out in the ocean expecting flat water.

"Why would you say that?" I asked her, setting down the bottle. The waves tossed me off balance, and I remembered why I wasn't fond of whiskey.

"Because I care about you, May," she said, her voice earnest but pleading. "And I want you to have a future. A real future. Here, in *this* country. You don't know what people will say if they see you together, attached. You and I walking arm in arm down the promenade is one thing, but you haven't been here long enough to see the difference. You don't understand."

The waves became hot and red, the earth's fire coughing, sputtering, pushing itself up through dry cracks.

"I'm so tired of people telling me what I don't understand," I burst out. My throat felt tight, as though I'd swallowed a mouthful of seawater. "I'm sick of it. How could you, Liv?"

"I'm sorry," she said quickly, her voice trembling. She moved to the window, shivering in the eye of the draft. "Maybe it was a mistake," she admitted, turning back to me. "I just heard what that man— Paschal Randolph?—was saying at the meeting. He said Irish folk had a chance at whiteness. Well, it made me realize something. Clement and I will never have that chance. I didn't want him to take it from you."

I shook my head, the ocean waves calming down around me. "But isn't that *my* choice to make? Am I not sovereign?"

"It is," she agreed. "You *are*. I just—" She closed her perfect mouth for a moment, searching for words. Then she said, "Once I was in a situation where I had a chance at something I wanted, and I let a man take it from me. I didn't want you to make the same mistake if I could help it."

I looked at her, realizing how close heartbreaking sadness and manic joy are to each other, and what a miracle it is to sip from a thimble of both, to slip like a nymph between worlds.

She looked no different than she had a moment ago, and yet I'd never look at her the same way again. I knew I'd do whatever it took to help her if I could, just as she had done for me. Our bond had become unconditional, and it broke me down.

I stood up and threw my arms around her, letting her hold me as I cried.

"You're not angry?" she asked, when at last I let her go.

"I'm not angry," I told her. As I wiped away my tears, the shadow of a chuckle escaped my mouth.

"You forgive me?" she asked, her usual confidence tinged with hesitation.

I nodded, ocean waves crashing over me but in a deliciously hopeful way, like I had floated off to a tropical island of white sand and ripe fruit. If Clement was staying away because of what Olivia had said to him, then maybe he really did care for me. Maybe he could look past my marriage.

Already there was a chance Rudyard would tell him what he'd seen my husband do in the dark. Now if I could only convince him that being considered white meant nothing to me, he'd have no reason to stay away. Maybe it meant safety in my new country, but whiteness wasn't my dream.

I remembered then what I wanted most. My farmhouse. My family. To be seen.

Well, I had work that earned a great wage, that I could use to buy a home and send for my family. And now, I had hope that Clement might be the man to see me as I was. Everything I wanted felt closer than ever, and I didn't need to be anything other than myself to reach it.

# CHAPTER 26

## Map

*R*udyard had told me when the next abolitionist meeting would be held at the Quaker meetinghouse. I was determined to make things right with Clement, whatever that meant. It was a vexing question, after all, tangled as it was with my feelings for him, feelings that would hardly earn the blessing of Friar Hoare, who had married me to Francis.

The night before the meeting, I went straight to my room after the seance ended. My thoughts churned like the river, restless and roiling with determination. I pushed open the window, letting the night air rush in. It bit at my skin, but I welcomed the chill, hoping it might quiet my mind.

Yes, I was still married. But if Clement knew how little that vow meant to me now—how I'd see it burned to smoke as swiftly as peat on the fire—perhaps he'd feel differently.

I leaned on the sill, staring out at the river, a silver serpent slithering toward the horizon. Once, I had heard it hiss. Its voice had been low and sorrowful, a whisper only I could hear. But now, nothing. Just the howl of the wind and the occasional creak of the house.

I shook off the thought, jiggling closed the paned glass window. I had a possible future ahead of me to focus on. Why waste my time on water's keening? I sat on the edge of the bed and began unlacing my boots, letting my thoughts drift back to Clement.

He cared for the abolitionist cause more deeply than anything else. Why wouldn't he? The weight of it hung on him like a talisman, as close as the chain around his neck. Even in the North, where slavery was outlawed, the stain of it crept like mold on rotting bread. The same vile roots—discrimination, fear, violence—spread their tendrils, choking those they deemed unworthy.

But when I'd see Clement again, I would tell him that I was on his side, and that together, we could tear down the whole miserable system that separated us in the first place. We could pull up the infected roots and plant new seeds.

Or we could keep to the tradition of the city and let fire do the work for us. Fire didn't ask permission. It destroyed, yes, but it also made room for something better. Olivia had said as much herself, that it was the city's fires that birthed its beauty, or perhaps its strong winds which spread them.

Each time flames licked through the streets, the city rose again, stronger than before. Mammy might have said widespread destruction was a bad omen. She'd be appalled to know I now wondered if it was a billowing, burning blessing.

I slipped out of my dress, the cold air grazing my skin as I stood in my shift. The thought of Clement's absence gnawed at me, but there was no use in unraveling it tonight. I crawled under the covers, pulling them tight around me. The chill air I'd let in lingered, settling into the room like an unwelcome guest.

The house groaned as it settled, the muffled sounds of moans and yelps and cries and giggles bombarding me within the bedroom walls that felt like jail bars, reminding me how very alone I was. I turned to the soft glow of the bedside lamp, letting its light blur and distort as my eyes unfocused. For a moment, I imagined it was the flame of a spirit's lantern, leading me toward answers, toward clarity.

But the vision didn't hold.

I pressed a pillow over my head to drown out the noise, but the weight of my thoughts pressed heavier. Was Clement staying away because of my marriage? Because of what Olivia had said? Or something else entirely?

I went over our conversations in my head again and again, letting them swirl through the ether like wind in a secret garden.

*And I certainly can't ask a pretty Irish girl out to tea.*

He'd called me pretty, just the once, but was that all it was? A passing word, meaningless as a petal carried on the wind? Had I invented an entire relationship out of nothing but longing? Did his interest in me only stretch as far as I was able to help his brother? It was worth it to me to fight for our future, but was it worth it to him?

The questions spun and tangled until exhaustion pulled me under. I teetered on the edge of sleep when the night shattered with a burst of profanities from Annie's room, followed by what sounded like a bird's violent squawking.

"Hang on! The rope snapped!" Annie's muffled voice rang out.

I sat up, my heart hammering. For a moment, I thought I'd imagined the sound, but then another sharp cry came, followed by Annie yelling something to whoever was in the yard below. I exhaled, letting the tension seep out of me. Lucky for me, I'd recently solved the mystery of the bird in the house.

I grabbed a second pillow and pressed it firmly against my ear, blocking out Annie's voice and the ceaseless din of the house. After a moment, the Queen Anne seemed to purr, once again, with contentment. Yet I shared in none of it. Was there some fundamental part of myself that couldn't ever grasp happiness? I pictured Clement and me holding hands, walking away from Diamond Street, toward a future without limits. But in this vision, was I happy?

Was he?

The answers eluded me, but I knew one thing for certain. I was done with sleepless nights listening to the sounds of faked fulfillment echoing through the walls, and I was done worrying over Clement. I'd get my answers soon enough.

I paced in front of the plain brick meetinghouse, my skirts brushing against the frost-covered ground. The sky was a dull gray, the kind of winter light that muted everything it touched. I rehearsed what I wanted to say over and over, the words scrawled across my heart in inky script, but as the heavy door creaked open, I felt those words scatter like autumn leaves.

To my surprise, it was Paschal Randolph who emerged first from the calm restraint of the meetinghouse.

"Miss May!" he greeted me cheerfully. "What an unexpected pleasure. Did you hear I'd returned to town?"

Before I could answer, he was already in front of me, blocking my view of the doorway. And then Clement appeared, stepping into the muted light with quiet gravity as he buttoned his coat. His eyes grazed over me briefly, and he offered me only a curt nod before turning to leave.

"Wait!" I called.

Paschal turned to watch, his head tilting like a curious bird, his posture an unnecessary barrier between Clement and me. Those who still lingered near the doorway peered in my direction, undoubtedly thinking me some half-wild Irish creature without manners. I ignored them, dodged past the medium, and caught up to Clement, breathless as I reached his side.

"What can I do for you, Miss May?" He sounded measured, distant, as though he had not just been hurrying to escape me. "I trust business is going well." For a moment, only the distant caw of crows broke the silence. "Rudyard keeps me appraised," he continued finally. So much ice in his tone, colder than the stars.

He still wouldn't meet my eyes, but his voice melted ever so slightly when he said, "I'm glad it's all working out for you." Just as quickly, it froze again. "Looks like Paschal's waiting for you." He nodded in the medium's direction.

Our breath hung in the air. I searched his face, desperate for a crack in his composure, for something to bridge the chasm that had grown between us. His eyes were a rich brown and utterly impenetrable. I shook my head quickly. "I came to see *you*," I pressed.

He let out a quiet, disbelieving scoff and turned to face me fully. "Why's that?" he asked.

Like iron drawn to a lodestone, we had moved closer together, and I felt the familiar heat of his body. His height cast a subtle shadow over me, the faint scent of tobacco and leather threading through the chill air. My eyes were level with the scarf wrapped snugly around his neck, though my attention drifted to the line of his jaw, the set of his lips. I'd never noticed a man's mouth before. Now I could see nothing else.

"I... I..." The words I had practiced slipped away like melting snow. "It's not working," I said at last. "The seances. They're drawing crowds, to be sure, but that packed parlor feels like a prison. I'm tied up behind a curtain and can't do a thing, and I'm distressed..."

"May," he said evenly. He pressed his lips, tilting his head toward the pale sun. "You should talk to your husband about this."

"But that's just it!" I cried, my voice thin and wispy even as I willed it to be thick and strong. "Has Rudyard not said anything to you?"

He met my searching eyes with a blank expression that told me no, Rudyard still hadn't told his brother the truth, about his own preferences or my husband's. Clement was ignorant as he'd always been to Rudyard's tastes, particularly the one I feared he might have for Francis.

"Francis is *not* a husband." This time I'd found my voice. "He's a captor!"

The area around the meetinghouse was quiet, the usual clamor of town mostly faded. The stillness stretched. Clement stared at me, his face unreadable. Then he asked, "What does my brother have to do with your marriage?"

I opened my mouth but said nothing. It wasn't my place to reveal Rudyard's truths, even if they might help Clement understand.

He frowned, no warmth in his eyes, only something colder. "Mediumship," he said slowly, "is for the lowest common denominator, a show of reckless manners and impropriety. What did you expect, Miss May?"

He'd said the words he must have known would bite the deepest, words like a pack of wolves sure to chase me away. I closed my mouth and stared at him incredulously, wondering how I could have even entertained the possibility of him returning my feelings. Before he could see the hurt on my face, I turned and walked toward home, brisk as I could without slipping on ice.

Shopkeeps still hawked their baubles, novels, hot chestnuts, and hair straightening serums, but none of it inspired a drop of curiosity in me. What good was lovely straight hair without someone to admire it?

Rubbish littered the streets, competing with the yellowing slush, which soaked through my boots. The smell of horses turned my stomach. These weren't the proud, wild horses of Ireland or the gentle ponies we'd shared apples with as children. The coats on these beasts looked dull, their necks drooped, and their glazed eyes stared at nothing.

My throat burned. I felt like I was seeing a completely different city than when I'd first arrived, like there was no way to ever see it fresh again.

Clement didn't love me. He didn't even care for me. I thought I might have heard him call after me, but I knew better than to indulge in such foolish hopes. Even if he had, my pride wouldn't let me turn around, tears stinging my face worse than the wind.

And then I was caught—stopped mid-stride by a sudden embrace. For one fleeting moment, I thought it was him. Perhaps I'd tripped and fallen and he'd caught me, just like the first time. Only this time, he would know me, *truly* know me, and he would be the one to apologize.

My breath hitched as I dared to glance up.

It was Paschal.

His expression was unreadable, his arms solid around me, but the sight of him made the cold settle even deeper into my bones. My heart broke all over again, a quiet shattering I didn't have the strength to hide. He held me as I cried—just for a moment, just enough to let the tears spill before I gathered myself again. I wiped at my face hastily, the idea of meeting Paschal's gaze unbearable. My whole face was tight and sticky, and I used my sleeve as a kerchief.

"Come now," he murmured, his voice soft and soothing, like the crackle of a low fire. "I have a carriage waiting. Let me take you home."

"I don't live far," I managed to say, my voice unsteady.

He waved off my words as though they were nothing. "You can't walk in the state you're in, my dear May. Come, come, let's talk about it. Maybe I can help."

Too tired to argue, too hollow to care, I let him lead me to the carriage.

THE SEAT, though padded, was chilly to the touch. I pulled my shawl tighter around myself. Paschal whispered something to the driver. Then, with a gentle snap of his reins, the driver urged the horses forward.

The sound of the wheels rolling over frozen ground and muddy ruts quickly lulled me into a calmer state. The rhythmic clip-clop of hooves soothed me. I let my eyes fall closed, imagining, just for a few blissful moments, that I was home. My family beside me. Warm. Loved. Enough.

When I opened my eyes, the world outside the window had shifted. Gone were the shops and houses, windows glowing faintly with oil lamps. The road we traveled was narrower and bumpier, the landscape more open.

"Where are we going?" I asked suddenly, contemplating jumping out of the moving carriage.

"Relax," he laughed. "It's just up ahead. I'll get you back in no time."

I swallowed, trying to push down the unease rising in my chest. The air outside was fresh and clean, tinged with the faintest hint of woodsmoke from unseen farmhouses. It smelled of winter, crisp and grounding, but it did little to quiet the voice in my head urging caution.

The carriage slowed and came to a halt along a wooded path. Frost and damp earth mingled in the air as I stepped down, my boots crunching softly on the frozen ground. Paschal extended his hand to help me, his touch brief and cool. My gaze lingered on his fingers for a moment, tracing their slender shape and smooth texture.

Mammy had taught me there are seven types of hands, each tied to a person's character. Paschal's was a mixed hand, a mark of a jack of all trades, sharp skepticism, and a knack for negotiation driven by self-interest. I saw it in the lines of his palm and felt it in the distance of his touch, a subtle impersonal chill that matched his nature.

*Run.* The voice inside me rang clear and urgent, but my feet stayed rooted. I couldn't trust in my family's wisdom any longer, for what if the old ways of Knowing were no more than old wives' tales, as fleeting and insubstantial as smoke, as mercurial as my Sight?

Paschal swept a few bare branches aside, gesturing for me to follow him along the narrow path. I trailed behind, descending to a beautiful, lonely strip of water, its surface glazed with a delicate sheen of ice and framed by snow-laden pines. He brushed a light layer of snow from a fallen tree and sat down as if it were a bench, his gaze fixed on the creek stretching before us. When no formal invitation came, I hesitated, then settled beside him, cramped but with nowhere else to go.

After a moment, I asked, "Why are we here?"

He chuckled in that strange way he did that was all head and no heart. "Folks refer to this creek by the name of Spook Rock," he began casually. He bent over to pick up a pebble poking out from the snow. He flicked it toward the sky and caught it.

"My wife told me a legend about this place. She's an American Indian. A native to this land. Grew up with all sorts of stories about places like this. The creek was named after two natives who fell in love. But, you see, May, their love was forbidden. They were from enemy tribes. And so they ran away together and rested right here on Spook Rock."

He looked out toward the creek as though it were milk and he a cat. "As the lovers embraced, the Gods grew angry. These two had disobeyed their tribes, so the Gods created a terrible storm that swept the lovers away. They drowned right here in this very spot. Folks say their spirits haunt the water. That's why it's called Spook Rock."

"That's an awful story," I told him point-blank.

His wistful expression hardened into something more calculated. "I hear you've figured out materialization. Folks are saying you're a miracle worker." He raised a brow, his grin sliding into place like a mask. "Full-body materializations six nights a week? That's no small feat. Must be exhausting, no?"

I studied him, searching for cracks in his mask, but his face gave away nothing. He was right, though. Those nights *were* exhausting. Perhaps that was why I could no longer read any spirit energy at all. Still, I thought I could read his motive. He wanted me to admit the truth. To confess.

"You know, don't you?" I said, deciding there was no point in dancing around it. "You know it's all a fraud."

His smile widened. "Of course, I do, Miss May! No one could master spirit materialization that quickly, not even someone as talented as you."

I frowned. "So why take me here? To tell me to quit?"

"Well," he said thoughtfully, "if you're exposed, it would set the Spiritualist movement behind considerably. We'd all be accused of fraud at that point. The setback would be enormous, perhaps insurmountable. But I'm not one to tell anyone else what to do. Are you enjoying the performance, at least? The perks of a good living?"

My frown burrowed deeper into my face. "No," I said honestly, my voice heavy with fatigue. "No. I despise it." I took a deep breath, unsure why I was confiding in him of all people. But who else could I turn to? He was the only one who might understand.

"I can't read beyond the veil anymore," I admitted quietly. "When I try, it's just… nothing. I'm completely alone."

The word hit the pit of my stomach like a stone down an empty well. *Alone.* I'd always thought I felt it, but the kind of loneliness I was feeling without my gift was a colder, shivery one. Even the feel of the word in my mouth was barren and dry.

"I've been seeing spirits for as long as I can remember," I went on, my voice cracking. "And now, all of a sudden, that entire world is gone to me. It's like a door's been slammed in my face."

The thought hit me harder than I expected, and shame coiled in my stomach.

Was it me? Had I slammed the door myself? Had they simply done as I'd asked and left me alone?

Paschal raised a brow. "I can't say I'm surprised. You disrespected the spirit world, May. You must have known there'd be a price."

Anger flared in my chest, but it was brief, fizzling out before I could latch onto it. Once again, he wasn't wrong. He was only echoing what I already knew—that my estrangement from the spirit world was my own doing.

"It's God that took it from me. It was the same for the Irish people. Farmers threw away their potato crops like they were nothing, and then God came down hard on us all with famine. I was a good Catholic back home, and I took to letting everyone see me as a spiritualist. I even started to believe it myself—believe I had some control over the ability, giving orders when I should have been listening."

His gaze meandered into a thicket of trees, where nothing stirred as far as I could see. "Well, now, that's not entirely what I meant. Spiritualists can be of any faith. Why not? Belief in life after death doesn't diminish faith in Divine intervention. If anything, it strengthens it."

His words lit a spark in me. "Can I ever get my gift back then?" I asked, hating the childlike desperation in my tone.

"Maybe," he said with maddening nonchalance. "Every lock has a key, after all."

He paused, his eyes fixed on the frozen creek. The wind blew clusters of snow across like tumbleweeds. Then he turned to me, his gaze locking with mine. For a moment, I wished he'd look back at the creek.

"Now, May," he went on, "there's one more thing to discuss."

The air grew denser, and the cold wind bit with sharper teeth. Even the creek seemed to whisper, its faint gurgling beneath the ice forming a haunting melody. Bare trees leaned in like skeletal sentinels.

"We can learn a lot from those who came before us," he said, his tone almost reverent. "They had ancient knowledge, you see. They understood the way of the world intuitively. Two lovers drowned right here, in this very creek, for not obeying the rules of their tribes. For trying to mix."

Revulsion twisted in my stomach. I couldn't bear his presence a moment longer. How blind and daft I had been to step into his carriage, to think for even a moment that he might have taken me here for my benefit.

I rose abruptly, the blood pounding in my ears, and everything clicked into place. I understood now why he'd told me that story. He had seen that I was in love, and that I was there to stay. He must have seen Clement and me together—perhaps as he was stepping into his carriage—and sensed it.

But this wasn't new. He'd wanted me gone long before now. Long before he'd ever even known me. His hypocrisy was overwhelming. That at least was clear to me now.

His words twisted and tore as he continued, his voice low and measured. "The Black man is destined to extinction if we continue on in this country. All that is ancient and wise within us will be gone."

My pulse raced, and my face felt so hot I could have fainted. I wanted to scream something but didn't know what to say. Actually, I had a few things I wished to say, but I would have regretted any of them. He had taken me to this creek as a warning. *Leave. Leave and never look back. There can be no love between you and the one you desire.*

I wouldn't hear another word of it. Everyone was so quick to decide what I should do, what I could feel, who I could love. But what about what I wanted? Did that mean nothing?

I began to run, a familiar urge to flee seizing my legs.

"What about your wife?" I shouted over my shoulder, my voice rising with bitter defiance. "You said yourself she's from a native tribe!"

My foot slipped on a patch of ice, and before I could catch myself, I slid down the hill. My hands and knees struck the frozen ground hard, mud and slush soaking into my dress. Pain flared in my elbow, scraped raw against the rough bark of a tree.

When I looked up, Paschal was there, standing over me, his expression unreadable. He extended a hand, his tone wearied but firm. "May, at least let me help you back to the carriage."

"I'm fine!" I snapped, ignoring his hand as I pushed myself to my feet. "I'm fond of walking."

And walk I did. Without waiting for his response, I turned and began trudging up the hill, unsettled by the eerie quiet of the country, void of the clatter of hooves and wheels, marked by a terrible legend's ghosts that I couldn't feel.

By the time I reached Maude's, the sun had dipped below the horizon, and the world was cloaked in the soft shadows of evening. My limbs ached with exhaustion, and my breath clouded in the chilly air. Through the large bay window, I caught sight of a pine tree glowing with candlelight. The doorway smelled of mulled wine and gingerbread, making my stomach rumble loudly.

It was Christmas Eve.

I had forgotten.

# CHAPTER 27

# Map

*I* wasn't surprised to find Rudyard having breakfast with the girls downstairs on Christmas morning. He'd become a fixture at the house, as natural there as the scent of Nellie's brandy punch or the creak of Maude's rocking chair.

At first, he'd arrive with the latest editions of the spiritualist press tucked under his arm, reading aloud to us about seances in New York and London, his voice brimming with intrigue. He'd come in early—by the loose standards of French Maude's—and slip into the rhythm of the household as though he'd always belonged.

By now, no one thought twice about his presence. The girls had raised their brows the first time he appeared, but any reservations dissolved with his easy charm and wit. He was both conspirator and gentleman, passing the butter and pouring the coffee, pulling out chairs for us as we shuffled in wearing nightgowns and housecoats.

This morning, like every other, he sat at the table as though he were part of the furniture, laughing with the girls about the previous night's escapades as though he'd taken clients of his own upstairs.

"Do we *really* have to work *tonight?*" Cora moaned as she forked some bacon onto her plate. "Come on Maude, it's Christmas! We never work on Christmas."

"Christmas is supposed to be our night off," Annie added, swiping the tray of bacon from Cora with a glare that said, *save some for the rest of us.*

From my spot in the doorway, I watched as Olivia noticed me and pulled out the chair beside her. I sat down silently, nodding my good mornings, though no one paid much attention.

"Ladies," Maude began, her voice carrying an unusual note of triumph as she rose to her feet. She held a newspaper in her hand. "I have here a copy of *The New York Tribune.*"

We met her expectant look with blank stares and impassive blinks.

"So?" asked Cora, striking a match for her pipe.

"*So,*" Maude continued lyrically, "I'll read you all something you may find intriguing."

She opened the paper, cracking it like a whip, and cleared her throat. "'No one knows what to expect next when the resident spiritualist Miss May calls upon the spirit world at French Maude's House of Ill Repute. Indeed, her seances exhibit the most stubborn aspects of human nature, combined with low, reckless manners.'"

Maude flapped the paper closed, peering, once again, at the passive faces around the table. "Well? Doesn't anyone have anything to say about what I've just read?"

"The big fancy journalists in New York City don't like our manners?" Cora quipped, blowing a smoke ring and leaning back, propping her feet up on the table.

"Yes!" Maude exclaimed, her tone suddenly bright and cheerful. "The big fancy journalists in New York City are writing about *us!*"

Our attention finally peaked as we clued into Maude's meaning.

"The most widely circulated newspaper in the state is talking about us," Maude said slowly, her grin widening as comprehension dawned on her audience.

We were making a real name for ourselves.

"Christmas, for many, is the happiest day of the year," Maude continued, her voice low and deep as she leaned over the table, addressing us like a preacher at her pulpit. "Or the loneliest," she said before a dramatic pause. "When all the poor, lonely men of Hudson see our lantern glowing upon red curtains like a lighthouse on the sea of Diamond Street, where do you think they'll set their sorrowful sails? All of New York knows about our shows now! This, my dear girls, will be the night of all nights. This will be the night that we strike *gold*! Give me tonight, and you won't be sorry."

The girls exchanged groans and weary eye rolls, like gold was fine and all but a regular Christmas party with brandy punch, mince pies, and mostly closed legs would be better.

I stayed quiet, though Maude's words stirred in my mind. She might have been right. A bird had landed on my shoulder that morning when I'd opened my window—a good omen, if the old stories held true, meaning we were all going to receive money.

Then again, perhaps that was only superstition. Perhaps in America it was meaningless.

"I'll pay you triple your wages, and you can have tomorrow off," Maude said flatly.

Cheers erupted around the table, the earlier resistance vanishing in an instant. The girls clapped and whooped, calling for Nellie's Christmas punch before Maude could even finish speaking. She made a face as she folded the paper into a smaller square and handed it to Nellie.

In the midst of the uproar, Rudyard cleared his throat and stood, the motion reminding us he was still here. Six heads turned toward him.

"Now that that's settled," he said as mildly as though his presence here were perfectly normal—just a casual Quaker breakfast guest at the most notorious bawdy house in the city, "Congratulations, all of you. I have to be going."

The groans returned, but Rudyard silenced them with a raised hand and a twinkle in his eyes. "But first," he added with a smile, "presents." He hoisted his bag onto the chair he'd been sitting on and doled out each carefully chosen gift, one by one.

"First is"—he checked the narrow box for the name—"Cora."

Cora took the box with a closed-lip smile, somehow no less flashy for the lack of gleaming teeth. She opened up the ribbon playfully. "A new pipe!" she exclaimed, holding it up for us to admire. The delicate white engravings shimmered as she turned it in her fingers. "I've been wanting one like this. Thanks, Rud," she smiled sweetly, her glossy black hair falling in a perfect curtain beside her face.

"It's made of meerschaum," Rudyard said, his voice warm with pride. "Imported from Turkey."

Next, he handed Annie her gift. "Red hair dye! Aw, you shouldn't have," she teased, holding it up as though it were a bar of gold.

"Isn't your hair already red?" I asked. The others broke into laughter, and I felt my cheeks heat as I sank back into my chair.

"This carrot top?" Cora said with mock incredulity, plucking a strand of Annie's hair and holding it up for show.

Annie smirked, unbothered. "You can use some if you like, May. Makes you look more unique for the fellas. Like a rare beauty." She giggled, clearly pleased with herself.

Rudyard turned to me. "I do have something for you, too, May," he said, offering me a small box.

I opened it slowly. The inside gleamed the same shiny silver as the Hudson River. "Ribbons," I said, my voice flat.

The table quieted, all eyes turning to me.

"Well thank him, why don't you?" Cora demanded, her tone half-joking but sharp enough to make me flinch.

I cleared my throat, feeling foolish. It wasn't that I was ungrateful. It was only that ribbons are what you buy a lass when you don't know anything about her except that she *is* a lass. The other gifts had seemed more thoughtful. "Thank you," I managed, forcing myself to meet Rudyard's gaze.

He paused briefly, nodded as if to say that was good enough, and moved on.

Next was Claire, who gasped with delight at her box of chocolates.

Little Madeline squealed over her new silk gloves, so excited she nearly spilled her coffee as she yanked them on. She refused to take them off, even as she continued eating her breakfast with sticky fingers. Then he handed Maude her present—a jar of jam, handmade by his mother.

Maude smacked her lips. "I'll have Nellie whip up some delightful tarts. *Thank you*, Rudyard," she said with a forced refinement, as though she were Queen Victoria accepting a sapphire necklace from Prince Albert.

Rudyard had even thought of Nellie, gifting her a new apron with pockets, knowing her complaint that even her chatelaine couldn't hold all her handkerchiefs, linens, and matches. Her hands were seldom empty, always busy with some task or another. In that way, she reminded me of Mammy.

I tried to swallow down the memory, though the bowls of oaten meal around me did nothing to help. The girls were a flurry of chatter, eating their breakfasts and fawning over their new possessions. Yet, my focus snagged on the look Rudyard gave Olivia as he handed her the final gift. It was warm and tender, as sweet as any tart Nellie could whip up. It spoke without words: *last but never least, for my dearest friend, whom I adore.*

Olivia took her time untying the ribbon, savoring the moment, and lifted the lid to reveal a set of paints so extensive she could fill a whole museum with paintings she'd create with it. There was every color, from bright apple-red to the color of wind in warm weather, to the gentle sepia of antique lace.

She gasped, and a delicate sniffle betrayed her struggle to hold back tears. She looked up at Rudyard, and he nodded, affirming that her reaction was worth every coin spent. That *she* was worth it.

"You mentioned you were interested in painting. You should make a go of it, Liv."

"What's Olivia going to do with *those*?" Madeline asked, her voice light but laced with a teasing edge.

Olivia stiffened, pushing the set deeper into her lap.

"You're a painter now, too?" Cora laughed, leaning back with an air of mockery.

"I thought you were a poet," Claire added, her brows furrowed with genuine confusion.

"Poet, painter, what's the difference?" Cora shrugged. "She's as scarlet as the rest of us."

Olivia stood so abruptly her chair almost fell backward behind her. She caught it, then set her jaw. Without a word, she turned and walked toward the door as fast as she could without losing her dignity.

I stood immediately, my chair scraping against the floor as I bumped into Rudyard. He'd moved at the same time, both of us reacting instinctively. For a moment, we froze, staring at each other. There was something in his expression—an indecision that mirrored my own. It was as if he wanted to tell me to stay put, to let *him* be the one to comfort her. But I didn't wait for him to speak. I turned and hurried after Olivia, the faint prickle of his gaze heavy on my back. I could hear him following close behind me, his hurried footsteps matching my own.

When we stepped outside, the cold air hit us like a wall. There, just a few steps away, stood Olivia. She hadn't gone far, I felt a bit foolish to see.

She stood on the sidewalk just in front of our house, hugging herself against the cold. Her head was slightly bowed, but when she caught sight of us, she straightened and quickly swiped at her eyes.

"Liv—" Rudyard and I said at the same time, approaching her. We looked at each other again. This time I sighed and motioned for him to go ahead. He hesitated for only a moment before stepping forward, his posture softening as he approached her. It was only fair; it was his lousy gift that had caused the whole situation in the first place. I nearly pointed that out, but the words caught in my throat when Olivia turned toward him and folded into his arms.

After a moment, she glanced back at me and reached out her arm. I stepped forward, wrapping her in a hug of my own.

She chuckled, wiping stray tears from soft cheeks. "I don't know why I'm so upset!" she declared. "I *am* a scarlet lady, after all."

"You're *more* than that," Rudyard assured her. She squeezed his hands. He did have a way of grounding her, I had to admit. Had I ever told her those same words? I should have.

"Say, I have an idea! Why don't we take the day together?" Rudyard suggested, his voice buoyant with sudden inspiration. "Your show isn't until tonight. The girls won't miss you *too* much, though they're crazy not to," he added, making her laugh away the last straggling remnants of emotion.

"But what would we do?" she asked, hugging her arms tighter around herself. "It's freezing out here."

This time, I knew how to help. "Grab your cloak," I told her. "I know just the place."

"You do?" she asked, not trying to hide her disbelief in the least.

"I do." I smiled. It was still a strange feeling to smile. Especially in the cold, I could feel my cheeks harden into an unfamiliar shape, like a lump of clay in a kiln before the bowl's been fully molded. I could sense my dimples pressing in and immediately straightened my face, wondering how odd Rudyard and Olivia might think I looked when I smiled, like I wasn't even myself anymore.

"Wonderful," said Rudyard brightly. "Lead the way. We just have to make one quick stop at the meetinghouse to tell Clement I won't be walking home with him. The meeting should be ending any minute now, and he'll be waiting for me."

Some words seem to go hand in hand with certain people. For me, my word was *dream*. The words "stop your dreaming, lass" sliced through my memory like a woodcutter's ax.

For Olivia, her word, naturally, was *poetry*. She'd read it, write it, paint it, *be* it, so that no other word could stand a fighting chance against it.

Rudyard's word was *insist*. He'd always be insisting on *some*thing, and not just the grand notions like putting on a seance at a brothel or talking to a notorious sex magician, but the little things like trying the biscuits with jam instead of butter or pairing the burgundy shawl with the forest green stockings.

And now, of all things, he was insisting all three of us visit Clement before setting off on our day.

"It'll be easier this way, rather than splitting up and trying to find each other later," Rudyard said casually, oblivious to how unbearable this task was for me. Olivia agreed with him, though her face at least softened with sympathy for me.

Clement was waiting for Rudyard just outside the meetinghouse, his broad frame stoic against the backdrop of falling snow. Time seemed to stretch and warp as we approached him. His stance was as strong and solid as ever, but when he caught sight of us, his entire body stiffened.

Oblivious, Rudyard cheerfully told him our plan. "I'll meet you back at the homestead," he said, placing a hand on his brother's shoulder.

I kept my eyes firmly on my boots. But the growing silence drew my gaze upward, and I caught the long, deliberate pause that followed.

"You should come," Olivia said suddenly, her voice breaking the quiet.

"What?" I blurted, startled into speaking for the first time since leaving Maude's. I turned to Clement, expecting to find him as surprised as I was. Instead, I met his gaze, and all I saw was fire—not the warm kind that draws you in, but the kind that burns cities to ash.

"Yes, please come," Olivia insisted. She must have thought she was doing me a favor, but the dove in me felt like retreating into her cage.

"You know what?" Clement said after a beat, his voice almost too casual. "I think I *will* join you."

My breath caught. "Oh, you won't like this place," I said quickly. "It's very Irish."

His eyes narrowed, just enough to show he'd caught the implication. "Well," he replied smoothly, "something different sounds grand. Besides, it's Christmas. I can't *not* spend the day with my brother now, can I?" He posed the question to all of us, though his gaze never left mine.

I tilted my head, caught between retreat and rebellion. The heart that beat inside of me may have been a dove's, but my anger was a lion's. He had insulted me so cruelly, I wondered if I knew this man at all. And if I did not know him and had merely created a version of him that fit my heart like a lock of hair in a distressed silver locket, then my entire worldview was open to questioning, and I could already stretch apart its wispy threads like a gossamer web.

I didn't have a chance to argue, even if I could have thought of a good argument. Rudyard clapped his brother on the back with an easy grin.

"Then it's settled! It's a merry Christmas after all, isn't it?" He looked at each of us, blind to the trio of hesitant, conflicted faces before him.

# CHAPTER 28

## 𝔐𝔞𝔭

*J*led them to Francis's newest local haunt, a tavern tucked
away off the main street, where Irish folks liked to eat and
drink after a day's labors. The exterior was made of weathered wood,
painted cream. The sign hanging above the door read Governor's
Tavern in faded gold and black lettering. The windows glowed
warmly, fogged by heat, and a few sprigs of holly and ivy were pinned
above the door frame.

Rudyard pulled the door open. Immediately the fiddle's lively tune,
mixed with half-sung, half-shouted lyrics in Irish and English alike,
burst through the door. The tavern was packed with likely every Irish
person on our side of the river, wearing their work clothes or their
Sunday best.

If you could bottle up longing, then I would have been sputtering
from too large a gulp. The beat of the drums and hum of the bagpipes,

the smell of pipe tobacco, ale, and cooking meats, the sight of rough hands clapping as naturally as a sparrow chirping at dawn were like Christmas gifts to me.

"It's perfect!" Rudyard exclaimed, his eyes wide with wonder as he took in the lively scene. A few folks were dancing jigs, while others warmed themselves by the large hearth, their wet clothes steaming. A burst of laughter punctuated the air, followed by the clinking of mugs and a toast to the season.

Olivia, noticing the saltwater flooding my eyes, slipped her arm through mine and said, "Come on, May, show me how it's done?"

I chuckled softly, remembering myself and wiping away a pesky tear. We held hands, dropping into the storm like rain, and dancing in that ecstatic way that's only possible when the senses are so overcome that there's no room for words, but something far more primordial. You're laughing so hard you might fall over like a drunk, and the pounding in your chest feels like the heartbeat of the earth, not the melody of the tin whistle or the fiddle.

Out of the corner of my eye, I saw Clement swept away by a gleeful, red-cheeked lass. She pulled him onto the floor, her laughter bubbling over like a spring, and he let himself be drawn into the dance. The sight of him laughing with her almost made me leave entirely. But Olivia caught the shift in my gaze and pulled me back with her own enormous smile and a laugh to match.

It was then that I made a choice. For tonight, we wouldn't be two fancy girls in a depressed industrial town in America. We would simply be lasses—sisters—dancing around the campfire in Connemara or County Mayo, bound by nothing. The sight of Clement faded into something small, the pain of a paper cut, tiny but insistent, nagging at the edges of my mind.

And then I couldn't ignore him at all—for he was suddenly standing right in front of us.

"Ladies," he greeted courteously.

My cheeks were flushed, and my hair was a wild mess, sticking to my neck and forehead. I smoothed back a curl as another one fell directly in my eyes. I could barely breathe as I felt his closeness and wondered if he was about to ask me to dance.

He glanced at me for a moment before turning toward Olivia. "Will you dance?" he asked her.

I felt sick to my stomach, and my heart hurt.

"You want to dance with *me?*" she asked him, eyes flitting in my direction.

"Go ahead," I offered, feigning indifference, though my shaking voice was hardly a chirp, and I don't suspect I was very successful.

I slunk away to the bar, which ran the length of one wall. Behind it, barrels of ale, stout, and whiskey were stacked. I ordered an ale from the ruddy Irish barkeep, trying not to look at them dancing or feel the pulse of my wound. Just like at the meetinghouse when I first met Paschal, I was left to watch the two of them immersed in conversation without a clue as to what animated them.

Was I a fool to feel something for him still? I finished my drink too quickly, and my stomach felt warm and rotten.

The floral scent of perfume drew me up from my slump as Rudyard plopped down beside me.

"Are you well, Miss May?" he asked, a cordial grin on his face. He swayed a bit in his seat, having clearly tasted the same ale as I had.

"Just grand," I said tartly, wishing to be left alone in my ungrounded misery.

"What a day, huh?" he exclaimed. "Phew! The Irish know how to have a good time, don't they?"

This actually made me chuckle. "You did seem to be enjoying yourself with that lass who pulled you to dance. Will you not have another dance with her now?"

He leaned back against the bar, more casual than I'd ever seen him before. The drink seemed to have a fondness for him, in return.

"She's not my type, Miss May. I think you know that." His tone was flat, his lips drawn tight, like he was hiding something jagged beneath the surface.

I nodded slowly. "You are as God made you, Rudyard," I offered sincerely.

"God can be cruel," he said coolly.

I sighed, knowing he spoke the truth.

"Have I ever told you how this city was founded?" he asked

suddenly, his voice shifting, more thoughtful now, as he met my gaze for the first time in a while. He signaled the barkeep for another tankard.

I tilted my head. "I don't think so."

"Mutiny!" he exclaimed again, slamming his new drink on the bar. "You know of Henry Hudson, our founder?"

I nodded, a subtle discomfort beginning to dance in my stomach. He seemed just a wee bit too wild, too reckless, too eager to dive into darker waters.

"Picture it: he's searching for a Northwest Passage. But he finds himself in James Bay, as far south as you can go on the Hudson Strait, with no outlet leading towards Asia. Winter closes in. He and his men are trapped."

There was a strange look in Rudyard's eyes, perhaps the flicker of a memory or a ghost, though there's hardly a difference. The hearth fire snapped and crackled. New patrons, just come wet and shivering from the cold, traded places with the ones who'd finished warming themselves by the fire. They seemed far away, as if we were the only two in the room.

"Now here's the part most people don't know. Facing starvation, the men eat moss and bark and become disabled from frozen feet. They grow wild, and act cruelly toward the Mohicans who had shown them the greatest kindness. The crew ties up Hudson and locks him in the shallop along with his son and the sick, then they set the little boat adrift and head for home. *But*—and you'll never guess what happens next."

I widened my eyes expectantly, his energy revitalizing mine yet exhausting it at the same time. Eager to finish the story, he didn't give me much time to respond anyway.

"When their ship stops for supplies, a native tribe attacks. Too exhausted to sail, they let the fickle winds blow them toward Ireland." Rudyard winked, his grin keen. "They eat candles and vinegar, no longer able to stand. But alas, every last mutineer dies before the ship even arrives in Ireland."

I sat back, quite stunned. Now the silent screams I'd heard upon the ferry to Hudson echoed in my mind. I'd had a Knowing then that something heinous had occurred along that river, and now its loose knot was tied. I had my perfect silver-ribbon Knowing yet felt little satisfaction for it.

My thoughts drifted toward home. I closed my eyes, and I was there, starving, freezing, the banshee's screech ringing in my ears. At last, opening my eyes, I said the only thing I could think to say that might make some sense to him.

"And those of modern, scientific minds balk at how people can place all their stock in God's will."

Rudyard laughed. "Yes!" he agreed. "It's true!" He might have noticed my eyes drift toward Clement, Olivia in his arms. "I'll tell you, May, there's no one in the world who cares like my brother. I know he can be a bit rough around the edges, but his heart shines like a full moon. Whoever he chooses one day, she'll be a lucky woman. Perhaps we're looking at her now." He gestured toward Olivia.

"Is that so?" I asked bitterly.

"No one better in the world than my brother Clement!" he assured me. "I was always mocked for being the sensitive one, the boy who would get lost in the heather and make up songs about trees, sparrows, and girls in white dresses. My classmates decided I was strange and different just about the same time they decided being the same was everything. I knew what they'd say behind my back, that God had made a mistake with me."

He swallowed before lowering his voice. He was speaking so openly, luxuriously, even. The most I'd ever heard him say was about spirit materialization. Had I ever had a conversation with him that hadn't to do with work? And I wondered still: the drink relaxed him for certain, but was it indeed fond of him?

"Then I tried to kiss a boy in the schoolyard," he continued, his tone shifting with a quiet pain. "That's when the teasing turned into an all-out panic, a refusal to be near me, like I'd caught scarlet fever. I basically spent my childhood alone until Clement came into the picture. His name at the time was Samuel, of course, and he was heartsick for his mother, whom he'd left behind."

He smiled then. It was a genuine smile, conveying love. I could see how much he cared for Clement, but I couldn't help wondering if he was sharing more about his brother's past than he ought to.

"Let me take that ale," I offered.

He swiped his drink away from me, unaware of the drops that spilled onto the sawdust covering the floor.

"I believed God brought him to our family," Rudyard announced. "My parents agreed. We'd all lost my brother a few years earlier, as you know. That's why our parents decided to legally adopt him."

The little dance of foreboding in my belly sped up to a jig. It was none of my business, and clearly Rudyard was speaking too freely under the influence of drink. And yet... my curiosity got the better of me.

"And change his name to Clement?" I asked, my voice careful, searching for pieces to fit together.

He leaned back, savoring another sip of his ale, before exhaling deeply, as though waking from a long, cold slumber. "Ah," he said, his tone taking on a mysterious lilt, "Now that's a story for another time."

I nodded, a part of me relieved that Rudyard had some meager sense of restraint, some hold on the secrets he might still keep. He knew everything there was to know about his brother, the information that had once saved his life. And yet I frowned, for could that information not also destroy it?

I watched Clement move stiffly but gracefully about the room, my best friend's hand in his. There was still so much to learn about him, and I wanted to learn it, if he'd only give me the chance. Perhaps we'd both judged each other too harshly. Perhaps a part of him was coming to the same realization. Why else would he have decided to spend the day with us?

# CHAPTER 29

# Olivia

Olivia stiffened at Clement's touch. She didn't know where to look. She didn't want to know the calluses in his hands or the spiced-earth scent of his white, uncollared shirt.

His movements were too controlling, and she wished women could occasionally take the lead. Stepping on his foot gave her a small sense of satisfaction.

"Ow!" he exclaimed.

She shrugged innocently and yelled over the music, "I've never done this dance before!" Yelling helped her hide her satisfaction. Not that she really cared if he sensed it.

The song ended and a new one began, slower and quieter.

Again, she felt tension in her muscles as Clement's arms tightened around her, holding her in time with the rhythm. She spotted

Rudyard, tankard of ale sloshing mercilessly in one hand as he chatted with May, whose head was slumped over her drink.

She exhaled sharply, then shifted her gaze up to Clement. His face was passive, unreadable. It annoyed her even more.

"Why did you do that?" she asked him.

"Do what?" he countered innocently.

Olivia rolled her eyes. "Ask me to dance and not her?"

He raised his eyebrows, clearly taken aback by her bluntness. She didn't flinch. Instead, she stared directly into his eyes, daring him to meet her challenge.

Maybe it was this glimpse into May's world. The songs seemed to tell stories almost eye to eye, mind to mind, heart to heart. And there was a camaraderie and a joy between the people in that tavern that she'd never witnessed before, not even in a book. Or maybe it was even just how infuriating this man could be, playing games with her friend who had the most tender, giving heart in the world. Whatever the reason, she didn't feel afraid of challenging anyone who needed a challenge. Actually, she felt pretty proud of herself for doing it.

"I actually…" He laughed nervously. Then he met her eyes and seemed to let something tight within him loosen a bit. "I wanted to ask you something."

She blinked. "Then ask," she said, unused to feeling taken aback herself.

He twirled her through the crowd of dancers, the motion dizzying, but it was hard to focus on the steps when her mind was tangled up in what he might ask.

"What *was* that before?" he finally asked. He looked at her intently.

Her brow furrowed in question. She looked back at May, her posture utterly defeated. Olivia didn't care about challenging Clement anymore. She only wanted to sit beside her friend and cheer her up.

"You wanted me to come today? You could've easily sided with May and told me I wouldn't like it here."

Olivia shrugged a shoulder, her movements now flowing with the ease of someone who'd danced this dance before. "You're Rud's brother. Why wouldn't I want you to come?" Her words carried a bite beneath their sweetness, a perfect shield against anything he might throw her way. She preferred it that way.

And yet, the music swayed and gripped relentlessly, dragging her heart to her throat and her mind to a place more savage than even poetry had ever dared take her. It was unbound, uncovered, unwritten. And somehow, it seemed to grant special permission to speak plainly. It seemed to coax her to set down her shield.

"You didn't need much convincing, did you?" she added. Her voice was softer now, more like a revelation.

Clement's grin was enough to ease her more than she cared to admit.

She sighed, wanting to let the tension slip from her shoulders and wanting to bear the weight of the evening at the same time.

"I wanted you to come for her," she said firmly, meeting his gaze head-on. "For my friend." Her lids felt heavy. "Though I heard what you said, Clement Stoker, and I only hope you agreed to this because you have every intention of making it up to her."

She watched him closely, her eyes steady. "What did you call her again? The lowest common denominator?" She raised a brow. "A mathematics insult? Really?"

Clement's laugh was a bit too cocky. She gave him the same look she always gave cocky men. It was a gaze she'd perfected to let them know she wouldn't take one bite of what they were serving.

"I'm sorry," he said, his voice dripping with mockery, "but aren't *you* the one who told me to stay away?"

Olivia scoffed. She wasn't the type to admit her mistakes easily— not when they came wrapped in such smug little jabs. She might have, just then, if only he'd kept his mouth shut. But of course, this man never knew when to stop.

"You know," he said, leaning in slightly, "for someone who cares so much about *status*"—he said the word as though it were trivial, and Olivia gave him another signature stare—"what about your own? Shouldn't you be doing more to prove to everyone else what you're capable of? You were born into freedom, and it seems your ignorance is not bliss. As far as I'm concerned, you're wasting your life, your precious freedom, at *French Maude's.*"

He nearly laughed the name of the establishment, as though it were the very height of indecency and ridiculousness. But she didn't flinch. She'd been called worse. She could take it.

"Rudyard told me you're an artist," he continued, his eyebrows raised in that way that made her want to wipe the arrogance right off his face. "Why not make something of yourself? At least art is not... well..."

"Whoring?" she finished the thought for him.

He shrugged his agreement.

She let out a short, humorless laugh. Then, stepping back, she straightened her posture, arms crossing as she shook her head, searching for the right words—the words that would make him understand just how little he understood her, and how much he needed to shut up.

"I *should* be doing whatever I damn well please, and whatever that *is*, is none of your business. I have *everything* stacked against me. Not just the color of my skin, but as a woman, I have to work not only twice as hard, like you, but three times as hard. And you—" she huffed —"how dare you come up to me and tell me what I'm doing wrong? You have *no* idea—"

She cut herself off, pressing her lips together against the serpent rising in her throat.

Clement stared at her, his expression unreadable at first. Then something flickered, a tightening at the corners of his mouth, a shift in his stance. Was it understanding? Resentment? She couldn't tell, and she was too tired to care.

Her heart pounded as her thoughts drifted to the broken pieces of her own history. She had watched her first love marry someone else. She'd spent seven years pushing down her dreams like a faulty jack-in-the-box. Then May had led her into a darkened room where finally, she was the one in the white dress. May had reminded her that creativity feels like a tryst with God, and maybe—just maybe—there was more to life than what she'd settled for.

Olivia knew, better than most, how love could blind you.

And this man? This man in front of her, who had clearly caught May's eye? He did not deserve it.

Clement exhaled, looking away for a moment before meeting her gaze again. "I—Maybe I don't."

That admission—unexpected, disarming—unnerved her more than an argument would have.

"You don't!" she said with quiet fury, doubling down. "You think May's just some fragile girl who doesn't know her own worth, but you're wrong. She's stronger than you'll ever understand. You don't see the kind of pain she carries."

She paused, taking a steadying breath, her gaze unwavering. "May has a good heart. She's been nothing but kind to me, and she's never asked for anything in return. But Francis..." She couldn't stop the disgust from creeping into her voice. "Francis keeps her trapped, keeps her small. He'd rather break her than let her live. And you—you think your pity or your 'help' will save her? Fix her? She doesn't need fixing. She needs respect. She needs—" Olivia swallowed. "She needs love. And she deserves love."

His breath came out slow and measured. "I didn't mean to insult her," he admitted. "I thought—" He stopped, exhaling sharply. "I don't know what I thought."

She pressed him with her gaze.

"You're right," he answered, the words quieter this time. "I didn't see her clearly. Maybe... maybe I still don't. I'm... You're right about all of it. What I said about you..." His gaze softened, and his lips remained parted, as though there was more he wished to say—though he didn't seem to know if he should say it.

Should she tell May?

Maybe. Maybe at the very edge of night, that temporal hinterland where whatever has passed dissolves into nothing, when words can almost be unsaid, blamed on fairy dust and flat ale and the moon.

The music swirled around her, wild and untamed, pulling at her heart. She felt that same wildness deep within herself, and now that she had given in to it, softened and opened by its rhythm, there was no going back.

If she told May, what would she even say?

Thankfully, she didn't have to decide.

Rudyard swooped in to save her.

# CHAPTER 30

## May

Rudyard's leg was bouncing up and down beside me, and I could tell he, too, sensed the rising tension between our companions. Their voices were growing louder, cutting through the quiet beauty of one of my favorite songs, *The Wind that Shakes the Barley.*

Like a knight springing to the defense of a damsel, Rudyard was suddenly beside them, stealing Olivia away for a dance just as the music picked up again. They spun away together, a prince and princess in their own dark fairytale, lost in their world, leaving me behind.

I reached for his tankard and swallowed the last few drops. I glanced around, wondering where Clement might have gone next, surely to dance with another lass.

But I was wrong.

Within moments, he was right there in front of me, his chest level with my eyes, his presence blocking out everything else.

"Will you dance?"

At least I thought that was what he said, though I could barely hear a word. He was shouting over the music, which seemed to have grown even louder as the crowd had thickened.

"What?" I shouted back. "I can't hear you!"

Clement smiled. For a moment I was lost in it, smiling back. Then I remembered he'd just asked Olivia to dance. I was tired of not knowing where I stood with him. I frowned and set down the tankard on the bar, crossing my arms defensively.

"Dance with me!" he shouted again, just as the music stopped.

"Aye, give the poor lad a dance!" one of the workers beside us called out.

"Go on now, give him a twirl!" another added.

I looked at Clement and couldn't help laughing.

His eyes were bright as he extended an arm toward me. "Please?"

I didn't have much time to think. The music picked up again, and next thing I knew, I was in his arms, twirling about the room, swept up by the winds of bliss in our own country of two.

It was the feeling of caramel sun in your eyes, so delicate that your lashes flutter like butterfly wings. It was a set of china, all your own, and the tea party where you serve sweet tea to your closest friends. It was love, I could almost admit it, and so it was God, a moment with God.

Of course, this love might very well have been one sided, but for that moment, I allowed myself to pretend that it wasn't.

His hand pressed against my hip, pulling me closer. His mouth moved toward my ear, lingering just a moment before he spoke. The warmth of his breath against my skin made my pulse quicken. I could smell the wool of his coat, the spice of his soap. I wanted to lean in closer, to lose myself in him.

But when you've been hurt before, you grow cautious. You grow fearful. It's always when happiness is so close you can almost taste it, when it feels just within reach, that you realize you're not ready to risk another injury.

He started to say something, but I pulled away, moving into a solo step I knew from home. He watched me, awe and amusement curling his lips. Around us, the patrons began to clap and stamp their feet.

He pulled me back toward him, our hips aligning once more, and for a brief, electric moment, I wondered—heart thundering in my throat—if he might catch me. If he might protect me from the inevitable fall I had felt coming for some time now.

"You're a miracle," I thought I heard him say, his voice low but insistent.

"What?" I asked. He might have said what I desperately wanted to hear, yet I hadn't dropped my defenses yet. Like Scáthach the warrior queen, I stood ready to protect myself, to keep out hope—that danger-ous, sticky feeling that never leads anywhere holy.

And I was still angry. Furious, even. How could he call me *a show of reckless manners and impropriety* one moment, and then turn around and call me a miracle the next?

His shoulder tensed beneath my palm.

"What you do... it's a miracle!"

Now it seemed he had to shout even louder for me to hear him. The band sped up. They were playing *Irish Washerwoman*, which made my heart sore for home, thinking of scrubbing all our clothes clean beside Mammy, wondering how many of my siblings' clothes she still had left to wash. I'd finished the flat ale much too quickly, and I was dizzy.

"Oh, is it?" I asked him, no longer dancing, no longer touching him.

He stared at me, wide-eyed, his mouth hanging open, as if my response had thrown him off balance. He hadn't expected me to stand my ground, to be the one to hold the line. In that moment, even I was surprised by my strength.

But I wouldn't have it. I wouldn't let him push me any which way as the wind might. I wouldn't let him call me harsh names one minute, and then something unspeakably beautiful the next, just because it suited him.

My people moved to a rhythm far older, far wiser, than a man's whims. It was a beat carved into the bones of the earth, a pulse that didn't bend or sway with the fleeting moods of anyone who happened to be standing in front of me.

Not even him.

# CHAPTER 31

# Rudyard

"You couldn't have moved out of Clement's arms and into mine any faster," Rudyard quipped. He gave Olivia a knowing look. "My brother's a good man, you know." And, he mused, with Olivia as his sister-in-law, they'd never have to be apart. But he could wait to push the matter.

"Sure," she replied, clearly dismissing the conversation. "Now come on, let's show these Irish folks how to dance."

They quickly became the center of attention. Neither of them knew the proper steps to the lively tune, but it didn't matter—they made up their own, fueled by their love of theatrics. As Rudyard lifted, dipped, and swung Olivia through the crowd, yelps and whistles erupted around them. For the first time in his life, Rudyard felt truly seen, admired. He suspected it was mostly thanks to Olivia, who could turn even the humblest moments into something grand.

When they finally pulled away from the dance floor, breathless and glowing with sweat, Olivia steered them toward the bar. "Two of your flattest ales!" she called out, causing the two of them to burst into laughter.

Rudyard wiped his forehead with the back of his hand, still grinning.

"You're so different from your brother, you know that?" she said suddenly, studying him.

He shrugged, feeling the urge to stick up for Clement. "Clem's really not a bad man. Actually," he said, smoothing a hand across his oiled hair, "he's the best man I know."

"Could have fooled me," Olivia replied, a sly grin tugging at the corners of her mouth. "I would have thought I'm talking to the best man right now."

She glanced at him sideways, her smile teasing but sincere.

Rudyard couldn't help but smile back, though her words sent a quiet shiver through him. No one had ever looked at him like this, like he mattered. No one had ever thought much of him at all. Now here he was, sharing a drink with a true friend, someone who thought the world of him.

The thought sobered him. His grin faded.

"What's the matter?" Olivia asked.

He shook his head, the new fragrance he'd treated himself to at the apothecary emanating from his hair. He hesitated, his fingers tapping against the side of his tankard. "Can I tell you something?" he asked finally.

She grew serious in an instant, her playful demeanor retreating. "Of course."

He looked into her eyes and knew she meant it. They were of one mind. From the moment he'd met her, he had recognized something in her—a fire he lacked but longed to stoke in himself. And in her eyes, he saw the same recognition, as if she, too, had found in him some quiet certainty she wished to claim as her own.

Somehow, the realization felt fresh again today.

He swallowed. "I wonder sometimes if I'm still on the right path, if I'm heeding May's advice from the other side or... chasing a fantasy."

"What do you mean?" Olivia asked, her eyes steady on him as she placed a hand on his knee. Her touch was grounding, but whether it made him more or less certain about what he was about to reveal, he couldn't say.

He chuckled softly, the sound brittle and almost apologetic. Then, raising his eyebrows in a wry sort of admission, he said, "I feel like a fraud, Liv. May—my late grandmother—*whoever*, told me to be myself. And I am. Well, I'm trying to. But something about it doesn't feel right. I'm… I'm ashamed, Liv. The love I have to give is shameful."

He glanced at her, gauging her reaction, but Olivia's expression didn't waver.

"My whole life I've drifted from passion to passion, or"—he laughed sadly—"interest to interest, all in search of something that would make others proud and wouldn't make me feel so phony. Something I could do as I grew older, when everyone else fell in love and moved on, and I would be left behind."

Olivia chewed on a nail. She seemed to be taking it all in. She hadn't run off yet, in any case. He took another slug of his ale, shook off the taste, and continued.

"I thought with spiritualism, perhaps I was finally on to something. The Spiritualist circles are filled with all kinds of people that might accept me—people that are different, themselves. But they're good, honest people who believe in change and purpose.

"I thought, if I could just find a way in, then maybe, just maybe, there could be a place for me among those good people, and I could be good, too. I could escape the shame that has followed me like a midday shadow since"—he laughed again, giving up his secret completely—"Andrew Hauffield's rejection outside the schoolhouse."

The confession hung in the air, raw and unadorned. For a moment, Rudyard wondered if he'd gone too far.

But then Olivia laughed—a loud, rich laugh that made his chest loosen. She swung her arms around his neck and planted a large, painted kiss on his cheek. Her hands laced behind his neck, and she looked him straight in the eye.

"Let me tell you something, honey. This world has no room for differences, so why even try to fit the mold? Be whoever you want. Never accept what they tell you. Don't just try. *Do*."

He'd been carrying his guilt like a yoke, convinced it was his alone to bear. But here she was, bold and unapologetic, and suddenly he wasn't so sure.

Fraud, Olivia seemed to say, wasn't just about sin or survival. It was a language everyone spoke—some louder than others.

And Olivia, with her jet-black curls, painted freckles, and silk dresses that shimmered like ripples on the Hudson, wore her contradictions like a crown. She knew what it meant to exist in defiance of the world's expectations.

He'd always thought of himself as weak, but Olivia made him wonder: was he just human? And what do all humans want most of all? Love. Acceptance. Belonging.

No, it wasn't love with Francis, but it was as close as he'd ever come.

It was rushing blood and excitement; it was a door cracked open. It was two people both wanting to be their own men in a world that would scarcely allow it. And it felt like a sign—the most profound sign imaginable—when Francis barged through the tavern door.

His heart surged, but he quickly glanced around the room. First to May, who was nowhere to be found, and then to Clement—also gone. When his search came up empty, he turned back to Olivia.

He returned her kiss on the cheek and walked toward Francis, his steps faltering only slightly as he approached.

Francis—handsome, clever, and dangerous in the way only someone who keeps their heart locked away can be. An insidious combination for a man like Rudyard, whose greatest longing was to feel seen, to feel *anything* at all without fear.

It wasn't love, but for now, it was enough.

"Francis!" Rudyard breathed. His chest was tight with the rush of seeing him, and he stood ready to throw his arms around him.

"Do my eyes deceive me, or did I just see my wife and your brother in here together?" Francis's voice was low, cutting cleanly through the blaring band. Was it a question or an accusation?

"What?" Rudyard asked, his pulse stuttering. In his mind he'd seen a warm hug, a passionate kiss, a stroll down the alleyway together... "No. Well, they were both here, yes, but not together, exactly."

Francis turned toward the door, jaw tight, eyes narrowed. "He's followed her out," he muttered. His body seemed poised to act.

"What?" Rudyard repeated blankly. He hated how foolish he always seemed to sound around Francis. He let out a weak laugh. "Oh! You think they're *together*. No, quite the opposite I'm afraid. They can hardly be in the same room. They think I haven't noticed, but—"

Rudyard stopped short as he noticed Francis's hands, fists clenched so tight his knuckles turned white. After a long moment, the crimson began to fade from Francis's face and neck.

"Oh," Francis finally said, relaxing a fraction. He ran a hand through his hair, chuckling lightly. "Well then, phew!" He cocked his head to the side, flashing an easy smile. "Buy me a drink?"

He didn't entirely like Francis. The man smelled of tobacco and cheap gin; he ate too much and too loudly; he was rude and even mean to Maude's customers and looked at Clement with a sideways glance. But when the Irishman had begun to talk to Rudyard in hushed tones and invite him to quiet corners in the black of night, the shadows had disappeared. Rudyard felt alive. He even felt passion, which had previously been an amorphous concept, a storybook trope, a thing he wasn't capable of.

He'd talk to Francis about who he was versus who he was

supposed to be, about farm life and Hudson's history, about Quakers and the country's great divide. Mostly, though, he talked about Clement, his dearest friend and brother, and how fortunate he was to have met him that scorching summer day when he'd arrived on the Underground Railroad and made Rudyard feel less alone.

They sat beside each other at the bar. "You looked like you were about to kiss me back there," Francis said, keeping his eyes fixed on his drink. "Best remember where you are, my lad."

Rudyard nodded, grateful for the poor lighting that hid his blush. In the darkness, nothing was amiss. He could crave the man's strong grip and rough hands and winter gaze. He could bite his tongue and swallow his words.

He had to.

If he didn't, Francis would walk away without a backward glance, leaving Rudyard in the same crushing loneliness he always feared.

Perhaps he could have loved Francis, in another life. Yet he knew that in this one, real love was a mystery. He didn't have a clue how deeply love could change a person, or how long it took to move on from it. All he knew was that love, especially with this particular man, would be a difficult feat.

# CHAPTER 32

## Map

It took me a moment to realize that the familiar figure that had walked into the tavern was Francis. The room was so dark, I couldn't be certain, and I hadn't expected to see him there at that time of day. Surely, he'd still be feeling the drink from the night before.

But I felt my spine turn to ice, and, as I knew better than most, there's hardly a smarter messenger than the body. Even in the shadows of a hearth fire, Francis loomed white and cold, like an *abhartach*, that blood-drinking creature whispered of in my childhood. Americans would call him a vampire, but that word lacked the chill of the old tales.

Without thinking, I bolted, my skirts rustling like startled birds. If Francis saw me here with Clement, it would mean trouble. He'd warned me to stay away from those who were "different," and here I was, drawn to Clement as if the very stars had tied strings between us.

Clement's voice followed me, muffled and distant, like a sound trapped in a dream.

I didn't stop. I didn't look back.

Outside, fresh snow blanketed the cobblestone, reflecting the copper glow of the oil lamps that lined the street. It was biting cold after the cramped warmth of the tavern.

"May!" This time it was Olivia. I could feel the wind of her skirts as she pushed past passersby to reach me. "May! Stop! Where are you going?"

Francis—if it had been him, I'd seen at all—was on the other side of the tavern door. All I wanted was to get as far from him as possible.

"I have to get back to Maude's," I murmured. Moments ago, I'd felt alive and infinite. Now I felt small and weak beneath the starless sky. "The show... I have to prepare."

Olivia's knowing gaze pinned me in place. "Should I come with you?"

"No, no. Stay," I insisted, the words tumbling out too quickly. "You still have time. I'll see you back home."

Home. The word felt empty and confusing. I didn't know where home was, and maybe I'd never known what the word meant at all.

I could feel her gaze linger for one more moment on the back of my head as my steps quickened, bringing a brief, welcome relief. I cradled my thoughts like a newborn, trying to make sense of them all. The icy snow numbed my feet, its sting strangely grounding amidst the surrounding silence.

But the silence didn't last long.

My heart suddenly lurched. I could feel something about to change, not with my "gift," as I'd begun to think of it now that it was gone, but with my skin. Every hair stood up along my arms, and I was chillier than ever. I steadied myself and took a deep breath in before watching a plume of air drift toward the heavens.

Even without any magic left in me, I could feel there was a magic to the world, a vase of purple gloaming, waiting to spill out across the horizon before me. I knew he was close because I knew *him*.

Maybe that's what love is, when you know somebody so completely that you can always feel when they're around, and that feeling is like when you look up toward the sky at the most heart-wrenching time of day.

I turned around, and there he was. My beautiful gloaming, my heart's compass.

He stood hunched against the cold, uncharacteristically shy, his broad shoulders shrinking into his coat as if he thought himself unworthy of the space he occupied.

He'd followed me. That had to mean something, didn't it?

Clement wasn't a self-proclaimed magician like Paschal, but fight the feeling as I tried, he was all the magic I sought in the world.

His own breath clung in the frigid air between us. He hugged his arms against the cold and smiled, timid and tender.

"I came to apologize." His words were the sweetness I'd been starved of, the home I'd been searching for. "The way I spoke to you earlier, outside the meetinghouse, was impolite."

His chuckle was soft and nervous. Unarmed. Open. He took two careful steps closer.

Tenderness and anger swirled in my breast. I wanted to see him smile, to feel him close, but first, I needed him to understand. I raised my eyebrows, taking a step forward myself.

"Impolite?" I asked. How could he think I gave a damn about manners? I cared for his thoughts and his feelings about me. Nothing else.

He swallowed hard. For a man who had no trouble drawing women toward him, he seemed at a loss. "I... I don't know. I don't know how to talk to you, May."

I scoffed. "That much is true."

He laughed, the sound soft and unguarded, and something in me began to melt. His grin widened, as though he'd just thought of something clever, something he knew I couldn't resist.

"That music back there"—he shoved his hands into his coat pockets—"well I heard it and I thought... well, I thought it sounded nice. And then I thought, maybe I'm for the Irish after all."

He bit his lip slightly, still grinning. My cheeks flamed, a rush of heat against the winter cold. I didn't need a mirror to know they'd turned the same blood red as the freckles on the bridge of my nose, and I imagined my nose like the Milky Way, framed by two blood moons.

I sighed, as though I was not just shedding breath but an extra layer of skin as well. I softened to him, to the moment, to the stars and moons. "So you think my readings are a miracle?" I asked indulgently.

"I do," he admitted, his voice low and reverent, "but that's not what I said. Not what I meant to say, anyway."

I stood breathless as all the planets spiraled around me, waiting to reconfigure based on his next words. The world might never be the same.

"I wanted to tell you that *you're* a miracle, May."

I realized only in that moment how close we stood to one another. I might have touched his cheek with only the smallest stretch of an arm. My tongue pressed against my teeth, holding back words that might shatter the most perfectly fragile moment.

He sighed as he carefully set his hands on my arms. Even through the heavy black wool of my cloak, his touch carried warmth. When I didn't pull away, he slipped his hands beneath the cloak's opening, resting them lightly on my elbows. The heat of him burned through the thinner fabric of my dress, sinking into me, stealing my breath. I glanced down at his hands, then back up at him. My resolve crumbled.

"You're a miracle," he repeated. "Not just because of your talent, but because you possess courage to do what you do, and you're thoughtful and strong and beautiful, and my thoughts keep circling back to you since we met, and I've never regretted anything more in my life than what I said to you outside the meetinghouse, and—"

I couldn't help myself.

His words. His sincerity. The urge to close the distance between us was more powerful than anything I'd felt when a spirit pressed into me, demanding to be heard. It consumed me, left me weightless, as if I were slipping between worlds. The sky was darkening to the sapphire shade in which I could once communicate with the greatest ease. I needed to feel that ease again. Just for a moment. Just for one perfect moment.

I stood on my tiptoes, the world narrowing, and pressed my lips to his.

His mouth wasn't cold or still. This kiss was as far from my first, my only other, as the sun is from the moon. It was warm and delicious —the kind that fills a hunger better than buttered bannocks. It was the wild splatter of a tallow candle and the heady scent of jasmine. It was the world reconfiguring in a perfect dance of love, a gateway into the seventh sphere.

It was pure magic. Pure lovely.

When I pulled back, I felt it—an ache in my chest that wasn't my own. I stared into his eyes and saw his sorrow, his anguish, like someone was tearing something vital from him. His smile was faint and wistful, his lips parted slightly, as though he had scrolls of poetry on the tip of his tongue, rolled up tightly, so that he couldn't recite a word.

I should have waited. Perhaps he would have spoken if I'd given him the chance. But again, I couldn't help myself.

I tilted my head up and kissed him once more, stronger this time. My hands found his jawline, and I rose to my toes to meet him fully. It felt as though I'd been bewitched, or intoxicated.

*Jasmine, jasmine, jasmine.*

"May," he breathed against my lips, his voice raw with longing. Then, softer, almost breaking, "I wish you weren't married."

I shook my head, a thousand wishes of my own piling on top of his. How could I make him understand?

"But I'm not," I whispered fiercely. "Only by the word of a priest. Not in any other way."

His expression darkened with hesitation, his brows furrowing. "Do you not..." He cleared his throat. "Well, I'll just come out with it. Do you not share a bed with him?"

The question made me chuckle, though his tortured gaze quickly quieted me. "I sleep beside him like a stranger. And that's only on the nights he returns. He's never touched me."

We were only down the block from Maude's. I could see the line beginning to form in front—drunken men drawn to spirits in silk robes like flies to honey. Whether they believed the women to be made of flesh and blood or ectoplasm, it didn't matter. Nobody cared about that sort of truth at French Maude's House of Ill Repute. It was a different truth they were after—the truth of a man's desire, of loneliness, of a circle in which pain can be forgotten and fantasy is king.

"Never?" he pressed.

I shook my head, starry-eyed. "Clement," I began, hesitantly. "Do you think you could ever care for a ghost?"

He laughed. "Only if you could, too."

I chuckled, but my heart felt like it might burst. My eyes flicked nervously toward the line, the men whispering and pointing as they noticed us standing so close. "I have to go," I told him. "Come back after the show. I have to tell you something."

He nodded reluctantly, his expression unsure, and I forced myself to turn away.

It was hard not to kiss him again.

I slipped in through the back door of Maude's, needing the heat of his hands on my elbows, already missing him, dreaming of a secret garden all our own. I was trembling so fiercely I wasn't certain I could sit still behind the curtain of the darkened room and keep my binding intact.

But I did sit, and I thought of the smooth feel of his mouth and the earthy smell of his hair, of a farmhouse with tall windows and light dripping through thick glass like honeycomb, of sparse but elegant decorations and a room for each of my siblings.

A cellar filled to the brim with all the food their wee tummies could hold, organized in sweet glass jars, and a big open kitchen and adjoining scullery, with black drawers like in a French castle, filled with all kinds of cooking tools and copper pots and pans and cast iron magic cauldrons.

I'd sort pretty little plates with floral trim and fill vases with garden roses the colors of blush and seashell. Then I'd gather more roses to tie with twine and hang to dry, so that each season I'd keep my memories safe in dried petals, heart-throbbingly beautiful in darker hues.

I dreamed so deeply in that shadowless place behind the curtain, that when Olivia opened it again, I was in tears, and all the sitters believed I was overcome from the spirits that chose to visit, and all the girls thought I was putting on an extra-special performance that night, holiday tip jar in mind.

The applause woke me from my reverie, but not from my dream. It was already sealed in my heart like wax melt on an envelope. That was the first time I'd allowed my heart to be soft without fear of it being trampled. Something about Clement made it feel safe. Made me feel like I could be me always and forever, no matter what.

*Jasmine, jasmine, jasmine.*

As the men began to choose their companions for the next portion of the night, shuffling off with hungry eyes and flushed faces, Olivia slinked over to me in a hurry, a single crease between her eyes.

"You have to get out of here for the night." She glanced over her shoulder. "You have to leave. *Now.* There's—"

It was too late. I could see what she was trying to tell me. Dr. Edmonds stood, hunched and dodgy-eyed, at the other end of the room. I had been so dazed in my binding, I hadn't noticed him sitting in the audience, undoubtedly watching our every move with clinical precision.

Seeing the color drained from my face, Olivia hissed her confirmation. "I noticed him just before the performance."

I wondered why the doctor would care so much about my case that he would leave his family on Christmas evening. Unless he had no family and the two of us had more in common than I'd thought.

The first time he'd come to see me, a spirit had knocked on the door of my mind—a woman, faint but persistent. I'd bolted the door against her then, unwilling to let her in.

Now, as I looked at the doctor, I saw only what everyone else did: a hunched, slight figure, his shoulders weighed down by something heavier than his neatly pressed coat.

He started toward me, and I forced myself to shake off the shock of seeing him. He'd already been watching me, that much was clear.

Best to get this over with quickly, to say whatever it was he needed to hear so I could find Clement.

He'd be waiting. What if I took too long, and he thought I was avoiding him, that I didn't care, and he went home? We'd miss one another completely. Olivia had read to me from *Romeo and Juliet*; I knew how tragically a missed moment could end.

"Mrs. McMurry, good evening," the doctor said, his tone stiff and formal, as though we were standing in his office and not in a room full of half-dressed lasses.

"Hello," I said, as if I'd just bitten into a rancid nut. My mouth tasted sour, and I had trouble standing still, my insides twisting into something slick and slimy like a snail. My eyes darted to Olivia, who tossed me a wistful look that said *good luck*. She had her own matters to take care of, which left me alone with the doctor.

He cleared his throat. "I wonder, Mrs. McMurry, if now that your duties are finished for the evening, we might talk for a few minutes in private?"

"Er, sure," I replied, my heart thumping. I cast a quick glance over his shoulder toward the window, hoping to catch sight of Clement.

"Is something the matter?" he asked pointedly, catching my drifting gaze.

"No," I said, more firmly this time, forcing my attention back to him. "Only, my name is May. Please call me May. Miss May, if you like."

"Very well," he replied, his tone clipped.

I gestured for him to follow and led the way into the kitchen. The wooden table stood unadorned and unoccupied, save for a vase of mistletoe and evergreen—one of Nellie's arrangements. Even in the dead of winter, she found ways to bring beauty into our brothel. Still the room felt cold, the air heavy and lifeless without even a pot of stew bubbling on the range or a loaf of bread baking in the oven.

"It was quite a performance," Dr. Edmonds said, settling himself into a chair. He crossed his legs with practiced ease, though his stiff posture betrayed his discomfort.

I stared at him calmly. "Aye, sir."

It was a tricky situation, and I was at a loss for how to move it along most smoothly. Admit that the show was just that—a performance, child's play with shadows and silk—and I'd be admitting to fraud and putting all the girls at risk. Coppers turned a blind eye to the inevitable brawls and raucousness that came from a night at French Maude's, for the bribe money was reliable income. And besides, they themselves weren't so righteous as to turn down the other favors that Cora, Claire, and Annie would offer.

But fraud? Fraud was something else altogether, and I had no illusions that the lawmen would be so forgiving.

On the other hand, claiming my truth, that I could—once could—speak to the dead, felt even riskier. Then I would be the one locked up, for certain.

I resolved to tread lightly, saying as little as I could while staying just vague enough to keep him from pressing too hard.

Dr. Edmonds watched me expectantly, waiting for more. When I offered nothing, he cleared his throat and pressed on. "Do you believe, Miss May, that the performances you ladies are putting on here are altogether moral?"

"Hm," I said, beginning to forget my sound plan right quickly. "Is morality a concern for a doctor?"

"Why, of course," he responded, taken aback.

My calm was edging its way out the door. "And yet here you are, at a brothel, might I remind you, on Christmas Day." I recognized the trapped dove look in his eyes, for I often wore the same one. "Do you not have any family to spend the day with, sir?"

He closed his notebook, adjusting himself in his chair. His lean body was tucked in neatly to his starched and pressed clothing, but I caught the faint sheen of sweat on his brow.

"This interview is yours, I'm afraid." His tone was agitated, and his throat moved slightly as he swallowed. Was it guilt? Shame? I couldn't put my finger on the emotion, but whatever it was, it set me at ease.

Perhaps I could shift my own fear in favor of amusement. Truth be told, it wasn't the most difficult shift, all the more so because by this point, I didn't have any special ability at all. I couldn't read or write like Olivia, I couldn't bring people together like Rudyard or run a business like Maude, and I certainly couldn't speak to the dead.

"You're right, doctor," I said, leaning into a soft smile. "Please, go on with your questions." Again, my eyes darted toward the window, hoping for a glimpse of a tall, shadowy figure. "Only if you don't mind hurrying them along. I'm feeling a bit tired."

"Very well," he said stiffly. "Let's move on. Do you enjoy your work here at this, ah, establishment?"

I paused, weighing the question. Deciding it was safe enough, I answered him honestly. "There are moments when I feel I'm enjoying it. There are parts of the job that I quite like." I thought of Olivia, mainly. Of getting to spend time in a sort of family. Then my mind went white.

"But that's the thing, doctor. This is work. On a good night, I earn two or three dollars, and I'm saving every penny to bring my family to America. Each ticket costs near ten dollars. I'll also have to buy a house and save up enough money to get my siblings settled once they arrive, and there are six of them, plus my mam and da, and I'd like to send for all of them at once so they can support each other on the journey.

"It's a harsh one, don't you know? They'll all be packed in steerage with the rats scrambling across their feet and no proper way to use the head. The smell below decks alone is enough to cause a disease that would make you very sorry indeed."

For a moment he looked like he might retch.

"Are you quite well, doctor?" I asked, feeling steadier now—and, admittedly, a bit amused.

He withdrew a white kerchief from his pocket and wiped his forehead. "Quite," he said shortly, though he looked anything but.

I had been honest, though. As much as I might have wished to dissolve like stardust into midnight when I'd be sitting there in my chair, bound and sealed in wax, I had a job to do. I needed to make enough money before either the police or the medical establishment or whoever else might be against me in this country of enemies and backfriends would shut down our show.

Even with the doctor sitting before me, the situation didn't feel entirely hopeless, so long as Francis didn't squander all our savings again or find my newest hiding spot for the extra bit I'd tucked away.

"I have just one more question for you tonight, Miss May, if you can spare the time."

I nodded politely.

"Can you describe what spirit communication is like for you?" He leaned in, genuinely curious, almost like a lad.

I licked my lips, hesitant. How could I explain it? Sometimes it split through me, like a lightning strike on dry earth. Other times it was more delicate, like the lace on a lavender petticoat. Lighter, like moth wings against my cheek.

"It depends," I said slowly, glancing up at him as I spoke. I wished to say as little as possible, nothing that could put me or the girls at risk. And yet, I wondered, if perhaps there was a way to explain what it was like in a way even the doctor might understand. Perhaps that might set him at ease enough to let me be.

"Spirits are always sending signs, trying to reach us by any means —by a memory, an animal, a word, a smell. Jasmine for love and marzipan for pain. The trouble is, people don't know their language. It's not altogether difficult to learn, but people just don't know about it."

I stared at him for a moment, searching for any hint of understanding. But when none came, I lowered my gaze to my lap, feeling a sudden rush of heat to my cheeks. My heart thumped with the uneasy rhythm of regret. Perhaps I'd spoken too openly. All I'd wanted was to rid myself of the doctor's presence and return to my night. I had no knack for words like Olivia or confidence in my will like Maude.

Dr. Edmonds sat still as stone but without the personality. That's when Madeline rode through the kitchen upon a man's back, whooping with laughter and her arms in the air.

The doctor stood. "Thank you for your time, Miss May. I'll visit again soon." With a slight bow, which looked rather foolish given the context, he left.

It was during moments like this, when I was suddenly alone, that my heart hurt the most. A gust of wind blew so hard the window rattled, and I found myself shivering, shaking, in fear for my freedom and the life I was trying so desperately to carve out of this unforgiving world.

I wrapped my arms around myself, my mind full of questions and my heart heavy with longing. What I wanted—no, what I needed—was someone to stand by me, to hold me, to assure me that I wasn't as alone as I felt. Loneliness must be the worst feeling of all. What was the point of any effort, any fight, if there was no one to share the rewards and the burdens with?

# CHAPTER 33

# Clement

*If only love were enough.*

Clement watched his breath dissolve. Vivid white plumes against a blue-black sky. She'd kissed him on Diamond Street, and rather than savor the moment, he'd done what he seemed to do best lately: panicked.

Panicked about the tiniest things he would have once brushed aside. His coat was fraying. The thread was unraveling around the right sleeve.

He hadn't slept enough recently. If he was being truthful, he had never slept enough, and the dark smudges beneath his eyes felt suddenly heavy as damp earth.

Worst of all, as he waited for May—what was taking so long? Was she still coming?— a new realization hit him. There was something real between the two of them, and he had no idea what to do with it.

If their love was one of the poems Rudyard had begun reciting ever since he'd started spending time with Olivia, well then, how does a poem end? It just... does. Whenever the poet chooses. There's no neat, tidy resolution like in a story, with its clear beginning, middle, and end.

So what happens next? Not in some grand, metaphysical sense, but literally, *next*.

Clement didn't even know how to find May after the performance, which must have ended by now. His discomfort grew with every sideways glance from the men who passed by. He shoved his hands into his pockets, tilted his head down, and began to walk around the block.

He never imagined himself in this position—pacing Diamond Street of all places, after dark no less. Yet here he was. The cold air carried the scent of roast ham and honey cakes, a sweetness that mingled with the faint acrid tang of coal smoke. Hearths glowed through diamond-shaped panes, and light flurries turned the sky a pearly sort of silver.

He knew the show would run about an hour long, and that she would probably meet him outside. But then what if she didn't come outside? What if she were waiting for him *inside*? For him to step up to the door and knock like a proper gentleman, and he was too fearful or lacking in sense to do it? What next, *then*?

He would have to go ahead and knock on the door. Stand face to face with his enemy, the husband of the woman he thought of when his brother recited lines from love poems!

He reached the end of the block. Checked to see if anyone was staring. Crossed the street to make his way back.

He'd never been in love before—not by a long shot. Between the endless demands of the farm and the railroad, there'd simply never been time.

Clement considered himself a rational man. He alone wouldn't lead all the enslaved to freedom, but he'd lead as many as he could. And then he'd keep working. Fundraising, organizing, spreading the cause. One way or another, he'd chip away at the hard, unyielding heart of this country.

But May was changing him.

At first, he'd wanted nothing to do with her. Women, he'd once thought, were distractions, shallow and impractical. And this one was a charlatan to boot.

But she'd proven him wrong when she'd mentioned his mother's necklace. After that, there was no hiding the fact that she was edging as close to his heart as that very pendant.

Clement sighed, another plume of breath rising pell-mell in the wind. He wondered whether this moment was a line in a poem, ephemeral and finite at the same time, or a moment in a story. And if it was the story, how close was he to the happy ending?

What if it was a tragedy?

Instinctively, he drew a hand to his pendant. Tonight, he wore it strung around his neck. He had never tucked it away in a drawer or jewelry box. Not once. Not even when his teachers told him jewelry was prohibited. The farthest from his throat he'd ever worn it was his pocket. But something about May made him feel like, with her by his side, no part of him would ever have to be tucked away secretly. Like he could live out in the open, under wide skies that were made for cloud-watching.

Clement routinely risked his life leading men, women, and children out of slavery, and yet it was only now that he felt this particular feeling of knotted intestines and heart palpitations, unsure how to meet one tiny woman outside her home.

Perhaps he was embarrassed to admit the truth; not only did he want to avoid May's husband, but he also wanted to avoid the stares of the other men in the brothel. Black men didn't go to the white brothels. They just didn't.

He paced in a circle. Walked around the block one more time. Walked around again, *resolute now*.

He was fiercely cold. Teeth beginning to chatter. A group of carolers glanced dubiously in his direction as they made their way around the block.

He sighed, deciding at last to follow the example of a poet he could admit had some particular level of skill—William Shakespeare—and throw a pebble at May's window à la *Romeo and Juliet*.

*Tragedy be damned.*

He hoisted his left arm behind his head.

"You're not about to throw that rock at my window, are you?" May asked, appearing beside him like a black cat in the night, all bright eyes and shining silk.

"Christ." He jumped at the sound of May's voice. He placed his free hand on his necklace. Felt the beating heart beneath it. *Steady.* "I was," he admitted after finding his bearings. He slowly lowered his arm, as though unsure if she were real. She always made him question what was real.

"Well," she said, her lips curving faintly, "French Maude will take the price of the repair out of my wages if you break it, so maybe we can walk on a bit and have a chat instead."

He laughed—an easy, genuine sound that surprised even him.

Something about her. He was for the Irish.

She was quiet as they walked, and it unsettled him. He broke the silence first. "Is everything all right? I was waiting..." His tone was diffident. Needy, even.

"I'm sorry," she admitted. "I was... delayed. I hope you weren't waiting long."

"No," he said, feigning ease. He shoved his hands into his pockets. "So, what did you want to talk about?" he asked at last, silently cursing the tremor in his voice.

They continued along Diamond Street, past the open shutters of the brothels revealing little bright squares of Christmas festivities behind frosted glass. They passed clouds of tobacco smoke pocketing around small gatherings of darkly clad men, lightly mixed with the scent of roast pigs and chestnuts and spiced wine. Past the whispers of passersby and carolers who noticed the pair.

"The truth is," May told him, bracing herself against a gust of wind, "I'm not who you think I am."

Clement stiffened. He didn't want her to be anyone other than who he thought she was. He *needed* her to be.

And yet, if it was love, did it matter? Wouldn't he still feel the same, regardless of what she said next?

He was the most level-headed, sober man he knew. He looked at the world through clear, indecorous lenses, as though it were made of bare winter trees, and leaves and flowers were frivolous distractions.

And yet here he was, not wanting the dream of May to end.

"The truth is," May breathed, "you think I'm a medium, but I'm not."

An empty, falling feeling. A rotten porch board giving out beneath your step. There was no way she could have lied to him about the necklace. It was just too specific of a reading.

Then again, he respected the power of the mind. It could fool its owner, sure enough. Perhaps she'd seen the glint of his chain when he'd scratched his collar or rubbed behind his neck. Perhaps she'd followed the sighting with an educated guess, knowing that if a Quaker wore a piece of jewelry, it must certainly be significant. Perhaps she was a master of intuition, and nothing more.

If she had lied, it would be a hard truth to swallow. But to feel so alone once again would be far harder. To forgive her for taking her gift of closure back from him might be the hardest of all.

"I can't read anymore," May said, her voice trembling. "It's gone."

He blinked, stunned. "Gone?"

"All my life I was one way," she went on. "I had my way of getting through the world, and I thought I was cursed." Her laugh was nervous. "And then one night, the curse was lifted. Like a witch had put a spell on me as a wean and then some mysterious hero destroyed her, and all her wee jars of curses opened and set each victim free. Except the only thing is, this curse doesn't feel like a curse anymore. It feels like it was a gift. I was never alone, you see, and always had the widest view, like a bird."

She stopped walking, turning to face him fully. Her eyes glistened in the dim light. "And it wasn't a witch in this story, but God. I was ungrateful for it. I didn't use it right. And now, He's taken it back."

Her tears spilled over, and before Clement could think, he stepped forward, wrapping his arms around her. She pressed her face into his chest, her sobs shaking her small frame. His hand moved instinctively, tilting her face gently toward his.

"It's been like that then, lass?" he asked in his best attempt at an Irish accent, which made her break into a fit of laughter. He'd never heard her laugh like that before, so freely, with so much mirth. It sounded rare and pretty, evoking a memory he couldn't quite place of seagulls in November.

They breathed together against the rush of wind. *Odd*, he thought, as the wind carried the scent of jasmine. Even the night sky had a tinge of its purple hue.

"May," he said at last, his voice low and steady. "What about your husband? God forgive me, but I need to know. He's truly never touched you?"

Her expression hardened, tears still clinging to her lashes. "No," she said bitterly, shaking her head. "Never. He's hardly given me a friendly pat on the back. He hates me. And I hate him even more."

Clement held her gaze, nodding once. That was all he needed to hear. He'd believed her earlier, yet he was still in shock. How could a man have a woman, and one as lovely as May, no less, and not touch her? Francis would have to be mad, or…

"But true as that is," she continued gingerly, "I'm the same as his property. I work for him as much as I work for Maude, and my word against his won't mean a thing to anybody with the power to change it."

A sour, burning feeling in his stomach. It took him a moment to pinpoint it as shame. Olivia had been right. He'd assumed too much about May. About her life, her circumstances. But there was one thing Olivia had been wrong about. He *could* fix this. May's predicament wasn't hopeless. This was New York—the most progressive state in the Union. There *was* a way out, if she was brave enough to take it.

"May," he said, his voice careful but steady, "why not petition for an annulment?"

She looked at him quickly. There was a glimmer of hope in her cobalt eyes. Then she looked at her boots. "Francis would never give it to me. I earn triple his wages after a seance. I'm his meal ticket, his safe escape from the poverty so many of us Irish face when we arrive here, thinking the streets will be paved with gold and learning quickly they're made of nothing but dirt and rubbish."

Clement shook his head. Wished he could put his words together faster. "May," he managed, "you don't need him to give it to you. If you can prove that you're a, well that you've never..."

Amusement flickered over her lips, cutting through the tension. "That I've not been touched?" she finished for him.

"Well, yes." He chuckled, then silently rebuked himself for chuckling. "If you can prove as much, then you don't need his agreement."

He could see the wheels turning.

"Maude has all her girls go to the physician once a week," she murmured. "I could go, too."

"Then you can prove your virtue," Clement said, his voice firm, "and be set free of the man."

Under normal circumstances, Clement would have regretted his choice of words. "Freedom" was not a term he used lightly. It carried a weight far heavier than the context of May's predicament. It was a term bound to the great stain on America, a wound that was always at the forefront of his mind.

But not tonight.

Tonight, his mind was lost in a dream of May, gentle as a hummingbird's breath.

"I don't even know what I would do with the freedom," May breathed. "Where would I go? Would I have to leave Maude's? How would I support myself?"

Clement inhaled deeply, forcing himself to see the situation through her eyes. Olivia spoke of freedom like a skeleton key forged from silver, something that could unlock every door if you jiggled it enough. But May—May had never known doors. Her life had always been an endless road, a stretch of dust and horizon with no locks to open, no walls to scale.

"Well," he said, no closer to an answer, "what would you like to do?"

Her face lit up cautiously. Flame in the breeze. "I've always wanted a wee farmhouse of my own," she told him, describing a few of the details she envisioned—the olive branch wreaths and silver sconces and fresh white paint. The woven carpet in the center of the living room. The family portrait she'd hang above the hearth, surrounded by dried roses and a vase of fresh lilacs.

Then she went silent, just as he was allowing himself to dream her dream.

"What's wrong?" he asked her.

"Even if I can have my marriage annulled, I can't leave Maude's. Nothing I want is possible without the kind of wages I make as her resident spiritualist. Without it, I have no hope of supporting myself nor my family, waiting for my help in a country that God's forgotten."

"You can't hurt yourself for your family," he said. The blank look on her face made him wonder if no one had ever told her that before.

"It's what's expected of me," she replied simply. "It's our way."

He nodded silently. He understood. He, too, bore the weight of expectation.

The question burning at the back of his throat remained unspoken. He glanced at the city around them. Looking back at its history, it was clear to see that many of its misfortunes came from forging ahead too quickly, overfishing the whale population for the sake of corsets and hoop skirts, umbrella and parasol ribs, lubrication for the moving parts of the century's iron marvels. Hudsonians hoarded their wealth, neglected investments in new industries, left the city financially distressed.

Clement was a man haunted by ghosts. One foot in the past at all times. He knew better than most that history repeats itself. How could he offer a hasty proposal, without seriously considering the downfalls?

And yet. In his mind's eye he saw wreaths woven from olive branches and silver sconces dripping amber wax above a large bed carved from the ash trees that grew behind his family home. He had carved it himself. Could feel the blisters on his fingers where his hands had gripped the knife.

There was still time to find a solution. He didn't need hope, for he was a man of faith, and that's what he believed.

# CHAPTER 34

## May

*I* awoke to a bright, sunny day alone in my bed. After all this time in Hudson, I still hadn't grown accustomed to sleeping quite alone. Francis rarely spent a night in our bed, and when he did, I felt even more alone.

I began to dress, my mind spinning quickly with ideas of how to best proceed with the annulment. I would take time on this day to think it through.

Traveling women understood the importance of time. We'd visit the wives of farmers only when their husbands would be out in the fields, or else we'd never make a sale. There was talk of traveling folk who took off with the wind, yet my folk always followed a cyclical clock, leaving our winter dwellings and taking to the road when yellow blossoms dotted the broom bushes and the mist thickened.

We'd disappear along with it, so that folks took to calling us *mist people*, much like the fairies. And for those who had lost someone over the past year, I'd watch them race to my family's wagon as it rolled reliably back into town. They'd been waiting, waiting, for an entire year if they were unlucky, until they knew the Conallys would return.

I continued to dress methodically through layers of corset, petticoats, crinoline, and corset cover, feeling quite caged and wee within the contraptions, more like a piece of machinery than a lass.

A part of me wondered if I should best proceed with the annulment on my own and avoid Francis altogether. Yet as much as I'd grown to hate him, he had suffered alongside me in Ireland. He knew me in a way that no one here could. The songs we sang by firelight, the wagons creaking under the weight of our lives, the roads that wound through Ireland's bones like veins. Without Flynn, Francis was all I had left of that life.

Most importantly, he had known and loved our John.

If I abandoned Francis completely, would I not also lose my last tether to John? To Lucy? To the lot of them?

I drew a tartan wool skirt from my trunk, its generous folds large enough to cover a wagon. A waste of fabric, Mammy would have called it. Pulling it over my head, I set to fixing and smoothing the flounces, a task nearly impossible to manage alone. Remembering Olivia's trick, I hopped up and down a few times to let the fabric settle into place.

My wee twin brothers would have laughed at such a sight. How I wished to squeeze them and inhale their sweet, mossy scent. Again, I thought of John—how he'd dutifully tell them not to tease me, and how he would have known exactly what I should do now, for he'd known Francis better than anyone.

When the three of us were children, I'd find the boys in meadows and burrowed in hedgerows. We'd shared an affinity for the wild buds of early February and March, which poked their heads out of the dirt when the earth was still dusty with snow, and you'd least expect to see bright yellow and vibrant purple.

There was a tenacity and freedom to the furze and daffodils of the

Irish countryside that the three of us had clung to. If those flowers could bloom, exactly when you least expected yet precisely when they were supposed to, if they could blossom along swampy bogs and icy pathways…

Couldn't anything?

Any*one*?

Did Francis's heart now long for the beauty of Ireland, for the love he'd buried in its cold dirt? It was a black, musty soil, he might remember still. Did he walk upon it in his dearest dreams, or would he resent it for the rest of his life?

I finished dressing but could not be bothered with my hair, so I pinned it back quickly and covered the mess with a bonnet.

Now that my gift had deserted me, I longed more than ever for contact with John. What if I could speak to him even without my sixth sense? Completely ordinary people prayed and spoke to loved ones on the other side of the veil. They trusted in angels and demons and even the lore that came from pre-Christian times—tales of the Lord and the Lady, the wee folks, and the *kelpies* and *pookas*.

Christians prayed to their God for help, Quakers sat in devout silence, and Hudson's pagans searched for the infamous Catskill witch who they believed controlled the weather.

These folks weren't able to hear back from anyone the way I could when I would use my gift, and yet still they spoke and sat and searched.

Could I not do the same?

I lit my bedside candle. I sat on my bed in the gray light of morning, leaving my gloves and cloak to wait in the chest. Then I asked my brother John what to do.

But the human mind is a strange and curious thing. Rather than listen for his answer, all I could do was compare. I thought how crisply I might have heard John's voice before, like the crunch of autumn leaves beneath my suede, scallop-trimmed boots. I no longer wore the sturdy, black boots of the wandering folk, nor the signature black shawl. I'd transformed into something else entirely, a picture of silks and bright trimmings.

Yet my heart still thumped and swelled as it always had. Perhaps I might have felt John's guidance had I opened myself to it. But my patience was short.

"I've been through enough already. Can't this just be easy?" I asked out loud, not sure who I was even trying to talk to.

Silence.

The failure stung more than I expected.

For comfort, I turned my thoughts to Clement. I pictured his striking amber eyes that appeared hazel in the sun and honey on a winter's night. I thought of his impressive height and broad shoulders, and his undeniable serious edge.

Perhaps that's what made me feel safe with him. My chin was always tilting toward the clouds. I needed someone who could help me keep my feet on the earth, who could convince me it was worth it.

I'd braved a look into his eyes after crying all over his coat. I'd checked for signs of being perceived too scornful, too emotional, too ungrateful, too much.

But I'd read no such signs in the lines of his face. Instead, I'd seen something unfamiliar in the honey of his eyes and the clenching of his jaw. Hope, perhaps?

I hadn't tried to hold back my tears as I would have with anyone else. Clement had never seen me this vulnerable before, yet in that moment, I couldn't find it in myself to care. Because this—this was one of the most difficult experiences for a sensitive person to endure. The loss of their craft, that is.

And suddenly, I found myself able to understand Olivia just a wee bit better.

I imagined a writer who spends each day chatting with a village of friends and foes in her mind, only to be robbed of her time, her resources, her will, what have you, until she gives up on giving life to the voices. Until they stop speaking to her altogether.

Her mind is no longer a kingdom, but a dusty, cobwebbed attic. Boarded up windows, boxed up and forgotten dreams.

But Olivia was creating again. She wasn't writing, but there was someone or something communicating with her once more, and it was holy as candlelight. Even if I could find another way to earn my wages, I couldn't take that away from her.

So I'd let my tears flow as Clement put his arms around me and held me close, breathing against the rush of wind. And as the scent of jasmine carried on the breeze, I'd closed my eyes and thought, *Of course.*

I was so immersed in the memory, I could swear the scent of jasmine lingered once again, ghostlike, in my bedroom. The feeling came not as an echo but as something alive and breathing, curling itself around my senses. It was then, as if summoned by the scent, that another thought arrived.

I'd believed there were only two paths before me: either go about the business of the annulment on my own or else ask Francis for his permission.

But there was a third way, wasn't there?

I could demand it. I could stand before him, not as the timid lass he'd married in Ireland, but as the woman I'd become since then. I could speak my truth, honor the years we had shared, and show him that I was no longer bound by the fear that had once wrapped around me.

The idea sent a shiver through me, equal parts thrilling and terrifying. I hummed with it, and at the same time, I blanched.

Would I be able to state my case without a tremor in my voice betraying me?

Was I, in fact, more the lass of last summer than I hoped to believe?

And if Francis said no, what then? Would I crumble?

A darker thought wove its web like a spider in the corner of my mind. *Dr. Edmonds.* If I asked for an annulment now, would it not bolster Francis's position? It was bad enough I'd called my husband a tyrant. But now, harassing him for an annulment might reveal an even greater piece of evidence to the doctor.

Dread coiled in my belly as I opened the taupe door of a very quiet Maude's.

And then, there he was—Francis, pushing past me, his face carved from stone. He moved toward the stairs, undoubtedly ready to sleep the day away.

But I couldn't let him.

"Let me get you some breakfast," I offered.

"Not hungry," he grunted, his voice like gravel beneath a heavy boot. Without so much as a glance in my direction, he mounted the stairs to our bedroom, two at a time, and slammed the door behind him.

I stood there, my hand pressed to my lips, as if that might steady the storm rising in me. What should I do?

"Oh, Miss May, you're up early! Would you like me to set out a bannock for you?" It was Nellie. Though her offer was kind, the thought of eating without an answer churned my stomach.

"No, thank you," I told her. Then, before I could lose my nerve, I followed him.

The door creaked open, and I stepped inside. He didn't look up. I stared at the familiar lump beneath the covers, a deep resentment making my clothes feel even tighter.

I took a deep breath and came right out with it. "Francis, I want an annulment."

For a moment I waited to see if the world would end. If the seasons would stop turning and the flowers would stop growing, and a great big crack would tear through the room, destroying all the furniture with it.

Francis didn't stir.

"Francis—" I started again, but he turned then, his eyes meeting mine with a blankness that chilled me.

"No," he said.

The world didn't snap in two, but my mouth hung open, and no sound came out.

"Why now?" he demanded, his voice low and biting as he sat up and threw the covers off. "It's for that Stoker brother, isn't it? You'd turn your back on your own people for him?"

He advanced toward me, his voice gaining venom with every step. "What would your mammy say? She wished for us to stick together, and now that you're here and proud of yourself for making a few extra dollars, you'll abandon your roots for some Jack who will never understand you the way I do?"

He moved closer, his presence so suffocating I had to take a step back. On another day, I might have raised my hands to shield myself.

But not today.

I wasn't afraid, and his words didn't deter me.

Once, I might have thought myself a meek dove and folded myself within my wings. But maybe my heart had grown bolder since falling in love. My wings would carry me forward as they always had. And Clement's? His would shield me.

My life with Francis was not what Mammy had wanted for me. Had she been here to see how her plan unfolded, to hear the harsh words from Francis's mouth and witness his carelessness with my wages—with our very lives—she would have been sorry she pushed the two of us together.

It was a match born out of desperation and scarcity of choice, nothing more, nothing less.

I only hoped Clement didn't care what others might have to say about our match, not Olivia nor Paschal nor whoever else might have an opinion, for surely there were some, and there would be more, who would pay a visit to the Catskill witch if that's what it took to keep us apart.

I hoped Clement felt what I felt. I would not have foreseen visiting a doctor—even with the Sight—but I was willing to. If an examination was what was required to free myself of Francis, I would make it happen.

I had hope in my heart, but it was a slippery thing. In a world where everyone seems against you, hope can be hard to hold on to. And when the one thing that defined you—both to yourself and everyone around you—is gone, it's even harder to trust that you'll still be enough without it.

I would wait until Rudyard came by, and I would ask him where to find Clement. Clement was the only one who could assure me that this was worth it—that *we* were worth it.

The truth was, aside from the meetinghouse where Clement prayed, lectured, and made his plans, I had no idea where to find him. A Quaker and a woman who lives at French Maude's don't exactly share a social circle.

Rudyard, on the other hand, did just that.

I was not surprised to find Rudyard at the breakfast table. He, on the other hand, seemed shocked to see me, even though I was the one who actually lived here.

For a second, I faltered.

I needed to ask him. I had to give myself this chance at love. At life. But the words stuck in my throat, and the question lingered, honed and aching: *what if I wasn't enough?*

# CHAPTER 35

## Rudyard

*R*udyard had ended his night at the brothel, as he often did, making himself useful by refilling glasses and trading notes with French Maude.

By late morning, he woke in Olivia's bed, with a pounding headache. He rolled over, expecting to see his friend sleeping soundly beside him. But instead, a patch of pale sunlight had claimed the space where she should have been.

He sat up slowly, rubbing the sleep from his eyes, his vision blurry as he peered around the room. The sunlight felt wrong in the heavy fog of his head. Nellie's greasy breakfast would be just the medicine he needed. Perhaps one of her delightful bannocks.

As he buttoned his vest, something caught his eye—a scrap of paper poking from beneath Liv's bed. He should have ignored it, but curiosity tugged at him.

He pulled out the paintings, each one unmistakably Olivia's work, entirely unique and original.

The first image he examined was a woman, cinnamon hair cascading over her shoulders, brown skin glowing beneath the soft folds of a silk gown. Her lips were a rich mauve, and her corset was tightly laced, intricate lace shoulders framing her collarbones like the wings of an angel.

Another one—a pair of legs, one extended forward, toes pointed, the other in the background, wrapped in creamy fabric held by two hands, one on the upper thigh, the other placed intimately between the legs.

Olivia, clearly, was through trying to fit a mold that wouldn't have her. She was carving her own, unapologetically.

He was lost in her world until the creak of the door broke his reverie.

Olivia stood in the doorway, her eyes wide as they fell on the spirit paintings laid out across the bed. "How did you—"

"Olivia!" He couldn't help himself; his excitement spilled over. He took her hands, not waiting for her anger or discomfort. "You're an artist!"

Her eyes shone, and her lips parted, though she didn't speak.

"I knew you must have talent when you told me you'd been drawing. I thought I'd embarrassed you when I gave you the paints in front of the other girls. I thought I'd ruined everything for you. Why didn't you tell me you've been painting?"

Her eyes softened as she stared at the artwork, unsure. "Do you really think I'm an artist?"

Rudyard beamed. He saw in Olivia something he saw in himself, yet he believed in her more. She had a secret life, a hidden tenderness, that he was honored to witness.

"Liv, you've given me a lot of advice in the short time we've known each other. Let me give some to you." He swallowed, trying to make his words catch up to his emotion. "*This* is what you should be doing. Let me support you. Let's go somewhere your talents will be appreciated. Let's leave Hudson and start fresh in London."

"You're crazy!" she laughed.

He felt saner than he'd ever felt before.

Francis was a door cracked open. Olivia, on the other hand, was the entire entryway.

"You've told me before you're not interested in marriage," he pressed, voice quiet but steady. "Neither am I. Let's leave together in early spring, when the sea will be calm for travel. We can sell your paintings at seances and galleries. We can go on tour. I won't give up, even if it feels hard at times. I know it will. But we'll do it anyway."

She opened her mouth, but the words that followed were not what he hoped. "But, May…"

"By the time spring arrives, May will have enough money to start fresh on her own."

He watched her think, the weight of her hesitation pressing on him like the heat of a summer day. At this point, the thought of her saying anything but "yes" was unacceptable.

He had fallen in love with Olivia—not in the frantic, desperate way that longing could burn, but in the way that he loved everything about her. She was a performer, a star so obviously rising, and an artist. Her paintings captivated him, drew him into her world, made him feel alive in ways he hadn't known before. The two of them were tangled in something bigger, something fated.

"I won't draw the traditional gothic Victorian woman, covered to her throat, white, pure by the standards of men. I won't do it, Rud. My subjects follow their own standards of purity."

He grinned, the pride swelling in him like something he couldn't hold back. "They're free and positively basking in it!"

He sobered quickly, locking his eyes on hers. "You've never tried to change me, never made me feel like I was less. I would never, ever, even think of doing that to you. Your art—your art is perfection. Overwhelming, in fact! I'm in awe of you, Olivia Johnson. I wouldn't have you change one stroke."

She hesitated, looking down at her work, still chewing on her lip. For a moment, Rudyard thought she might withdraw, but she didn't. She didn't take her hands away, didn't gather her paintings and sketches and hide them again under the bed. She was still there, still listening, still open.

Maybe, just maybe, she wanted to be convinced.

"I don't know, Rud," she said softly, but the words were tinged with something that wasn't quite doubt, but more like the softest invitation to press a little further.

"Olivia," he said, and the seriousness in his voice was palpable. "We've talked about London before. We always spoke of it like a dream or a distant possibility. Now we can really do it. Your art is how we turn our dream into a reality."

She chewed her bottom lip again, staring at the drawings, and for a heartbeat, he wondered if she might say no. But then she looked up at him, and there was a glint in her eyes, something playful, mischievous even. It was the same twinkle he'd seen in her when she performed, when she held the room in the palm of her hand. And now, she held him just as tightly.

Rudyard and Olivia sat next to each other at the breakfast table. Olivia's cheeks were rosy. She smiled at Rudyard as she poured them both coffee. He grinned back as he spread jam on their rolls.

"What are you two so smiley about?" Annie asked matter-of-factly, shoving a buttered roll into her mouth.

Before he could decide how to answer, May blew into the breakfast nook, fierce and fast as a squall. Her strange, usually sleepy eyes were bright and focused. Focused on *him*. Ignoring everyone else, she marched straight to him.

"Where can I find Clement right now?" she asked.

To Rudyard's horror, the other girls shared knowing, almost satisfied glances. What did they know that he didn't?

Cora smirked. "You owe me a dollar, Annie!"

Annie grimaced and shrugged.

Rudyard felt a stab of jealousy. When had May and Clement grown so obviously close that the girls placed bets on them? When had they become so friendly as to meet in private? *For pity's sake!* Last he'd seen them together, they'd hardly looked at one another.

Rudyard swallowed his coffee a little too fast. It was scalding and he choked.

"So May's in love," Annie said, unperturbed. "Doesn't prove he loves her back."

Rudyard's mind started reeling with excuses for how he had missed their connection, how he normally would have seen something so essential in his brother's life.

But his gut feeling was undeniably strong. The truth was, he had failed to show up for his brother. Failed to consider May as a woman rather than a ticket to another world, because that would have forced him to give up Francis.

Francis, tall, with jet-black hair and icy eyes, pale skin that always appeared a bit rough and raw and flushed against the wind. Francis, who made Rudyard accept his own desire for the first time in his life. With Francis, he was beginning to see the beauty of wildflowers against a newly thawed world.

But what if he'd been so enthralled, he'd missed something important?

May was entirely unbothered by the exchange between Cora and Annie. "Rudyard?" she pressed, her voice a gentle tug on his focus.

He blinked, his thoughts still tangled, uncertain about what had just transpired.

He could feel the weight of May's gaze on him—those wide eyes, blue like winter skies, almost gray in the dim light, peering up at him with that directness that unsettled him more than it should.

Her hair was pinned back sloppily beneath her bonnet, and her porcelain skin had that same wind-swept blush as Francis's.

Rudyard had no choice but to consider the woman standing before him, demanding an answer as to Clement's whereabouts.

"Clement? Oh, he's probably at the homestead right about now, taking care of the chores," Rudyard said as casually as possible. "I'll go with you, if you like," he offered, too curious and uneasy to linger around the table and gossip.

"I have to go alone," May insisted.

"Why don't you let him walk you, at least?" Olivia suggested. There was a strange tightness in her voice, as though she, too, felt something stirring in the air.

"No, thanks," May said firmly. "The walk will do me best on my own. I need to clear my head."

"Bet that's not all that needs clearing," Madeline sniggered.

Reluctantly, Rudyard gave May directions to his home, then watched helplessly as May charged out the house in a whirl of plaid skirts.

He knew she was attractive. He wasn't attracted *to* her, but he wasn't blind, either. Any mention of her in the spiritualist press referred to her as "the pretty little spiritualist of Diamond Street."

May wasn't just attractive, she was captivating, and there was no mistaking that in her quiet, steady way, she had become something more in America. Where once she might have been poverty-stricken and invisible in Ireland, here, her suffering had shaped her into someone else—someone that others envied, even admired.

But it wasn't just that. It was the flush of her cheeks. It was her eyes, wide and alight with something that made her almost glow. And now, he could see it—*it*—the thing that had changed her. Love. She was in love, and that was what had transformed her from a mere figure of beauty into a muse.

And if May was in love with Clement, that meant Clement must be in love with her, too. The realization hit him like a blow.

He'd ignored the growing distance between him and his brother, dismissing it as nothing more than the result of busy lives—he with his late-night seances, Clement with his work on the railroad.

But now, Rudyard couldn't deny it any longer. His brother was slipping away from him, and it wasn't just The Fugitive Slave Act that set him walking alone at night, through rain and snow, his head in a fog.

How could Rudyard, in good conscience, plan to leave for London, knowing his brother might be making a terrible mistake?

He didn't see any of the ways that May and Clement could work together as a couple. He saw the hatred his brother would face. He saw an immigrant in a brothel steering Clement off his path. He saw a married woman and scandal, even bloodshed. He didn't need May's gift to see any of it. He just needed to know his country. Even in a state like New York, at the forefront of progression, the people were divided.

He looked to Olivia for guidance, but she wouldn't meet his eyes. She stared down at her bacon, all eyelashes and red cheeks.

Rudyard excused himself and walked upstairs. He knocked on Francis's door, knowing the Irishman never joined the girls for breakfast. He slept deep into the afternoon, his night beginning only after the brothel's hours ended. Then, his lover would slip between gambling parlors, taverns, and those shadowed brick coves where men like them gathered before returning to the warm bedsides of their wives. Wives. *May.* Clement.

Rudyard had to do something about this *now.*

"What?" came an agitated, muffled reply.

Rudyard opened the door sheepishly. "I think we have a problem."

He told Francis about Clement's odd behavior and May's demand in the middle of breakfast, about how he actually might have missed something flourishing between them, perhaps beautiful yet thorny like a black rose.

Francis listened in silence, a state in which Rudyard could imagine him to be endearing. It was only when Francis opened his mouth that Rudyard was forced to remember how little he liked the man.

Francis set his heavy jaw. "That's that, then," he said coolly. "I told you I saw something at Governor's Tavern, didn't I?"

"You did," Rudyard said cautiously.

"I knew it from the start," Francis went on. "She asked me for an annulment last night. I thought to myself, 'Now how does a daft wee creature like May know a thing about annulments?'" Francis pounded the nightstand with his fist. The basin bowl with its pink rose design, water pitcher, and oil lamp that rested on the stand all clattered.

Rudyard's chest felt heavier than his head when he'd first woken up.

"Don't worry," Francis said, with such kindness that Rudyard faltered. "I'll take care of it."

"How?" Rudyard asked, a sense of dread stewing in his gut.

Had he done the right thing? Why wasn't he more certain?

Francis reclined against the headboard with his hands folded behind his head. His stomach had grown so large, the mound of it could be seen through the blanket. Then he sat up and pulled Rudyard to him in one swift motion, kissing him on the lips.

It was a passionate kiss. Yet Rudyard wasn't sure if it was the right kind of passion. He wasn't sure if it was good.

Francis's stubble rubbed painfully against Rudyard's sensitive skin. Rudyard's stomach churned from the rancid scent of last night's ale on Francis's breath. His whole body reeked of it.

Rudyard, finally released, backed away from the smell. He waited for Francis's response. What was he planning to do?

"I have an idea," was all Francis said.

With the taste of old alcohol in his mouth, Rudyard nodded, stood up, and walked to the door. He turned back to Francis, who had begun packing tobacco into his pipe. That's when he noticed the dried roses decorating the gilded mirror of May's vanity. Where Olivia kept her perfumes strewn about, May, instead, kept a journal, open to a page where it seemed she'd been practicing her letters.

Francis lit his pipe with the flame of the oil lamp, turned to his other side, and blew a ring of smoke into the vase of fresh flowers on the opposite bedside table. May's table.

How had Rudyard never noticed these traces of May in her own bedroom? She was a sweet girl and a good person. She helped people. She'd helped *him*, hadn't she?

He'd just wanted to be a part of that world, helping people find peace as she did. But as he looked around, he shuddered. He was a part of something, yes, that's what he'd wanted, but was he a part of something good?

He closed the door quietly behind him, his shadow growing longer with the day.

How was it that he could be happy for his brother and eager to destroy that happiness at the same time?

But that's how people are, isn't it? Rarely consistent when it's to their benefit, bound to experimentation when there's no room for risk, replaying cycles and relationships with a revolving cast of characters, always hoping to get it right in the next scene. That's what Olivia would say.

People are gamblers, whether it's cards or dice or lives in their hands. Perhaps that's what Francis would say.

But what did *he* have to say?

He didn't have any wisdom of his own, only questions.

How was it that he could jeopardize Clement's love? He couldn't find the words, but on some level, he knew the answer. He was the sum of his contradictory choices and weak in his convictions—the kind of person too easily seduced and distracted, too eager, undiscerning.

The kind of person poets ignore and gamblers play and history forgets.

# CHAPTER 36

# Map

*M*y walk to the Stoker homestead was a cold but pretty one. As the sounds of daily life in Hudson faded, I breathed in the sky and let my mind wander, thinking of the world in the way one of Olivia's poets might—*The stock-dove shall hatch his soft twin-eggs and coo, While I kiss to the melody, aching all through!*

I began to return to myself. I felt light and hopeful, and so eager to see Clement that I had to force myself to keep my eyes open to the world before me rather than the one that was so charmingly unfolding in my mind's eye.

Past the bare fields and snow-dusted hills, smoke billowed from the four chimneys of the Stoker farmhouse. It stood tall and handsome, all brick, with a velvety black trim along its windows and doors, perched atop its own hill. Sheep and cattle grazed the fields.

It was a grand house, the likes of which a wealthy farmer in Ireland might own, and my da and brother would sweep for.

I lifted my skirts and ran straight up the hill to the front gate, then turned and looked out at the view. I could see Spook Rock Creek and the dirt road, the sun so bright, I had to squint against it.

My heart began to thump in the way it would before a spirit came forth to speak to me. I felt a rising panic in my throat. It was all too beautiful, too beautiful to be true, too beautiful to be mine.

The tears came before I could stop them.

"May?" I heard Clement call. His voice sounded distant even though he was right beside me, holding me as I wept on the frosted earth. "May, what's the matter?" he asked with a tenderness I'd never heard in his voice before. "What are you doing here?"

"This was all a mistake," I told him. "*This* is where you come from. Where you belong. Not with me. I'm nothing but begged rags and life on a wagon. You have all I ever wanted, and now I see that's how it's supposed to be. I'm not meant for a life like this."

"May, look at me," he commanded.

When I didn't, he gently moved my chin to meet his eyes. He held my gaze firmly, resolution shining in his eyes and hardening his jaw.

"You're meant for any life you like. *I'm* not meant for a life like this, yet here I am." A pregnant pause. "I believe I have God's blessing, and it's taken me a while to see that, but I still have to worry every single day about who's judging me, about upsetting a Know-Nothing or someone else who would gladly see me in harm's way."

I shook my head, not understanding. "You don't think I have obstacles of my own? I have the entire medical establishment breathing down my neck, waiting for any excuse to call me a lunatic and lock me away. I have no property. In fact, I *am* property, belonging to a man so disgusted with me he won't even touch me."

Clement breathed deeply. He looked off, as though wondering how much he should say. Then he looked back at me, a decision in the set of his jaw.

"May, I can't be your doorway out."

I felt like I was drowning, dissolving, rotting into the earth.

He swallowed. "You want to know the real difference between us?

In one or two generations, your children, or maybe their grandchildren, can be white if they want to be white. They don't have to be Irish if they don't want to be. My kids will never have that chance.

"When we first met, you told me you could see my ancestors with me. Well, my mother was enslaved. Her mother was enslaved. That means I carry slavery with me everywhere I go. I can't escape my past. It's always a part of me. With me. Darkening me.

"You want to be American? You can be. You want to be settled? You can be. You can have whatever you want! You just don't see it."

My tears felt dry and sticky against my flushed cheeks. "What I want most, I can't have," I whispered. "There is just one doorway I wish to walk through, and now I know it's not open to me."

He didn't answer right away. He held me there, gently, before speaking again. "I need you to think carefully. What is it you truly want most? Tell me. One doorway. Is it a house? Your family by your side? Tell me, May."

I searched his eyes for an answer, though I alone had to decide what happened next. What if he was right? What if I really could only choose one path?

The choice I made felt more like a compulsion than something I could actually ever say no to.

I kissed him, with all the passion I'd been holding in my entire life. All the lives I'd brought closure to, all the loss I'd ever felt—it all came pouring out in my kiss. Fresh tears fell and clung to my face. I tasted salt.

"Isn't it obvious?" I asked at last, when we separated and I caught my breath, our foreheads still pressed together. "I want *you*."

His voice was low as he asked, "You want me *how?*"

"I want you in the way Francis never wanted me," I told him.

"Don't say that name to me," he said, his voice tight. "How do you want *me?*"

My lips parted, but I couldn't speak.

"Like this?" he prompted. He kissed me again. "Or like this?" He kissed my neck, softly, as though breathing in the scent of wildflowers. "Or like this?" he asked again, kissing the top of my shoulder peeking out from my cloak.

"All of it," I said, my voice full of something I hadn't known I could feel.

I'd crossed the threshold between life and death too many times to count, but I'd never fully crossed over a line of fire into a burning love before. But it didn't scar or threaten. Quite the opposite. It was new and sweet, like morning dew.

Clement pulled away, gazing at me, his amber eyes fierce and dark. "Marry me," he said.

I swallowed, certain I was dreaming. "But—"

"I've had time to think about this, May. I thought during silent worship, and again as I mended the fence. In fact, it's been all I've thought about. I even found myself thinking about it as I gathered my tools, preparing to go back inside the farmhouse—until I saw a figure in the distance. Striped, slight. I knew it was you the moment my stomach lurched. You were walking up the hill, and I knew then, without question, it was you. And that..." He exhaled. "If I really am what you want, more than anything, then you have all of me."

He grinned.

"Can it all be this simple?" I asked him.

When there's love like you've never felt before and life as you know it is over, you must start anew. Like the lovely buildings of Hudson that replaced the old, decaying ones most severely destroyed by fire. There's no other choice, though desperation plays no part in the decision.

I'd never be the same after falling in love with Clement.

If he would have me, I would begin again with him by my side. If he wouldn't, I'd have to relearn how to breathe. How to feel. How to see. How to see in the dark.

All I could hope was that he *would* have me. That the key fit. It would certainly make my new life easier if it did.

"Marry me, May. If you're sure, then I will be your door."

And as he said those words, I felt more doors opening up to us. That one "Yes" resounded, and nothing felt hopeless anymore. Not my dream to be settled, nor my obligation toward my family.

I looked at him, and I knew he felt it, too.

"Send what you've earned back to your family. I'll build us a house right here on my family's land," he said excitedly, his smile widening. "Don't give up on your gift. Once you leave that house you've been living in, your gift will return. I'm confident about that. I don't know *why* I'm so sure. Maybe you've influenced me."

He grinned again, and as much as I wanted him to keep speaking, I wanted him to keep grinning even more.

"And then use it, May. Use your gift to make a difference; contribute to the world and help others find peace, just like you've helped me and Rudyard and everyone who's been lucky enough to meet you. We won't need much money. Send all you have to your family. Bring them here."

I heard the proposal. I heard the invitation to bring my family over and all move into a big house together. And then I heard Clement's encouragement to use my gift, and my mind shifted from fresh white to stark black.

Yes, I'd helped others find closure, yet the most I'd ever felt at home in Hudson was minutes before, when I'd breathed in the splendor of the view from the hill of Clement's home and known, in the deepest part of me, that I didn't belong there.

I was never meant to be a part of it. That's why God had given me this gift. I was never destined for domesticity, though I could lose myself forever in the fantasy of it. I was destined to give and not receive. To wander. To See.

Paschal had shown me how mediumship could be more than just roadside fortune telling. Olivia had shown me I could use my gift to change the way people thought about women. Now Clement was telling me I could make even greater changes, fight for them by his side, and all I wanted was to be enough as I was—a woman of two worlds, an admirer of beauty I could never own or even be a part of, with a wanderer's thirst for freedom and grief in my heart for the settled life I could never know.

People called America the melting pot, but it felt harsher to me, more like an iron cauldron—and I, a dove trapped within, too gentle to escape yet destined to flap my wings all the same.

"May?" His voice brought me back. It didn't mock me for getting lost in a dream like my da's would have, nor scold me for it like Francis's. It simply called me back, too kind to be real, too full of love to be directed toward me.

"And what about us?" I asked, the words spilling out before I could stop them. "Would I become a Quaker? Would you become Catholic? And what of my reputation? Would your people accept me, knowing my past? How would it all come together, then?"

He took a deep breath before answering. "I don't know if we have to change each other or have it all figured out just yet."

There were some who called Hudson a ghost town, a relic of former glory. The local papers said, "Gone are the days of mushroom-like growth, carts and wagons rumbling down the streets, the blasts of hammers upon house and ship."

I'd had a similar thought myself, when I'd believed Clement didn't love me. The sight of the city sickened me, and I thought I'd never see anything lovely about it again.

And yet, at this moment, I couldn't imagine a grander place in all the world. The river was wide and deep as any river ought to be, and the tide still ebbed and flowed.

Perhaps perception is everything. One day God gives me a gift that fates me to a wandering life, and the next, He gives me a man that tells me I don't have to change or have everything figured out. How could He offer me such a gift and not intend for me to receive it?

I looked into Clement's eyes, and something inside me shifted, and I said yes.

Yes, I would marry him. Yes, we would build a home together. Yes, I would find a way to fit into his world, even if it seemed impossible.

For him, I would try. And for me, he would try. We'd have enough to figure out along the way, but neither one of us was a stranger to long journeys.

WE HELD hands as we walked to French Maude's to collect my money and few possessions. We talked of our plans. I would live in the spare bedroom at the Stoker homestead while we waited for the annulment to become official. We would begin building the new house on the property, with our bedroom window facing west, so we could watch the sunset every evening and remember how beautiful our life was when we decided to marry. We'd move in after the wedding and start a family, bringing together old and new.

It was only once we reached State Street that reality sank in, like boots in the slush where the carriages rolled by. We began to walk slower, past the wreaths, ribbons, and holly wilting in the cold. Past the general store, the window fogged over, Mr. Theobold shoveling his shop entrance clear of snow. He stopped only to give us a nod and a long blank stare. Passersby gave us similar looks.

I tried to keep my gaze toward the rising chimney smoke in the clear, endless sky, but the farther into the city we walked, the more difficult it became to ignore the pointed fingers and gaping mouths. My heart thumped, and suddenly—impossible to know which one of us initiated it—we unclasped our hands.

I stopped walking, turning to face him. "Clement, I choose you. I don't care who sees it."

"That's easy for you to say," he replied, surprising me with the edge in his tone. "I'm the one who will face the hatred. It will be directed toward *me*. May, you don't know what it will be like to be with me. You can't imagine."

I shook my head, refusing to listen. "No, I don't know what it'll be like to face the world together, but I'm here, willing to learn. Will you not take my hand and walk with me to collect my belongings?"

His eyes searched mine, as if seeking a reassurance I couldn't possibly give. The future was a fragile thing, a shifting mist no one could grasp. I wondered if his resolve was as strong as mine. Did he burn for me as fiercely as I burned for him? Did thoughts of our future consume him the way they consumed me? I wanted to believe they did, but doubt rustled in the silence between us.

His throat bobbed as he swallowed, and then, with a quiet determination, he took my hand, and we walked on.

My breath and heartbeat filled my ears, loud and insistent, drowning out all else. We stared straight ahead, past the men and women who rubbed their eyes and thought maybe they'd been mistaken, blinded by the snow that had begun falling in sheets as heavy as rain.

At last, we reached the front steps of Maude's, the tallest house on Diamond Street, its presence looming. The brass knocker gleamed faintly beneath the snowfall, and the windows flickered with the light of a dozen candles. This was a place where countless stories had ended and begun, but tonight it seemed to hold its breath, waiting for ours.

"Are you ready?" I asked.

We looked at each other for a long moment, the snow gathering on our shoulders. Then, together, we turned our eyes toward the house.

The brass door handle jiggled from the other side, a sharp metallic sound that broke the stillness. The door began to creak open, and the sound of muffled voices inside grew louder. Arguing. Tense, biting words spilled into the cold night air.

Perhaps it was instinct. Or perhaps something deeper stirred in him—a need, a fear. Whatever it was, it propelled his next movement. Clement let go of my hand. This time, there was no doubt who had pulled away.

# CHAPTER 37

# 𝔐𝔞𝔭

𝒯he sun sank behind the blue silhouette of the Catskill Mountains, painting the sky in shades of creamy purple, like a bruise spread across the horizon. The shouts inside French Maude's carried out into the evening air. Olivia's voice rose first, then Maude's, sharp and scolding, followed by the rough, grainy voices of men.

I looked at Clement, daring him to prove me right, that it was all too good to be true. Before I could open my mouth, the door was wide open, and three coppers sauntered toward us with open handcuffs. Could they really be tearing us apart? There was no law against the two of us being together. Was there?

The stout officer leading the charge puffed out his chest, the brass buttons of his coat straining against his girth as he closed the cuffs around Clement's wrist. He spewed some semblance of charges, making sure the gathering crowd could see and hear that it was he, Police Constable Duffy, who was making what he clearly considered a historic arrest.

"What are you doing? He's done nothing wrong!" I shouted.

"Now see here, tiny miss. I have word this fellow is an escaped slave, and it's my duty to be seeing he gets back to his rightful owner, as per according to the law."

His words landed like a slap, jolting me from whatever dream I'd been living in. The world felt slippery beneath my feet, unreal, as though I were floating somewhere above my own body, watching this scene unfold like a story told secondhand.

"No," I whispered, shaking my head. "That's not true. He's a free man! You're making a mistake!"

But Duffy ignored me. He closed the cuffs around Clement's wrist with a loud *snap,* his movements deliberate and theatrical. Clement stood tall, his jaw clenched, refusing to give Duffy the satisfaction of a reaction.

Until he struck.

With a sudden, forceful movement, Clement drove his elbow into Duffy's gut, doubling the man over with a wheeze. The moment felt triumphant, almost like justice, until the other two officers descended on him with fists and clubs.

Time seemed to slow, a blur of movement and sound. They swarmed him like a flock of leathery-winged *sluagh,* Ireland's most terrible creatures. Clement was handcuffed and helpless, yet they preyed on him just as the *sluagh* prey on the dying, feasting on their weakened spirits.

There was no room in my body for everything I felt, just a sinking, draining confusion. One officer drove his knee into Clement's stomach, and I felt the blow in my own middle. He doubled over, the wind knocked from him. I stood frozen as another officer struck Clement across the face, the crack of bone against flesh splitting the air. He fell to his side with a heavy thud.

Clement turned his head, barely lifting it from the dirt. Blood trickled from his lip, his breath coming in short, shallow bursts. He found my eyes, and for the first time, I didn't know what he was trying to tell me.

*Run? Stay? Don't look?*

I wanted to reach for him, to throw myself between them, but the moment I moved, one of the officers stepped forward and shoved me back. My heels slid against the icy ground.

Another kick. Clement gritted his teeth, but I saw it then—the moment pain overtook him, the moment even his stubbornness couldn't hold back the groan that escaped his throat.

Something in me shattered.

And still, they didn't stop.

The third officer kicked him in the back, and Clement's body twitched like a fish pulled from water, desperate and flailing.

"Stop it!" I screamed, the sound raw and unfamiliar, a jagged shriek born from the bottomless hurt within me.

But they didn't stop.

The officer kicked again, his boot slamming into Clement's ribs. He wheezed, his body curling instinctively against the pain. I screamed again, louder this time, my voice tearing through the cold air. My screams echoed in my ears, filling the space left by the silence of the crowd that had gathered to watch. No one stepped forward. No one intervened.

"Somebody help him!" I cried, my voice cracking. "Please!"

But no one moved. I stood there, trembling, my fists clenched so tightly my nails bit into my palms. Every fiber of my being screamed to do something, to act, but I felt paralyzed, trapped by the weight of my helplessness. Why wasn't anyone coming to help?

It took both of Duffy's henchmen to hoist Clement up, his weight sagging between them. His legs dragged uselessly as they shoved the tattered and bloodied version of him into their carriage. I ran to the window, breath ragged, my fingers pressing against the cold glass as the others gave the driver his instructions.

Clement's head slumped forward, his chin grazing his chest.

"Clement," I whispered.

His head lifted—slowly, like it cost him something—and his eyes met mine. That burning intensity was still there, but it was different now, raw in a way I couldn't name. My breath hitched as I searched for the right words. *Are you well?* seemed altogether foolish.

So I said nothing. I only held his gaze, willing him to understand. *I'm not afraid. I'm not running away.* But my breath came too fast, uneven, and I wondered if he could see through me, if he knew which of those assurances was a lie.

"I'll find Rudyard. We'll meet you at the jailhouse. We'll get you out." My voice was steadier than I felt.

He looked away.

"It will be quite right," I promised, though the words curdled in my mouth.

His head shook—just barely—but he didn't speak. He didn't meet my eyes again.

"Rudyard will know what to do," I insisted, desperate to tether him to hope, to remind him of the life we would still have together. But I knew—*knew*—something inside him had splintered. Something vital.

The carriage lurched forward.

"He'll tell them you're his brother!" I called after him. "You'll be released before morning!"

The words felt childish, foolish, weightless as the carriage carried him away, dissolving into the thickening night. My world was darkening with it. Deep, velvet purples and black lace shadows swallowed the last of the day, and my vision swayed at the edges.

And then—

"I wouldn't be so sure of yourself, dearest wife."

I turned to see the shadow of Francis, hovering by the doorway. My body went cold, the marrow in my bones thick and heavy.

"You did this?" I asked. My voice was barely above a whisper. "Francis, how could you?"

He shrugged, broad shoulders rising and falling like this was nothing to him. He had changed since arriving in America; his once defined, almost regal features had thickened, softened with drink and indulgence. He looked rough now, grizzled.

"It was easy, actually," he said. "Your Rudyard was a big help to me. He told me all I needed to know. More than that, actually, but it was worth listening to him jabber on for the sake of learning your Jack's wee secret."

I gaped, caught in the sticky memory of Rudyard's loose tongue at the tavern. I'd felt, then, that Rudyard was too trusting, too affected by the drink. But I hadn't stopped him. I hadn't suggested he hold his tongue. I'd only listened.

Was I to blame for Clement's arrest? My stomach churned.

The joyless semblance of a smile left Francis's face completely. He spat his next words. "Your mammy would disown you if she could see the scum you've given yourself to in America."

I rushed at him then, pounding on his chest fiercely. He pushed me off as easily as a dove feather, brought to his clothing by a breeze. Then he lifted his arm to strike me.

He hadn't fallen into a rage. It seemed he was more interested in hitting me simply for the sport of it. But before he could, the two of us were startled by a pronounced throat-clearing. I turned toward the door, and then nearly to stone.

*Edmonds.*

Dr. Edmonds stood in the entryway, his shoulders slightly slumped, his brown hair slicked neatly to one side. His expression was grave as he adjusted his tortoiseshell glasses. "I think I've seen enough," he said in a clipped tone. "Miss May, may we speak for a moment?"

His brown eyes appeared kind but set. Unmovable.

I knew I was in trouble.

Still, I followed the men inside with shaking shoulders, powerless and numb without Clement by my side.

I stared at the hallway, the grand staircase with its intricately carved banister, the paintings of lovely things—women and picnics and cherry blossoms—hanging in perfect rows on the wall.

And then I saw them.

Olivia, the other girls, French Maude—all standing, shamefaced, in the parlor.

They'd been there the whole time, just inside, ignoring my cries for help.

"What's all this, then?" I asked, scarcely able to breathe.

Francis had a wicked smile on his face.

I looked to the group, though I already knew the answer. Francis had won. He'd done away with Clement, and now he would do the same with me, leaving Hudson with a clean slate according to the morals he'd made up on the coffin ship to America, when he'd promised himself things would be different, no matter the cost.

Maude, normally first to speak, remained quiet. Olivia opened her mouth for a moment, but she didn't say anything either, even when my eyes pleaded with her.

I turned to the doctor. "Are you sending me back to Ireland?"

"To Ireland? Heavens, no!" he said. "I intend to help you, Miss May. Right here in Hudson. Now you don't need to pack a thing. Your clothes will be provided for you at the asylum."

"The asylum!" I cried.

I'd fretted over the possibility since the day I'd landed in America, yet somehow it never seemed real to me. It was more like a banshee; you can hear it, and you know it means something, but it's still a piece of folklore.

I frantically turned to my so-called husband. "Francis, please. Tell him I'm not insane. The asylum is no better than the workhouse—you told me so yourself! Would you really send me there to rot? To rot like John?"

Now Francis's icy demeanor began to melt and simmer. "Why don't you shut your mouth and leave John out of this?" Noticing the eyes on him, he straightened and asked the doctor for a moment alone with me.

With a little too much force, he led me into the hallway. He leaned in close, nearly whispering. "You thought you could just up and leave me? Too good for me now that you're a famous *spiritualist*?" He said the word with such venom, it sent a chill up the sides of my neck.

"Well, I'll tell you something," he continued, standing even closer to me. I smelled sweat and gin, could barely breathe for the reek of it. "John can't do a thing for either of us now. He left me alone, and then you did the same when you wouldn't talk to him for me. You Connallys are all the same, looking out for your own and no one else."

Now his whisper was a hiss, his lips nearly touching my ear.

"There's nothing anyone can do for you, May. I'm your husband. I'm the one that can get you locked up, and the only one that can get you out." He moved back, calmer, like a snake that had finally shed a layer of itchy skin.

I wanted to shake my head, but I was too frightened to move. Instead, I focused on holding back my tears. What good would they do for me now? Francis nodded to himself, then led me back the few feet into the parlor, where everyone had been waiting in a rare silence.

With a cordial voice he told the room, "And now, sweet wife, I'm certain you won't forget what I've told you. Get well, May. Good day to you, everyone. Doc, I leave her in your care."

He picked up a sack that lay packed and ready by the doorway, hoisted it over his shoulders, and moved toward the door. "Don't worry, May," he said just before leaving, "I collected everything in the safe, and that extra bit you were keeping beneath the mattress." He winked. "I'll hold on to it for you for when you're cured."

And then he was gone, for it was in his blood to travel. I'd known that from the beginning. I had been the one to want a house when he had wanted Ireland, rolling hills and snowdrops and no walls, only miles.

Only sun and stars and wind.

Only love that was forbidden.

"I'll go with you now," I said to Edmonds.

Perhaps I *was* mad. Perhaps I had never had any talent at all, whether a curse or a gift. Perhaps all I'd had was my own sick mind.

Clement was gone. Ireland was gone. Olivia. Maude. All of it lost to me.

"Don't fret, Miss May," Edmonds said cheerily. "So long as we see improvement in your case, your friends will be able to visit in a few months' time."

*A few months.* The thought curled in my chest, overwhelming and unwelcome, like a storm cloud gathering above the sea. Long enough to turn the tide of the world, to twist a fate, to keep me forever from my love and the life I had dreamed of.

I thought of Romeo and Juliet—their hurried love, their tragic end

—and tried to recall how long they had endured apart before reaching for poison and dagger. Surely it was less than a few months.

I told my feet to follow Edmonds, but they didn't listen. He stood just outside the door when he turned, realizing I wasn't behind him. I turned back to Olivia. She wouldn't look at me.

"Liv?" I begged.

Slowly, she tilted her head up to meet my eyes. I could see her face was flushed and her eyes were wet before she looked away again, batting her lashes.

"Olivia," I pressed. "Promise me you'll find Rudyard and get Clement out of jail and somewhere safe."

She crossed her arms, head firmly turned sideways. I took a cautious step closer to her.

"I can't make sense of this, of you just standing here watching, but if our friendship ever meant anything to you, you'll help me with this. Do it fast, Liv," I begged softly. "Please, just do me this one favor. Promise me. Before they send him to… away."

I couldn't quite bring myself to say "Louisiana." Naming the place would make it all too real.

Olivia looked at me, deep sorrow in her eyes. She opened her mouth as though she were about to say something. Then her eyes flitted toward Maude, who stared back hard, and Olivia sucked in her lips with a nod. Her gaze returned to its original position on the floor, but I could see her eyes were glistening, and I wondered what would happen after I left. Would she let herself cry, or would she take a heavy breath and return to work?

# CHAPTER 38

# Olivia

Olivia could taste the bitter sweetness of atropa belladonna, the deadly nightshade, the same poison that had nearly claimed the life of her beloved heroine, Juliet. Her fingers were stained with the same inky blue.

She didn't care about the men at Governor's Tavern who stared at her as she burst through the door, looking for Rudyard through red-rimmed eyes. A few scraggly drinkers tried to say something about a tavern being no place for a lassie, but her scowl quickly silenced them.

"Liv! What are you doing here?" Rudyard asked. At first, his face lit up, but as she stepped closer, his expression darkened.

She could feel the heat radiating from her skin, burning beneath her coat, even as a gust of wind swept in through the swinging door behind her. She felt specks of fire in her liquid eyes.

She'd wanted to trust him, truly she had. But that had been foolish.

She should have known to hold back. She'd caught him snooping beneath her bed and hadn't even been upset! How could she have been so naive? She'd been betrayed by one man who claimed to believe in her, before. That betrayal had changed her life. It *should* have taught her to protect her heart. *Fool me once, shame on you. Fool me twice...*

"How could you?" she demanded. "Turn in your own brother? What? Was it for the reward money? Was that how you were going to take us to London?"

Rudyard squinted, his head tilting to one side. "My brother? What are you talking about?" The blood drained from his face.

She'd caught him. Figured out the whole scheme on her brisk walk to the tavern. Would he admit it, or play the fool?

"I've been here since just after breakfast, Liv. If something's happened to my brother—"

Olivia blinked, shaking her head. "Since breakfast? What? Why?"

Rudyard looked down at his cider but didn't answer.

*Francis.*

She didn't know how, but she was sure Francis had done something. He was the only person she hadn't considered who might have played a part in Clement's arrest. And he made a lot more sense as an explanation than Rudyard. There was a reason her friend was sitting at a tavern, drinking pitifully alone, and it probably didn't have to do with betraying his brother.

*Shit.* She'd messed up.

"Rud..."

His breath quickened as some form of recognition crossed his face. "Olivia. Where is my brother?"

Olivia was too shaken to breathe, but she could see now that Rudyard's ignorance was real. *Shit, shit, shit.* She might actually be able to trust him. And *shit.* She would have to be the one to break the news to Rudyard. She couldn't have come in a bit more tender?

"You really don't know?" she asked to buy herself time.

"Know *what*? Turn Clement in to *whom*?"

His face whiter than white, Rudyard looked like he was about to fall over. Olivia chewed on a fingernail. How could she tell him that his brother had been arrested? That May was on her way to an asylum

330

where they'd never hear from her again, because only her husband, now long gone, could set her free? She didn't know how to tell him, so she just went ahead and did it.

Rudyard took it all in. The red veins of his eyes emerged, and his breath came shallowly.

"Can a person really be so cruel?" he asked miserably. "It's all my fault." He tried to step down from the stool, but his legs buckled beneath him. He would have fallen on the floor flat as a pancake if she hadn't caught him.

"Just hang on a second, Rudyard," she grunted, struggling to keep him upright as she guided him back onto the stool. "What do you mean it's all your fault? This was Francis, not you."

"No!" he yelled through gritted teeth as his fist pounded the thick, dark timber of the bar. "I told Francis about Clement." Again, he tried to slip from his stool, fighting against his inebriation, but Olivia pulled him back.

"You *what?*" She wasn't sure if she was more furious or disappointed. How could he have trusted that man? He sold his own wife to a brothel! What made Rudyard think he wouldn't do worse?

But when she looked at him—really looked at him—her anger wavered. His eyes, rimmed red, brimmed with unshed tears, and she felt more pity than anything else. Rudyard was as foolish as she had once been, as heart wrenchingly human.

"I have to go!" he burst out, struggling once more to rise, though his body betrayed him. "I've been an idiot. A complete idiot! I will never be able to fix this. I didn't think he would—well I never imagined—" His voice caught, his jaw tightening against a sob.

Then, suddenly, his hands were gripping her shoulders. "Liv, what do I do? How do I fix this?"

She would have expected his anger. His guilt. But the panic and anguish in his voice took her by surprise. His eyes were ponds of sorrow, and the tenderness in Olivia began to grow like weeds, though she had not forgiven him yet.

Her feelings toward Clement had always been complicated, but no human being deserved what he had coming.

And May most certainly did not deserve what was coming for her, either. May wasn't insane. She was just about the only sane person Olivia knew, for the spirited Irish girl went after what she wanted and didn't give up.

Once, Olivia had held a dream in her heart, and then she'd given up on it. In retrospect, that was about the most insane thing she could have done.

She exhaled slowly, pressing her lips together in thought.

Behind her, a voice slurred from across the bar. "Hey sugarplum, why don't you walk those sweet drumsticks over here?"

Olivia rolled her eyes, keeping her attention focused on Rudyard. "Damn," she muttered. "I just need a moment to think."

"Come on, you cheap strumpet," the man pressed, voice thick with drink and self-importance. "You can do better than the likes of that invert."

Olivia felt Rudyard go rigid beside her. "Just ignore him," she said to her friend, whose cheeks flamed a deep scarlet. "He's up the poll."

The drunkard swayed closer, his glassy eyes struggling to focus. Any second now, he'd either pass out or hit the floor with a hard *thunk*. Olivia sighed, exasperated, and turned to face him fully.

"Hey, why don't you shut your sauce box and quit barking up a knot."

The man sneered. "Angry dollymop."

"Gibface asshead."

She delivered the insult with ease, then spun back to Rudyard without another glance. He blinked at her. She lifted a hand to shield her eyes in thought.

After a moment she asked, "Do you have any kind of proof that he's your brother? Anything we can take to the jailhouse to get him out of there?" She knew they'd need to rescue May next, but at this moment, Olivia didn't know how. She hated it, but she trusted her friend's resilience. May would get by, but Clement could be on a carriage heading down to Louisiana by the same time tomorrow, for all they knew.

"Come on, Rud, think," she urged. "If his case goes to trial, we both know what sort of odds he has."

Rudyard raked a hand through his hair, shaking his head. "I—I don't know. I don't have anything."

"Another cider?" The barkeep, a stout Irishman with rolled-up sleeves, looked expectantly at Rudyard. The fire behind him crackled, logs hissing as the flames licked them clean.

Then, just as Olivia was about to push Rudyard for more, his expression brightened, as if a spark of hope had been kindled beneath his gloom. He ignored the barkeep entirely.

"Liv, I might have an idea."

# CHAPTER 39

# Clement

*C*lement's cell was small, barely larger than its wooden cot and thin, straw-filled mattress. He had been given a coarse wool blanket, a once-white linen sheet, and a bucket. That was it. A single grated window let in dim light along with an unforgiving draft that sliced through his clothes, burrowing deep into his aching muscles.

Everything he wore felt stiff and uncomfortable, the damp air settling into the fabric, making it heavier. Colder. His shirt clung to his skin where sweat and blood had dried, and the uneven stone floor was so frigid he could feel it through his boots. Puddles of moisture gathered in the cracks and corners, the chill creeping steadily up his legs.

Behind him, Constable Duffy locked the gate with a loud scrape of rusted metal.

Clement was alone.

Again.

He rolled his shoulders, testing the bruising beneath his skin. His ribs throbbed from the scuffle, a swollen, persistent pain radiating across his side. His jaw felt stiff where he'd been struck, and his wrists, rubbed raw from the shackles, stung in the chill.

He sat on the cot and let his forehead fall into his hands, his thumbs pressing against his throbbing temples. He would be here for the night. At least. His breath came shallow, rough against the calluses of his fingers. He dragged a hand over his hair as if trying to wake himself from the nightmare.

A throat cleared.

Clement's head jerked up. He wasn't alone after all. The same squat officer who had arrested him stood just beyond the bars. Watching. His eyes were too wide and droopy at once, like a hound who had been scolded but wasn't sure why.

"Can I get you something to drink, sir? Something to eat, mayhap?"

Clement furrowed his brow, glancing around as if the copper might be speaking to someone else. But no. The constable's gaze was locked on him, full of something that almost looked like pity.

A dry, humorless laugh escaped Clement's lips. "No," he said plainly, voice hoarse. Not half an hour ago, he had driven an elbow into this man's stomach, and now he was offering him refreshments?

"Well, er, if you change your mind, I'm only right outside your cell. I sleep at my desk, you see. So I'm just right here if yous should be needing anything."

Clement blinked.

Duffy shuffled away. The creak of his desk chair followed.

Clement exhaled sharply, rising to his feet. He crossed the cell in two strides, pressing himself against the cold iron bars of the grated window. The street was empty, but he caught a faint whiff of tobacco smoke, heard the distant roll of a carriage, the clatter of hooves against the rocky road, and a few stray yelps—perhaps from children playing nearby. A mother's shrill call confirmed the suspicion.

Life outside continued.

His, however, had come to a halt.

He turned away from the window, restless. He paced. Stretched his limbs, testing their limits. Tried a half-hearted pushup, but the strain in his ribs made him stop. He hummed to himself, if only to fill the silence. At last, when pain and weariness wore him down, he sank onto his thin bedding, letting it sag beneath him as he gave in to the thoughts clawing at his mind.

May.

Her name lodged itself in his throat. Nearly choked him.

Francis had been there at Maude's. He must have been the one to fetch the constable. But it must have been May who told Francis about his past. No one else outside the family knew.

A sickness curdled in Clement's gut. He closed his eyes, inhaling as much as his bruised ribs would let him. Maybe she and Francis had been more husband and wife than she had let on. Maybe she had never truly cared for him. Maybe the entire affair had been a ploy for the $1,000 bounty. Maybe May *was* a charlatan, as he'd suspected.

Maybe he had been a fool.

Anger flared hot in his chest. He kicked over his bucket. It slammed against the brick wall and crashed loudly, waking Duffy from his slumber.

"Everything all well in there?" Duffy called, hesitant.

The meekness in his voice only made Clement angrier.

He let out a harsh breath, fingers tightening around the cot's edge.

It had been a mistake to trust her. A mistake to feel courageous with her by his side. She had watched him get dragged away. She'd pretended to care. And then... nothing. She was gone from his life as quickly as she'd entered. A squall blown in from the east. A month, one mere month, in the length of a year.

What other explanation was there? The only thing separating them now was a set of iron bars. And yet, she wasn't here. Certainly, this clod of a watchdog would have let her in.

A rising sob threatened to break free, but he swallowed it down. He would not give these people the satisfaction. Instead, he thought of Rudyard. He had to stay strong for his brother. Rudyard must have heard the news by now. He had to be working on Clement's release. Maybe their parents were involved, too.

The thought brought little comfort. Clement had never relied on their parents the way Rudyard had. He respected them. He was grateful for what they had done. But the truth was, Rudyard had been the only person Clement had ever truly considered family.

Though Clement was more afraid than he had ever been since arriving north, he knew his brother must be suffering too. He had always been by Rudyard's side through his erratic moods, his periods of lavish planning and excitement followed by the barest, bleakest darkness. But now, who would be there for Rudyard? Who would make sure he was well?

Alone with his thoughts, Clement realized just how much he had hardened. Against the cause of abolitionism, against intimacy, against anything or anyone that threatened to steer him off course. He had no room left for trust.

Yet, through everything, Rudyard had always stood by him. Shy and awkward among the other boys at school, Rudyard never wavered when it came to Clement. He had never made him feel unwanted.

Now, as Clement sat in the cold, damp cell, worry for his brother tightened like a fist around his heart. Clement loved him completely. The brother he had not known as a young child, but no less a brother. And now, Rudyard was alone too.

Clement leaned back against the damp wall, letting his head tip against the cold stone. He had no idea how long he'd have to be there. It was always darkest before dawn, but dawn came late in midwinter, and he feared the darkness would swallow him first.

# CHAPTER 40

## May

*M*adness.

Francis had accused me of madness; therefore, I was mad. That's how the doctor saw it, and that's all that mattered in the trajectory of my life. What I believed didn't count for a stitch, and so, I began to believe it less.

In fact, I tried to block my thoughts as much as possible, for when I did think, I felt muddled. I questioned myself, even my sanity. If the important, educated people with their gold-headed canes and gentle, quilting, tea-party-throwing wives thought I was of unsound mind, then perhaps I was.

Mammy had wanted better for me, yet I'd been fated to marry a man who was impotent with me but flagrantly lustful with another. I was jailed in marriage and in the world at large.

Back home was a kind of prison, too. We were locked in bodies that could never know enough.

But that first day in the asylum, I realized I had never truly known prison at all.

At precisely nine o'clock, we were escorted to our sleeping quarters. I was placed in a dormitory with the other women deemed unthreatening. The dangerous ones were locked in individual cells, under the watch of a night-keeper, afforded no privacy.

The keepers came and went as they pleased, their presence marked by the ever-grating scrape of the jail lock. Officially, they were here for "protection."

But I soon learned what that really meant.

A tall, bony woman known as Sally warned me. "The doctors think insanity comes from sexual deviancy," she said in a gruff voice, her gaze sharp as flint. "They think a man keeps you chaste. But in the morning, we whisper about what really happens."

The women stripped, abused by their so-called keepers.

"Don't let them think you need a keeper," Sally advised. "The dormitory's bleak and cramped, but they don't touch you as much when you're with the others."

That night, I lay awake, cold and rigid with fear, clinging to the one thing in the world that was still mine, which I hoped to save for Clement.

Sally had been admitted for melancholia, but after nightmares began plaguing her sleep, the doctors changed her diagnosis to mania. That meant she needed a cell. A keeper.

She must have been twice my age, but for reasons I couldn't fathom, she had taken an interest in protecting me. She pointed out which keepers took liberties, who to avoid, how to survive.

There was a quiet confidence in her, but her condition was deemed chronic and delicate. She spent much of her time in bed. She did not speak of leaving. She did not seem to want to.

I couldn't understand why.

But in that hollow place, I welcomed the friendship nevertheless.

Outside of Sally's kindness, the days were my worst nightmare.

I woke to the piercing clang of a bell, my eyes bleary and red, my head wrapped in a dull, unshakable ache. That sound sent a shudder through me, made me want to cover my ears, to scream, to run, to tear at my own hair, or all four at once.

It was a reminder that whatever life we had known before was a privilege of the past. Fate was no longer in our own hands, nor even in God's, but in the hands of a faceless state.

The bell signaled the start of a routine that grinded us down, that turned time into something shapeless and endless, made certain that if we were not yet mad, we soon would be.

With the bell began the cries and screams of the other prisoners, yet I fought each morning to appear calm on the outside, to give the nurses and doctor every reason to believe I did not belong.

It was almost laughable, in a very mad kind of way, that all my life I had wished to belong to one world entirely, and now, belonging had become my enemy.

How could Sally accept her place here?

Even after two years in that place—enough to make any sane woman lose her mind—it became clear to me that Sally was one of few women who was entirely of sound mind.

There was a sadness to her, certainly, but was she not a woman?

All of us were sad, but I could not fully believe that that made us mad.

I told her as much one evening, as rain lashed against her window and I sat beside her bed.

"I must be," she insisted. "I'm afraid there's more to my story than you know."

*Perhaps.* There always was more to a woman's story, wasn't there?

But whatever it was, I could see she wasn't mad.

Most of the others were too far gone to see the walls that contained them.

I could already imagine the kind of spirits they would become.

I thought again of the *sluagh*, those restless ghosts born of a westerly wind and shadow, more fearsome than Death itself, ill-begotten, with no loyalty or mercy.

These women were as lost as victims of the *sluagh*, their souls already doomed to fly eternally in disfigured clutches.

And if I stayed here, mine would be too.

My husband's part in my incarceration was deemed especially insidious, stripping me of the status of "amenable patient."

I was not allowed into the courtyard, not even the walled garden.

I was utterly, miserably trapped.

I'd stare at those lonely white walls and laugh bitterly at myself, for the thing I longed for most in those moments wasn't my own little farmhouse filled with laughter and pretty furniture, but no walls at all.

I wanted the sunrise peeking through the calico cover of the wagon I grew up in. How pretty the world always looked as it shifted from gray to copper to pink to blue.

How pure lovely.

Sometimes, when hunger kept me awake at night during the famine, I'd slip outside barefoot to watch the stars. Mammy would nearly give out to me in the morning for my muddy skirts, but I didn't care.

All I wanted now was to be back there.

To breathe the fresh air.

To feel the dew on my feet.

To drink up the sight of mountains.

You could feast on that beauty, so much so that it almost... *almost,* filled the hunger.

Dr. George Worth Edmonds checked on me daily. Perhaps he thought if he could reform me, he might make a name for himself, or at least salvage the reputation of his profession, which was losing devotees as rapidly as the church.

At first, I hated the doctor like I hated Francis. Cowards, both of them.

I knew what Francis had been through; I'd stood by his side through it all. Yet, I still couldn't forgive him for the choices he had made. But over time, I began to see a more sympathetic side to the doctor. He thought the very worst of me, yet he acted with kindness, listened patiently to my complaints.

Once, I asked for some tea, and he brought it to me himself, not bothering to ask one of the nurses or maids. The scent of mint and chamomile filled his dingy office, a fragrance so much like home that it nearly undid me. I breathed in the steam, letting it stir the last hidden bit of joy buried deep within my tired body.

He smiled. "It's not just all of you across the pond who can prepare a good mug of scald," he jested, winking.

He'd used an Irish expression I hadn't heard in so long. It was a balm, and for the briefest moment, a smile touched my face. Then, just as quickly, I frowned, remembering that he was my enemy and my captor.

Still, from that day on, he always had a mug of tea waiting for me during our check-ins, along with a sweet.

And slowly, these check-ins began to feel more like chats.

One afternoon, as the last sliver of sun sank behind the Catskill Mountains, I turned to him. "How would you feel," I asked, "if you were in my shoes? Locked away without a shred of evidence?"

The light through his small window cast long shadows across the floor. It wasn't barred like those in the dormitory. Next to that little square of sky, the iron bars of my own window had become my only connection to the outside world, to the wild rhythms that used to guide my path before gray meals and bells and rusting keys replaced them. Before the building's corridors echoed with locks opening and closing, and my entire existence felt like an echo of life itself.

"Well," he said, "that's not entirely true. I had your husband's word."

I ignored him, keeping my eyes on the window until the last drop of shine vanished from the sky, until there was no more light left to long for, to draw courage from, to remind me I was still alive.

I decided I would answer my own question with complete honesty. Maybe it seems strange to confess my intimate thoughts to someone who was more or less a mutton shunter, but I was so lonely, so lost, so forgotten, that I undid the tight stitching of my lips and spoke to the only person who would listen.

"All I thought in that moment when you took me away in your carriage was one thing," I began. "All I saw was one face."

In an instant, my reputation, my profession, my future were all destroyed.

I'd never rescue my family from a hunger he couldn't imagine.

At least, that's how people would go on to tell my tale.

Sure, The Weekly Star would make a fortune selling papers of the "pretty little spiritualist" who went insane—perhaps it already had—but I didn't care.

I looked at him then, resolved to the fact that there would be no more sun until morning.

"What you call insanity, Doctor, I called a curse. But I knew more clearly than ever before what I wanted, and that's what I'm holding on for. My story won't be a ghost story or a tragedy. No, my story will be a love story."

He peered at me oddly.

And then, out of nowhere, I felt compelled to add, "Unlike yours."

His body went rigid. His mouth twitched ever so slightly, and my breath caught.

He had never told me he was married.

How had I known?

A familiar heaviness wrapped around my neck like a wool scarf, and in the corners of my vision, a murky smattering of symbols and colors flickered to life. They were bright, and I had to squint to see them, so trained had my eyes become to the asylum's matte whites and grays.

"You were happy together," I told him quickly, still trying to make sense of what was happening, how in the dustiest place I'd ever called home, I suddenly saw glitter everywhere.

Instinctively, he inched backward. He cleared his throat, and though the air in the brick building was always cool, his forehead glistened.

"How do you know that?" he asked, failing to sound calm. He was waiting for a practical explanation. Surely a nurse or he himself had mentioned her in passing.

A devilish smile curled my lips, and I couldn't slow down. I felt color—blood—enter my lips, and my teeth felt sharper. "You had what I've always wanted, Dr. Edmonds. You were so happy. Yellow flowers…"

"I'd bring her daisies every day they bloomed." The words rushed out of him almost at the same time as mine.

Then my voice trailed off, as the spirit of his late wife told me what became of her.

"When she passed, you fell into a deep, deep melancholia. She's showing me your pain, and your loneliness. You miss her every day."

"Every day," he whispered back, his eyes shining like a freshly mopped floor. I could feel the thick pounding of his heartbeat, faster and faster. Then a prick, like the tips of two silver swords against my cheeks. *Dimples.* I was grinning.

Clement's words came back to me. *Don't give up on your gift. Once you leave that house you've been living in, your gift will return. I'm confident about that.*

He had been right—my dear Clement.

The doctor met my eyes for the first time since I had begun his reading, and we focused on each other, on something deeper than the surface, and there was a moment of understanding.

*And then use it, May. Use it to make a difference, contribute to the world and help others find peace.*

God was giving me the chance to take back my fate.

"You're different from the other doctors because you care. You do. You've felt what your patients feel, and you want to *help* them, not *restrain* them."

*My story won't be a ghost story, or a tragedy. It will be a love story.*

That's what I'd told Dr. Edmonds only minutes ago, though it felt like years had passed and I'd shrunk and wrinkled into an old wise woman like Grandmammy.

I thought of all the ways a person could love if they were free to do so. They could love a woman or a man, a gift or a curse, whatever story they told themselves, so long as it was *theirs*.

I felt so light I thought I would float right out of my chair.

But it was the doctor who rose so suddenly, I wondered if I had made him levitate—if God had blessed me with a slew of new abilities I didn't yet comprehend. Then I saw the panic in his face and realized he'd risen all on his own. He was out the door before he could reveal anymore of himself to me, the lass who was supposed to be his patient, not his healer.

I don't suspect he was overly concerned with me at that moment.

If he had been, he might have seen the panic in my own eyes. My ability had returned so quickly, I didn't know how it would fit inside this changed version of me. I felt more ghostly than ever, cradling hope in transparent arms.

Hope. It meant so many things to me then. A dream. An impossible longing. A homecoming. Danger. *Everything.*

Would this version of me be able to control my ability, or, in my weakened state, would it take control of me?

# CHAPTER 41

## Rudyard

### 1833

"*P*lease, Mother and Father. Please!" Rudyard's hands clenched at his sides, his breath coming fast. "We can be his guardians, can't we? I know we can!" His heart pounded so fiercely it felt as though his ribs might shatter.

Rudyard's parents, Molly and Phillip Stoker, were leaders in the Quaker community. Their farm's harvest was always plentiful, their table never empty, their hands never idle. They had the means to raise his new friend as their own; he was certain of it.

Unfortunately, his parents didn't seem to share his certainty. They exchanged a long, weighted glance, wrinkles pressing into their foreheads, their expressions drawn tight. His father bounced on his toes—a habit of his when uneasy. His mother's lips thinned to a line.

"Don't you see?" Rudyard insisted, his voice rising. "God has answered our prayers!"

The moment the words left him, he knew he had struck the right chord. He saw it in the way their faces softened, the way their furrowed brows smoothed. He may have spoken too boldly—his elders often reminded him that a Quaker ought not to be so forceful—but he didn't care. He *knew* he was right.

That very afternoon, Rudyard held Samuel's hand as they followed his parents to their lawyer's office on Front Street.

At first, he was certain. He was walking in with a friend, and he would walk out with a brother. He squeezed Samuel's hand, grinning so hard his cheeks ached.

But time passed. The light outside shifted. His grin faded, and he began to feel a twisted knot in his stomach. He'd felt this knot before, only once, when his parents had told him that his baby brother was with God.

His fingers, still clasped around Samuel's, began to feel cold. The boy didn't talk much, but that didn't matter. Rudyard had felt warm and light and happy around him, from the moment they met in his family's parlor.

"Don't worry," Rudyard whispered. "This will work."

Samuel only offered a small smile and an even smaller shrug. He looked exhausted.

Then, from inside the office, his mother's voice: "But, Timothy, New York is a free state." She sounded distressed.

"Yes," Mr. Cook agreed, "but Samuel has arrived by illegal means, and even a formal adoption cannot guarantee his safety."

Rudyard glanced at Samuel, whose eyes widened, glistening with a look too heavy for someone their age. His hands, white-knuckled, twisted the fabric of his sleeves, but otherwise, he was still—terribly still, as if afraid of what might happen next. Rudyard tightened his grip on Samuel's hand.

"Timothy," his father spoke now, his voice firm, "I know you're a lawyer, but you're also a Quaker. We believe in the words of God above any words on paper, written by human hands, do we not? Is there nothing we can do?"

Rudyard let go of Samuel's hand, stepping quietly toward the door. The faint murmur of voices from inside was like a weight pressing against his chest. Would he remain an only child, hope crushed?

Inside, Timothy Cook leaned over his desk, his round face harsh in the dim candlelight.

"There might be a way to combine the two forms: the words of God and the laws of man. But," —he lifted a finger— "what I advise you to do is between us and God. You must reflect first. How much do you wish to provide guardianship for this boy? There are surely other families, perhaps that look more like him, that could take him—"

"He's *not* just a boy. He's my *brother*." The words burst out before Rudyard could stop them. It didn't matter that his parents had told him to wait outside, to give his elders privacy.

A heavy silence stretched out like an eternity. The clock on the mantel ticked once. Twice.

His stomach turned to lead. Slowly, he stepped back from the door, bracing himself for chastisement, for scolding, for disapproval, for disappointment. But he didn't regret saying it, because it was the truth.

To his surprise, his parents only nodded. Their faces looked long and hard. The candlelight made shadowy stripes across them, like rough bark on a beech tree.

"You might as well come in," his mother sighed. "You, too, Samuel." She motioned for the boys to join them, taking each of them in one arm.

Rudyard felt warm and excited once again. When he looked at Samuel, another smile tugged on his sore cheeks.

Mr. Cook nodded, then explained what needed to be done.


ON THE NIGHT of the half moon, when the town's streetlamps were never lit, Rudyard set off with his father to follow the lawyer's advice, as "dubious" as it was. He didn't know the word, but when he looked up at the Black church on Main Street and saw the bob in his father's neck, he began to have an idea.

His father would have preferred to do this alone, but Rudyard had insisted on helping. Samuel was going to be his brother, for pity's sake!

He felt brave as he followed his father's soft footsteps into the church.

They began to search the back room for the vital records. For a moment, he froze. He thought he'd heard someone coming, but it was only a mouse scurrying by.

"Are we criminals, father?" Rudyard dared to ask.

"Not by nature," his father responded wryly. He paused, then knelt before Rudyard, placing a large hand on his son's shoulder. "But my heart does not rebel against me, for I know my God, and I know all men are created equal in his image." His eyes asked a question, and though Rudyard didn't exactly know what his father meant, he nodded.

He watched his father hold the lantern close to the sheaths, frown, then pull his reading glasses out from his pocket, clean them off, and place them on the bridge of his straight nose. He turned the pages with careful, deliberate hands, the whisper of parchment loud in the silence.

Outside, a crow cawed. His father tensed, and Rudyard's stomach tightened. Had someone heard them? Would the Reverend return early?

He held his breath as his father scanned each name, lips moving silently over the words.

*Faster, faster,* Rudyard willed.

He ignored the deep ache in his knees, the hunger curling at his ribs.

A sense of purpose filled his chest. A sense of pride. This was *right.* This was good.

Then, at last, his father's voice—"Clement Cornelius Alingham."

His father exhaled. Rudyard's entire body went limp with relief.

"My brother." His voice cracked, and warmth flooded his chest, arms, legs.

"Born October 31, 1826. Died November 7, 1826. Cause of death: pneumonia," his father confirmed.

Nobody knew Samuel's birthday. As his father explained, enslaved people in Louisiana did not typically keep records or calendars. Instead, they measured their ages by the agricultural year—planting time, harvest time, and so forth. But looking at Samuel and speaking with him, they assumed his age to be about seven years, the same as Rudyard's.

His father traced a finger over the next line. "Parents: Martha and Peter Alingham." An address was scrawled below. "I don't know if the family still lives here. It's been seven years," he murmured. "Perhaps we should return on Sunday and try to find them."

Rudyard's eyes and throat stung. He stared at his shoes to hide his feelings. He felt too much, all the time. He didn't want his father to see.

"I'm going to lose another brother, aren't I?" he asked, trying not to let his voice squeak.

When his father didn't answer, he wiped his eyes and looked out the stained-glass windows. When the light came through, it would be another day. Another loss.

"After all this, it'll be too late!"

His father placed a firm hand on Rudyard's shoulder. "We'll go now," he agreed softly.


THE DOOR of the Alingham cottage cracked open just wide enough to reveal the gleam of steel. Rudyard froze.

A rifle.

His father didn't flinch. He merely lifted his hands, palms open, his voice low and even. "Peter Alingham?"

The barrel of the rifle barely wavered, but the shadowed figure stiffened.

Rudyard felt his heart pounding against his ribs as his father continued, "We've come about your son. Clement."

A pause stretched between them. Finally, the rifle dipped—just an inch.

A woman's voice broke through the dark. "Peter." Mrs. Alingham gripped her husband. Her fingers sank into his arm, and he lowered his rifle before nodding for them to come inside.

As soon as Rudyard crossed the threshold into the little cottage, exhaustion began to make him feel dizzy.

He took a seat on the couch, his eyes heavy, and tried his best to listen to what the elders were saying. Mrs. Alingham was speaking slowly and plainly about the child she'd lost.

Clement Alingham's death had been recorded in the church's vital records. But his father explained to the room, "What is written can be unwritten."

If the Alinghams would give their blessing, Rudyard's father would return to the church that night and erase their son's name from the book.

The elders spoke just a little while longer. Then Mr. Alingham nodded, shook his father's hand, and mumbled something about chopping wood.

Mrs. Alingham was the one to lead Rudyard and his father into their bedroom.

Her hands shook as she opened the top drawer of her dresser and pulled out a small wooden box. She opened the bottom drawer next, removing a tarnished silver skeleton key. She could barely keep her hand still enough to fit the key into the lock. Rudyard thought of offering to help, but his father gestured for him to wait. After a moment, she managed.

The box opened with a puff of dust, the smell of age filling the air. Rudyard peered in. He saw a stack of ancient-looking papers, yellowed and dusty, and at the bottom, a piece of parchment that looked perfect, almost new. *Clement's birth certificate.*

Rudyard's father carefully took the paper from Mrs. Alingham's hand and gave it to Rudyard. Then he cupped her shaking hands before promising her it would be safe.

"I'm going to take this straight to my lawyer to complete a legal and binding adoption. The story will go that you and your husband were under financial duress, and our family"—he placed a hand on Rudyard's shoulder—"agreed to adopt and raise your youngest son."

Rudyard had trouble breathing as he watched Mrs. Alingham try to smile. Instead, a small sob escaped her, her shoulders shaking as she sat down heavily on the bed.

Her lips pressed together, trembling. "We haven't spoken his name in years." Her voice was barely more than a whisper. She released a broken exhale, as if the words themselves hurt. "It's grown thorny with neglect."

Her fingers curled against her dress, twisting the fabric. "Peter and I still visit his grave each year," she admitted. "Never together. We make up excuses—'I'm going to the store,' or 'Peter's visiting his brother.' But we know."

She swallowed hard, staring at the floor. "I see the toy he leaves, something from his childhood. He sees the dried daffodils, my favorite flower. And we say nothing."

Her breath hitched. She pressed a trembling hand to her mouth.

Her voice quivered as she stood, her hand gently resting on Rudyard's cheek.

He closed his eyes, savoring the warmth of her touch. For a moment, he felt as though she might say more, but the words didn't come. Instead, she led them back toward the front door.

Rudyard couldn't shake the feeling that she had more to share, something lingering just beneath the surface. She seemed both sad and joyful at once. Was that even possible?

Finally, she spoke again, her voice steady but tinged with a quiet strength. "His death won't be in vain. A child will be saved because of him. He'll have a safe home after what he's been through, and our Clement will live on."

Rudyard's chest tightened.

What did that mean? What had Samuel been through?

He knew about slavery. His father had spoken of it, had called it a sin, a violation of God's will. But those were words.

This was something else.

This was a mother breaking before his eyes, pressing a trembling hand to her mouth to hold back sobs. This was a father who had answered the door with a rifle, because the world had given him reason to be afraid.

This was a child's name spoken for the first time in years—Clement.

And somewhere in Louisiana, another child—Samuel—had lived through something terrible enough that a mother believed his suffering had *redeemed* her son's death.

Rudyard's stomach twisted.

*What had he been through?*

Then, in a moment that stunned him more than anything else from that night or morning, Rudyard's father stepped forward and held Mrs. Alingham as she sobbed.

He wrapped his arms around this woman he had just met, the same woman whose husband had greeted them with a rifle not long ago.

Rudyard stood frozen, torn between confusion and relief. He was getting a new brother. But would his parents love Samuel as much as they loved *him*? As much as they had loved his baby brother? And would they love him as much as Mrs. Alingham had loved Clement?

With a lump in his throat, he decided it didn't matter. Love wasn't bound by blood or name. It was a choice, and he would choose Samuel. They would choose each other. And together, they would make sure neither of them ever felt the sorrow he had seen in Mrs. Alingham's eyes tonight.

1850

RUDYARD RACED toward the Stoker family home, Olivia by his side, her skirts lifted with a graceful urgency. When they entered the house, his parents were sitting down to tea at the long, wooden dining table.

"It's late, Rudyard," his mother said sternly, though there was a twinkle in her eye. His father raised an eyebrow at her, looked sideways at his son, then frowned at his slice of cake.

Rudyard swallowed, suddenly feeling the weight of the moment. His family stood at the edge of losing a son, not for the second time, but the third. And this time, it was all his fault.

"I brought a friend." Olivia stepped into view, turned to his parents, and curtsied. A grin touched the corner of Rudyard's mouth at the sight of Olivia acting proper. "Come, Liv," he beamed. "We don't stand on ceremony here."

Though his parents paused, their gaze lingering on Olivia with a hint of surprise—especially at this late hour—they welcomed her with their usual warmth. His father asked their housekeeper to prepare two more cups of tea.

His mother took Olivia's coat. "My, you're pretty," she remarked. "Rudyard's been in such a good mood lately. You must be the reason why."

Rudyard was amused to hear her tone was warm, and Olivia chuckled.

"Oh no, Mrs. Stoker. I'm afraid I can't take credit for that—"

Rudyard cleared his throat. "Of course you can," he interrupted, placing a hand on the small of her back. "Olivia has become my dearest friend."

He smiled at her. "But," Rudyard continued, facing his parents, "we did come for a reason." The air in the room shifted. Rudyard felt a familiar knot in his stomach. "I have to tell you something."

He filled them in on Clement's arrest, his voice steady but the dread in his chest growing with every word. Olivia, much to his relief, picked up on the details he missed, offering what little clarity she could. His parents listened in silence. His mother's fingers found and curled into the fabric of his father's sleeve. His father exhaled, long and slow, before turning toward his desk.

"I see," his father murmured at last. "You're certain of all this?"

"Yes," Rudyard said, his throat dry. "I am."

A pause. Then his father moved, retrieving the birth certificate from among his records.

"Let's go," he said as his mother moved for his hat and jacket. "We'll head straight to the jailhouse with proof of Clement's birth in the free state of New York, and all will be well."

Dread sank deeper into Rudyard's stomach. His father smoothed the paper between his fingers, his face unreadable. His mother stood beside him, but her grip on his jacket was tight, white-knuckled.

"This should be enough," she said, though her voice held none of the certainty of her words.

Rudyard swallowed hard. "Should be."

His father's jaw tensed, his gaze flickering toward the door as though already imagining what lay beyond it. Discrimination knew no borders. They all knew that.

But whatever happened, Rudyard had to be the one to face it first. This was his fault. He wouldn't burden them with more agony than necessary.

"Father," Rudyard said, his voice firm but laced with guilt. "Mother. This is something I need to do alone."

The guilt gnawed at him. He had trusted the wrong man, and now the worst had happened. His father couldn't work the system in his favor this time—not if Rudyard ever hoped to redeem himself. His father had already pulled the necessary strings once before, risking the laws of man to give Rudyard a beloved brother and companion.

Clement had been saving everyone else practically since the day he arrived in New York. Now, it was Rudyard's turn to save his brother. To right his wrong.

His father frowned. "I don't understand," he said, his voice a mix of confusion and concern. "You don't have to bear this burden alone. It isn't your fault—"

Olivia parted her lips, a finger poised in the air, but Rudyard hushed her with a glance. The part he'd played in his brother's arrest was a secret he intended to keep from his parents—for now, at least.

"It *feels* like it is," he cut in, his voice rawer than he intended. He exhaled sharply, schooling himself, steadying his tone. "I don't mean to shut you out, but this is something I have to answer for. I have to look him in the eye and tell him I won't fail him."

His mother's brows knitted, but she said nothing, only gave his father's arm a gentle squeeze, just where she had clung to him a moment ago.

"Go tomorrow then," his father advised, his tone shifting in response to her touch. "Bring Timothy with you."

Rudyard and Olivia headed upstairs for the remainder of the night. His father called after him. "You'll free our boy, Rudyard."

Rudyard paused, swallowing a bitter lump in his throat. He didn't look back.

It was first light when the Stokers awoke their son and his house guest. Neither were used to waking early, but they had a mission, so they rubbed the sleep from their eyes, dressed, slugged coffee, and made their way to town, birth certificate in hand.

They had proof that Clement was free, born and raised in Hudson, New York, October 31, 1826, adopted by Molly and Phillip Stoker on Nov 11, 1833. Their first stop was the law office, neatly stationed on the first floor of their lawyer's home in the center of town.

When Rudyard and Olivia arrived, Timothy Cook was already halfway out the door, leather gloves and cane in hand.

"This will free him, won't it?" Rudyard asked.

Timothy grimaced and shook his head.

The truth was, it wouldn't be so simple. Rudyard felt his body sway like the pendulum of a grandfather clock, in a daze of déjà-vu, as the middle-aged lawyer explained that The Fugitive Slave Act was national law, and once a man stood accused of escaping, the government might well like to make an example out of him.

The arresting officer might want to make a name for himself.

Most fearsome of all, the arrest wasn't a mistake, in the sense of the law. Clement *had* escaped slavery, and there was someone in their country who believed his property had been stolen from him, with a cruelty in his heart that would more likely have hardened than thawed in the past seventeen years since Clement had made his way North.

"But we'll fight this, and he'll be released eventually, won't he?" Rudyard pleaded more than asked.

"By the grace of God," the lawyer said as he shuffled Rudyard and Olivia out the door, like children, with his cane.

Rudyard, Olivia, and Timothy entered the jail.

"I'm here to see my brother, Clement Stoker," Rudyard told the stout officer right away.

His eyes narrowed on the man, whose belt was tight around his middle, holding both a worn truncheon and a whistle. The buckle was off center. His frock coat appeared poorly tailored and rumpled, his trousers too baggy, his sideburns overgrown, and his bowler hat did little to hide his balding head. Something about his demeanor just *screamed* bald.

"I'm afraid that's not possible..." the constable began.

Rudyard's cheeks burned and his stomach thundered. He felt like he could punch the man right in his paunch.

"Let us all slow down for a moment here," Timothy said with unfathomable calm. "We have here Mr. Stoker's birth certificate and adoption papers, proving him to be a free man."

The officer's mouth dropped open. He swallowed. "Right. Let me send a telegram. Come back tomorrow, eh? Why don't you? I should have it sorted by then."

Rudyard's nails dug into his palms. He was nearly out of his mind with anxiety. The air felt heavy in the dimly lit prison, and all he wanted was to see his brother.

But then, a light tap on his back broke his focus.

He turned to find Timothy's cane held horizontally, gently guiding him toward the door.

Rudyard squinted, hoping to catch a glimpse of Clement, but his heart sank when he saw only bars and shadows.

Olivia, standing beside him, gave him a look—a silent plea to surrender, just for now. And so he did.

"Trust your lawyer," she whispered, her voice soft but firm.

Rudyard nodded, his throat tight, and allowed Timothy to take the lead.

That night, he stayed at Olivia's. He couldn't face his parents without better news. He needed this to be resolved, needed to be able to give them something to hold on to. Let Timothy be the one to tell them. In another day, it would be sorted. *Please, God. Let it be sorted.*

The next morning, the three of them returned to the prison. The air was even heavier today, filled with the expectation of a resolution that felt far too elusive.

"Can I see my brother now?" Rudyard asked.

The officer—*Duffy*, even his name screamed of an unpolished nature—looked across the three sets of eyes watching him, then shrugged. "Well now, lucky you, the mayor did respond to my telegram. Seeing as you have the documents, it's supposable that one of you can go in."

"Go *in?*" Rudyard's voice rose, incredulous. "Shouldn't you let him *out?* He's a free man. You've made a mistake to begin with!"

Duffy met his gaze with indifference. "Well, not so fast," he chastised, his neck and chin thickening as he spoke. "I do have a piece or two of information to share with yous about that very happenstance."


SEVERAL MINUTES LATER, Rudyard approached the dingy cell. He could hear the sound of his own breathing, the light tapping of his shoes against the scuffed plank floors of the hallway.

Clement shot up from his cot at the sound.

Rudyard looked at his brother. He was wearing the same clothes he'd been wearing when he was arrested, stained in plum-colored blossoms, as though time had stopped for him with the drying of his blood.

But for Rudyard, the days and nights had never been longer. He could only offer a half-smile, Duffy's news stealing away the rest of it.

Duffy unlocked the cell with a grating *clank* of iron against iron.

He lingered for a moment with the gate open, head sunk, until Rudyard cleared his throat.

"Some privacy, perhaps?"

"Oh, uh, sorry," Duffy grumbled before closing the gate behind him.

Rudyard glanced over his shoulder, making sure that Duffy had indeed returned to his desk at the other end of the hallway. When he was sure they were alone, he wrapped his brother in a strained, lifeless hug. He sat down on Clement's bed, the wool blanket rough and thin under him. Clement joined him, the silence between them settling like an old, worn thing.

"There's something you should know," Rudyard said at last, his voice echoing against the bare walls.

As Duffy had explained, the worst had come true. Even with the birth certificate, Clement could not be released. The coppers of Hudson had already sent word to plantation owners in the south of a potential fugitive—strapping, with light-brown eyes and a small birthmark resembling a raven on his left shoulder. They would have to wait two weeks to see if anyone responded to the report before they could release their prisoner.

"Weeks," Duffy grumbled from his desk chair. Rudyard peered at him through the bars of Clement's cell. He looked as much a fixture of the jail as the oil lamp beside him.

"As I was saying..." continued Rudyard, shaking his head.

"Weeks, huh?" Clement said more to himself. "Fine. So I'll have to stay here a while longer." He shrugged one shoulder, letting it fall heavily. He lowered his voice to a dark, hoarse pitch. "Unless my enslaver claims me."

Rudyard rubbed his forehead. Guilt was gnawing at him, sending waves of nausea through his body. He couldn't hide the truth any longer. The closer he came to losing his brother, the more he knew it was time to be honest about who he was, and what he'd done.

"That's not all," he said, trying to shake away the tightening in his chest. "There's something else."

Clement swallowed. His gaze darkened, but he didn't interrupt. He waited.

"Oh, for pity's sake. This is my fault, Clement. I'm the one who told Francis where you're from."

Clement didn't answer immediately. The silence stretched on long enough that Rudyard began to sweat. Finally, Clement's voice broke through, low and unreadable. "Why would you do that?"

"I'm sorry. I'm so, so sorry. I should never have trusted him. I thought—"

"You thought he wanted you," Clement finished, his tone unexpectedly gentle.

Rudyard felt a fierce blush spread across his cheeks. "You knew?"

Clement met his gaze, his eyes soft, understanding. "I've had a feeling for years. And you weren't as subtle with him as you thought. Then when May told me he never touched her, I started to piece it together..."

They grinned at each other, that familiar brotherly grin that almost made them forget the serious trouble they were both in, for Clement's freedom wasn't all that was at stake. Indeed, it was a complicated case.

As the family lawyer explained only minutes before, now that a birth certificate had been introduced as evidence, if Clement were to be claimed by an enslaver in the south, his adoptive family could and would be sued for fraud.

"I will never forgive myself," Rudyard said. Reality closed in, and their grins vanished.

"You should," Clement said to his brother's surprise. He drew in a breath, and let it go with a peculiar air of luxury. "It's time we all stopped lying." A corner of his mouth curved upward. He looked straight at Rudyard. "It's this awful lying that got us here in the first place. Take May's advice, Rud. Be yourself. You don't have to hide and settle for the lowest types of people."

Clement had always been truthful. It was Rudyard who had introduced materialization at French Maude's, Rudyard who had spun the even more elaborate fraud of who he was. Clement fooled everyone else with his hard exterior, but Rudyard had always seen through it. Even now, Clement shared the burden with him, though it was Rudyard's to bear.

If only he had given his blessing to Clement and May. If only he had trusted in the truth of their love. Then he wouldn't be sitting here, facing the very real possibility of losing his brother. Instead, he might have been preparing for London, in search of what he truly needed. Clement and May would be together—yes, a terrifying thought, but a far happier one than the reality they now faced.

What Rudyard couldn't understand was why Clement wasn't angry with him. Not even disappointed. He seemed... relieved.

"How are you not angrier with me?" Rudyard asked at last.

Clement shook his head, searching for words. "Honestly?" he asked. "I'm relieved. I thought it was May who turned me in. Or, rather, May who told Francis to. But she didn't." He exhaled sharply and rubbed the stubble on his jaw. "The only thing I can't figure out is why she hasn't come to see me. Have you spoken to her?"

Rudyard swallowed, unable to meet his brother's gaze, ever intense and scanning.

"She's a tiny thing and you might miss it without really knowing her, but she's feisty. She's strong. If she wanted to see me, she would be here."

Rudyard's eyes pricked. His brother was waiting for a response he couldn't bear to give. "I have something else to tell you," he admitted, a headache forming with the words. Clement's eyes locked on him. Rudyard swallowed. "It was just after your arrest. Olivia told me. May was distraught, and she would have come straight here, had she not been... delayed."

Clement's stare didn't waver. "Delayed *how*?"

Rudyard exhaled sharply, making a strained, choking sort of sound. *Out with it, for pity's sake.* "A doctor from the insane asylum came for her. Clem, he took her away. It was Francis who arranged it." He paused. "I'm sorry," he ended weakly.

Clement's rage reanimated his features, darkening his eyes and tightening the sharp lines of his jaw. He stood up, pacing, clenching his fists as though searching for an outlet for the blood boiling in his veins.

"Clement," Rudyard tried quietly.

Clement kicked the cot with enough force to send it crashing against the wall, the mattress sliding limply to the floor. "I'll find him," he breathed hotly. "I'll ring his neck. I'll beat him senseless."

"He's gone," Rudyard told him, dizzy from watching his brother's cramped pacing. "I don't think he's coming back," he whispered next.

The assurance did little to cool Clement's temper. "Then it's up to you and Olivia. You've got to help her. You've got to get her out of there. Promise me."

It was no use trying to convince Clement that his own safety was more urgent. He wouldn't listen. He stopped pacing, turned to Rudyard, and stood very still. "She can't be trapped in there," he insisted. "She can't be caged."

"What about *you?*" Rudyard pressed.

"I can't believe she's trapped in there and I can't do a damned thing about it," Clement said, more to himself, anger spilling from his tongue in rolling, boiling hot bubbles. "Forget about me, for the love of God." He exhaled hard, eyes locked on his brother, his throat bobbing. His expression shifted from fury to something more fragile —frustration, helplessness. "You don't understand her, Rud. She's a Traveler. She can't be locked up like that."

Clement was right. Rudyard *didn't* understand. Perhaps if he'd gotten to know her better, really considered who this woman was... but he hadn't. He hadn't allowed himself to. To acknowledge her as real, as complex, as deserving, would have meant facing something unbearable.

How could he lie with the husband of a woman who was more than just an idea?

A young, gawky copper cleared his throat outside the cell, puffed up with self-importance. Rudyard's time was up. He sighed heavily before mumbling, "I'll get her out. I promise."

Outside the jailhouse, the afternoon sun struck his eyes like a blade. He squinted against the brightness, raising a hand to shield his gaze. Olivia was waiting for him, chatting with Duffy as though he were an old friend rather than their enemy. *A bit cavalier*, Rudyard thought, but he didn't bother to question her. It was her job to butter up men; perhaps it had become second nature.

Duffy, of course, was falling for it—dazzled, as men so often were. Just as Rudyard had been.

Charmed and duped. By soft words. By firm hands. By gnawing curiosity.

He cleared his throat and offered his arm to Olivia. As they walked, he wondered: could second nature ever be reversed?

# CHAPTER 42

# Olivia

Olivia and Rudyard walked arm in arm into Governor's Tavern. It was so early the floors were still being mopped from the night before. Each footstep felt like a sticky ghost of the last time they had all been there together—all four of them.

Now Olivia saw no dancing, no lively music, only the hacking of a drunk in the corner and a sad bout of arm wrestling going on at a small shadowed table.

The barkeep, wisely, didn't say a word about a woman in his establishment during regular hours. She dared him with her eyes, but he only nodded at her. She idly pulled at a glossy curl, tossing him a smile when she saw him steal a glance.

Rudyard stared at her impatiently.

She shrugged. *Old habits.*

"Two hot toddies," Rudyard ordered.

They sipped. The steam curled upward, spiced and soothing, but she felt no joy in it. Not today.

It was always the little things, the tiny details no one else seemed to notice, that told her she wasn't dead to the world yet. Her life had cracks, but somehow, light always seemed to seep through. But now? Now, she didn't know where to go or how to find happiness when everything wasn't just cracked but broken, the pieces too jagged to fit back together.

"How'd he take it?" she asked after a long sip.

"Not bad, actually," Rudyard said simply. His clipped tone told her not to ask any more about it. She pressed her lips together, needing more.

"So we just wait?" she asked after a moment.

He nodded glumly. "And somehow"—he sighed—"we have to find a way to get May out of Dr. Edmonds's asylum without her husband to vouch for her or any way to visit."

Olivia wished she could shed her stiff, suffocating dress and crumple into a ball like a page of poorly written poetry. She had made exactly one true female friend in all her life. She had thought she was powerful, fooling the men who came to see her. They thought they possessed her, but for that hour each night, *she* possessed *them*—a spirit, a deceiver, a creator.

But what if she had been looking at the world backwards, as though through a mirror or the reversed image of a daguerreotype? What if her fraud had left her powerless when the doctor came to take May?

Her stomach turned at the memory of May's face. She'd looked so bewildered and lost, like the day they'd met. But what could Olivia have done differently? Under Maude's orders, she couldn't say a word in May's defense, lest the entire house fall under arrest for fraud.

Olivia had told herself the sitters at Maude's needed her. May wasn't the only one who brought light and closure to the seances. All of the girls did. The sitters relied on Olivia, too. She helped give them proof of life after death, in a time when everyone knew death with a seething intimacy. Hardly a parent knew life without the loss of a child. Hardly a lover knew life without the loss of their affinity. It was a harsh world, made beautiful only by a collection of small moments, carefully written down in blue or black script or preserved in a portrait. Olivia had found the magic that most people missed.

And she had let it go.

She was as much a fool as she had been the first time she let her imagination run wild.

*Nobody* had relied on her. It was *she* who had relied on her audience.

And now? Now she had nothing.

"Are you sure we couldn't ask a nurse to let us in?" she suggested, knowing she was grasping at straws.

Rudyard shook his head. "They don't allow visitors, at least not right away. I knew a woman from our community who was checked in last spring. No one's been allowed to see her since."

They finished their drinks, ordered one more round, and then, finally, there was nothing left for them there.

By the time they stepped outside, Olivia wasn't sure if minutes or hours had passed. The wind swirled, blocking the noise of the city street. In the silence, Rudyard placed a hand on Olivia's arm. She breathed in the moment, because moments were the only real things folks were entitled to.

How wonderful to be touched by someone who wants nothing from you but to see you soothed.

Was *that* all she'd ever truly wanted? To be reached for, without expectation?

Her eyes fluttered open. She felt as though she were outside her own body, like one of May's spirits, and she imagined her lashes as two butterfly wings billowing against the falling snow.

And then, suddenly, it struck her. If they couldn't reach May, someone else had to.

"Rudyard," she gasped. "We're not allowed to see May, but what if there is someone who is?"

His eyes met hers. His head tilted to the side, and she was sure he could read her mind. There were so many reasons why the plan wouldn't work—too many, really. But it was a plan, nonetheless. It was a moment of hope, a crack when everything had seemed broken. And not all cracks are bad. Some of them let in light.

# CHAPTER 43

# Map

*I* gritted my teeth at the sound of my dormitory's door locking behind me. It had been days since the doctor had spoken to me, leaving me with a gnawing pit in my stomach. As I sat on my cot, a chill wind entered through a crack in the decaying brick wall—my only company.

What had been going through the doctor's mind since his late wife's visit? Thanks to Rudyard and his obsession with the spiritualist press, I knew there were doctors taking an interest in Spiritualism, shedding their white coats like seal skins, calling themselves believers and the seance a scientific experiment.

This must have been what bothered the doctor most.

Believers insisted on total darkness during their seances. The doctor was no stranger to darkness. I could see how it had coated him since his beloved wife passed. He still saw the world in shades of black and gray, a flat photograph of what once was. Perhaps he wondered: spend one hour in the dark, and could not anything seem possible?

He wasn't alone in his skepticism. Rudyard had also told us that clear examples of fraud were coming out of the woodwork, and Edmonds must have wondered whether I, too, was a fraud or simply insane. I suppose as a doctor, he must have felt inclined to believe the latter.

Now I wondered if his question had changed. Had *he* gone completely mad?

I knew about his late wife. Perhaps I had found an old obituary, but how would I have known about the daisies?

And I was changing before his eyes.

Each day I felt stronger, more confident, more driven to help others heal. Surely he overheard snippets of my conversations with the other patients in the dining hall, when I said things like "Your sister doesn't want you to grieve over her anymore. It wasn't your fault," and "Your grandfather wants you to know he's with your mother and father, and he knows it's been hard for you on your own, but you've got a fire in you that will see you out of here if you only spark it."

He'd quickly change direction, for as much as he must have wanted to chase me away and forbid me from filling the "deranged" minds of patients with lies, these women were making progress. A cloud of gloom was lifting in the asylum. The air was softer, like a kiss on the forehead, and I imagined he noticed the absence of echoed screams when he took his afternoon tea in his office.

He must have chastised himself for even entertaining the idea I might be legitimate. He wanted to debunk me, he just didn't know how. In the meantime, he wanted nothing to do with me.

I'm certain he was only too glad to pass his medical obligations to me over to a visiting doctor, whom he had certainly never heard of before, and of whose unusual practices and theories he knew nothing. This doctor would only be visiting for the day, yet perhaps Dr. Edmonds hoped that in that time, he might offer a fresh perspective on my case.

It was morning when Dr. Edmonds called me into an office I'd never been in before, keeping his distance as though worried I'd see into his soul and extract more secrets if he moved any closer. Then he spoke, gesturing to the door.

"This is Dr. Randolph. He specializes in cases like yours. He'll be examining you today." As a cane tapped through the doorway and a tall figure followed, I gasped. I had nowhere to run. No one to shield me. Just a pair of sharp, shadowed eyes fixed on mine, pinning me to the whitewashed walls of the room.

He must have been pleased to have me there, alone in that cold, stark room, with nowhere to run.

Like Edmonds's office, this room had large windows, except these windows were as barred as the little ones in the dormitory. A wooden desk sat in the heart of the room. Beneath the scattered quills, ink pots, patient records, and notebooks, there were scratches and ink stains. Against one wall stood a cabinet of glass jars—tinctures and herbs, likely laudanum and ether, a doctor's "medicines" of sedation. Against the other wall lay a raised wooden plank covered in a gray linen sheet—the examination table.

How much time had passed since I'd hoped to lie on one of these tables myself and prove my virtue? I couldn't dwell on the answer long, for my eye caught on what hung above the table—a doctor's more ominous tools: restraints, a stethoscope, forceps.

In this office, Paschal could do whatever he wanted to me, and nobody would turn an ear toward my screaming. Perhaps even worse, he could say whatever he wanted to me, and nobody would stick up for me. He was, after all, my doctor, the man who was supposed to care for my well-being.

But I knew better. I knew better than most that doctors were just men. Human beings. Some cared for their patients and some cared for themselves.

I *was* frightened. Our "protectors" took liberties behind locked doors, after all. But I wouldn't let Paschal see me squirm. I still had my pride, even in that terrible prison they called an asylum.

He sat behind the desk, gesturing for me to sit on the rickety wooden chair in front. I sat, clasping my hands tightly together on my lap. When he didn't speak, I began to fidget.

"You must be pleased to see me here. Got what you wanted," I said at last.

He stared at me with his hands clasped across the desk. To my surprise, he frowned.

"I didn't want this," he said, almost wounded by my accusation.

Then his shoulders relaxed, and when he spoke, his tone was so casual, one might have thought he was asking me for directions to the privy. "I have to tell you, May, Clement's former enslaver has identified him. Seventeen years ago, a mother and son escaped his plantation. He kept records. Knew about an unusual birthmark or some such marker on the boy. Now he's coming up to New York for the trial. Our man is lucky, really, to get a trial at all." He shrugged as if discussing a horse race with a clear favorite. "But I'm afraid the odds are not in his favor. The date's already been set."

I had expected Paschal to gloat about getting rid of me. Or perhaps to scold me for setting the spiritualist movement so behind. But not this.

I felt sick, like all the air in the room had been sucked out. A vision of Clement, strip-searched by coppers, invaded my mind with a burst of light. I could hear their voices calling out descriptions as they lifted his arms, turned him this way and that, cataloging him like stolen goods. I could see them tracing the delicate shape of his mother's necklace, their fingers dirty and careless. *Now where does a Quaker go about finding something like this?*

"You've got to do something," I breathed, my voice barely there.

Paschal only stared. That same infuriating, unreadable stare, as though I were a curiosity under glass. At last, he spoke, and his words surprised me even more than his first. "You're not pro-slavery, are you?"

I glanced at him, dumbfounded. He sounded perfectly genuine in his curiosity, as though he were just beginning to come to that conclusion.

I began to understand why he didn't want me staying in Hudson and playing spiritualist. It finally started to make sense. I was Irish, after all. My people were competing for jobs with his people, and there weren't enough to go around. Not if the enslaved were freed and traveled north. That was the story, anyway. If I stayed, wouldn't I just convince the people of that tale? What was to stop me from telling the world that the spirits sided with the Irish, with the politics of the South?

I wanted to tell him he was a damned, ridiculous fool, especially for a man so clever. Instead, I answered simply. "No. I'm not."

He nodded, uncharacteristically quiet. "Then I'm here to help you."

"Why?" I asked him. *Why now?* was what I really wondered. *Because our politics are not at odds, am I finally human enough to deserve my sovereignty?*

"Because it's what Clement wants. He asked me to help you."

I blinked. "Clement wants *your* help?" I let the words settle, unable to make sense of them. "You're not even fond of each other."

His lips twitched. One of his smiles, I supposed. Each one meant something different, but none of them meant joy. "We're beyond personal preferences, May," he said, like he was explaining something simple to a child. "My brotherhood with Clement is deeper than affection. He's a human being at the gates of hell. He's not doing well, if we're speaking plainly. We need to get you out and help him next. He won't think of himself until he knows you're safe."

I pictured Clement alone in his cell. Was he wearing iron? Were they feeding him proper food and keeping his cell clean? I feared the worst.

"Get me out?" I asked. "How did you even get in?"

"I heard about the trial date and went to see Clement myself. At first, the copper in charge wouldn't let me speak with him. Said it could be considered witness-tampering... or something. He didn't seem quite sure, in fact, about *why* I couldn't see our man.

"Luckily for me, Rudyard and your lovely scarlet friend arrived shortly after. This whole charade was their idea. They'd gone to look for me at my hotel. My wife told them I'd gone to the jailhouse. And then there we were, all three of us together. That Miss Olivia is a charmer. Had no trouble distracting the copper."

He smirked, shaking his head. "Poor bastard's a lonely sort of wooden spoon. As soon as your girl started chatting with him, he forgot everything else, and Rudyard and I walked right over to Clement's cell."

I gaped at him. "She distracted him right there in the station. In front of everyone?" I whispered.

Another strange smile, sprinkled with satisfaction. "She just listened to him talk. What did you think, May?"

He raised an eyebrow at me. I sighed. Oh, how this country has changed me. Hudson had turned me into a lass that a sex magician thought impure of mind.

"Poor man, too," Paschal continued, not fazed for long. "He feels nothing goes right for him, and his wife doesn't appreciate all he does for her. I overheard a bit. It's like I say, an affinity should come and go as we change and adapt. It's rare indeed for a person to find their other half for the rest of their life, and yet we so readily sign a marriage contract." He shook his head, amused at the folly of human attachment.

"Anyway," he continued, "Clement made it clear we needed to help you first, so I'm doing this for him as much as for you. For him, really. Why keep up pretenses at this point?"

He sighed, and then, with a flourish, he spread his hands and bared his very white, very small teeth. "Clem directed us to a forger and now here I am, the visiting Dr. Randolph, at your service."

I was stunned, unable to fully wrap my mind around it all.

"Clement knows a forger?" It was the first question that left my lips, for the Clement I knew was honest and forthright, at times to a fault.

"And he told you to lie?" Had the jailhouse changed him so greatly?

Paschal shrugged. "The price of love is never too high, I suppose."

We might have exchanged a genuine smile then, but it happened too quickly to be certain.

"Clement doesn't lie to himself, anyway," Paschal added. "He's an honest man, albeit a bit of a prig. It's the system we're in that forces us all to lie, at some point or another. When we start lying to ourselves, that's when the trouble begins."

I bit back my smile, hesitant to reveal too much.

This man, this self-alleged descendant of Madagascar royalty, was a mystery to me still, and I couldn't lay all my cards out on the table. My heart pounded. Like it or not, I had to trust him, at least somewhat. He was the only person on my side. The only person allowed into my brick prison.

I exhaled slowly, forcing down the lump in my throat. No point in dwelling on what I couldn't change. I had to focus on what came next.

"And what am I supposed to do now?" I asked. "The doctor won't even look at me, let alone listen to me. He believes I'm insane."

Or worse, I brooded. Perhaps my situation was more dire than I'd realized, and the doctor was *lying to himself* about my sanity.

Paschal shrugged, less energetically this time. I could see he was growing bored of this favor he had promised to a man he didn't care for.

"Prove him wrong," he said. Then he smiled, and for the first time, I saw a spark of joy. "Make him think he's cured you."

I swallowed.

"Without your husband's permission," he continued practically, "the only way to get out of here is to petition for your freedom from the higher ups."

I frowned in question.

"The Superintendents' Association," he clarified. "It's an organization made up of thirteen organizers and superintendents of America's insane asylum. Write to them. State your case, clearly and simply. Prove that you are a cured patient, ready to rejoin society as such. Avoid any show of passion. That'll work against you."

I blinked. I didn't want to tell him, didn't want him to think me daft, but what choice did I have?

"I can't write."

"Oh," he said, unfazed. "Miss Olivia. She's something of a writer, isn't she? We'll have her write the letter. Best to have it in a woman's script."

"Right," I said slowly, wondering where Olivia truly stood in all of this mess and what lengths she would travel to help me. She hadn't spoken up for me when Edmonds came to collect me, after all. That memory still left me hollow.

"You're going to play the part of a cured patient. Admit to the lunacy diagnosis. Act like a 'normal' lady." He leaned in closer, so near I could smell the sheep's milk in his pomade. "Have your abilities returned yet?"

My mouth parted in shock. Not at the question, but at his certainty. It wasn't *if* my ability had returned, but *when*.

"Aye," I breathed.

"Then you are *not* a normal lady, Miss May. Not by a long shot." His voice was low, threaded with something almost reverent. Then, with an arch of his brow, he added, "Don't give up on your talent. So long as you plan to use it for *good*."

*Good*. The meaning was clear. It meant politics. He wanted me on his side. If I *had* to remain in the picture, he'd make me an asset. It was progress, I supposed.

I stared at him, mouth still so ajar Mammy would have warned me against catching flies. A smirk touched the corner of his mouth.

"The letter is important," he continued, slipping back into business. "You'll need it for your doctor to release you. But that's the easy part. That's bureaucracy, you see. A bother, but nothing personal. The doctor, on the other hand... He does seem to know you already. You'll have to convince *him*, too."

He was right. Dr. Edmonds was the real challenge.

Rudyard had once remarked that the difference between believers and skeptics was that believers didn't need to experience something to have faith, and skeptics wouldn't believe even after seeing it with their own eyes.

Well, Dr. Edmonds *had* experienced it. And the flicker of hope in his bespectacled eyes had told me that he *wished* to believe. Maybe he could not admit as much, but deep in his heart, he did.

Now, I had to tell him that my readings had been nothing but symptoms of madness. It would tear him apart. He might try to accept my supposed cure, but once the seed of doubt is planted, it's nearly impossible to keep seeing the world in the same black-and-white, dead-and-alive kind of way.

I had my work cut out for me, that much was certain.

With one last sigh, I accepted Paschal's advice.

# CHAPTER 44

# Olivia

*O*livia whirled through her bedroom, rifling through drawers and shelves in search of her quill pens and parchment. She hadn't used them in so long, she'd forgotten where she last left them. Without the circles, without May, there was no joy in creating, no muse to be courted in silky white dresses.

Eventually, she remembered stashing her supplies at the bottom of her trunk after Nellie had organized her desk, wondering if the maid might have spotted them.

She pulled out a journal and pen, then sat at her desk. Taking a steadying breath, she began to write. *To the esteemed members of the Superintendents' Association...*

The words flowed with a startling ease, and Olivia couldn't help but wonder if she had more in common with that frizzy-haired forger Clement knew—C.L. Blood, of all names—than she'd care to admit.

When she finished, she carefully tore out the letter, folded it, and slipped it into a folio.

She had just reached for the doorknob when another idea struck her, making her bite back a grin. She glanced over her shoulder at her journal and pen, still scattered across the desk.

She shouldn't...

And yet, she found herself sitting on the edge of her chair once more, chewing on her thumbnail. She started sketching the faint outline of a man with a profound gut and impervious light eyes. She smirked, pleased, and kept going. When the drawing was done, she held it up, nodding in satisfaction. Then, she began to write.

Unlike her last attempt at a story, this one flowed like a river. It was a long one, however. By the time she'd finished, the feathery shadow of her pen had grown longer, and the sun was dipping west.

She quickly folded the drawing and story together, tucked them into the folio, and set off toward the post office.

"Two envelopes, please," she said to the teller. "And would you look up the addresses for me? One is for The Superintendents' Association, and the other is for *The New York Tribune*."

"My, you have friends in high places, Livy dear."

Olivia's stomach dropped at the familiar rasp. She exhaled before turning around, a fake smile plastered to her face. "Maude, what a coincidence running into you here."

Maude squinted, eyeing her up and down, arms crossed. "Come now," she sighed. "Seven years, remember? I've known you long enough to know you're up to something, and that something, I already know, is a mistake. What's going on, Olivia?"

Olivia straightened. "I'm just mailing a couple of letters," she said with feigned cheer. She sniffed, then looked away. *Shit*. She always sniffed when she was lying. Maude would know that.

Maude smacked her vibrant lips. "Olivia, baby doll, are you getting involved?" She didn't have to specify what she meant.

Olivia exhaled sharply. She knew what she had to do. Why couldn't Maude just step aside for once and let her do it?

"Look, Maude, you know I respect you more than anyone in the world. But I can't just stand around idly while May—*our May*—rots in the asylum! I was careful, Maude. You can trust me." She glanced behind her at the teller, who had already begun assisting the next customer. Maude discreetly tugged her towards a silent corner, away from listening ears. "I signed the letter in May's name. This won't get traced back to us," Olivia whispered.

Maude folded her arms again, considering. "And the other letter?" she asked.

Olivia sighed. The one destined for *The New York Tribune*. "Anonymous," she shrugged, praying to whatever entity did or didn't exist that Maude wouldn't ask to see it.

"Let me see it."

*Shit.*

Olivia's hands shook as she slowly withdrew her drawing and story, animated by the hope that Maude might see the humor in them. But she didn't let go, even as Maude pulled them stiffly from her fingers. As the madam looked over the documents, her eyes bulged.

"Olivia. Under no circumstances are you to mail this! No, no, *no*." She was about to rip the pages down the middle, but Olivia snatched them back. She looked Maude in the eye, a challenge, though she swallowed a lump in her throat. "Olivia," Maude said slowly, "if you send this out, that'll be it for us. I can't bring scandal into our home."

Olivia sniffed again—*damn it, damn it, damn it*—but she didn't back down. Her eyes didn't waver, and she wouldn't give the pages back.

"Livy, baby, I'm going to ask you one last time. Hand me those pages, or go back to the house, and pack your things."

Olivia's breath hitched. Her hands trembled as she clutched the pages, fingers wrinkling the parchment. She looked at them. Then she looked at Maude. Her savior. Her captor. Her surrogate mother. Her friend. Her boss.

Tears welled in Olivia's eyes.

And she made her choice.

# CHAPTER 45

## 𝔐𝔞𝔭

wo weeks passed before I heard a single word from beyond the asylum walls. I kept careful track of the days, not just for myself, but for Clement. His trial loomed closer, and my nightmares were filled with shadows of what could happen to him within his dark cell. Was he as buried to the outside world as I was? Was he, too, locked away from visitors, from fresh air, from any proof that the world still turned outside?

Paschal's words haunted me. *Prove Dr. Edmonds wrong. Make him believe you're cured. Act normal.*

It should have been simple. But in the wee hours of the night, when the tiny square window above my cot revealed the most perfect hues of purple and copper, I thought of Ireland. I thought of the wagon's warmth, my siblings' bodies pressed close, their slow, steady breaths. And that was when the loss would settle over me like a thick fog, pressing, suffocating.

I longed for a sign that everything would work out in the end.

More than anything, I longed for the raven who'd once let me stroke his feathers, the one who had always *meant* something, even if I never knew what. His absence now felt like a warning. Each night, I searched the window for him. Each night, I found nothing but the hollow dark.

The lonesomeness dug into me like a silver dagger. I'd curl up and let the tears come in silence, feeling my da's voice slither through my thoughts. *You're good for one thing only—playing the part of a ghost.*

Maybe he was right. A ghost was better left alone. A ghost couldn't be loved.

I'd seen too many people try and end up little more than ghosts themselves, never living their real lives still before them. They were drowning, when they could have been floating, deliciously buoyant and at peace. That was all that ever came from my readings: sending people to a watery grave on earth, anchoring them to the dead instead of the living.

At night, frustration gnawed at me. I thought about the friends I'd made in America, how the one who was not quite a friend, Paschal Randolph, seemed to think I could get myself out of there, how it's so rare in life for anyone to believe in you, and how in Hudson, it seemed quite a lot of people *did* believe in me.

And yet, their belief wasn't enough.

I couldn't make heads or tails of how to appear normal. I wasn't clever enough. I'd never be clever enough for any of them. My thoughts spiraled in on themselves until I accepted what I had always feared: that I was exactly where I was meant to be. Away from everyone. Away from the land of the living.

Love was for those who deserved it.

That's when Dr. Edmonds called me into his office.

"A letter has arrived," he announced, his voice clipped. "From the Superintendents' Association."

My spine went rigid.

"Apparently," he continued, "they received your *remarkably* articulate letter admitting to a correct diagnosis of lunacy and a full recovery due to my care."

He peered at me over his spectacles, waiting.

I swallowed. *He knows.*

Dr. Edmonds knew I couldn't read or write. He knew I had received no visitors. My pulse pounded against my ribs as I willed my expression into one of innocent surprise.

"One of my friends must have written it," I said carefully. *Truthfully.* There was no sense lying to him.

His brows furrowed. "You must have very astute friends, to know exactly what to say and to whom, in order to have you released."

My heart beat out of my chest. I didn't know how to lie. I never had, and I cursed the world that forced a person to lie just to be free, just to be themselves.

"What does the Association's letter say?" I asked.

He sat down quickly, as though a moment slower and he'd change his mind. "Miss May," he began, resuming a formal tone with me. "It says"—he slid his reading glasses up the bridge of his long nose and scanned the document—"that the Association sees no reason to keep you in the care of the state, so long as your doctor, being me, attests that the patient, you, of course, is now sane, acknowledging, naturally, that you have no mediumistic abilities."

He held my freedom in his hands. All he had to do was sign a piece of paper. I was so close. I could feel the breeze through my hair, the fine wool of my former skirts, the cobblestone beneath my boots.

I let out a breath. *Don't let him see how desperate you are.* "Will you do it?" I asked. I couldn't stand another night in that prison, just as I couldn't stand another night away from Clement. We needed to be together. Together, we could face any challenge. Alone, I was withering.

Dr. Edmonds studied me, his fingers steepled beneath his chin. "Do you mean to say that you are no longer a spiritualist? That you are not now, nor have you ever, communed with the dead?"

The question made my stomach twist. I had only just been given a second chance at traipsing the line between worlds. I had banished the spirit realm and mocked its existence with a lie. Now the spirits were giving me another chance. If I lied again, would I lose my gift forever? Would it be worth it? I would be a free woman, but would I even be *me* anymore?

I set my jaw. There had to be more to me than that.

"That's exactly what I mean to say."

He blinked, his brows knitting together. "Mrs. McMurry—"

"May."

"Miss May." He sighed. "This very morning, I overheard you telling Miss Price that her deceased cousin was in the room with her."

I swallowed. It was true. Her cousin had been there, bond still strong through the veil of death. I cursed myself for being so obvious about it, but how was I to know he'd been watching?

"Dr. Edmonds," I began, then closed my mouth.

His lips twitched. His eyes narrowed. "How did you know about the daisies?"

A shiver ran through me. My throat felt dry as old parchment. I wanted to speak earnestly, to plead my case, but any display of emotion would damn me as hysterical. I was trapped. *I cannot lie, and I cannot tell the truth.*

He drummed his fingers on the desk. "Is she here now?" he asked. "What does she say?"

I clenched my hands into fists. "Please," I whispered, "don't ask me that. I am cured." My voice was weak and feeble.

"What does she say?" he demanded, pounding a fist against his desk.

I flinched, my breath shuddering in my chest. My eyelids felt heavy, my pulse too fast. I had to get this right. There was no room for error with the late Mrs. Edmonds. Slowly, I breathed in, then out. I let my mind slip into that liminal place, between the world of the living and the world beyond.

She was there. Waiting.

I nodded to her, then opened my eyes.

"*Dearest*," I murmured, "*you're allowed to change your mind. Just as you did about me.*"

Dr. Edmonds stilled. His ink-dark eyes widened, and for a moment, I could see him perfectly as he must have looked as a young man, in a garden of fresh love, rather than this sullen, clean-shaven, thin-lipped and pale-faced doctor before me, worn down by the weight of his choices.

"Please," I begged, "tell the Association that I'm sane. Tell them I renounce spiritualism. Tell them whatever it is they want to hear. I promise you I will not practice any longer. I will hold no more seances. Just please tell them what I ask you!"

He hesitated. There was kindness behind the ink of his eyes. I'd seen him act kindly here and there, when he'd lay a hand on a patient's shoulder or serve me tea. I only hoped that the depth of his capacity would extend toward me now.

Would he do what I asked?

At last, he shook his head and stood up.

"I cannot lie for you, Mrs. McMurry. May."

My heart sank.

"I can't tell the Association that you have no mediumistic abilities, because I believe that you do."

Had I heard him right?

"My wife," he said suddenly, his voice quiet. "I didn't propose at first. I wanted to open the asylum. I had too many plans for my occupation. I didn't think I'd have time for a wife."

I barely breathed.

"But she convinced me that it would work out, that she would support me no matter what." He looked me square in the eyes, his face filled with sorrow, his eyes still sunken but keen. "I changed my mind." There was a half chuckle, like he couldn't figure out if he was nervous or in awe, tragically sad or achingly happy. His eyes were shining.

"You must change it again!" I urged, my voice thick with desperation. "If you know that I'm sane, you must tell them what they want to hear and let me out of this place. I need to get out of here!"

He shook his head, faster this time. "I cannot lie. I'm a doctor. I have morals."

"But—"

"I cannot lie, and I cannot admit the truth. If I tell the Association that I have faith in your abilities *and* your sanity, it will be the end of my profession. I didn't neglect my wife to become a doctor, just to leave the whole medical field behind!" He was speaking through gritted teeth, though the shadow of a question lingered in his tone.

I was at a loss for words. He felt as trapped as I did, but we were not the same. He had the power to help yet lacked the courage.

Again, I thought of Clement, knowing I'd found a rare and brave man, but he was taken from me before we'd even had the chance to properly love one another.

I thought of my family in Ireland, next. How could I even dream of Clement, when a life with him would require me to give up my readings? He hated everything to do with spiritualism, and it was getting involved with me and my charade that got him arrested in the first place. Sure, he'd called me a miracle, but if I married him, wouldn't he want his wife to take on a more respectable and domestic role?

And how would I ever earn enough money for my family as a wife to someone who gave his time to those less fortunate, quite literally, freely?

I sighed, for none of these lingering thoughts even mattered. I was trapped, and so was he.

Dr. Edmonds stood, mumbling an apology as he turned away. I did not look at him as he left.

And after that, I refused to read for anyone.

No matter how strongly I felt a spirit pulling at me, clawing through the veil, I ignored them. Grit my teeth against them. Every one of them.

I refused my meals. What was the point of eating? My family was a world away, starving, beyond saving. If they had no hope, then neither did I.

Hunger? That was nothing. I was no stranger to hunger. I hungered for closeness, for fresh air and the sight of stars, for wind that reddens your cheeks and blows life through your lungs, for a love I thought once, once upon the briefest of times, I might deserve. Those hungers were fierce and fearsome.

But hunger for food? That was run of the mill.

I was ready for it all to end—the monotony, the grating turn of the keys, the screams that had settled into my bones like an old hymn. I could no longer tell which ones belonged to my dreams, which to my memories, and which still echoed through wretched halls. They had all blurred together, a chorus of sorrow that I could not silence, no matter how I tried.

I was still thin.

It wouldn't take long for my hunger to send me across the world to where I belonged, like ashes rising from an open fire, driftless in the windswept abyss.

By the time word reached me that my family was gone, and that Clement was gone, and that I had failed them both, I would already be gone, too.

# CHAPTER 46

# Clement

*C*lement sat with his back to the cell wall. He rubbed his forehead, sick to death of the sound of Duffy's strangled snores.

The law could be unkind. No news to him. His birth father would be unwavering in his will to reclaim what he believed to be his property, if not to keep, then to sell. Profit from.

Clement pressed his fingers to his eyes, rubbing hard against the memories. In the light of day, they were easier to forget, scattered like nuts and bolts rather than heavy machinery. But even scattered, there were too many of them.

There was the plantation. His mother and siblings (he knew who they were, yet they were strangers). The hunger. The kind that made him wait by the kitchen door for Cook to throw out scraps, racing the dog for crumbs. The graveyard not far from his enslaver's mansion, where folks claimed to see ghosts on black horses, wailing, never going to reach heaven.

Nuts and bolts. But every day, one or two worked themselves loose, and he was forced to relive it all over again. Forced to rub his eyes against the shadows on the walls.

He shrugged stiffly to himself.

Didn't matter how old he was. The most painful memories still gripped. Gripped from the inside, deep in his body. Transformed into the most insidious parts of himself, hardest to touch and to heal. They were like ghosts that walked with him. Most painful of all, they lingered for a reason.

The thought sank into his shoulders like two strong hands. *The ghosts lingered for a reason.* Hadn't that always been obvious? They were waiting to be set free. A ghost longs for freedom. Why would death change that? Spirits couldn't be so different from the people they'd once been.

What would May say? He pictured her lips, could almost hear the soft, low cadence of her voice.

*All energy, all spirits, want to move, to be recycled, to be released from obligation and returned home.*

He stood so abruptly, the cot banged against the wall. He waited. More snoring.

He walked toward the window.

That's why he did his work. That's why he'd risked his life, the laws of man be damned. Oppression cycled through generations. It kept moving indefinitely, like water from the river to the clouds and back to the river. If he didn't stop it, who would? If his pain didn't end, his mother's never would.

A particularly obtrusive snore echoed from Duffy's chair. Clement sighed bitterly, frustration like a belt squeezing his chest. He hadn't done enough. He couldn't have. Why else would his mother and grandmother still walk with him?

*When you're dead, you're dead.*

The day had been blustery when he'd uttered those words in Theobold's shop. He had yet to discover that May was anything more than a month. Even as he'd said those words, something had felt off, like he'd tried to fit God into a garment too small.

It was *his* freedom that his family waited for and guided him toward. They wouldn't rest completely, they wouldn't loosen their grips, until he, in turn, let them.

Now with his back against the dirty wall of his cell, he wondered: *If I am returned to this old enslaver, and I die in chains, what will happen to them?*

Wondered still: *If I die in this cell, in chains but by my own hands and my own volition, what will happen to them, then?*

He'd been imprisoned for two months now, entering the month of March and still waiting for his trial. His father had warned him at an early age to prepare for March, The Dying Time, when some would sacrifice themselves for others. Forgo food so their loved ones would have enough to live on.

Clement laughed wryly at God's sense of humor. He'd been thinking about The Dying Time when Rudyard had first told him about spiritualism.

And now, he was thinking about sacrifice.

He moved to his bed. Squeezed the coarse wool rag of a blanket between his fists. Rubbed his head violently. May had told him his ancestors were with him. Were they with him even here, in this jail, when there was no right decision to be made?

Without ceremony, he tore off a strip of the bed linen, raggedy enough not to require too much effort. A noose began to take shape in his hands.

He wouldn't use it.

But what would it feel like once it was complete? An escape?

Would May be imagining her own escape? From her own kind of jail, in her family's own insidious cycle?

He pictured her face, heart-shaped and prettier than any he'd seen before. Her blue eyes that sparkled when she smiled, her honey laugh, her wild curls. He thought about touching them. Soft as ferns. About hugging her. Her narrow body against his.

It felt like they belonged to each other and set each other free at the same time. *Iron lock and skeleton key.*

He thought about his family's farm. The way the hay fields looked electric at sundown when the sky was cobalt, and the clouds were indigo and gray.

Fishing with Rudyard and his father in the summer and skating in the winter.

He thought about giving it all up, the bleakest memories and the nostalgia, the ghosts and the warm blood, the kind of hatred that sickened his stomach and the kind of love that he'd almost believed he'd fight for with his very last breath.

His hands trembled as he looked at his creation. A simple knot. Barely more than a glorified ribbon.

Powerful enough to end it all.

# CHAPTER 47

## Rudyard

*R*udyard woke at dawn to rooster crows. He stretched his stiff limbs, dressed warmly, and slipped into his square-toed shoes. He silently drank the coffee his mother had made him, then stepped outside.

First task: feed the animals.

The wind nearly knocked him over as he filled a sack with grain. He opened the buck pen and scattered feed over the hay. Before he could blink, one of the bucks tore through, sending the entire sack of grain spilling onto the ground.

*For pity's sake.* He'd forgotten to close the gate.

As he lunged after the buck, the others swarmed the spilled grain —grain meant for *all* the livestock, not just them. The family was already running low, waiting on the pastures to recover.

Then the bucks turned toward the fence.

His eyes widened, and he wiped a hand down his face. *For pity's sake!* He hadn't mended it yet. There was just too much mending to be done—the fence, the barn, the gate, not to mention the plow and wagon.

He cursed under his breath as the bucks barreled toward the break in the fence and bolted outside the acreage.

For a moment, he just stood there, hands on his hips, staring at the mess he'd made.

At least it kept his mind off the terrible news he'd have to give Clement later.

He turned on his heel and ran for the house, yanking his father away from breakfast. Together, they chased the bucks past sluggish harvests and withering winter crops. His father clutched his lower back as he trudged through muck. He'd been working extra to make up for Clement's absence, and the strain was making his sciatica worse.

By the time they wrangled the last buck back into its pen, the sun was already high.

"I'm sorry," Rudyard said weakly. "I'm trying."

His father pressed his lips together in a sort of nod. He looked resigned. Rudyard's heart broke all over again.

"Father, I know I'm not born to be a farmer. But I promise, I'll get better. If I have to."

Again, his father nodded, placing a firm hand between Rudyard's shoulders.

"Get some rest. I can do this," Rudyard promised again.

He stayed out for the rest of the afternoon, making sure all the animals were fed, though they never seemed as happy to see him as they did when Clement brought them their meals. He collected the eggs, only dropping two. *Two out of six. Not the best odds.* He milked the cows and spilled the milk, cursed, and milked them more. He checked the sap buckets on the maple trees. *Hardly anything yet.* He patched the fence and missed the nail only once, hammering his thumb instead.

By the time the workday was done, his mother helped him pick out the splinters and pressed a hot compress to his swollen hand. "We appreciate you working so hard to fill your brother's shoes," she told him.

"Hm," Rudyard breathed, a half-smile curling his mouth. "If only that were possible," he added sardonically.

He could think about Clement all day long, about how his imprisonment was all his fault, and about how lousy he was at farmwork, but would any of it atone for what he'd done? Would any of it shove the words he'd told Francis back into his foolhardy throat?

Probably not.

He kissed his mother absently before heading into town to call on Olivia for what had become their daily visit to the jailhouse.

The walk was his most miserable yet. His mind spun over how he would deliver the news to Clement.

It would destroy him.

At least he would have Olivia there to soothe him, afterward.

At last, he arrived at French Maude's, but there was no Olivia in sight.

She wasn't sitting on the step outside as usual, and for that matter, when he knocked on the door, none of his so-thought friends would open up for him. He peered through the windows. The drapes, normally open by now, were closed. He thought he might have even spotted Nellie's hand swiftly pull them closed as he approached.

At last, a male voice from inside yelled at him to go away. He'd never heard the voice before. It was thicker and even deeper than Francis's, but no less of a gnawing reminder of his lover's absence.

Abandonment felt like a better word.

He swallowed down the rising tide of it and turned away, boots heavy against the cobblestones.

And where on earth was Olivia? Had she abandoned him, too?

He made his way to the jail alone, head reeling. Paschal and Olivia had done their parts to help May McMurry, May Connally, or was it future Mrs. May Stoker? Rudyard couldn't keep track. Was he losing his very mind?

How was he a farmer one day—the worst one, no doubt—but a farmer, and then a fraud within a movement that he actually, ironically, believed in, and then nothing? Nothing at all. He wasn't a friend or a brother or a lover. He had learned to wear new hats only to discover he looked bad in hats.

By the time he reached the jailhouse, his breath was uneven, his thoughts unraveling faster than he could stitch them back together.

He knocked, smoothing a hand over his hair. It had begun to darken to a sandy brown over the course of the long New York winter. He hoped the blond streaks would return in summer like fresh golden hay, and then scolded himself for thinking about such frivolous things as hair color.

What was taking that bumbling dunce of a copper so long anyway?

At last, Duffy arrived to let Rudyard into the jailhouse.

"No Liv with you today?" Duffy asked.

"Not today, I'm afraid," Rudyard told him, a false pleasantness stiff on his lips. Since when was Duffy on a nickname basis with her? Honestly, Liv was supposed to be *his* friend, yet where was she when he needed her and why was she cozying up with his brother's simpleton captor?

To Rudyard's distaste, Duffy's face actually fell.

"Well"—he shrugged—"bring her next time."

Before Rudyard could turn around, he smelled rosewater, and Duffy's face lit up. Olivia was hurrying toward them.

"Sorry I'm late," she breathed to Rudyard.

"Liv!" both Rudyard and Duffy exclaimed at the same time. Rudyard cleared his throat territorially. "I didn't think you were going to make it. I—"

"We always visit at this time."

Rudyard blinked. So they did.

"Ah, I was actually going to tell you. I need to speak with Clement alone today. Can we catch up afterward?"

"Course you can!" Duffy beamed. "I'll keep Miss Olivia company."

Olivia smiled in agreement. Rudyard shot her a suspicious glance. Whatever was going on with her, he'd have to wait to find out. For now, he had to focus on his brother.

Duffy cheerfully unlocked the cell door for Rudyard. "No more than twenty minutes today," he told the two of them. "The commissioner from Manhattan is coming up this evening. Can't have yous around when he does." Duffy's eyes flicked to his, just briefly, before he stepped away, leaving the brothers in private.

The first few minutes passed in easy small talk—updates on the farm, their parents. Neither met the other's gaze for long. Something unspoken thickened the air between them, settling damp and heavy in the corners of the cell. It lurked, waiting. Once it was said, there'd be no unsaying it, no boarding it back up like a hole in a fence.

So instead, Rudyard told Clement about the bucks escaping. Clement chuckled, shaking his head. Rudyard considered telling his brother about the cracked eggs and spilled milk, as well, but time was running out. He had to swallow his nerves, *for pity's sake and damn it all*. But why couldn't he ever have *good* news to share?

"So," he forced himself to say, "Olivia wrote the letter to the Superintendents' Association."

"As though she were May? Was it believable?"

"Absolutely," He straightened, remembering that, actually, he did have one good thing to tell his brother. "I would have brought it here to read to you, but Olivia thought it best to send it out right away. She writes remarkably well. The letter made a sound and logical case for May's sanity."

Clement exhaled, a full-bodied sigh of relief. "They're going to let her out of there. They have to."

Rudyard looked away. One good thing, and one only.

Mistaking his hesitation, Clement added, "I know you have your doubts about us, but Rud, we're meant to be together."

Rudyard's throat tightened. God help him, his brother still believed.

Clement still believed he and May might come home to one another. Believed that if she were freed, it would send a ripple big enough to reach him, to free him too. As if fate itself had conspired to bring them together, and the world—ruthless, monstrous thing that it was—would not dare stand in their way.

But his brother was wrong.

"I spoke to Timothy after our visit yesterday," Rudyard began flatly.

"Oh yeah?" Clement's expression sharpened. "What does he have to say about my case?"

Rudyard nodded to himself, repeatedly, as if that might somehow delay the inevitable. It wasn't too late to change the topic. He could ask Clement if his hair looked darker now or still sandy. It'd be foolish, ridiculous, but at least it'd be a distraction...

"Rud?" Clement pressed. "Whatever it is, just come out with it. I can handle it."

Rudyard swallowed. Could he?

He exhaled slowly, then finally delivered Timothy's update. Clement's former enslaver had arrived in Hudson for the trial. It had been moved up—to tomorrow. If the man, whom their lawyer had identified as Judah Barrow, proved his case and won, the Stoker family wouldn't just lose Clement. They would more than likely face arrest themselves.

The case was already slated to be a clamor in the papers, and likely the politicians in the south would want to make an example not just out of escaped enslaved people but those who harbored them, as well.

Clement was silent. He sat back on his cot, eyes fixed on the sliver of light squeezing through the barred window. "You bring anything to drink?" he asked at last.

Rudyard hesitated, then carefully pulled the flask from his breast pocket. He'd never seen Clement take a drop of alcohol before, but figured correctly that today might be a good day to start.

"Perhaps it's not so bad," he tried weakly. "Timothy believes you still have a strong chance. Even with the evidence against you, you'll have a New York jury. Most of its members will be on your side."

Clement took a long drink, wiping his mouth on his grimy linen sleeve. Rudyard stared. His brother didn't look frozen in time anymore. He'd grown a beard over his normally clean-shaven face. The hair on his head had grown as well, and he looked tired and poorly fed, despite the meals Rudyard had been bringing him. Clement sighed loudly.

"And if the trial doesn't happen, then you and our parents are safe?"

For a moment, Rudyard couldn't breathe. He felt panicked, yet he couldn't identify why. He stared at his brother. "Why wouldn't the trial happen?"

Clement took another slow drink. "Rudyard, you've been a great brother to me. I don't want you to doubt that."

The words landed like a gut punch. Rudyard snatched the flask back and took a sharp swig. His pulse roared in his ears. "It'll work out," he lied.

Clement turned his head fully to face him, smiling more like a father than a brother. "It won't," Clement said simply. "I know you, Rud. You wouldn't survive a day in prison."

He was still smiling, but Rudyard felt the twist of pain inside him, breaking him like a horse.

"Maybe not," Rudyard admitted. "Which is why we've got to win this trial."

Clement exhaled sharply, dragging his hands over his head. "You don't get it, Rud!" he snapped. "The trial is a show. A circus. Nothing more. We would never win."

"We *will* win," Rudyard persisted.

"Not if there isn't a trial."

Rudyard froze. The aggression in Clement's voice knocked him off balance. His mind scrambled to make sense of it. "I don't understand," he said at last, his voice cracking.

Clement licked his chapped lips. His laugh came unevenly, as if coated in bitter syrup. "I'm going to tell you something, Rud. I never wanted to. I never wanted to talk about it with anyone. There was no reason to. But why take secrets to the grave? I guess I pretended I wasn't sure, but a while ago, May confirmed what I knew to be true." He let out a long, cold breath. "Judah Barrow is my father."

Rudyard gaped. "Your father?" He began to mutter to himself, processing as much as questioning. "What kind of father?" and "That's why—" until Clement stopped him.

"I need you to listen to me and not argue. I *will not* see that man in court. He kept my mother enslaved until her last, miserable day on earth," Clement continued. His voice was level now, but that made it worse. "He left me an orphan, long ago. I won't see his face, and I won't have him see mine. I can't give him that satisfaction." His jaw tensed. "I won't die enslaved."

The words landed with the weight of finality.

Rudyard broke.

"This is all my fault," he sobbed.

What if this was the last time he ever sat with his brother? At some point they'd gone fishing together, and ate breakfast together, and trudged up the dirt road to town together, and he hadn't known it was the last time. What was fair about that?

But Clement didn't need to say it outright. Rudyard understood now. Without Clement, there would be no trial. Without a trial, their parents could not be arrested for aiding and abetting an enslaved man who was never legally proven to be anything but their adopted son, born and raised in the free state of New York.

"Listen to me, Rud. I forgave you months ago. But what I can't forgive is this country. This whole system that allows one man to claim ownership over another. That's what I blame. Not you. Not my brother."

Rudyard was shaking his head, but Clement kept going.

"Tell May I loved her. Tell her she was always enough, and I loved her the moment I met her. Tell her to move on and find someone else. Someone who can appreciate her." His voice dropped to barely a whisper. "And please, get her out of there."

Rudyard shook his head harder. Stubbornness was an unfamiliar thing to him. He'd never had much cause for it before. Even when their parents hesitated over the adoption, they had been easily swayed.

But this?

He *had* to be stubborn about this. "You'll tell her yourself," he said, his voice thick.

Clement gave him a dark look. It said *you still don't get it, do you?*

Duffy reappeared, keys jangling. He unlocked the door. Rudyard rose unsteadily, still staring at his brother. His limbs felt useless, his breath foreign in his own lungs. Before he stepped through the door, he forced out one last thing.

"You'll tell May yourself. And I don't mean from the other side. You'll tell her yourself, and then you'll marry her."

He turned and walked out without looking back, even as he felt Clement's dark gaze pressing into his back.

He pushed past Duffy without a word. He wouldn't break down in front of his brother's jailer, no matter how pathetic and unimportant Duffy was. The man could barely even speak English.

But if Rudyard broke down now, he'd never stop.

Not when light would break out over the eastern horizon and he'd wonder if Clement's Light Within would still be shining on earth, witnessing the miracle. Not when spring would return to the valley and winter would begin to feel like a memory or a fever dream. Not then and not ever.

He was concentrating so hard on being strong, he'd made it halfway down the block before realizing he'd forgotten his companion. He rushed back toward the jail, then knocked vigorously on the door. Duffy opened it, a dazed look in his eyes.

"Where's Olivia?" Rudyard asked.

"She said she had to get to work. Told me to say goodbye for her."

# CHAPTER 48

## Olivia

The wind howled, making Olivia shiver.

"Do you care to wait inside today, Miss Olivia?" Duffy asked, holding two hot mugs of coffee.

"No," she said politely. "We'd better give them their privacy."

"Right as always, Miss Olivia." He nodded, admiration crinkling his eyes, and sat on one of two chairs beside them.

"Well, well," Olivia said, impressed, as she carefully settled into her seat and cradled her coffee. "You'd better not let word spread about the treatment around here, Constable. You might need to build yourself another jailhouse."

Duffy blushed, all the way to the top of his balding head. Even his bowler hat couldn't hide it.

"You make me smile, you know? You've been coming around here with your sweet, painted freckles on your face, reminding me of the schoolgirls from when I was young."

"I'll bet they chased after you," Olivia coaxed.

"Oh, no, miss. It was me who chased after them. My mother would whip me rotten for it."

Olivia felt a pang for him. Rudyard was doing all he could to help Clement. This was Olivia's chance to help them all. She'd been buttering Duffy up for months now, and it seemed to be working.

She'd hooked the fish; now she just had to reel him in.

"Officer Duffy," she began, her voice soft, "I can tell from our short time together that you're a good man. You care about others, about the law! It's, well, honorable." She fluttered her lashes at him, and he sheepishly brushed the air away with one hand. "But you know," she continued, "there's one thing that's been troubling me."

"Now what's that, Miss Olivia?"

Olivia sucked on her red lips, collecting her thoughts. "You see, I know you were just doing your job when you arrested Clement, and believe me, I respect a man who does his job. But—"

"Olivia," he interrupted solemnly. "I know where you're going with this, and I suspected we might be talking about this come some point. Truth is, I have no heart for slavery, and Clement Stoker seems like a fine fellow, and he's got himself some nice friends." He looked up at Olivia with large eyes. She nodded her gratitude.

"No," Duffy shook his head, "there's no joy at all in keeping Clement Stoker a prisoner. If the case were still in my hands alone, I'd let him walk out right now I would. But headlines are out there now. It's national news, it is."

Olivia held her mug with one hand in her lap and reached for Duffy's hand with the other. She felt a wave of grief, of helplessness, but she refused to admit defeat this early. Even if Clement's freedom really was out of his hands, he felt remorse, *genuine* remorse. She could work with it. One way or another.

"Oh, Olivia," he sighed. "I do feel I might have made a deal with the devil. If only I could turn back time and arrest Francis McMurry when I had the chance instead."

When he'd had the chance?

Olivia paused, loosening her grip on Duffy's hand. She'd known it was Francis who had turned in Clement, but hearing the story from Duffy's mouth felt like a revelation. And why would Duffy have arrested Frances? More than a few questions stacked in her mind.

"When was that?" she asked carefully.

"Oh, the day I cuffed Mr. Stoker," he offered freely. "Believe you me, that Irish villain was the last person I'd expected to see walking into my station that afternoon."

Olivia wasn't entirely sure why, but the details felt important, like breadcrumbs leading her where she needed to go. "What happened?" she asked, leaning forward.

"Well, I sat myself up and drew out my weapon, I did! But he made an effort to set me at ease, placing his own gun on the floor and holding his hands in the air. He made me a proportion, you see. 'Let's you and I leave each other alone. I'll get out of town quietly and give you a parting gift. But you've got to take action immediately, today,' he says."

Olivia hid her wince at Duffy's uncomfortable impersonation of the Irishman. "He asked you to arrest Clement Stoker," she confirmed evenly.

"That's right. As I say, Olivia, I have no heart for slavery. But McMurry, you see, well he became something of an obsession for me after the gunfight. I'm sure you heard about it?"

Olivia nearly gasped as the dots finally connected in her mind, like a constellation aligning. She remembered the afternoon Maude had presented her with the juicy bit of gossip about the Irish drunkard who had escaped the crime scene outside Central House with nothing more than a shallow stripe across one cheek.

Of course, it had been Francis. How had she not seen it before?

"I let the whole gang of drunkards slip through my fingers in broad daylight, in front of a bawdy crowd, no less! No one was taking me serious after that. Now I do feel a bit rotten about hopping into bed with a villain, but at the time, there was my reputation to consider, and ding dang it, I wanted that scamp out of my town. I was at a crossroads, so you see. So I asked myself, 'What would my wife have me do?'"

Olivia blinked. *His wife?* "I didn't realize you were married."

"Well, she don't visit much," he said simply. "Anyway, after the fight, I went business to business asking for clues as per the large Irishman's whereabouts, and 'anyone seen a man with a scar on his left cheek?' I even spent a bit of my own wages on spies to hunt down the gang. When the money ran out about a week and change later, I waited all night outside the taverns, hoping to catch me a glimpse of that scar."

Olivia nodded slowly, unsure whether to squeeze Duffy's hand or pull back.

"McMurry knew I'd take his deal. He told me he knew the whereabouts of a fugitive slave, right here in Hudson, breaking the law before my own enforcement, making a mockery of me. He said once I made the arrest, all yous throughout the country would be knowing me as the copper who enforced The Fugitive Slave Act, who earned a pretty bonus and provided for his family."

He bared his crooked teeth in something between a grimace and a self-loathing grin. "Look, Miss Olivia, if I had a thing to say about it, the country would be rid of the entire business. But it's no secret that police constables in Hudson barely earn enough to pay the rent."

"Did he tell you what was in it for him?" Olivia asked, her brows knitting as she tried to make sense of everything he was saying.

"In a way," Duffy said, shaking his head. "His smile was as icy as his eyes when he told me. He said, 'The man's a bother to me. That's all you need to know.'"

*That was all?* Olivia snagged on the words like a dress hem caught under a boot. A bother. As if Clement's entire existence had been nothing more than an inconvenience to Francis McMurry.

"I had a mind then to stand up for what I thought was right," Duffy went on. "To let bygones be bygones and arrest the criminal standing right in front of me, unarmed, no less! At the least, give him a good kick in the berries! Pardon my French. But Miss Olivia, I hadn't had a real 'win' since I started on the force. Matter of fact—no jest, Miss Olivia—I've had some pretty big losses. I made sure he'd leave town as soon as I made the arrest, but then, I shook his hand and let him get away, I did."

His head drooped despite the strong coffee. Olivia studied him, searching for something she wasn't sure she'd find. He looked small, slumped in his chair, and for a brief, fleeting moment, she almost pitied him.

"I get it," she said at last, though she wasn't entirely sure she did. Then she pulled her hand away and started chewing her nails.

"I'm sorry, Miss Olivia. I wish—"

She did, too. She wished all the time she'd spent buttering him up could have meant something.

She stood up before he could finish his sentence and handed him her empty mug. "Thanks for the coffee. I'd better get to work. Say goodbye to Rudyard for me?"

She walked away quickly, eyes straight ahead.

# CHAPTER 49

# Rudyard

*R*udyard pounded on the door of French Maude's.

"We're closed!" boomed the low voice from inside French Maude's. "Now get out of here, you half-rat pervert, before I get my shotgun and force you!"

Apparently, Maude's new man took his position more seriously than Francis ever had.

"I just need to speak with Olivia!" Rudyard called. "I'm not a pervert. I'm her friend! We were just together, and she left before I had a chance to say goodbye."

A few children giggled at him from the road, kicking a dented tea kettle back and forth like a ball. He frowned. Children had never cared for him, even when he'd been one.

"Liv! Liv!" he called, trying his best to ignore them.

Finally, Maude herself shuffled out the door in her lace corset, wrapped in a wool shawl, shushing him.

"Would you be quiet? You want the entire block to hear you? Come in, come in."

She looked around as though making sure no one of importance was watching as she hustled him inside. Then she brushed past the skeptical glance of her new security, chased the girls out of the parlor, and motioned for Rudyard to sit down. The girls left in smokey clouds of wagging hips and a mixture of clicking sounds and indigent "hm's." Only Claire greeted him with a friendly, "How goes it, Ruddy baby?" before she disappeared up the stairs.

For a moment, he thought of Christmas. Sitting around the table with them, handing out gifts. The dark side of nostalgia pressed down on him.

Once the room was cleared, he turned to Maude. "Where's Olivia?"

"Shh!" Maude said, looking around again. "Look, honey, Olivia is gone."

He blinked. "Gone? Gone where?"

She sighed, as though the question was an obvious bother. "Gone, hm? Just, gone. To another house I assume. I don't know. I had to send her away. I had no choice. All this scandal here—my business can't take it." She put a smooth, fleshy hand on Rudyard's thigh. "My heart, you see, is very weak."

"You dismissed her?" he asked incredulously. "She was your best girl!"

Maude cleared her throat. "Yes, well, I did what I must." She leaned back in, whispering, "She wrote a letter for May." Then she sat back as though everything was now clear.

Rudyard blinked again. "She wrote a letter. So what?"

Maude rolled her dark moon eyes. "Look, Rudyard, we all had a good time, did we not? We made a real good business. We had fun! Sure, we did. But I told my girls the jig was up! That was it. I can't have us all go to *prison* now, can I?" She said the word as though it were a secret, like a dungeon beneath a trapdoor in a faraway castle, or something sticky she wished to flick off her fingers. He wasn't sure which.

"I'm responsible for these poor girls," Maude went on emphatically. "They trust me. No one was to get involved in May's case. And then I follow our darling Livy to the post office and ask her nicely what she's mailing, we go back and forth, back and forth. Turns out, she's writing a letter for May! To have her released from that lunatic asylum! I can't have it. You understand, honey. Word gets out we at French Maude's helped the pretty little spiritualist who turned out to actually be insane... we'll be next on the accused list. Don't look at me like that. You'd do the same if you were responsible for these poor girls!"

But Rudyard was already on his feet. He left without another word.

Outside, the sky looked so gray, it might have been made of granite. He strode down Diamond Street with blind determination, going door to door, asking after Olivia.

The whole seance experiment had been his idea, his grand hope to find a place where he belonged. Something different. Something exciting. Something good.

And yet, the one person who had made him feel like he *truly* belonged had lost her job because of it. Because of *him.*

Each man who answered seemed grumpier than the last. He knew it was early to be pounding on doors along Diamond Street, but he only had one day before the trial and the tragedy that might precede it.

*One day.*

He reached the last house on the block. Its man was the meanest of all. He pushed Rudyard out, even as Rudyard insisted that he hadn't come straight from the taverns, desperate for a bit of evening delight.

Rudyard stumbled backwards, down all three steps, hitting the back of his head on the wooden slab of sidewalk. He turned his head. A shallow pool of blood darkened the wood beneath him.

For a moment he felt like the world had stopped, its edges gone fuzzy. Then he registered a pulsing pain. His cheeks burned hot and red as he cautiously felt the wound. His throat constricted even tighter at the sight of blood dripping down his fingers. He felt so wretched and lost. The only two people who cared for him unconditionally were gone.

*Free May.*

Clement's words were a curse.

Shouldn't May take some of the blame for his plight? May agreed to the seances, for pity's sake!

He blamed May for loving Clement, himself for needing Francis, and his brother for not being open with him sooner. Of all the people in the world, he felt closest to Clement, and he hadn't even known who his birth father was. Clement had never trusted him with that information. Yet for some reason, he had trusted May with it.

Maybe, he'd been right to trust her instead of him.

"Don't be crying now." He heard a voice as smooth and intoxicating as lavender mead. "You'll make me cry, and I look ugly when I cry."

"Liv!" he smiled. Warmth and relief flooded his entire body. "What are you doing here? I went to Maude's. She let you go?"

Olivia stretched out a hand and helped him off the ground. "Your head!" she gasped, focusing on the bloodstain on the sidewalk. "We've got to get you to a doctor! Come, I know a guy." She tried to pull him along, but he pulled his arm back.

"I'm fine, I'm fine," he insisted, pawing gingerly at the gash on the back of his head. It was small. The sight of the blood, though mildly dizzying, was worse than the injury. He dusted off his pants, carefully stretched his back, and smoothed the sides of his hair, flicking away a bit of mud.

"You sure?" Olivia asked skeptically, placing her hand gently on the back of his head. "Gregory can be such a brute."

Rudyard flinched at the sting of her touch on the wound but nodded, surprised by how centered he felt from that simple act. He hated how much any fleeting act of kindness could sway him. He was weak—too easily moved by a gesture, too easily distracted from the weight of his own self-doubt.

"Will you sit down at least?" she asked him.

His brows knit as he looked toward the door, checking for Gregory.

"I sent him in already," Olivia assured him.

They sat down on the steps, knees touching. Olivia used her lovely orchard green kerchief with lace trim to dab at the wound. Rudyard met her eyes, and in that quiet, shared moment, he understood the significance of the gesture. The stain would not come out easily, if it all.

"Maude let you go?" he asked her again, gently moving her hand away. The kerchief was a mess. He made a mental note to replace it.

"Forget her," Olivia said, her gaze drifting away.

Rudyard studied her, taking in the disheveled image she presented —still in her nightdress and housecoat, right in the middle of Diamond Street. It wasn't unusual for the area, but it seemed off for her. She looked so forlorn, as though the street itself had drained the life from her. With freckles scattered like brushstrokes on porcelain and ribbons tangled in her hair, she resembled a delicate doll—still, fragile, and abandoned.

She shivered, breaking the spell. "It's freezing out here. Come inside. We can talk by the stove."

Hesitantly, he followed her past the scowling Gregory, into an empty kitchen. It seemed a prerequisite for bawdy house security to be imposing and angry. How had he not seen it earlier?

The kitchen was more cramped than the one in Maude's Queen Anne. The ceiling was lower, with soot-stained beams running across. Someone had spilled flour on the creaky wooden floor and not bothered to clean it up. The air smelled heavily of old cooking grease, overcooked vegetables, tobacco, and body odor—a far cry from Nellie's delightful bannocks and bacon.

Olivia placed the kettle on the stove.

Once there was a time when silent moments couldn't exist between them. Now silence split and stretched like ice over a pond.

"Toast?" she asked.

"No," he said simply.

She had never been one to cook, and he had never been one to refuse food. They looked at each other a moment, then down.

A couple of girls sauntered into the kitchen.

"Oh, Olivia, who's your pretty friend?" one asked, batting the scattered remnants of fake lashes.

"Olivia has no friends," the other said breezily. "Didn't you hear? She was fired at French Maude's. None of the other girls stuck up for her."

"She was probably reading when she should've been canoodling," snickered the first.

The second one plopped into a chair. "Make us some tea, will you, baby?"

Rudyard saw Olivia's gaze drop, her posture shift. She looked... meek. He'd never seen her meek before. He had only ever seen the Olivia he'd wanted to see, or was it the Olivia he'd *needed* to see? A friend who could take charge, chase dreams, speak her mind because he could never speak his own.

And yet, Olivia's jaw was set tight, and she looked breakable. She looked human. And somehow, that messy, marvelous, complicated humanity made her radiate a beauty he'd never seen in anyone else before.

A familiar heat unfurled in his chest—stubbornness. He recognized it now.

"Enough of this!" he snapped, his voice shaking with indignation. "Enough. She's more beautiful and talented than either of you could ever hope to be, and you know it, and you know she'll take your clients so you're putting her down."

The girls gaped at him, pale mouths hanging open.

It seemed utterly ridiculous that he'd ever let anyone shame or diminish him before. They were all just people, human, no better or worse than anyone else, flawed and trying. But these girls needed to try harder. No, he certainly wouldn't let anyone push him around anymore. And while Olivia was with him, he wouldn't let anyone push her around, either.

"Just leave!" he concluded. "And make your own blasted tea. She's not a maid, for pity's sake!"

With stuck-up noses, insulted humphs, and a few choice slurs directed at Rudyard, they left. The second they were gone, a giggle slipped from Olivia's mouth. She slapped a hand over it, but her eyes danced. Then, to his surprise, she wrapped her arms around his shoulders.

"I *am* glad you came," she said, her hands lingering around his neck.

He looked away, suddenly awkward.

"What's wrong?" she asked, slowly sliding her hands down.

Rudyard grimaced before filling her in on his conversation with Clement.

Her brows knitted with concern. "You don't think he'd really take his own life, do you?" She handed him a lukewarm cup of tea.

He took it, attempting to thaw his pink hands against the cracked china. "I think he might. He was so reluctant to tell me about his parentage. I think..." He set his cup down on the pantry and slouched into a chair. "There's a lot to his story. More than I know. I think he'd truly rather die than return to that chapter."

He'd had time to think as he'd searched for Olivia, or perhaps it was the head bump, but finally he was able to see clearly. His brother, noble to the end, would choose death.

Olivia pulled out a chair for herself. She placed a warm hand on his, stroking it absently with her thumb. "You've been using that lotion I gave you," she smiled.

He looked up, suppressing a grin. "Every morning and night, like you said."

They both sighed.

"I'm sorry you lost your job," Rudyard said. "You must know I feel responsible."

"You've got to let it go, Rud. This isn't your fault. None of us knows God's plan."

He looked at her abruptly. "God? Since when are you religious?"

She smirked, lifting her cup. "I'm not," she said, taking a sip. "But *you* are."

He stared at her.

"What?" she asked. "Why are you looking at me like that?"

Before he could answer, one of the girls from before waltzed back in, rolling her eyes. "Any chance you two are almost done gabbing in here? Some of us who actually live here would like to make a cup of tea."

Rudyard stood abruptly. "We're just leaving." He turned to Olivia, his eyes alight. She recognized the look instantly. *The wheels were turning.* Then, to her shock, he plucked the teacup right out of her hand and set it aside. "We're going to need something stronger than tea, anyway."

"Right now?" Olivia asked, a line appearing between her brows.

"Right now! We need somewhere private to talk, too. How did I not think of this earlier? Here I've been, trying so hard to belong, but I do belong somewhere, and I think that's what I've been missing."

She turned her head, brow furrowing in confusion. He saw the flicker of hesitation in her eyes, but excitement was contagious, and he knew she felt its pull despite herself.

"And Liv?" He shot her a grin. "You're going to need to take the night off work."

# CHAPTER 50

## 𝕸𝖆𝖕

*L*ike me, it was Sally's husband who had her confined to Dr. Edmond's Insane Asylum, citing her erratic moods after the death of their newborn. Two years had passed for Sally within those walls before I met her. Her will to live was so fragile that, on some nights, she couldn't summon the strength to lift a spoon to her lips, retreating to bed without supper.

She was tall but weightless, as if the wind might carry her away at any moment, her pale hair shimmering through the air like dandelion seeds. Quiet and aloof, she seemed to exist on the edges of the world. And yet, she was lovely. Pure lovely. More so than many women I'd met outside, the ones who'd chased me off their porches with freshly picked broom or tell me I didn't belong because of where I came from.

There were many Irish girls in the asylum, as a matter of fact. At first, I thought to tell them I was from a settled family. But I reconsidered, for when they'd ask me where I came from, I knew I wouldn't be able to lie. It was just the same when I rode the boat to America. I knew that any county I picked, surely with my own luck, one of them would have grown up in that very county and asked me all sorts of questions only a settled person would be able to answer.

"I'm a Traveler," I told them proudly when they asked where in Ireland I was from.

I hoped that in that prison, in that country, we might be united by something more urgent than our roots.

But of course, it didn't matter that we were all deemed insane. It didn't matter that we were all locked away in the same jail. Even there, they wished to keep their distance from me. Perhaps even more so, to differentiate themselves from me, to be seen as better than someone else.

*Sure, we're Irish, but not like the likes of her.*

They called me "dirty Tinker" and pulled my hair, ignoring me at mealtimes when others, who didn't know what it meant to be a Traveler, came up to me for a chance at solace.

I was glad to have Sally by my side when the Irish girls would torture me, for she wore the fierce expression of a woman with nothing to lose. All she had to do was stare at them down her straight, ghostly-white nose and they'd take their big hands and noisy temperaments elsewhere.

But two years in an asylum will put a strain on you, no matter how pure lovely you were when you came in. Sally was no exception.

"How have you survived this place?" I asked her one afternoon in the dining hall. It was a large, echoing room with high ceilings and a cold stone floor, worn smooth by shuffling feet.

"You get used to it," she said, shrugging as she hunched over her gruel and coffee.

I wasn't convinced.

"Look," she sighed, setting her spoon down. "In the darkest moments, I remember what an old friend once told me: 'Live, live, live.' She'd been through something awful back in Montreal. I don't know the details. All I know is, she survived, and that's what she told herself: to live. Something about the way she said it stuck with me, and now... I find myself repeating it, too."

I can't say it didn't surprise me to hear she'd had a friend so close. Sally could be loathsome. Even Dr. Edmonds didn't spend much time with her. She had a way of staring at you when she didn't want you around, that made you wish you were anywhere else in the world but there, underneath her avalanche gaze.

Not long after that, an old friend of hers started visiting each week. She wouldn't tell me if this friend was the one from her story—or anything else about this woman who appeared out of the blue. All I knew was that she'd be beaming when she came back inside. Her hair tousled, her cheeks almost rosy.

One morning, my curiosity got the best of me. I watched through my small window as Sally and her visitor took a quiet walk around the grounds. Her friend wore a hooded cloak that hid her face, but just before I turned away, ashamed for peeking, I saw a flash of red as the visitor pulled back her hood.

I gasped.

Then a kiss—a tender one—light daffodil yellow and blood red merging together, like the top curves of a heart. I watched their hands linger on each other, tracing shapes, soft as whispered words.

A hailstorm began to pound against the window, blurring my view. Even from where I stood on the second floor of the brick building, I could feel the cold coming in strong.

Perhaps in the confusion of the strange and sudden weather, or perhaps because another patient fell into a fit of hysterics and needed several bodies to subdue her, the nurses didn't seem to remember Sally at all. No one went to collect her as they would on a typical day.

Sally stayed out in the storm long enough that I began to worry, for as rough as her personality could be, her health was undeniably delicate.

It was supper before I saw her again. She was shivering so fiercely she could hardly reach the stale bread to her lips.

"Shall we have some dessert?" she asked casually when she caught me staring.

"I'm not hungry," I told her. Three days had passed since I'd taken my last bite.

"Oh," she said, just noticing I hadn't touched my mush at all. "Well, good then. Forget the bread pudding. I'll go make my coffee, perhaps. My blood could use some warming." She placed an icy hand atop mine and her eyes lingered over my face for a moment.

I looked down at her veins, blue and purple and swollen. When I looked back up, a trickle of blood had fallen from her nose.

"You're bleeding!" I breathed.

A drop of blood landed on her tray, turning her mush a darker shade of brown.

"Oh." She placed a hand over her nose, tilted her head back, and sniffed. "It's nothing, only a nosebleed."

She tried to scoff, but instead, a deep, agonizingly long and congested cough exploded from her chest and lungs.

"Sally, you need to tell someone." I moved in closer so I could whisper. "You need a doctor."

I knew the sign better than anyone. The memories were ice around my heart. Lucie in the hospital, her lips white and cracked, choking on lemon water. The blood that dripped from John's nose, just before Francis wiped it away. The cry of the banshee.

I couldn't catch enough air. I couldn't bear that cry once more, and I'd be damned if I had to see another person I cared for taken by the illness.

"You sound like my husband," she said stiffly.

I snapped my mouth closed.

How could I go on forcing her into something she didn't want to do, when all the world was always forcing us already? I was her friend, was I not? I'd betrayed her once already when I'd spied on her private moment from my grimy window. The image of Maude's hands running through Sally's fine, feathery hair burnt a hole in my conscience.

I wasn't supposed to see that earlier, and I certainly wasn't supposed to play the part of a controlling husband now. Hadn't we had enough of those already? Enough roles forced upon us. Enough pretending.

416

Sally rose from her seat and drifted toward the kitchen. "Amenable" patients were allowed to make their own tea and coffee, just as they were allotted a bit of time out of doors. I frowned and followed as she stirred her coffee, slow and deliberate.

Counterclockwise.

Widdershins, as Grandmammy would say. Stirring against the sun. *Unlucky.*

Sally glanced at me through her narrow hazel eyes. "I'm going to take my coffee in bed tonight. Good evening to you."

A thousand things rose in my throat. Warnings, pleas, apologies. But I only nodded, watching her slip into the dark.

And then—*I saw it.*

A green aura flickering around her head.

Green, the color most people associate with birth, forgetting it's just as much the color of death. Green is springtime and the last bright burst before autumn; it's both growth and decay; it's a bridge between this world and the next. I could see the color consuming my friend already, coiling around her head like a crown of poison ivy.

I nearly reached out, nearly stopped her.

But I didn't.

I LAY ON MY COT, staring at the wooden planks above, my body hollow with hunger. Soon, even the ceiling blurred, my breathing weighted and labored. Something began to make sense when I finally stopped *forcing* it to.

Sally had told me I didn't know her story. But I was beginning to piece it together.

A woman she loved, a husband who called her insane, and now the woman returning.

Perhaps it was my arrest that had reminded Maude of the woman she'd loved and lost, once upon a time. Perhaps there was more to the story I didn't know. What I was certain of, nevertheless, was that there was more to be written still.

I bolted upright, and I ran. I raced through the halls, feet pounding against the floor, my nightgown snapping at my ankles. I reached

Sally's door, knocking softly at first, then harder, *harder*, until my fists ached.

No answer.

I pounded. A riot of sound.

Her keeper yanked the door open, dazed from sleep, smelling rotted with gin. Attendants rushed in, keys jingling an iron death melody.

We were too late.

There was my friend, lying dead on her bed, the air musty with the scent of sweat-soaked linens, coffee spilled all over the floor. I stared at her, more broken than I thought imaginable.

"Pneumonia," I whispered.

I could hear a swirl of movement around me—a nurse fetching a male attendant to move the body, Dr. Edmonds rushing in to record the scene, the gossip of the gathering patients, and then... a thin wisp of green, hovering about her pale lips.

In death, there is no aura. But here one remained, as flimsy a shade as desiccated nettle, but there, nonetheless.

"She's alive," I whispered next.

No one heard me. The rush of movement carried on until finally I screamed, "She's still alive, damn you all!"

They must have been stunned to hear me shout—the wee deranged lass who had put so much care into appearing docile, amenable, normal. Nobody moved as I ran to her, placing my ear to her chest.

Silence.

No. Not quite silence. There it was. The faintest rhythm, dim and distant.

Back when my gift first flickered in the presence of Edmonds, I wondered if it would return unchanged. Now, I had my answer. Something *had* shifted. Sally still lived, but her sickness clung to me like a spirit untethered, wrapping itself around my lungs, swirling, liquid, insidious, as if it were searching for another host.

My hands moved instinctively, pulling at the illness as though I could lift it from her, unravel it into the ether. Slowly, I worked up toward her head, my breath coming in ragged gasps, unsure if the sweat breaking out under my palms was hers or mine.

The male attendant arrived, but Edmonds extended an arm to stop him. I didn't need to see it. I *felt* it. My time in the asylum had been gruesome in many ways, and yet, deprivation creates space for the divine; it only takes one candle to make a space holy.

Sally and I were green, destined to walk the bridge between life and death in all the ways that could break a person's spirit, yet strengthen her heart. Perhaps that's why my gift returned here, of all places. Why it came back stronger, with a lion's courage. From nothingness, I found a well of power. I found order. I found God.

Clement's words came to me. *And then use it, May. Use it to make a difference.*

I held that power, that order, that holy wind. And I *used* it.

My hands hovered over her head, and for a moment, I thought the fever had broken. But just as quickly, it surged back. Hotter. Wilder. Her skin burned beneath my touch. Salt bloomed on my tongue. My strength wavered. The next world loomed so close, I could feel its breath on my neck.

*Stay*, I willed myself. *Long enough to save her. Long enough to pull her back.*

I would do Clement proud, even if it killed me.

"Come back, come back, Sally." I wept the words. Pleaded them. Prayed them. I almost fell to my knees from the weight of them.

Then, a whisper.

*Hold me.*

My breath hitched. My eyes darted to Sally's lips. They hadn't moved.

*Hold me,* she repeated.

A Knowing stirred deep in my bones. Deep as anything I'd ever felt before. Deeper than roots. I opened my mouth, and a gust of wind rushed in.

*I don't want to die.*

My fingers tightened around her. "You won't."

I turned to Edmonds. He was staring at me, unreadable.

I could save her, but if I did it, there would be no going back, no claiming I was just like everyone else, no convincing the doctor I was cured. I might never breathe a free breath again.

"She's alive," I said. "And I can keep her alive. But you need to heal her body."

His throat bobbed. "How much time?"

The nurses and attendants looked dubiously from him to me.

"I—I don't know." The weight of my choice pressed down, but I *knew* it was right. I only prayed my strength was enough.

Edmonds exhaled, reaching for her forehead. "Her fever is high, but if she makes it through the night, she may manage."

*Hold me. Hold me through the night.*

I did.

When people have a will to live, they live. When they don't, they slip away. I kept her tied to me, held her spirit against mine until the first light of dawn. My memory of that night is foggy, but I know I dreamed. I dreamed and woke and dreamed again. I saw gun fights, flame-red curls and full painted lips, large hands and feet. I felt crippling fear, a shame that made my skin crawl, a numbness like bare feet in frosted grass on a cold November dawn.

And then, at last, morning.

I ducked out of line for the dining hall and went straight to Sally's room.

Dr. Edmonds was asleep on the chair beside her. I swallowed hard. Sally lay motionless, long and thin as a whisper. My arm trembled as I reached for her forehead.

*Tepid.*

My breath shook as I sighed with relief. I hadn't wanted my friend to die, nor had I wished to keep her spirit tethered to me.

Though my time in the asylum had nearly broken me, as I looked at Sally fighting to *live, live, live*, I knew I had fight left in me still. I knew I had a whole heart, full as a bucket of moon water on May Day, and a mind that raced like a stallion across the endless fields of home, and a fiery spirit of my own, longing for its twin.

I sat on the edge of the bed and watched her sleep, her mouth slightly ajar.

It was enough.

I leaned close, lips nearly brushing hers, and exhaled.

Her eyes fluttered open.

They were such a dull hazel they appeared brown, but wide, and she took in a large gulp of life as she saw me sitting there. Then her arms flung around me, her body racking with sobs. I clung to her fiercely, wee thing that I was in her long grip.

When I pulled away, Dr. Edmonds was awake. He had his eyes fixed on us. I wasn't sure what exactly he'd seen, but he stood up, nodded at me, and left the room.

"You wanted to see me?" When I stepped into the doctor's office, he was scribbling away, nose in his ledger. He didn't seem to notice me. When he did look up, his eyes were a bleary red, as though he hadn't slept at all. He placed his quill down and sighed.

"I went to see your friend," he said.

I licked my lips, unsure if I was about to be rebuked or praised. "How is she?" I asked tentatively.

He rubbed under his nose and leaned back in his chair, before slapping his legs. It was a pell-mell display of conflicting emotions. "Perhaps I should ask you," he said at last. "It seems she should be *your* patient."

I tried to apologize. Clearly, I'd gotten myself into even more trouble. But he wouldn't let me.

"Miss May," he interrupted. "All my life I thought of things a certain way. I thought everything had an explanation, that everything is made of something we can see, with the right tools." He shook his head. "I don't know... Could it be possible there is more than meets the eye, and we simply haven't created the right tools to see it yet? Maybe it's time I do my own investigating.

Perhaps... my wife would still be here if I'd been open to the idea."

My brow furrowed, for I hadn't a notion what he meant. He motioned for me to sit, so I did, smoothing the plain linen over my thighs.

"She poisoned herself, my late wife," he told me. "She suffered from melancholia. We tried for ten years to have a baby, and we never could. She told me once she didn't feel like a woman if she couldn't have a baby. Do you know what I said to her?"

I swallowed, for indeed, I had a hunch.

"I said nothing," Dr. Edmonds admitted. "I left the room." I felt a strange mixture of fond memories and bitter regret wrapped up in his soft chuckle. "The next morning, I awoke beside her. She didn't move, and I smelled almonds and knew. My wife had taken her own life, and I hadn't done a thing to help her. I felt her last shallow breaths and couldn't save her."

He rubbed his tired eyes, looked at me a moment with his jaw quivering, then stifled a sob.

"Perhaps there was something I could have done. Science would say she was as good as dead, beyond the point of no return, but perhaps I might have used your methods to... to..." He trailed off. Just when I thought he was done, he forced the words out. "To anchor her spirit to the material world. To hold her until I could convince her she'd made a mistake or rid her body of the poison. Perhaps I could have saved her, had I known."

I smiled sadly. "But it wasn't your fault, Dr. Edmonds. We only know what we know when God sees fit to show us." His expression flickered. "Your wife knows how much you loved her," I continued, "and she knows it was just as hard on you, not having a child. You wanted one as much as she did."

The only difference, as far as I could see, was the choice each of them made because of it.

And what choice would I make? I hadn't eaten so much as a bite in over three days. My stomach was a tight, twisting creature inside me, the hunger curling deep.

There was relief in his laugh. "I did. I wanted a child so very much." His voice was thick. "She told you that?"

"Aye," I said. Because she was with us even now, her hand resting lightly on his hunched tweed shoulder.

He shook his head, and for the first time since I'd met him, he smiled. A true smile. A warm, *living* thing. It changed his whole face.

"Miss May," he said, sitting up and clasping his hands together, voice charged with something new. "I'm going to write to the Association and tell them what I've learned from you. Then I'd like to work with you, if you'll have me."

I went still, his words catching me off guard.

"We could make an incredible team," he went on, eyes bright. "This world of alternative healing is a great mystery to me. There is so much I've ignored, so much healing I've never considered. It's overwhelming," he said almost gleefully, "but perhaps it's time a man of science stepped onto the scene. Maybe I've missed something remarkable. Maybe it's time science catches up."

He looked at me with the same hungry eyes as the Irish people, except his were shining, lit with curiosity.

My mind whirled. My vision blurred. Was it the weight of his words? Or the hunger gnawing through me?

"Are you well?" His brow furrowed. "You look pale."

He rang his brass desk bell. A maid entered purposefully, clad in her somber gray uniform with a plain white apron tied around her waist. He asked her to bring us some tea and sustenance. Before I knew it, a tray of buttered toast and pastries was before me, a far cry from the stale, tasteless fair served to the patients.

I lifted a honey bun, my mouth watering immediately.

How strange to live in a world where I could decide to starve or decide to eat, just as simple as that, while my family had no choice at all.

Some say there's only one world. The spiritualists argue there are two. But I'd wager there are infinite worlds, layered over one another like gauze, more than we could ever know. And as I sat in the doctor's office, warm pastry in hand, I wasn't just *one* world apart from my family, but many.

*Back to the land of living*, I thought, as someone else might say *cheers*.

I bit in. Cinnamon. Nutmeg. Cloves. Warm honey. It was just about all I could bear. I closed my eyes, savoring the spiced tickle in my neglected mouth. The honeybun still melting and sticky on my tongue, I took a sip of hot, black tea, the heat dancing in my chest.

For better or for worse, I was coming back to earth, back into my body.

Then I set down the cup and pastry, swallowed the last taste of comfort, and looked up to find Dr. Edmonds watching me with his lips slightly parted.

"Am I free to go then?"

He exhaled, his shoulders sinking ever so slightly, and his sharp gaze dulled. "Of course," he said. Then, after a pause, "Will you think over my offer?"

I nodded, my mind tangled with too many thoughts to unravel. My heart was split. Half of it was trapped in a jail cell with Clement, the other pulled across the ocean to Ireland, to my family.

All I had wanted since setting foot in America was a place to bring them. A home. Wages. Stability.

Hadn't I?

Or had I grown greedy? Had America changed me, made me hunger for more than just survival? Because now I wanted more. I wanted to explore this new depth of the Sight, the part of me I hadn't known existed. I wanted to *own* it, wield it, not let it wield me. And, more than anything, I wanted Clement Stoker to be my husband.

But… How could I choose my own happiness when my family still suffered? How could I fail them for my own selfish desire?

"I will think about your offer," I told Dr. Edmonds, though I knew I wouldn't have the luxury of time. One way or another, I would have to choose. "But before I go," I continued, swallowing the lump in my throat, "there is something I'd ask you."

"Anything," he said. And he meant it. He *owed* me, and he knew it.

I took a breath, steadying myself. "I need an annulment."

Whatever future lay ahead, I knew one thing for certain: I would not be tethered to Francis when I stepped into it.

Dr. Edmonds straightened in his chair, his brow knitting slightly.

"I need a doctor's examination to prove my marriage was never, well... complete."

The heat in my cheeks spread to the tips of my ears. I stared hard at my slippers, humiliated to even ask, but there was no time for shame. My life was unfolding before me like watercolor bleeding across a canvas, and I could not afford to hesitate.

Dr. Edmonds frowned. "Do you mean to tell me your husband never consummated the marriage?"

"Not once," I muttered, still unwilling to meet his gaze.

He grimaced, his long face growing even longer. "I believe you."

Without another word, he reached into a drawer, pulled out a newspaper, and slapped it down in front of me. I could make out enough letters to see it was *The New York Tribune*, folded to a page in the middle. I couldn't read the full article, but the image nearly knocked me off my chair.

A cartoon.

A high forehead, a crooked nose, a strong jawline, icy eyes... unmistakably Francis. And he was kissing another man.

My breath caught.

This was Olivia's work. Every line, every stroke, was hers.

I tore my gaze away and met Edmonds's eyes. "What is this?"

"The morning paper," he said. "Written by Anonymous."

I shook my head. "I don't understand."

"It's an exposé," he clarified, tapping a finger against the page. "On an Irishman who lied about his wife's sanity in order to be rid of her and, well, *that*." His mouth twitched downward as he glanced at the illustration. Francis's lips had been exaggerated, made comically large, busy against his lover's mouth.

I swallowed, stunned.

"This article is going to put my asylum into question," he admitted. "Probably much more."

I stared at him, my lips curving into the smallest of smiles. My heart swelled with love for Olivia—fierce, brilliant Olivia, who had wielded her weapon of choice against the man who tried to destroy me.

"Maybe that's a good thing," I said.

Edmonds considered that. Then, slowly, he nodded. "Maybe it is." After another moment's thought, he straightened, reaching for a fresh sheet of stationery. "Why don't we forgo the examination?" he suggested, dipping his quill into ink. "I think this story can suffice as proof enough."

I let out a quiet breath, the last vestiges of tension uncoiling from my shoulders. I watched as he set to work, drafting the necessary letters to secure my freedom. Not just from the asylum, but from Francis, from the lie of our marriage, from everything that had held me in place.

As he wrote, I hesitated, then asked, "Can I say goodbye to Sally before I leave?"

He nodded without looking up. "I'll have the letter ready when you return."

I stood, my heart light, my steps steady. For the first time in a long while, I was walking toward something, not away.

Sally lay in bed, her gaze fixed on the low beams of the ceiling. The pitcher of lemon water I'd requested sat untouched beside her. Fever had left her, but I figured some old Irish wisdom wouldn't hurt her any.

I sat beside her and took her hand. "I'm leaving today."

Her grip tightened, her fingers cold against mine, but she didn't turn her head. "What will I do without you?"

Her voice was hoarse, almost wistful, as if she were resigned to the space between us. She looked both soft and gruff, like someone caught between two worlds. Softened by her fingertip touch against the Veil, hardened by what had put her there. The unfairness of it. The cost of brushing against death in exchange for one single day with the person she loved.

I swallowed, the tightness in my throat making it hard to speak. There was something I needed to say. Something I couldn't hold back any longer.

"You should come with me," I began, my voice barely above a whisper. "You don't belong here." My throat burned with the intensity of what I wanted to confess, but I bit my lip, watching her face crumple beneath the strain of her own fears.

Her eyes drifted away from me. Her lips remained closed and pale, but the soft tremble of her hand in mine told me she was listening.

I drew a slow, unsteady breath, the words bitter on my tongue before they'd even left my lips. But I was leaving, and if I didn't tell Sally the truth now, I knew I'd carry the weight of it with me forever.

"I have to tell you something."

Sally pressed her lips together. Her eyes were misty, haunted by memories I wasn't sure I was ready to uncover.

"I saw you in the garden yesterday. With Maude."

She remained frozen, and I felt her pulse quicken under my fingers.

"I *saw* you, Sally," I pressed gently, my heart thumping in my chest. "And what I saw was not insanity. It was love. I knew it before but now I know it with all the certainty that exists in the world. There is truly nothing wrong with you."

A soft, broken sound escaped her as she covered her mouth, her eyes squeezing shut, stifling a cry.

"How can I feel this way," she whispered, her voice shaking, "and still be of sound mind?"

By the desperation in her voice, I knew she'd asked herself this very question too many times before.

She exhaled shakily, her body sinking deeper into the mattress. "My husband caught us together," she admitted, her voice so quiet I had to strain to hear it. "He's a good man. His very job requires him to do the right thing. He never wanted to take a bribe like the others. He just cared about what was right."

A bitter smile tugged at the corner of her lips, but it was flimsy, slipping from her face. "But when he saw us..." She shook her head, the words caught in her throat. She was barely holding back her tears now.

I reached for her hand again, my fingers trembling, not just from the cold. "Will you tell me about it?"

For a moment, she hesitated, but then the words came spilling out like water from a washbasin painted pink with roses.

"I met Alice—Maude, as you know her—at the police station, of all places. I was waiting with a picnic basket for my husband to meet me during his lunch break, when I saw this fiery-haired woman bailing out one of her girls." She chuckled. "Well, you know us both, we're not meek by any means, but somehow we spoke shyly to each other at first."

I tried to imagine it. Sally, who rarely let herself go, and Maude, who said whatever she wanted, whenever she wanted, and it was usually lewd and forthcoming. They were opposites, yet it seemed they had drawn close anyway.

"After that," Sally continued, "I began showing up at the police station at noon more often, and then a quarter to noon, and so on. Alice did the same. She became the only madam to be seen outside the police station in broad daylight on such a regular basis. She told the other madams that having a friendly relationship with the coppers was one of the keys to a successful brothel, and she wasn't wrong."

A sly smile ghosted across Sally's face. "It served Alice well that she became better acquainted with my husband, though she'd always call him Fluffy Duffy when it was just the two of us."

I gasped, jolting her from her storyteller's trance. My heart pounded as if it might burst from my chest.

"Do you mean to say your husband is *Police Constable Duffy*?" The words came out like clogged smoke, a sound that didn't feel like my own.

Sally froze, the air between us thick with an unspoken question. She was wondering how I knew him, what Duffy meant to me.

"Oh," she murmured after a beat, "of course you must have crossed paths with him at Maude's." She sighed, her expression hardening. "Well, suffice it to say... he found me in bed with Alice, a frilly mess of petticoats over my face." Her face softened. "You know, that's the only time I've ever been in love... just that once."

Her expression darkened, and her gaze drifted past me, as if she were lost in the memory. I could feel the tension building between us, a storm of emotions waiting to break. Should I tell her the truth about Duffy? About what he did?

"But after that..." she continued, "I stopped showing up at the police station early, and didn't answer the door when Alice knocked. Until one day, my husband closed down French Maude's for two weeks, before his assisting officers forced him into taking her bribes again." She gave a hollow laugh, her fingers tracing the edge of the blanket absently. "He couldn't give them a good reason why he wouldn't, of course, unless he wanted his reputation to go up in flames."

Her voice lowered, and I could barely hear the next words she spoke. "He always cared so much about his reputation." She whispered it more to herself than to me, as if she were finally admitting it.

"I see," I murmured, my voice tight.

Duffy. The man who put Clement in handcuffs, whose actions had twisted my heart into knots, and whose puffed and proud shadow still clung to the edges of everything I'd learned. My hands clenched involuntarily, and for a moment, I felt a flare of something—resentment? Fear?—that I didn't know how to untangle. She'd called him a good man. How could I stay silent while she defended him?

And yet, this moment wasn't about me. It was about Sally. Her pain, her lost love, her anger and her grief. Not mine.

She exhaled, her gaze drifting back toward the ceiling beams. "I always wondered what Alice thought when she heard what became of me—carted off to a brick prison only blocks away that might as well have been miles. Then when she came here to see me after they took you, I finally got my answer."

Sally's eyes shone with something too raw, too strained. "She was crying so hard, the rouge streaked down her cheeks, turning her tears the same red as her hair. She told me she'd tried to visit right away, but no one would let her in. Eventually, she gave up, hoping that one day I'd be released, that I'd know where to find her. But after you were taken, she tried again. By then, I'd been deemed 'amenable,' so they let me see her in the courtyard."

Her hand was cold and bony beneath my fingers. I felt the pulse of her desperation, her sorrow—a wild thing that had nowhere to go.

"For what it's worth, Sally, I've never seen Maude—er, Alice—with anyone else. She must have a fierce love for you. I can understand why she gave up at first. She didn't have a way in. But what I can't understand is how *you* could give up on a love like that? Why didn't you try to get yourself out of here?"

She sniffed and wiped her nose with the back of her hand. "My husband convinced me I was insane. When he told me to seek treatment, I didn't fight him. I trusted him."

Then she looked at me, and I had never seen her eyes so large, so dark, like the heart of the ocean itself. Emotion glistened. Not just fear. Not just regret. But a kind of understanding too complicated to name. "You're right. I gave up." A harsh breath left her lips. "Now look at me."

She dissolved into tears, and I held her hand tight, my fingers like weeds tangled in the mouth of a great fish.

She knew what kind of man Duffy was, on some level. I didn't need to tell her. What difference would it make for her to know he'd harmed someone else? Revealing it wouldn't change anything; it would only add more weight to Sally's already heavy burdens.

I thought I was the only one keeping a secret between us, until Sally made one last confession.

"I must admit… I befriended you when you arrived because I knew who you were. I'd overheard the nurses talking, and I knew you were the spiritualist from French Maude's." She inhaled sharply. "And I was kind to you because I wanted to hear about her. It had been two years since I last saw Alice. I only wanted to know if she was well. I only wanted to feel close to her again."

A few months ago, I might have felt betrayed to hear such a thing. I might have felt used and overlooked. But I knew now how love could make a perfectly sane person do insane things.

"It's fine," I assured her.

Sally swatted at her tears. "I *am* sorry I didn't tell you. But I want to thank you, because it was you who brought me back into Maude's mind. When she watched you get taken away, she thought of me again, and she came to see me, and I know now that we've never fallen out of love."

I squeezed her hand. "Then don't give up now. Get yourself out of here. Come with me. Find Maude and be happy."

Maybe it was her brush with death, or maybe it was because she had me there to hold her hand. Maybe it was the sounds of the words *Maude* and *happy*, like poetry or a lullaby or wind that carries the scent of jasmine.

Whatever her reasons, she said yes.

Sally leaned on me as we made our way to Dr. Edmond's office. Though she was weak and needed rest, she somehow looked more vibrant, young and sweet than I'd ever seen her before, like her shield and armor had disappeared with the fever.

Inside the office, I gripped the arms of the chair, bracing myself for a fight. Dr. Edmonds would refuse, I was sure of it. He would tell me Sally, like so many other women locked away by their husbands, would need petitions and signatures, months of bureaucracy before she could see the outside world again. My heart pounded, and my breath felt shallow as I prepared my argument.

But then he simply said, "Mrs. Duffy's husband filed for her release a year ago. She's here of her own accord."

The room seemed to tilt. My fingers went slack, slipping from the chair's worn wood. I turned to Sally, searching her face, but she only stared at the floor, her expression unreadable.

For a moment, I was speechless. It was what he'd revealed, but also the sound of my friend's name in his mouth. *Mrs. Duffy.* I'd only heard her called by her given name. By the frown on her face, I believe she cared little for the surname, herself.

Still, I was glad I hadn't told her the entire truth. It was one thing to think about Duffy's cruelty, to let it simmer inside me—but to name it, to connect it directly to Clement's suffering while sitting beside her, *Duffy's wife*, would feel too painful.

Edmonds turned his attention to her. "Mrs. Duffy, you're free to leave anytime you'd like."

She could have left. A whole year wasted in this place. *Why?*

"Did you know this?" I asked her, my voice trembling with an emotion I couldn't place.

She nodded solemnly. Her voice was small when she said, "I couldn't go back to him." Her arms tightened around herself.

Now I understood the emotion for exactly what it was: outrage—at Sally for not leaving, at the world that had left her nowhere to go, at the system that had convinced her she never could.

I set my jaw. "I think you have a better option now."

"Very well," said Dr. Edmonds. His letter to the Commission was set, and he assured me he'd post it today.

OUTSIDE HIS OFFICE, Sally turned to me. "I don't know how to thank you." Her tone was almost desperate, like a child on the edge of something too big to comprehend. I had spent three months in this awful place. She had been here two years longer. Freedom would not be as simple as stepping outside.

"No need to thank me. Just take care of yourself," I told her. Then, after a beat, "And trust yourself. You've been waiting a long time for this moment. You know what to do, and who you are. You deserve this." I thought of Maude, her fiery red hair and matching personality, her open arms and shimmying shoulders. "But you'll be in good hands."

Sally would go on to live life to the fullest. I truly believed that.

What worried me now was Clement.

With some hope, the doctor's word would save me, but even he didn't have the power to bargain with society's prejudices to free my fiancé. My stomach churned over and over at the possibility that I might never hold him again.

# CHAPTER 51

# 𝕸𝖆𝖕

efore Sally and I closed the wrought iron gate of the asylum behind us, I turned for one last look.

The asylum was the largest house I'd ever lived in, yet the one that felt the smallest.

We wore the same dresses as the day we entered. Sally's still fit like a glove, but mine had grown roomy. I ran my fingers over the soft, durable wool of my tartan skirt and wondered: where had our clothes been kept all this time? Was there some great hidden closet, hoarding the remnants of people's former lives? One room for the living, and so many more for the dead.

But I couldn't linger. I had to get to Clement. Perhaps his trial date was already set and looming. I couldn't even think of the alternative, that while I was trapped in the asylum, it had already passed.

"Do you want me to go with you?" Sally asked. She looked handsome, her light blonde hair like reeds blowing easy in the gloaming. She was unsteady on the cobblestone, though, and I hoped she'd take time to mend.

"No, I'll fare well enough alone. But what about you? Where will you go now?"

A crooked smile poked at the corner of her mouth. "Don't worry about me," she said. "I know where to go."

"Are you certain you don't want me to walk you?"

"I'm just around the corner, May. I'll rest when I get there, I promise."

We hugged goodbye, strong and quick, for though Hudson was a city, it often felt like a wee town, and I knew I'd see her again soon.

I watched her strut down the road. Even in her weakened state, she was a formidable figure. I almost called out to her to wait for me, for I knew well where she was going, and I could hardly wait to see Olivia again. But time was slipping through my fingers, fast as it could.

Still, I allowed myself a moment.

I closed my eyes and turned my face to the sky. The air was cool, but not bitter. Cold, without the ominous cracking of ice. A single snowflake melted on my nose. Then another. And then, within seconds, the sky was *full* of them.

I raised my arms, turning in slow circles as the wind wrapped around me. Though my body had weakened, I felt light and agile as a deer. The snow wreathed and swirled, tugging at me like a lover's hands, and I made no attempt to stop it.

I was home. Not in Ireland, or at French Maude's, or even at the Stoker homestead. I was simply at home within the moment. In shades of moss and stone and old keys. On a quiet city street framed by white-peaked mountains. In a driftless chase and a tartan wool dress. In the rush of air through my lungs.

It lasted only a few moments, but sometimes, in the company of a great and wise unknown, those few moments are enough to shift the earth beneath your feet—enough to unburden an impossibly heavy heart.

I opened my eyes, ready to see my heart's desire.

I stood tall and moved from one prison to another.

The jailhouse was guarded by two young but sober-faced men. Just on the other side of the brick wall, my beloved was waiting, possibly in chains, in darkness, or worse. It was the *not knowing* that made me stand very still.

How was it that, during all this time apart, we'd only been separated by a couple of brick walls and a few muddy streets?

How was it that, at that moment, I felt farther from him than ever?

I stepped forward. "I need to see Clement Stoker."

It was what Olivia might have called anticlimactic. The guards denied me outright, saying no one was allowed in or out—save for the defendant's lawyer, who was preparing Mr. Stoker for the *morning's* proceedings.

"The morning's?" I repeated. Their blank stares did not waver.

I went on to make such a fuss about getting in that the police constable himself came outside to handle the commotion.

"I need to see Clement Stoker. I need to see him *right away!*" I begged, my voice cracking with urgency.

And then our eyes met.

It hit me like a slap in the face.

*Constable Duffy.*

My breath caught in my throat. I couldn't move, couldn't speak. My mouth hung open in shock.

He didn't seem to have the same trouble. His gaze flickered with recognition—he must have known me as the one who had loved Clement, who had cried for his release. His lips curled in a tight, contemptuous line. "Oh, pox on me," he muttered under his breath, looking like he'd tasted something foul. "I shouldn't say a word. Proving my wife right, I am."

He took a step closer, and instinctively, I stepped back.

"Look, lady," he murmured, his voice low, almost weary. "I can't let you in here. Why don't you go find your friends?"

"My friends?" I blinked in confusion, then it dawned on me. "You mean Olivia and Rudyard? They've been here?"

He exhaled sharply, wiggling his mouth in thought. Would he help me? Or turn me away? At last, he jerked his head toward the street. "Try Governor's Tavern, mayhap."

I closed my mouth, nodding quickly, then hurried toward the tavern. It loomed ahead, a den of stale smoke and lingering stares. I pushed past the sorry drunks and half-rats at the entrance.

Inside, the place was a dim echo of its Christmas liveliness. Without the crowds of the day, the raucous laughter, card playing, dancing, and the like, the room seemed little more than another cramped and dingy cell.

I scanned the room. Olivia and Rudyard were nowhere to be seen. Biting my lip, I marched to the bar.

I was barely breathing when I arrived. The barkeep—same one who had been there on Christmas—raised an eyebrow at me.

"Have you seen two people? A woman of ravishing beauty with a fancy hairstyle and a blond man dressed to the nines?"

He considered me, then gave a slow nod. "Aye. They were here." His gaze slid sideways, as if wondering what business I had with two people so different from me. "They were talking about the Clement Stoker case," he added, casual but watchful.

I tried to steady myself. "Did they mention the trial date?"

He shrugged one shoulder. "Aye. Trial's set for tomorrow. It's all over the papers." He rapped his knuckles against the bar. "We're expecting quite the crowd around here. Preparing triple batches of grog, I am. Your friends didn't seem too keen on it though. Looked like they had a bad case of the morbs over it, truth be told."

*Tomorrow.*

I swallowed. So it was true. Less than a day remained before I might never see Clement again.

"Do you know where they went?" I chewed my lip, nauseous and faint, a wispy thread of a woman who had been so briefly, so safely, in love.

The barkeep only shook his head and poured me a beer, sliding it across the bar. "*Sláinte*," he said. I chugged about half, grateful for a bit of extra courage. A small fire sizzled in my stomach.

"They were talking about God, for what it's worth," he added, eyeing my glass. "And the fancy lady was to be taking the night off from work. They spoke quietly, aye? But I heard mention of a meeting."

A meeting.

I inhaled sharply, setting the beer down with a dull *thunk*. They were at the meetinghouse. They had to be.

I thanked him tremendously, then turned, shoving my way out into the cold wind.

Snow flurried around me in silver streaks, dissolving the heat from my skin. I pulled my shawl close, bracing myself, and I prayed that tonight, God would be on all our sides.

The meetings at 343 Union Street were typically quiet, contemplative affairs where one person spoke at a time.

Back home, Quakers had the loveliest reputation. There were those who took advantage of our plight, buying souls for the price of a meal. We called them soupers. But the Quakers didn't charge for their charity. They set up soup kitchens in Ireland because it was what they believed to be right. They fed us in the famine, and now still, across the world in New York, it was clear they'd continue to stand on the right side of history.

They were peaceful folks with strong convictions. Which was why I stopped dead in my tracks when I heard yelling from within their house of worship.

The sound quickly subsided, with gentle hushes followed by a low crescendo of voices. I hesitated, my hand hovering near the door-frame. How much had changed since I'd been imprisoned?

"Impossible. We are peaceful people," someone argued.

"We are in general, but do abolitionists have that privilege?" It was Rudyard speaking.

I almost squealed for joy and rushed in right then and there to ask him for news of Clement, to demand he tell me there'd been a big misunderstanding and the trial date was still unsettled. Or better yet, dropped completely.

But something in the room's atmosphere made me wait. Through the window, I could see the meetinghouse packed wall to wall, hot breath fogging the panes. Familiar faces mixed with strangers.

"We must act *now*," Rudyard pressed.

The knot in my stomach tightened. Time was as scarce as I'd feared.

"Why not conduct a peaceful protest outside the jailhouse in the morning, once a crowd has formed? We can make a real statement without using violence." I recognized the face as another member of the religious society. I'd seen him at the one meeting I'd attended, but that was all I knew of him.

That, and the fact he was wrong to wait. I could feel it.

"The morning will be too late," Rudyard insisted. His voice held something unfamiliar—an edge of desperation.

That's when I wondered if Clement, like Sally, was also clouded in that murky green. I closed my eyes as if I could reach out to him through my mind, past the brick walls and iron bars. But there was nothing. Just a silence so deep even the Quakers couldn't understand.

I gritted my teeth. Then I threw open the door and strode inside. "I have an idea."

Rudyard gaped at me. Then Olivia stepped forward, having been hidden by the crowd, and before I knew it, they were both rushing toward me with open arms.

Oh, how sweet it felt to be embraced by friends, by people who knew me, who saw in me something I had yet to see in myself. Olivia breathed something about her letter working, about how she'd missed me, how sorry she was for her silence when the doctor came to take me away. Rudyard babbled some kind of apology of his own.

But once we pulled apart, neither of them spoke. They just looked at me, waiting. Perhaps hoping that I'd know—*Know*—the answer to our shared plight.

I looked around at the faces that filled the wee room like ghosts in the lantern light. It was a full moon; the streetlamps would not be lit. But in that room, the sky was beginning to darken, for even the moon faces a worthy opponent in winter darkness. I found myself to be at the center of the low light, with all eyes on me.

*Right*, I told myself. *Speak from your heart.*

"It will be dangerous," I told the room, "but do we fear danger in the face of what is right?"

A murmur spread through the gathered crowd.

"But who are you?" a woman asked. Others echoed the question.

"She's Clement's fiancé," Rudyard clarified.

Gasps and whispers followed. Whether they were more shocked by *me* or by the fact that Clement intended to marry at all, I wasn't sure.

"And she's May Connally, the well-known spiritualist," added an unwilting voice.

It belonged to a woman, simply dressed with gray-blonde hair. Her face was long, drawn, and kind. Her eyes were a dazzling green, the same shade as Rudyard's when he'd stare into the sun and rub the back of his neck raw when he was thinking hard on something.

*His mother.*

For a moment, I forgot what I was doing, and my mouth hung open.

"Let's hear what she has to say," Mrs. Stoker said calmly.

Her word was all it took. The whispers ceased.

I swallowed, steadying myself. "Tomorrow will be too late," I said. "I'm sure of it."

That silence—when my mind had reached out to Clement and found nothing. Had we already lost him?

"We meet at midnight," I continued. "Whoever is willing to fight, if necessary. We'll get rid of the guards, steal their keys, break Clement free, and help him flee."

I braced myself for skepticism. It was a scrappy plan, surely outlandish in the eyes of these prudent, patient Quakers. Perhaps it was something my family would have done, had one of our own been jailed. But I saw no other way.

Mrs. Stoker had been staring intently, one eyebrow arched, as I spoke. I tried not to meet her eye, but somehow couldn't avoid it. Beside her sat the man whom I presumed to be her husband. He was tall and lean like a beanpole, stern-faced except for his caring light-brown eyes. He let his wife do the talking—so different from how my parents acted together.

Back home, the man spoke, and the wife listened, tidied, cooked, and minded the coin. Yet I had always known the truth. Traveler women were fierce and fiery as any, and in secret, they led.

Hadn't Mammy risked Da's wrath to see me to safety? Hadn't her dull eyes worn that same look of determined defiance that I now saw in Mrs. Stoker? A look that said, *I'm doing what's right. Go on, try and stop me.*

"But how will we distract the guards?" someone asked.

I hesitated.

My only answer was violence, and I was no stranger to it. Violence seemed to follow me like a shadow, sometimes silhouetted in the crinoline bustle and corset of a fine lady and other times in ambiguous darkness. Violence to myself, violence of the tongue, sharp and split like a snake's, violence of hunger pains and love torn apart.

And yet, I could relate to the Quakers, for my soul craved peace.

But how can desperate human beings fight against evil, against captivity and law, with peace alone?

"I have an idea," Olivia said. No one questioned her. "Leave that part to me."

# CHAPTER 52

# Olivia

When Olivia raised her hand toward Maude's familiar Medusa door knocker, a wave of second thoughts washed over her. The last time she'd seen Maude, she'd been fired. Maude had been agitated. Maude had barely met her eyes.

Then again, Maude hadn't had much choice.

Olivia understood. The madam couldn't afford to entangle her business in scandal, nor her reputation in fraud—at least, not when there was a chance of getting caught.

Still, Maude wasn't exactly a woman of the law, either. There was a chance she'd come around. Olivia wrapped her fingers around the knocker, meeting Medusa's brass eyes.

She'd learned long ago that Alice Antonia Maude, otherwise known throughout New York City, the Hudson Valley, and the Catskill Mountains as French Maude, was shrewd. Her hair was a fiery red, more blood than marigold. In her prime she was considered a great beauty, or so she claimed, but no one knew for sure because she had worked all the way in Montreal.

What Olivia *did* know for certain was that Maude had warned every girl who worked for her to be careful. She had seen enough lives ruined. *Her own* had nearly been. When she was sixteen, as it goes for most working girls at one point or another, Maude had found herself with child. So had one of her dearest friends. Together, they'd gone to Abby Cole, known among the working girls in Montreal as the best abortionist in town.

Only Maude had survived.

The next morning, Maude found her friend in a pool of blood on her mattress, operation wounds putrid and infected.

Olivia shuddered, thinking of the fate so many women in her position were forced to meet. No wonder Maude had been cautious. Firing Olivia couldn't have been easy, but from Maude's perspective, it had been necessary.

And yet, Maude had once told her something about that visit to Abby Cole—something she had confessed to Olivia and Olivia alone, making her swear never to tell a soul.

"It's best to hide one's soft spots, honey," she'd crooned.

But in that moment, Maude had revealed hers.

She hadn't always been sure she *wanted* to survive. But when Maude had found herself alive and unencumbered after her best friend was taken, she'd considered it a sign from God.

Olivia had nearly choked when she'd learned her madam was devoutly religious—in her own way, of course. Maude believed God had saved her for something more. That's why she had made her way to New York City, set on marrying a rich older man and living life to the fullest.

She had, in fact, met many such men. Two that had even said they loved her. None that would leave their wives for her.

Not that she had been heartbroken. Neither one was truly to her particular tastes. "Aside from the thickness of their wallets," she'd told Olivia with raised brows.

"Their wallets, hm?" Olivia had teased.

Maude had clucked her tongue. "Yes, baby, their *wallets*."

And anyway, after the second disappointment, Maude was done waiting to see what God had in store for her.

*Live, live, live.*

That had become her creed.

And now, Olivia only hoped Maude still had the same optimism, the same *fire*, when it came to listening to *her*.

The sound of Maude's booming voice made her snatch her hand from the polished knocker. "I'll just be gone for a couple of days, shopping for the house and so on!"

*Hm.* So Maude was leaving, no doubt for New York City. Shopping for *talent*, more likely. Olivia knew Maude well. Her old friend would be feeling pretty desperate by now for a new girl of higher caliber than what Hudson had to offer. She'd be looking for a little fish from the big pond.

"Ta-ta!" Maude bellowed.

That's when Olivia realized Maude was about to step outside. She squared her shoulders. Whether she forgave the madam or not, she had to ask for this favor—for Clement, for May, for all of them. And she had to do it *now*, before Maude left for her trip.

The door swung open, and the flame-haired woman's face fell.

"I'm not here for my job back," Olivia said right away. "I'm here because I need your help."

At first, Maude looked at her as though she were a sign from God. Then, her rouged cheeks drooped into a frown. "Olivia, I think we both know we can no longer help each other. We've had this discussion," she chastised.

It had been weeks since Maude had fired her. Olivia studied her, seeing her now with different eyes.

Maude's features had grown rounder and flatter since the day they'd met, with stray white hairs highlighting her autumn mane, still long and lustrous. Without her hair, you might not recognize the ravishing working girl who took Montreal's laboring-class men by storm in 1820. But Maude still had her tricks. A beauty mark ever-painted on her cheek. A dress stuffed just so. The confidence of a woman who had *built* herself, brick by brick. A woman who had survived a visit to Abby Cole, seduced two rich men into declarations of love, left New York City to become a *big fish in a little pond*—and succeeded.

Olivia didn't realize she had been staring until Nellie spotted her.

"Olivia! You're here!" The petite woman rushed forward, slipping past Maude and wrapping Olivia in a quick hug.

Maude balked as Nellie ushered Olivia inside, past the other girls, who sat glumly at breakfast, barely glancing up.

"I've been wondering what to do with the rest of your things," Nellie added.

Maude's mouth remained open as Nellie led Olivia toward the pantry. "What *things?*" she asked, clicking her tongue as if she had tasted something unpleasant. Nellie crouched down, pulling open a low drawer and revealing a stack of papers.

"I found them in your desk," Nellie explained. "Some under the bed, in the dresser, under the rug, and a few in Miss May's old bedroom. I would have thrown them away, but—"

Maude swiped the stack.

"You don't need to see those!" Olivia reached for her drawings.

She hadn't thought to collect them as she'd packed her suitcase in tears, remembering she'd left them behind only when it was too late to go back.

Maude held them away, staring with fixed focus. Charcoal sketches of the women, of their languid poses and knowing eyes, of their world rendered in shadow and light. She looked through them, one by one, until a small wet dot blurred the charcoal on a sketch of a thick thigh, garters fastened with roses. Maude inhaled sharply, as though mortified by what had just happened. She dabbed at her cheek with the back of her hand.

Nellie, still hovering beside and slightly behind her, reached into her pocket and offered Maude a rag.

Maude shook her head. "That rag looks filthy."

She dabbed the stray wetness from her cheeks with the back of her hand. Olivia watched from the doorway, scarcely daring to breathe.

"I'll pack these up for you?" Nellie asked her.

Maude's exhale was shaky. Olivia waited for her to say something, somehow nervous and sure at the same time.

"Nellie, would you give us a minute?"

"Maude, I—" Olivia began, unable to wait.

"Please, Livy. Let me." She gestured as though she were summoning courage up from the ground. "Olivia, you and you alone know me as a woman of God. I've never met anyone else who could understand that." She smiled faintly, though her eyes were shining.

"When people meet me, they see me at a surface level, as a scarlet lady or madam or former beauty or businesswoman. But still waters run deep, my dear. I know my relationship with God is the deepest of my life. When I stare at my reflection, I see a woman who is blessed. It was only when I let you go that I began to feel uneasy." She laughed lightly. "Even worse, my clothes seemed to fit a bit tighter around the middle."

Olivia chuckled softly, then quieted as Maude became serious, looking into her eyes with a tearful smile. "Didn't I tell you I always knew you could make something of yourself?" Maude murmured. She traced the edge of one of Olivia's sketches. "Of course, I'd hoped you'd make one hell of a madam." She smirked. "But I think God has another plan for you."

She looked back at Olivia with something like admiration. "When I left New York City, I wanted to be a big fish in a little pond. That day I found you scribbling at your makeshift stand on Warren, I said to myself, 'that girl's another big fish.'"

Olivia huffed a small laugh, strangely flattered to be called a fish.

"I was right," Maude went on. "But you're meant for a different pond entirely."

It took Olivia a moment to realize what Maude meant. She was talking about her *art*.

"I'll buy them all. Since I'm your first customer, I expect a fair price."

A lump rose in Olivia's throat. "Does that mean..." She swallowed. "I'm welcome here again?"

"Livy, you've always been welcome here, and you always will be. But take a more experienced woman's advice, hm?" Maude met her gaze with a knowing smile. "Don't stay." She looked back at the drawings. Then she nodded to herself. "We'll hang them here."

Nellie clapped from where she was hiding on the other side of the wall. "Oh, great news, Madame!"

"Yes." Olivia smiled, wiping a tear from the corner of her eye. Nellie extended the rag to her, but Olivia politely declined. She looked at Maude, whose lopsided smile felt like home. Before she could second-guess herself, she threw her arms around the woman's neck.

"The pictures are yours," she said. "Consider them a gift."

Olivia had run away from home at fifteen. She'd never wanted another mother, but if she had, there was a place for that here. Maude's girls came to her with their boy troubles and fear around jealous ex-husbands or children writing for more money. Maude had always been there to lend a soft pillow shoulder to lean on. Now she was scooping Olivia's dreams into her hands and nurturing them there. However far they took her, Maude would always be waiting with open arms, a home for her to come back to.

When at last Maude gave her a friendly pat on the shoulder, Olivia took the cue to pull away.

"Now, back to business," Olivia said, shaking off the emotion. "I *did* come here for a reason. We have something else we need to talk about." She took a breath. "I need you to cancel your trip."

Maude let out a deep sigh of relief. "Oh, thank God. I *really* didn't want to go, anyway. Nellie said she'd take care of her, but if you want something done right, you do it yourself, am I right?"

"Do what? Take care of *whom*?" Olivia asked.

Maude lifted her chin toward the staircase. "Come upstairs, will you dear? There's someone special I want you to meet."

# CHAPTER 53

# Olivia

"*E*veryone ready?" Olivia asked her former coworkers, her former boss, and her boss's *someone special*.

"I've never looked better, baby!" Annie declared, her husky, smoked-out voice dissolving into the starry sky as she fluffed her hair.

"These guards won't know what hit 'em when they see Cora's bubbies out and about like a lady on Parade Hill!" laughed little Madeline, her grown-up way of speaking ever incongruous with her age.

Cora presented the girls with a quick shimmy. "No one on this side of the river can resist these ripe fruits," she agreed, her faint Vietnamese accent drawing Olivia's attention to the comedy of a scarlet lady's vocabulary.

"Did anyone bring any nibbles?" Claire asked.

"Eat later," Olivia said. "Focus, ladies. There are only two guards outside the jailhouse." She peered across the street. "This'll be our easiest job yet."

"Go get 'em, Livy Baby," Maude said with a tender fist beneath Olivia's chin. She stood back, taking Sally's hand.

And then, it was just Olivia and the other girls.

Her heart pounded against the whalebone of her corset. She took a deep breath and grabbed Annie's hand, who grabbed Claire's, until all five of them stood in a linked chain. They strutted across the road together.

She hadn't lied, exactly. Distracting the guards would probably take little to no effort. It was the *probably* that made her palms sweat. There was too much at stake—Clement's life, May's heart, the institution of slavery gaining another victory.

A squeeze at her right hand made her glance up. Annie was smiling... *warmly*.

"We've got this," she assured her, squeezing her hand once more.

Olivia smiled back. Maybe they really *could* do this.

Two guards stood outside the building. One was older, maybe Duffy's age. The other was young and gawky. *Very* young. He had pimples on his face, and his mouth hung slightly open as he watched them approach.

"I'll take *him*," she whispered to Annie, who sidled up to the older copper with the others.

Olivia turned her full attention to the boy. She softened her stance, let her lips part just so. "You look like you could use a break," she coaxed in her silkiest voice.

The boy swallowed hard. "We—we—can't," he stammered, glancing anxiously at the older officer. His Adam's apple shifted in his long, wiry neck.

"Oh, relax, Willy Boy," the middle-aged man grunted, clapping the kid's back. "What's twenty minutes in the dead of night? No one's coming here."

"But, Uncle, we're not supposed to leave!"

The two exchanged words in low, tense voices while the girls played their parts—laughter, teasing, a brush of fingers over fabric, a breath too close to an ear. Olivia absently tangled her fingers in the boy's curly hair, her mind already elsewhere.

Her mind on Clement.

Was he awake? Could he hear them? Did he sense, somehow, a spark of hope stirring in his heart?

A grunt from the doorway made her blood run cold.

Duffy.

He pushed the door open, rubbing the sleep from his eyes.

Annie, Cora, Madeline, and Claire were already around the corner with both guards in tow, Willy Boy gazing back at her with a mixture of longing and nerves. A shrill whoop pierced the air in the distance, and Duffy's gaze shifted to her, sharpening when he found her standing alone, a little too still in the chaos.

His brow furrowed. "Olivia?" he said. "What are you doing?"

She looked at him with pleading eyes. He looked back with a matching expression.

And then she changed. She steeled her jaw. Lifted her chin. And spoke plainly. "Officer Duffy, I know you better than you think. Better than you know yourself, maybe."

Duffy blinked. It was a patently ridiculous statement, one he should have laughed at outright.

And yet, she was counting on an unfamiliar warmth in his chest. Smooth. Rhythmic. Like the lead of a slow dance. Didn't all men wish to be understood? Was it not Duffy's ballroom dream?

Francis had understood him. He'd seen right through the man. Known what he wanted and how to give it to him. But Francis had purely selfish intentions. He saw the *worst* in Duffy and knew how to bring it out.

Olivia would do the opposite.

"Trust me," she said, her voice low and steady. "I thought about what you told me. You don't want to be remembered as the copper that sent Clement Stoker back south. You'll go down on the wrong side of history, mark my words. But you *can* be remembered as the copper that did what was *right*. Who helped an innocent man keep his freedom."

She took a slow step forward. "You're not like the coppers in the south." Her voice softened just enough. "I know you're not. You're better."

He stared.

*Keep dancing.*

He swallowed. "Miss Olivia," he said at last, his voice hoarse. "I got me a *job* to do. This ain't about me *or* what's right."

She glanced to her side, where May and Rudyard were waiting in the shadows for her signal. She hoped they wouldn't come out too soon, that they might achieve what they set out to do *cleanly*, without ruining a man's reputation.

"Then no one has to know you didn't do your job," she told him sincerely. "Let Clement Stoker go, and we'll spread the story of how courageously you fought against the group of abolitionists that bombarded your jailhouse, when even your own two guards abandoned you."

Duffy was sweating even though the air was cool.

"Come on, Officer Duffy." She leaned in just slightly. "How do you want to be remembered?"

His throat bobbed. "My wife would've wanted..." He hesitated, then tried again. "I mean, I have to stay strong for her. The doctor said that with consistency—" He said the word slowly, like he was making sure to get it right. "Well, I do love her. She's my reason for going on."

Olivia swallowed. She really didn't want to have to embarrass him.

Duffy exhaled hard, bracing himself. "Thing is, Olivia," he said, his voice laced with both desperation and resolve, "if I see this through, it'll bring her back to me. She's not right in the head, you see. A *maniac*."

His voice turned pleading, as if begging Olivia to understand. "This victory will *cure* her. She doesn't understand the challenges of this job, the hardships I face each day and why I spend my own money to track down criminals. She wasn't proud of me, but after tonight, she will be. She'll hear about my bravery and finally answer my letters. She'll finally come home."

Olivia's stomach twisted. "Officer Duffy, please," she whispered. She knew who was hiding in the shadows. If Duffy saw them, it would shatter him.

"I can't," he said firmly. "Liv, I'm sorry. I can't. It's not what my wife would want."

For a moment, Olivia faltered. She wasn't used to her words falling flat. She glanced at the darkened street beyond the doorway, grasping for an angle.

"Are you sure about that?"

Duffy squinted at Olivia, as if wondering how she'd spoken without moving her lips. Then he stiffened as it became clear whose lips *had* moved.

"Sally?" His voice cracked on her name.

He took a tentative step forward, his gaze locking on the figure who emerged into the dim light. She was taller than him, draped in glimmering blue silk, and she radiated a cold composure.

Duffy hesitated, arms half-raised like he wasn't sure if he should reach for her. Her arms were crossed, and the set of her jaw sharpened. Maude stepped into the light beside her, gripping Sally's hand just a little too tightly.

Olivia looked away. She hadn't wanted him to see them like this.

"You're still angry," Duffy murmured, the life draining from his face. He clutched his hat, his fingers trembling as he fumbled for the right words. "I haven't proven myself to you yet."

"Nonsense," Sally snapped.

Olivia winced on Duffy's behalf. She *did* sound pretty angry.

"This was never about you, can't you see that?"

*Poor Duffy.* His eyes registered a glimmer of hurt, but no mark of understanding.

"I was never insane," Sally continued, her voice steady, rising with conviction. "I'm not mad for feeling how I feel. Or for loving whom I love."

The color drained from Duffy's face completely, as though he'd just seen a ghost. In a way, Olivia figured, he had—the ghost of his love, his marriage, his life, his *why*.

His voice was low, almost tremulous, as he ventured, "I do see you're cross with me. But you don't know what these years have been like for me, either. Did you get my letters?"

Sally didn't answer, her arms still folded tight across her chest, her silence heavier than any rebuke.

Olivia couldn't help pitying him, forging on despite his wife's icy demeanor.

He cleared his throat, desperation seeping into his words. "Every morning, I wake up and put on this vest." He patted his chest awkwardly, like he was reassuring himself it was still there. "The one you sewed for me. With all the pockets. For my watch, for my papers." His voice cracked a little, but he didn't stop. "I go to work. I fight the petty crime of this city. Do you know why? Because I'm making it safer for you. For when you'd come home."

It might've been touching, Olivia thought, if he weren't standing there like a scolded dog, half-wringing that poor hat to death. As it was, Sally's silence hung between them, thick as fog, and Olivia could tell there wasn't much hope left for him to cling to. She wished Sally would go easier on him. His wife had been everything to him, and now, she was the ghost of everything, which left him with nothing at all. Olivia knew what that felt like.

"I wrote to Dr. Edmonds to let you go," he said, almost pleading now.

"But you'd convinced me I was insane!" Sally shot back, releasing Maude's hand and stepping closer to her husband. "How could I go back to you when I knew I wasn't 'cured'?"

Duffy's shoulders slumped further, his face crumpling. "I just wanted you to be well, Sally. That's all I wanted."

"You wanted *you* to be well," she countered, her tone lethal. She exhaled, her composure returning as she stepped back and took Maude's hand again. "Well, I'm well now."

Duffy didn't respond. He turned his back on Sally, Maude, and Olivia. He didn't need to say it—his defeated posture said enough. It was over. All of it.

He opened the jailhouse door and whispered, "I'm sorry." He glanced at Olivia."You're like a Madonna with the breeze through your hair."

Olivia blinked, startled by the odd remark. She lifted a hand to her loose curls, still tinted auburn from her latest madder-root dye.

"If I had your talent," Duffy went on wistfully, "I'd paint a picture of you right now, Miss Olivia. With your red hair glowing in the moonlight and your painted-on freckles. Like a daughter I never had." He gave a small, broken shrug. "Like a life I never had, 'suppose."

Olivia pressed her lips together. "I didn't want it to turn out this way," she said softly.

"Just do me one favor, Miss Olivia?"

She waited, hoping that, though one door had closed for him, another one would open.

Duffy gave her a long look. Then, quietly: "Make your story believable."

In this case, it was the door of a jailhouse. She might've said something. Might've found a way to soothe him. But as she followed him into the building, she saw Clement.

There he sat behind the bars, and when he saw them enter, Olivia didn't miss the glimmer of hope that lit his eyes.

With a smirk, she signaled to May and Rudyard. At the same moment, Duffy unlocked the cell.

# CHAPTER 54

## 𝔐𝔞𝔭

𝒪livia signaled. My heart beat with a wild wondering. What would Clement think of me after all this time? I'd grown thinner and paler. I'd held another person's spirit in my body. I was on the cusp of no longer being Mrs. McMurry.

I thought of Grandmammy's old wisdom. "Change a name, change a fate."

Who would Clement see when I ran through those doors, and would he still want me?

My breath shook as I inhaled.

I decided right then to charge forward like the unsung heroines of Grandmammy's stories. She used to call them soul dwellers, for they live forever in the souls of all who hear their tales, offering guidance should we call upon their spirits.

I thought of her selkie women and witch goddesses and the like, the wild ones who belonged to no man's world but their own. If they'd been given this moment, had this chance to reunite with their hearts' desires, they wouldn't hide in a panic. They wouldn't hesitate.

No, I was certain they'd succumb to nothing less than ecstatic fury, and grasp for freedom with the nimblest fingers.

So that's what I did.

Clement's mouth fell open.

The sight of him standing there alone in his cell, a beard grown in, white shirt stained as gray as a storm cloud, nearly broke me. My throat tightened as though I'd swallowed sea water.

But the crushing look in his eyes told me I'd had nothing to fear. He still wanted me.

I crashed into his arms so fast he stumbled back. We missed the bed entirely, toppling to the freezing stone floor, but neither of us cared.

"What's going on?" His voice was lost in my curls. He kissed them, again and again, his hands greedy as they cupped my cheeks, traced the shape of my face. His eyes devoured me as though he'd just woken up from a horrible nightmare and fallen back into the most blissful dream imaginable.

That was the look I'd been waiting for since I was a lass, seeing some of our own wandering folk with their wives.

"What happened?" he asked again as he kissed my mouth, my cheeks, my hair. "I could hear bits and pieces on the wind but—"

I kissed his lips, my fingers pressing into his cheeks.

A sharp clearing of a throat cut through the moment. *Liv.*

"So nice to see you two back together, but in case you forgot, we have our girls with the guards and judging by the look of those boys, they won't be gone too long. Duffy'll send them the wrong way once they return, and if that doesn't slow them down, the roads should." She tossed a look toward the door. "But anyway..."

Disbelief didn't fade from Clement's face as he released me and gave Olivia a quick hug, spinning her around in the process, and then did the same for his brother. They stared at each other, speaking volumes through their eyes in the way that only best friends— brothers—can.

"Right," Clement said, flushed and grinning. "Let's get the hell out of here."

Rudyard looked at Olivia, giving her an impressed look that said, *he curses now.*

Clement shoved him playfully as we bolted toward the open sky.

"Wait!" Duffy shouted before we could leave. The four of us stared back at him, paralyzed by the possibility he had changed his mind.

"You have to make it believable," he said again, swallowing hard.

Rudyard and Clement looked at each other, nodded, and then quickly did what they had to do.

A knee in the stomach, a fist in the eye, and one across the jaw.

As Duffy buckled and gurgled and spit blood, he smiled.

I didn't exactly enjoy watching, but I didn't mind it, either, seeing as the matter aided Clement's freedom.

I glanced at Olivia. She'd apparently developed a friendship with the copper while I'd been in the asylum, but her slight nod in my direction told me she was well enough. I imagined she might have felt satisfaction in seeing Duffy do what was right. In this moment, he had a lion's courage. Perhaps he would become immortal in the minds of the citizens of Hudson, maybe America at large.

Olivia already had Duffy's next steps planned out.

In the morning, she would scatter drawings of the "fearless Police Constable Duffy" being attacked by a mob of abolitionists.

Clement's lawyer, Timothy Cook, would arrive ready to defend his client, only to find Duffy asleep in his client's cot, with an uncle and nephew pair of guards explaining the story of how they were regrettably, unavoidably lured from their post—"fancy ladies are running amuck these days!"—and their boss was, again, *most* regrettably, attacked and left unconscious.

A carriage would arrive, sent from the mayor himself, to take Duffy to the hospital, where a pretty nurse would tend to him night and day until he was recovered, and then tend to him in a completely different way, a *hero's* way, once he had.

The newspapers would carry the story far and wide, illustrated with mysterious drawings from an anonymous artist. It would tell of the violent jailbreak of accused fugitive Clement Stoker, now at large, and of the police constable who had single-handedly defended the law against a ruthless mob of abolitionists. The gang was said to have fled south, toward New York City, their mission clear—to aid Clement Stoker in reaching his final destination: London.

Olivia had thought through every detail. Of course, London was nothing but a *will-o'-the-wisp*, a fool's fire. In Ireland, Grandmammy spoke of these flickering phantom lights—how they danced over bogs and marshes, leading lost travelers astray. That was Olivia's plan exactly. Let the ones pulling the strings go chasing ghosts across the clandestine routes to New York City and its harbors, perhaps even beyond. While they searched, we would take our own path, quiet and unseen, toward the true journey's end.

Sure, no one would question the constable's honesty, seeing him in such a state as he'd be in. But the rest of Olivia's plan would indeed be truthful.

Most importantly, Sally might come to see the officer as the hero he had always tried to be, as the hero Olivia had hoped he could be. Sally might yet find a way to forgive him, even if she couldn't love him, and let the ghosts of the past float on.

As Clement ushered the final blow, Olivia and I exchanged a slight smile at the thought of what was to come.

She reached for my hand and squeezed.

Duffy's story would live on.

If the Stoker homestead had not been so near the edge of town, we'd never have made it that night. The snow had melted just before a cold spell had closed in, turning the ground to sheets of ice, visible only because they reflected the moon. Olivia leaned on Rudyard, and I on Clement, though we could barely keep our hands off each other.

We had to move quickly, before the guards returned to find Duffy tied and beaten. He had a fine tale ready to spin, but there was no doubt the higher-ups would be called upon to hunt down the so-called *mob* that had freed Clement. Our escape window was a wee thing, narrow as a keyhole. Perhaps they were after us already.

We were drunk on hope, until we reached the hill.

A steep slope led down to the homestead entrance, the path completely iced over, hard enough for skating.

I halted at the top, staring. "What do we do?"

Cautiously, I placed a boot on the ice, testing the slick surface. It was just as treacherous as it looked, all shine and moonlight.

But the brothers only grinned at each other. Before Olivia or I could protest, they dropped to their knees and pushed off, skidding all the way down, yelping and laughing like children.

"You must be out of your damn minds if you think we're going down that way!" Olivia called after them.

"No problem," Clement teased. "You could always wade through the snowdrifts, ruin your pretty shoes and gown."

Olivia let out a sharp cluck of her tongue and folded her arms, tossing me a look that said, *This guy? He's the one for you? Really?*

A grin spread across my face, a wicked sort of thrill curling in my chest. I felt as mischievous as the fay.

"Oh, no," Olivia groaned. "No way, May. Are you serious?"

I took her hand. "Together," I said.

She let out a long, reluctant sigh but dropped to her knees beside me, fingers gripping mine. The night had been full of miracles. This was just one more. She shot me another wary glance, but her eyes gleamed with something else entirely.

From below, Rudyard cupped his hands to shout, "Come on down! We'll catch you!"

One last breath and down we slid, yelping and screaming, wind in our faces. For a breathless moment, we were weightless, flying, the world nothing but ice and stars.

We unclasped our fingers at the bottom as Clement caught me while Rudyard caught Olivia, and we tumbled into fits of laughter, giddy with relief.

Still breathless, we made our way up the shoveled path to the farmhouse. Clement and I stumbled and giggled and caught ourselves and kissed, too lighthearted to speak of what had passed while we'd been apart.

For now, we wanted nothing more than this. To relish in each other's company, our shared freedom. This sweet hinterland of unsaid words and endless possibilities. If we remained quiet, then maybe, just maybe, nothing painful had happened at all, and nothing had changed.

But soon, the weight of what had passed and who we'd become couldn't be entirely ignored. By the time we reached the house, we had shyly exchanged a few stories from our time apart, as though we were getting to know one another again. I told Clement about the annulment, the return of my gift, and Sally and Maude, and he told me about what would have to come next for us if we stayed together.

We couldn't remain in Hudson, of course. Our safest path was north. Canada. We would travel north along the Underground Railroad toward a new "Heaven" or "Promised Land," as free soil was called.

As I listened, I thought about what I'd leave behind. Olivia, Maude, and Sally. I *was* ready to leave the reunited lovers but felt sorry to do so without giving them my thanks or bidding them farewell. A memory of the last time I'd been forced to go without saying goodbye still clung to my chest and ribs—a greasy, heavy feeling, one I wished never to feel again.

Clement's parents must have been waiting on pins and needles, for by the time we neared the front door, they came running out, lanterns in hand. Mrs. Stoker was first to embrace Clement, while Mr. Stoker wrapped his arms around Rudyard. It was too dark to see their faces, but I'm certain I wasn't the only one crying.

"Thank God it worked!" Mrs. Stoker sobbed into Clement's chest.

"I knew you could do it," Mr. Stoker told Rudyard, emotion tugging on the lines of his face.

Then they switched, before everyone took a step back, laughing with relief. More hugs went around. The Stokers each thanked me, then Olivia.

"Well come on in, all of you! The kettle is on, and you must be freezing!" Mrs. Stoker said as she wiped the tears from her pale but lovely face.

Clement and I were last to enter. "We'll join you in a minute," he said to everyone. They made their way into the parlor, while Clement and I lingered by the front door. Once it slid shut, he turned to me, a teasing smile playing at his lips. "You'll have to tell me another time how you know my parents."

I grinned, reliving the moment I had barged into the meetinghouse with my will sturdy as iron. "It's a pretty grand story."

"May…" His voice dropped, laced with a hint of concern. "There's one more thing we need to talk about."

I took a deep breath. My will had been iron, but my heart felt much weaker. I wasn't sure how much more excitement I could stand in one night. I exhaled, unable to believe I'd woken up that morning in the asylum.

He gingerly took my hands, his thumb brushing my knuckles. Then, with careful deliberation, he met my eyes. "Are you sure you're ready for this trip? I've taken the railroad before, and I can tell you with certainty, it won't be easy."

I opened my mouth to answer.

Before I could, a sharp knock sounded at the door. A weight of panic dropped into my stomach. The others must have felt it too. Mr. and Mrs. Stoker, Olivia, and Rudyard came running, breathless.

*Coppers.* Maybe Clement's former enslaver had already heard, had wasted no time convincing the authorities to hunt him down. Even with Duffy's yarn, no one would be shocked if the law came knocking at the Stoker homestead.

A voice called through the heavy farmhouse walls. "Open up! It's me!"

Clement's grip on my hands softened. I let out a breath, my shoulders sagging in relief. *Maude.*

Smoothing my skirt, I hurried to unlatch the door. The wind howled as Maude and Sally pushed their way in, slamming it shut behind them.

"It's wild out there!" Maude announced, removing her cloak and

460

hanging it on the rack as though she'd been to the Stoker residence a hundred times before.

Delight filled my chest, scraping at the old sorrow that had stuck to the bones of my ribs. I threw my arms around each woman's neck, breath catching as I held them close. "I'm so glad to see you both."

"Well, I'm certainly glad to hear that. Hell of a time getting over here! You know that path down the hill is all iced over?" Maude bellowed.

"We made do just fine," Sally said, taking hold of Maude's arm and laying her cheek on the shorter woman's shoulder. By the looks on everyone else's faces, I wasn't the only one who didn't want to know what that meant.

"Thank you, both, for your help," Clement said, his voice steady with gratitude. "I'd be a few breaths away from hell if it weren't for you." His amber eyes were warm as the fireplace crackling in the empty parlor.

All of us stood packed together by the door, still too caught up in the moment to move. For another minute, we exchanged relieved laughter, sharing our perspectives on the night's strange twists.

"What are you doing here, anyway?" Olivia finally asked. The hallway grew quiet.

"It's a bit awkward, you see," Maude began, glancing at Clement and then shrugging two round shoulders.

"Well, I'll just come out with it. May, Sally told me everything. I know how you saved her life, and I know you've got that quack doctor wrapped around your fingers now."

She paused, watching for my reaction before continuing.

"Why not come back to the house with me? By this time next week, you'll be filthy rich and famous—the pretty little spiritualist who convinced the great Dr. Edmonds that she's the real deal. Think about what that'll do for our seances. You could even return to individual readings, if that's your preference. The girls will get over it. They can be real sourpusses, but they'll cope."

She leaned in, her voice lowering with a conspiratorial edge.

"Just think, in no time flat you'll have the money you need to bring your family over, start your own house if you like. I'm not trying to hold you back, just get you started."

She finished with a sly smile.

"Fox sisters, who, right May? Us ladies of influence need to stick together, hm? What do you say?"

I turned to Clement. He appeared stoic. Only a slight tremor in his throat belied any feelings one way or the other. "What do you think?" I asked carefully.

Clement sighed and gently took my hands. He lowered his gaze, speaking as though we were the only two in the hallway. "May, I can't make this decision for you. You know how I feel about you, but this is your life. You have to be happy with your choice."

Grasping for guidance, I looked to Olivia. Rudyard had his arm threaded through hers, and the two of them stood silently. "Liv?" I asked.

Olivia took a moment before opening her mouth, then shrugged one shoulder. "There's no denying you'd make a fortune. It's what you've always wanted, ever since you arrived, isn't it?" She gave Clement a look of sincere apology. He didn't seem angry with her for telling the truth, but he looked away nonetheless.

I let out a narrow breath. Now my choice had grown even more confusing. I could stay with Dr. Edmonds and develop my skills; I could learn to help people in all new ways. Or, I could stay with Maude and Sally, almost like two new mothers there to support me; I could become independent and free my family from the gates of hell.

These choices made sense. Both of them.

I looked at Clement.

Even though he wouldn't meet my eyes, I could see the expression in them, and it said everything I needed in order to feel sure. I saw sincerity, sacrifice, and above all, longing. I saw time, once again as something wild and untamed yet trustworthy. I saw myself, wanted and seen and cherished more than anything, blossoming in a garden of myth and magic.

My features and lineage might have been fay, but I felt more like a witch. Not the Catskill witch, for that woman already existed, perhaps at the summit of the mountain I used to gaze at from my old bedroom window. Yet I could likewise change the weather, for I could thaw winter from the hearts of those who would see others in chains.

My work was unfinished, had barely begun, and it would be too great for Diamond Street.

"I'm sorry," I said to Maude, the words coming out quieter than I intended. "You'll have to go on without me."

I could feel Clement looking up at me with a dark-fire stare.

"Well." Maude shrugged. "Never a dull day at French Maude's. Expect the unexpected." She turned to Sally. "Did I ever tell you I almost called the place 'House of the Bizarre?'"

"I prefer French Maude's," Sally said, kissing Maude sweetly on the cheek. My eyes widened, for I'd never seen Madame Maude blush before.

"You're sure?" Clement asked, drawing my attention back to him. "It's a convincing argument, May. And you have to be certain. What we're about to go through—"

"Believe me, Clement," I interrupted with a smirk, "I'm no stranger to hard travel."

He kissed me, a plume of cold air left between us. We stood close together, eyes locked, as the rest of the group took the hint and started talking amongst themselves in hushed tones.

"You can never come back," Clement pressed, taking my hands once again, lacing his fingers through mine. My stomach leapt, and my skin tingled. "Not to Olivia or Hudson or anything you've come to love here."

I thought for a moment, his words sinking deep into me. I would miss Olivia terribly, but I could continue learning to write and then send her letters, and she could always visit *me*. Now that we'd done something impossible, anything felt possible. Maybe it would be years before I saw my friend again, but I wasn't afraid our goodbye would be final. More importantly, there was nothing and no one I had come to love in Hudson more than Clement.

"All I want is to come back to you, each and every day," I said, my voice soft but certain.

"Then you will," he said, hands quite at home on my arms now. He just couldn't stop touching me. It felt too right. "We can head directly north, toward Montreal, or if you like, we can head northwest, stopping over in Stockbridge to rest."

"Randolph's farm?" I asked, taken aback. "I thought you hated him."

Clement sighed. "I did. But perhaps I misjudged him. Perhaps we wouldn't be standing here, together, if not for his help."

We stared at each other, wondering what words were left unsaid.

Finally, I was the one to speak. "I'm not so sure, in any case," I admitted. "About never returning to Hudson. There may well be a day that we *can* come back. Clement, I feel something coming to this country. Something big. I can't say exactly what it is, but it will change everything. All that you've been working for, all this time… it won't be in vain."

He kissed me again, as though wanting my words to be true but mostly just wanting me. In my heart, I could feel the thunderous, bloody tinge of war between brothers. Even closer, I could feel apple blossoms, lilacs, and gorse like dawn clouds hovering low.

Rudyard put on a show of shivering by the door. His mother was deep in conversation with Olivia, their arms linked. Maude, Sally, and Mr. Stoker were talking nearby. Mr. Stoker rocked from his heels to his toes, his teeth slightly bared—perhaps an attempt at a smile. It did little to mask his discomfort at standing among the reunited lovers. But God bless him, he tried. He loosened his collar.

"Pardon the interruption, everyone," Rudyard said, rocking back and forth on his own heels. I hadn't seen the likeness between him and his father before, but in this gesture, I did. "It's unlikely anyone will be out looking for Clement tonight, not on a night like this." He hugged himself. "*Burr.* But I wouldn't linger too long, nonetheless. Sunrise will be here before you know it! Come on, then," he said as he gave his brother a loud clap on the back. "Father will marry you."

Clement and I looked sharply at each other. I hadn't realized until that moment that if we were to marry with any friends or family there to witness it, we'd have to do it tonight.

"I'm still married, I think," I whispered to Clement.

He nodded, then placed his hands around my arms. "Rud's right, May. We'll do better if we're married when we cross the border. It'll

464

make things easier in Canada. You trust that doctor of yours to get the paperwork?"

I nodded.

"Then it will all work out," Clement promised.

I hesitated, glancing toward his parents. "What about your parents? They don't care about my religion?"

Clement frowned slightly. I had reason to worry. Marriage outside his faith wasn't permitted.

"Oh, not at all, dear!" his mother said, making no pretense of having given us privacy. One eyebrow arched. "That rule never felt right to us, anyway."

I turned toward his father, who nodded. "She's quite right," he agreed. "We've always known Clement to live life his own way. We wouldn't expect him to choose anyone who wasn't just as extraordinary as he is. He's chosen well."

Clement wrapped his parents in one large hug, then returned to me, his lips brushing mine in a quiet reassurance. But...

He looked at me, searching my face. "What's wrong?"

"I just—"

How could I tell him I was afraid? The last time I'd been married, nothing had turned out as I'd hoped. I wanted to say yes, to be his wife now, but something inside me urged me to wait. Not because I doubted him, but because this moment, as full of love as it was, wasn't the right one.

"Clement," I began, my voice soft but certain. "I want to marry you in Canada," I said finally. "Not here, not while I still have unfinished ties behind me. I need to feel safe, and settled, and—"

I closed my eyes and tried to imagine it. His father saying the words: *You may now kiss the bride.* Clement's kiss would be hard, yet tender. I'd feel the pressure of his teeth, the crashing of ocean breakers, the promise of what was to come. It would leave me breathless, my chest tight with anticipation. I'd feel nothing icy like when Francis had gazed at me across the altar in Ireland. I'd simply feel... alive. A woman of flesh and bone and coursing hot blood.

I wanted that feeling more than anything.

And yet, I knew it wouldn't be enough.

He studied me for a long moment before nodding. "Then we wait." He took my hand, pressing his lips against my fingers. "But I consider you mine all the same."

Warmth spread through me, and I squeezed his hand in return.

We all filed into the parlor, following the warm glow of the fire.

The room was as pure lovely as I'd imagined it, spacious and well-lit, with three tall windows dressed in undyed linen curtains. The floors were polished, the walls a soft, muted green, and the furniture was simple but elegant. A spinning wheel sat in one corner beside a basket of knitting. A bookcase filled with well-worn books stood in another corner. Iron tools hung above the brick fireplace. Its mantle was free of clutter, save for a few burning candles.

It was the sort of home I'd always imagined for myself, and though it wouldn't be mine, I knew that it existed somewhere, and therefore, it could exist for me, too.

Before I had a chance to compliment Mrs. Stoker on her home, she took Olivia and I upstairs to fetch us new petticoats and dry stockings. The men went their separate ways, and by the time we returned to each other in the parlor, the sight of Clement made my heart race all over again.

His face was thinner, but his beard was gone, and his skin was still moist from a bath, his white shirt and vest perfectly laundered as though they'd been waiting for him. He looked almost like his old self, so that I could almost imagine nothing horrible had ever happened.

His mother had placed our sopping hemlines and stockings to dry by the fire, and it was there that I got to know the Stokers a bit better —sharing stories, laughter, and quiet moments, filling the spaces between us with warmth. Clement and I spoke of what had happened while we were apart, our words stitching together the time that had been lost.

And for the first time in a long while, I let myself believe in the promise of tomorrow.

Olivia and Rudyard stepped away to prepare a light meal and tea in the kitchen. When they came back, they had an announcement.

"We've decided," Rudyard began. He turned to Olivia with a broad smile.

"We're going to London!" Olivia finished.

They told us how they planned to make their mark on the city with Olivia's spirit drawings. Spiritualism was blossoming in London. Even the queen had begun participating in seances, and Olivia planned to become *the* spiritualist artist, documenting what she would see in the circles and selling her art to newspapers, shops, and galleries.

"Olivia's art is one of a kind." Rudyard beamed. "She has a completely fresh perspective that will set the art world on fire. It's different, a new standard of beauty, representing not just the pure, pale, and chaste Victorian woman, but, well, I'll let her art speak for itself. And it will."

Olivia clutched his arm, laying her head on his shoulder. Their plans were grandiose, so great they might swallow the two of them whole, but how happy, how pure lovely they both looked.

"I'm so pleased for you," I said earnestly into Olivia's hair as we hugged. "You were always destined for greatness. I'm going to miss you terribly though."

We laughed and batted away tears.

I'd once wondered if there was some fundamental part of me that was missing—the part that let a person be happy—but I didn't wonder that anymore. It seemed the completely wrong question in a world with so much meaning. I could have a friend like Olivia. I, of all people, could be strong and capable. She pressed her lips together sadly, but her eyes still smiled, telling me she felt the same way about herself.

"Liv, can you do me one favor before you take London by storm?" I asked.

"Anything."

"Will you introduce Dr. Edmonds to Mr. Randolph?"

I couldn't be the one to work with the doctor, but perhaps I could be the link between two great, albeit vastly different, minds. They weren't quite as immiscible as oil and water, destined never to mix, but more like earth and air, elements of the mental body, driven by the mind, possessing the ability to balance the other out.

Clement slipped an arm around my waist. "And take care of my brother." He and Olivia looked at each other sternly for a moment, then softened simultaneously. "I know he's in good hands," Clement added.

"Mhm," Olivia answered facetiously, the corners of her mouth curved upward. "And you take care of my sister. She'd *better* be in good hands."

They grinned. Olivia took his hand and squeezed it. He kissed her cheek in return.

"I'm sorry," he said to her, more in earnest, "for what I said to you in Governor's Tavern. You were right. It wasn't my place to say what I said."

"I *was* right," she agreed gladly. "Water under the bridge. In any case, I *am* making something of myself, aren't I?" Her eyes twinkled in that blue-black, midnight way that made me shiver, like I was camping out under the stars.

"Despite the odds," he agreed.

Olivia turned back to me, remembering what I'd asked of her. "I promise," Olivia assured me. "I'll make sure Randolph and the doctor meet."

"Thank you, Liv," I said, taking her hands wistfully.

"What is it?"

I sighed. "I want you to find love, too," I admitted.

Olivia shook her head. "Don't worry about me, May. I don't want love. I want success."

I squeezed her hands. "You'll find it then," I said, convinced well enough.

"I know," Olivia smiled. "Now that's enough talk from all of us. You'll be on your way at first light. Let's get some sleep."

We were given the guest bed to share, and I lay beside her for what felt like hours, staring at the ceiling, listening to the quiet creaks of the house settling. Olivia's breathing had long since turned slow and steady, but sleep wouldn't come to me. My thoughts spun too wildly.

The night would be our last moment of stillness before the journey ahead. Before the uncertainty of what Canada would bring. Before Clement and I could truly start our life together.

Carefully, I slid out from under the covers, my bare feet silent against the wooden floor. Olivia shifted slightly but didn't stir. I held my breath and tiptoed toward the door.

Clement's room was at the end of the hall, the glow of firelight flickering beneath the threshold. My heart pounded as I pushed the door open.

He was sitting at the edge of the bed, his shirt unbuttoned at the collar, his elbows resting on his knees. When he looked up, his expression softened, like he'd been waiting for me. "I had a feeling you wouldn't sleep," he murmured.

I closed the door behind me. "I had the same feeling about you."

He stood and reached for me, his hands warm against my arms as he pulled me closer. The scent of firewood and soap clung to him, and I let myself sink into his warmth. "We'll be married soon," he murmured against my hair. "When we're safe."

I nodded. "I know."

His lips found mine in the quiet firelight, slow and certain, and I let myself get lost in him, in the promise of what was to come. With Clement, I was happy. I belonged. We'd both faced trials that most others could not have withstood. We'd been hungry, discarded, disempowered, and belittled. We'd loved and lost and now loved again, and we wouldn't waste a moment.

We would follow every wind that carried the scent of jasmine. We would sleep in shiny blankets of raven wings, stop searching for mountain witches and cultivate the magic within our own inner gardens. We would *live, live, live.*

"I want to make you another promise," he said, standing to stoke the fire. He watched me carefully as I sat on the edge of his bed. The air filled with the warm scent of oak and maple, mingling with the furniture polish. It smelled earthy and satisfying. It smelled like home.

"When we get to Canada, I'm going to give you the farmhouse you've always wanted. I'll build it myself, and we'll live there and start our own farm. We'll save every penny and bring your family over, and together, we'll continue to fight for what's right. I was half ghost before I met you, May. Now I feel entirely alive."

I blinked back tears. "Whatever the world throws our way, we're together," I said, though my trembling voice betrayed lingering doubts.

"What is it?" he asked, stepping closer.

"It's just..." I was afraid to ruin the moment, yet I couldn't shake the familiar feeling of being too gentle for this world, for him, for our journey. "What if I can't be the person you need me to be? What if I'm just a dove, trapped in an iron cauldron? You think I'm capable of more, and maybe I am, but I'm afraid of disappointing you, of not being enough."

He laughed. I gave him a punch on the arm, less gently than I'd intended.

"Forgive me for laughing, May, but all the cauldrons *I've* come across are places of transmutation. You and I will change the world, set a fire under its belly. And doves are fierce, too, by the way. Gentle, but fierce." He raised his brows in a mock stern gesture. "And they don't just wander, they soar to new heights."

As he said his next words, he ran his fingertips along my spine, sending a delicious shiver along every bone. "And you, my love, will unfold those dove wings, and soar higher than either of us can imagine."

His hand paused at the nape of my neck, his brow furrowing as he cupped the spot where my figure charm clasped. We each carried a piece of where we'd come from, tied close to our throats like a whisper we couldn't part with. His past, bound in the weight of old silver and gold; mine, in the worn grooves of a charm smoothed by generations. Two stories, hanging by threads, drawn toward each other like spirits aching to be known.

"You know, I haven't had a chance to tell you yet," he breathed, "I was at a low point in jail. I wondered if I was enough myself. I questioned whether I was more of a burden to the people I love than anything else." He swallowed, but he didn't look away.

I placed my hand over his, pressing his warmth into the cool of my neck. He rubbed the side of my neck, behind my ear, gently pulling at the roots of my hair, before sliding down to my collarbone. As he moved, I kept my hand over his, reassuring him that I was there, that there was nothing he couldn't tell me. He breathed in, our bodies relaxing under the touch.

"There were moments I thought about ending it all." He paused, the gravity of his words washing over me.

Perhaps God had a wry sense of humor, for I'd contemplated the same thing, myself. For three days I'd taken no food. What if we'd both perished, like Olivia's beloved Romeo and Juliet, and all the joy that was meant for us never had a chance to exist at all?

Not everyone steps into darkness like that in their life, but we had, and somehow, we'd managed to step back into the light, and find each other.

"Clement," I whispered, voice unsteady, "I don't see how you could ever think of yourself as a burden."

"You were the only thing that changed my mind," he said simply, lacing his fingers with mine.

"I was?" I asked, hopelessly breathless.

"When you stepped into the jailhouse, and I saw you standing there before me, I thought I was dreaming. Then you knocked me over and kissed me and I realized I was awake. I knew God was on my side when I held you and touched your wild mess of curls and kissed you feverishly."

He recreated the moment, tipping me back onto the bed, his fingers knotting in my hair until it was a hopeless tangle I'd never tame before morning.

"When we're settled," he continued with a patience I'd nearly lost myself, "you'll find a spiritualist community that will help you grow your skills." His lips brushed the nape of my neck, trailing slow and deliberate down my back.

"And you'll get to know the abolitionists and work on the Underground Railroad," I continued for him, "and together we'll fight for what's right."

As I lifted his shirt, my breath caught. A raven-shaped birthmark marked his shoulder.

"What's wrong?" he asked. I traced it with my fingertip, a realization dawning. "Oh, that? I've always had it. God-forsaken thing almost got me sent back to the south, too."

My pulse quickened. "It was you," I murmured, more to myself than him. It wasn't God-forsaken, at all. It was *God-given*.

I met his calm, questioning gaze. "When I came to America, I felt a raven's presence. I didn't know what it meant at the time. There's an Irish belief that ravens are drawn to Seers, and I thought maybe it had come to me as a reminder of where I came from. But I didn't feel certain. And then a raven came to my bedroom at Maude's, the morning you introduced me to Paschal. Now I see it was leading me to you."

He quirked an eyebrow, a wee smile touching his mouth. "Does that make me a ghost, then? If I was able to visit you in a vision?" He brushed his fingers along my jaw as though he were drinking it in.

I smiled, closing my eyes and leaning into his touch. "I don't know," I teased, making both of us laugh.

"Well," he said, unfastening my dress with careful hands, "then we'll write the next chapter of my ghost story together."

Once, I had wondered who would care about my story. It wasn't always a living one, after all. My life had teetered on that delicate edge between reality and myth, what was and what will be. But now, I felt a shift.

"It's not *your* ghost story," I corrected, smiling against his lips. "It's ours. And it's not a ghost story." I kissed him, slow and deep, feeling the truth of it settle in my bones. "It's a love story."

He grinned, his eyes glinting with mischief. "Then prove it."

AND SHE DID, and he did, and though they didn't sleep before they set out on their journey north, they dreamed, and woke, and dreamed again. There was no difference at all, for though they wanted more, they were perfectly content where they were—ecstatic, even. For the first time, they were each entirely alone together, free of ghosts, free of sorrow, freely in love.

# AUTHOR'S NOTE

Sometimes, as authors, the stories we are meant to tell choose us. We may feel like it's not the right time, or like we should not even be the ones to tell them, but they come anyway, whole unto themselves or in fever dreams or like will-o'-the-wisps, beckoning us to chase after them. They ask us if we're willing to give our time, sweat, love, empathy, and at least a chunk of our sanity. They can't promise much in return outside of a window into another world, one that together—these stories and their willing writer—hope to share with readers.

One of the questions my early readers asked me most often was: *Why did you write this story?*

In many ways, the answer lies in what I've just described. But more concretely, this novel began with my fascination with Irish Travelers, an ethnic group indigenous to Ireland. The more I researched, the clearer May's voice became. She would whisper little thoughts to me while I was washing dishes, folding clothes, or taking my children for a walk. It didn't take long to realize she was a romantic.

*Okay*, I thought. *There will be a strong romance in her story. But with whom?*

I didn't know much about writing novels, but I did know that the most compelling romances often follow characters who face a major obstacle in being together. As I delved deeper into the time period (I can't remember a time when I wasn't captivated by the Victorian era and the Irish potato famine), I came across a documentary called *Frederick Douglass and the White Negro.*

The film follows Douglass's life, including his time in Ireland, where he felt he was treated as a fellow human being. The documentary juxtaposes this with his return to America, where tensions between Irish immigrants and the Black community were rising— leading toward two particularly violent peaks in American history: the New York Draft Riot of 1863 and the Civil War.

Deeper research led me to lesser-known historical figures, including Paschal Randolph. His vividness grew in my mind as I read *Paschal Beverly Randolph: A Nineteenth-Century Black American Spiritualist, Rosicrucian, and Sex Magician.*

Stacks of books soon filled my home office. I knew I wanted to set this story in Hudson. After years of yearning for a settled life close to nature, I'm now building a homestead in a small town neighboring Hudson, so it felt like the right place for May to land. Its proximity allowed me to immerse myself in research, while its rows of gorgeous, historic buildings required no great stretch of imagination. The more May spoke to me, the more I saw her struggles mirrored in my own experiences as the child of an immigrant.

Setting her story in a brothel, however, was a surprise. As I explored Hudson's history, I realized how central the industry was in 1850. Bruce Edward Hall's *Diamond Street: The Story of the Little Town with the Big Red Light District* introduced me to Hudson's infamous past and its colorful cast of characters, including the real French Maude and Police Constable Duffy.

From there, my research spiraled outward. I learned about the Fox sisters and Hudson's role in spreading the burgeoning religion of

Spiritualism. I examined the intersection of Spiritualism, feminism, and accusations of insanity—particularly through Alex Owen's *The Darkened Room: Women, Power, and Spiritualism in Late Victorian England.*

I delved into the murky past of Henry Hudson himself, the town's Quaker heritage, and the grim history of the Hudson Almshouse, also known as the Hudson Lunatic Asylum.

Inspired by all these threads, and by Frederick Douglass's story in particular, Clement Stoker took shape—a man who was stoic, focused, passionate, and deeply caring. Soon, he and May were having burning, candlelit conversations in my mind.

With this story, it is not my intention to attempt to take ownership over histories that are not my own. The discrimination that African Americans faced in America is still deeply and agonizingly felt in the lives of their descendants today. Rather, it is my hope that this story joins the many voices raised up in the song of lore and folktale, illuminating a lesser known area of history, and that those who have been silenced or ignored continue to step forward to share their own stories and the stories of their ancestors as they have never been able to before.

You may notice that I've modernized some historical vernacular for clarity. For example, the Know-Nothing Party was not officially named until 1855, but I chose to use that term instead of its earlier name, the Native American Party, to avoid confusion for contemporary readers.

Though my characters are fictional—some inspired by historical namesakes—their struggles, triumphs, and dreams reflect the real histories that shaped them. And those histories continue to shape the world we live in today.

# ACKNOWLEDGMENTS

Thank you to my beta readers: Leah Sikora, Amos Margulies, Kate MacRitchie, Giada Rose, Jessica Filip, Elle Caldwell, and Mackenzie Letourneau. You are the most wonderful, dreamy, intelligent group of early readers I could have ever hoped for, who bore with this manuscript in some pretty messy states.

Thank you, in particular, Friel Black, for your relentless encouragement, faith, and reading so many drafts that I've lost count. You're my sister and kindred spirit.

Thank you, Katie Morrowick, for digging in deeply with me. You were the kind of editor I had always dreamed of working with, and you're a true polymath. Thank you, as well, for imagining the cover with me. Working with you was more delightful than buttered bannocks.

Thank you, Jennie Ryan, for helping me find and polish my character's hearts and voices, even when your hands were full. Your intuition is sharper than a selkie's teeth, and your nit-picky notes were my favorite.

Friel, Katie, and Jennie: The three of you gave me hope when I was hopeless. It is no exaggeration to say that this book would not exist without any of you.

Thank you to my kind and thoughtful sensitivity readers: Dinasty Kelly and Farai Harreld.

Thank you, Avery Virginia. I could not have hoped to speak with a medium as intuitive, insightful, and generous of time and spirit as you are. I tell everyone that you're the real deal.

Thank you, Gillian Culff, for reading my first chapter and encouraging me to be as brave and open as my protagonist.

Thank you, Ellen Dugan. Your phone call not only made my day but gave me the push I needed to see this book through.

Thank you, Brenna Cameron Lopes, for being unimaginably sweet and understanding and helping me visualize May.

Thank you, Yishai Margulies, for coming through for me at the very last minute with your grammatical prowess.

Thank you, Amy Parkhill, for receiving a large brunt of my over-thinking with patience, kindness, and wonderful ideas.

An extra thank you to Giada Rose for your final-hour reread and for bringing the book's atmosphere to life in your stunning cover design. I love that I could offer you nothing more than the vague request for *"dreamy, romantic, dark, moody, eerie Victorian vibes,"* and you returned with the perfect cover that gives me butterflies.

Thank you to my in-laws and great aunt-in-law for always believing in me.

Thank you to my husband, my best friend in the world (all worlds), who encouraged me to keep going no matter what and always made sure I had the time I needed.

And thank you, dear reader, for taking a chance on the words of a new author and hopeless dreamer.

# ABOUT THE AUTHOR

Hadas Knox lives in upstate New York with her husband and three children. Her writing is inspired by history, mythology, folklore, fairy tales, and motherhood. Her Oracle Deck, *Folklore Oracle*, debuts in July 2025. She is currently working on her next novel, a medieval Irish historical romantasy. *Dove in an Iron Cauldron* is her debut novel. Connect with her on Instagram @hadas.knox.